BLIND THRUST

A JOE HIGHEAGLE NOVEL BOOK 1

Horrific earthquakes are devastating the Front Range between Denver and Colorado Springs in an area long believed to be seismically quiescent. They are being generated by ruptures along cryptic, mysterious, deeply buried thrust faults (blind thrusts) that, unlike many faults, do not break the surface during large-scale seismic events. Somehow the cause of the unusual earthquakes must be unraveled and the cataclysms stopped before they result in more carnage and devastation. But are they the result of natural tectonic adjustments, hydro-fracking, conventional subsurface sequestering, or clandestine operations?

Environmental Geologist Joe Higheagle is on a mission to find out the answer. But he soon finds himself in a deadly duel of wits against powerful forces. With his team of techie sleuths, Higheagle goes toe to toe against his adversaries while grappling to collect, analyze, and leverage the scientific data needed to prove his case. But at every turn he is thwarted by his shadowy enemy and, with the cataclysms worsening, he may not have enough on his side to solve the mystery and save Colorado from more devastation.

Can he solve the enigma of the earthquakes and gather enough evidence to stop those responsible? Will the tremors continue to wreak death and mayhem across the Front Range? Or will Higheagle and his outgunned team be defeated and ultimately crushed by their adversaries? If the earthquakes are not stopped, thousands more will perish and more towns and homes will be destroyed, leaving countless injured and homeless as well as untold financial damage across the Front Range. But can the resourceful Higheagle and his team stop those responsible? In the end, all they can do is try.

Praise for Bestselling, Award-Winning
Author Samuel Marquis

"A promising thriller writer with a fine hero, great research, and a high level of authenticity."
—Donald Maass, Author of Writing 21st Century Fiction (for The Coalition)

"Marquis is brilliant and bold...It's hard not to think, 'What's he going to come up with next?'"
—SP Review - 4.5-Star Review (for *The Slush Pile Brigade*)

"With *Blind Thrust* and his other works, Samuel Marquis has written true breakout novels that compare favorably with—and even exceed—recent thrillers on the *New York Times* Bestseller List."
—Pat LoBrutto, Former Editor for Stephen King and Eric Van Lustbader (Bourne Series)

Praise for *The Slush Pile Brigade*
#1 *Denver Post* Bestselling Novel
Award-Winning Finalist Beverly Hills Book Awards

"This high-energy, rollicking misadventure will change the way you look at the publishing industry forever. The plot is unpredictable...twists and turns and counterturns abound. So, too, does the humor...The dialogue is superb...Marquis laid the groundwork as a thriller writer with *The Slush Pile Brigade* and hopefully his following novels build up a James Patterson-esque empire."
—Foreword Reviews – Five-Star Review

"There's a lot going on in Marquis' book, as the author smartly builds off a solid premise...A fresh concept and protagonist that breathe life into a conventional but exciting actioner."
—Kirkus Reviews

"*The Slush Pile Brigade*, by Samuel Marquis, is a hilarious and exciting read filled with one crazy turn after another...The author slams on the accelerator early in the story and doesn't let up, forcing the reader to flip the pages frantically. And once it's over, it's still hard to catch one's breath."
—SP Review - 4.5-Star Review

"Twists, turns and double crosses in literary theft quickly expand to threaten the globe in *The Slush Pile Brigade*, a promising debut from an up-and-coming thriller writer."
—IndieReader Book Review - 4.5-Star Review

"Marquis makes the whole bewildering journey entertaining with his quirky friends who accompany Nick on his mission. The fact that Marquis himself wrote a novel called *Blind Thrust*, bring out the book-within-a-book theme, and the New York City scenes and dialogue feel authentic throughout. Read *The Slush Pile Brigade*...for the enjoyable romp that it is."
—BlueInk Book Review

Praise for *The Coalition*
Winner Beverly Hills Book Awards – Political Thriller

"*The Coalition* has a lot of good action and suspense, an unusual female assassin, and the potential to be another *The Day After Tomorrow* [the runaway bestseller by Allan Folsom]."
—James Patterson, #1 *New York Times* Bestselling Author

"This ambitious thriller starts with a bang, revs up its engines, and never stops until the explosive ending...Perfect for fans of James Patterson, David Baldacci, and Vince Flynn, *The Coalition* is a standout thriller from an up-and-coming writer."
—Foreword Reviews – Four-Star Review

"An entertaining thriller about a ruthless political assassination...Marquis has woven a tight plot with genuine suspense."
—Kirkus Reviews

"*The Coalition* by Samuel Marquis is a riveting novel by an uncommonly gifted writer. This is the stuff from which blockbuster movies are made! Very highly recommended."
—Midwest Book Review - The Mystery/Suspense Shelf

"Reminiscent of *The Day of the Jackal*...with a high level of authentic detail. Skyler is a convincing sniper, and also a nicely conflicted one."
—Donald Maass, Author of *Writing 21st Century Fiction*

"Author of 2015's *The Slush Pile Brigade* and *Blind Thrust*, novelist Samuel Marquis has accomplished something rather rare. In *The Coalition*, Marquis has injected fresh air into the often threadbare genre of political conspiracy and assassination thrillers."
—Dr. Wesley Britton, Bookpleasures.com (Crime & Mystery)

"Marquis knows his stuff: [his] conspiracy is prescient and plausible, and well-drawn. Each one of his characters has uniquely interesting motivations. If you're in the mood for an engrossing assassination thriller with a unique twist, *The Coalition* is a very good place to start."
—SP Review – 4.5-Star Review

"*The Coalition* is an entertaining conspiracy story driven by the diverse motives of a varied and complicated cast of characters."
—IndieReader Book Review

Praise for *Bodyguard of Deception*

"*Bodyguard of Deception* grabbed my attention right from the beginning and never let go. The character development is excellent. Samuel Marquis has a knack for using historic details and events to create captivating and fun to read tales."
—Roy R. Romer, 39th Governor of Colorado

"Readers looking for an unapologetic historical action book should tear through this volume."
—Kirkus Reviews

"As usual, Marquis's descriptions are vivid, believable, and true to the time period...*Bodyguard of Deception* is an intriguing launch to his new trilogy. Warmly recommended."
—Dr. Wesley Britton, Bookpleasures.com (Crime & Mystery)

"Old-time spy buffs will appreciate the tradecraft and attention to detail, while adventure enthusiasts will enjoy the unique perspective and setting for a WWII story. A combination of *The Great Escape*, *Public Enemies*, a genuine old-time Western, and a John Le Carré novel."
—Blueink Review

"The world hangs in a delicate balance in the heart-pounding *World War Two Trilogy* opener, *Bodyguard of Deception* by Samuel Marquis. Put together with an intricate plot to follow and a commitment to realistic detail, there's a lot going for the read...a wonderfully nail-biting experience with good characters and solid intrigue."
—SP Review – Four-Star Review

"A fast-paced, riveting WWII espionage thriller. *Bodyguard of Deception* is as good as the best of Daniel Silva, Ken Follett, Alan Furst, and David Baldacci and brings back fond memories of the classic movie *The Great Escape* and Silva's finest novel, *The Unlikely Spy*."
—Fred Taylor, President/Co-Founder Northstar Investment Advisors and Espionage Novel Aficionado

"*Bodyguard of Deception* is a unique and ambitious spy thriller complete with historical figures, exciting action, and a dastardly villain. Fans of prison-break plots will enjoy this story of a loyal German struggling to save his homeland."
—Foreword Reviews

By Samuel Marquis

THE SLUSH PILE BRIGADE

BLIND THRUST

THE COALITION

BODYGUARD OF DECEPTION

BLIND THRUST

A JOE HIGHEAGLE NOVEL BOOK 1

SAMUEL MARQUIS

MOUNT SOPRIS PUBLISHING

BLIND THRUST

Copyright © 2015 by Samuel Marquis

MOUNT SOPRIS PUBLISHING

Trade paper: ISBN 978-1-943593-04-0
Kindle: ISBN 978-1-943593-05-7
ePub: ISBN 978-1-943593-06-4
PDF: ISBN 978-1-943593-07-1

Second Mount Sopris Publishing, premium printing: May 2016
Cover Design: George Foster (www.fostercovers.com)
Formatting: Rik Hall (www.rikhall.com)
Printed in the United States of America

To Order Samuel Marquis Books and Contact Samuel:

Visit Samuel Marquis's website, join his mailing list, learn about his forthcoming novels and book events, and order his books at www.samuelmarquisbooks.com. Please send fan mail to samuelmarquisbooks@gmail.com. Thank you for your support!

ATTENTION: ORGANIZATIONS AND CORPORATIONS
Mount Sopris Publishing books may be purchased for educational, business, or sales promotional use. For information, please email the Special Markets Department at samuelmarquisbooks@gmail.com.

Dedication

For my father, Austin Marquis (June 1924-April 2015), who served his country in the Pacific Theater in World War II and was a great dad.

And for my wife, Christine, and our children, Sam, Clapton, and Cassidy, whom I love more than words can describe.

Blind Thrust

A Joe Higheagle Novel Book 1

Cry 'Havoc!', and let slip the dogs of war.
—William Shakespeare, *Julius Caesar*

CHAPTER 1

ON THE DAY of the first catastrophe—October 23, 2008—Joseph Higheagle stared down at one of the greatest paleontological wonders ever discovered.

It was a breathtaking sight.

The two fully articulated, freshly exposed dinosaur skeletons were preserved just as they had died, locked in a desperate struggle. The fleet-footed predator *Allosaurus* gripped the upper neck of the *Stegosaurus* with its massive jaws and serrated teeth while the plate-backed herbivore tore at the attacker's abdomen with its dagger-like tail spikes. In the bright sunlight, the primordial beasts appeared not only entangled in battle, but as though they were grappling to break free from the tomb of arkosic sandstone that had encased them for the past 150 million years, both attacker and defender literally leaping out of the friable rock. Gazing down at the powerful scene, Higheagle could almost feel the great Saurians' final frantic moments on earth, a stirring reminder that, on rare occasion, fossilization can perfectly capture nature's organic creations in the very throes of death.

The historic dig site known as "Felch Quarry 3" was located in Garden Park, Colorado, six miles north of Cañon City. Joseph Higheagle and his grandfather were participating in a weekend dinosaur "day dig" as part of the Denver Museum of Nature and Science's fall field expedition, funded through a grant by Quantrill Ventures, Inc. In addition to the two volunteers, three University of Colorado graduate students were busy exhuming the stegosaur's hindquarters while a pair of museum field assistants carefully exposed the allosaur's skull.

Higheagle wiped away a rivulet of sweat trickling down his face. Though late October, the temperature was a stifling eighty degrees. His back ached, and so did his knees despite the thick kneepads he wore. His lungs burned like an icy fire from all the bitter alkali dust, and his belly rumbled from lack of food. But he was oblivious to his hunger pangs and physical discomfort. Like everyone else, he was entranced by the spectacular lost world coming to life before his eyes.

"As you can see, ladies and gentlemen, our friend *Allosaurus* was not just *any* hunter—he was the T-Rex of the late Jurassic," declared the expedition's leader, Dr. Christopher Williston, Chief Preparator and

Curator of Vertebrate Paleontology at the Denver Museum of Nature and Science. "True, he was smaller and less agile than a tyrannosaur. And he differed from his Cretaceous counterpart in having less powerful jaws. But he was still the fiercest predator of his day. As for the countermeasures available to his plant-eating adversary, please note that *Stegosaurus* had broad, overlapping plates running along her back, an armored throat, and nasty tail spikes to protect her. Her throat protection consisted of hundreds of small hexagonal bony pieces closely packed in the neck region. This afforded her natural chain-mail armor across her upper chest. Locked in battle, these two magnificent creatures must have been a sight to behold."

Higheagle compared the stegosaur's tail spike to the allosaur's claws and teeth and concluded that if he had lived in the Jurassic, he would have much preferred to be the meat-eating theropod.

"I'd hate to be caught out in the open by that bad boy," he said to his grandfather.

The crinkly-faced chief and former tribal lawyer smiled as he gazed down at the bones of the ancient Saurian warriors. "Old Spike Tail gave him a run for his money though."

"If I were a dinosaur, I would want to go like these two—fighting till my last dying breath."

"Just like our ancestors."

"It was a good day to die. They must have killed one another right in this very spot."

"Actually, I don't think they died from their battle wounds," interjected Dr. Williston, brushing away some sandy grit from the allosaur's partially exposed jaw bone with a fine artist's camel brush.

Higheagle was surprised. "What makes you say that?"

"The specimens are so well preserved that they must have been buried quite rapidly. I'm thinking some kind of catastrophic event, like a flash flood or collapsed riverbank. Note the full articulation of the major bones and overall lack of abrasion. One minute these creatures were locked in mortal combat, the next they were buried in a liquefied sandy soup. It's only by a stroke of luck that they have been exquisitely frozen in their terrible embrace for 150 million years until we stumbled upon them."

"I like that they kept fighting to the very end," said the old chief with feeling.

"Nature—red in tooth and claw. Welcome to the real Jurassic Park, gentlemen."

The hot, sweaty bone digging team resumed unearthing the antediluvian combatants with dental picks, awls, and brushes. Working methodically, Higheagle and his grandfather exposed some more of the stegosaur's right front limb, careful not to flake away any bits of bone as they dug. Every few minutes Williston and one of his museum assistants would apply a fresh coat of rubber cement to the newly exposed skeletal remains, impregnating the bones with glue to harden them and make them easier to extract. The ancient bones could not be completely disinterred and transported to Denver until they were cut loose from the pedestal, the pillar of matrix underlying the fossils, then carefully wrapped in protective jackets of burlap and Plaster of Paris.

"Hey look someone's coming!" exclaimed one of the grad students.

Higheagle's eyes darted to the dirt road at the base of the bluff where he saw an unexpected sight: a fleet of gas-guzzling Humvees charging up the road, kicking up an iridescent plume of dust. *Who the hell is that?* he wondered. The rest of the group stopped digging too and stared down with a mixture of curiosity and mild disapproval at the sight of the new interlopers.

The fleet of oversized vehicles came to a halt. A gargantuan man with an outfit straight out of *Cowboys and Indians* magazine—perfectly pressed Wrangler jeans, a fur felt Silver Belly "Gus McCrae" Stetson hat, handcrafted silver bolo tie, and costly Lucchese hand-tooled cowboy boots—stepped from the lead Hummer. He stood as erect as a clock tower. His chin and aquiline nose projected forward with a supremely confident air. His eyes shone an intense gunmetal gray. The man took a gander at his surroundings before waving up to the group of crouching bone diggers.

"Who the hell is that—J.R. Fucking Ewing?"

Higheagle smiled; he found his grandfather's penchant for using colorful language quaintly amusing. "No, Grandfather, that there is Charles Prometheus Quantrill."

"Holy shit, the famous billionaire? Your client?"

Higheagle nodded.

"What the hell's he doing here?"

"He's come to make sure his money's well spent," answered Williston, looking jittery as a newborn colt with the unexpected arrival of their important new guest. "He's funding our dig. In fact, he's the museum's biggest benefactor."

The old chief grinned through gnarled, yellowed teeth. "Well, just tell him my grandson and I are working for free. That ought to make the son of a bitch happy as a clam."

The museum curator gave a nervous laugh. "Yes, I'm sure he'll love to hear that." Then to Joseph: "You didn't tell me you knew Mr. Quantrill."

"I do environmental consulting work for him."

"Who are you with again?"

"HydroGroup. We're doing the work at Quantrill's haz waste plant, refinery, and wind farm in Elbert County. He's the one who told me about the dig. But he somehow cleverly failed to mention that he was the one funding it."

"I've never actually met the fellow. They say he's rather remarkable."

"Trust me, that's an understatement."

"In that case, how do I look?"

"Like fucking hell frozen over," chided the old chief.

"Oh dear." Williston ran a fussy hand through his mop of tousled, dust-speckled hair and turned to address his museum staff and grad students. "Okay, here he comes everyone. Please be on your best behavior. Mr. Quantrill funds the museum to the tune of two million dollars per year. Needless to say, we would very much like to keep the grants coming."

As if on cue, the Fortune 100 CEO came walking up the dusty footpath trailed by an army of attendants, security personnel in dark suits and impervious sunglasses, and servants carrying foldout tables, chairs, silver serving platters, tureens, and portable hot plates bearing who-knew-what-kind-of sumptuous food. Higheagle found himself staring in awe at the man. He had worked as an environmental consultant for Charles Quantrill for the past three years, and had met him on several prior occasions including a business meeting a mere two weeks ago. Yet he was still mesmerized by the entrepreneur like everyone else. Despite the man's laughable rhinestone cowboy attire, he provided a towering, commanding, charismatic presence and was in such fabulous shape that he looked nearly a decade younger than his actual age of sixty-five.

"Dr. Williston, it is a pleasure to finally meet you, sir," he said in his trademark West Texas twang that simultaneously carried a down-home affability and unmistakable edge of command. His diverse entourage assembled patiently behind him along the rocky outcrop, the pungent aroma of the catered lunch toying with the nostrils of the hungry field crew.

"Mr. Quantrill, what a pleasant surprise."

They shook hands. "I apologize for dropping in unannounced, but I was in the area and wanted to see the new dig for myself. I left a message on your voice mail back at the shop—I hope you don't mind."

"Why of course not. We're thrilled to have you."

"I see you've put my young friend, Joseph Higheagle, here to work."

"Yes, sir. He's doing a wonderful job."

"Joe, how the heck are you? I sure am glad you took my advice and decided to come on out to the dig."

"I'm doing well, Mr. Quantrill. It's quite a site."

"I can see you're having success." He glanced down appreciatively at the entwined Jurassic combatants grappling to break free from the dramatic *bas relief* beneath their feet.

"It's all been Dr. Williston and his capable crew. We just try not to get in the way."

"We?"

"My grandfather and I. Oh, I'm sorry I forgot to introduce you. Mr. Quantrill, this is my grandfather, Chief John Higheagle."

The big man turned towards the elderly Cheyenne with the turquoise and vermillion braid wrappings fluttering in the breeze. He again stuck out a bony hand. "Pleasure to meet you, Chief. You don't mind if I call you, Chief, do you?"

"I don't mind."

"I reckon you know I think highly of your grandson."

"Glad to hear it. All he ever did growing up was cause me goddamn trouble."

At this, Quantrill's massive sculpted face broke into a wide grin. "Is that a fact? Well I'm pleased to report that the young rascal has always done a bang-up job for me. So much so that I've placed him in charge of all my environmental work. He keeps everything clean as a whistle and the regulators off my back. Am I keeping you busy enough, Joe?"

Higheagle smiled bashfully. "Yes, sir, you certainly are."

"Good, good." He turned back toward Williston. "Now I brought y'all some mighty tasty chuck. Red hot Texas barbecue—had it flown in from Fort Worth just this morning. Where should I have my boys set up, Doc?"

"It smells delicious. How about over there?" He pointed a hundred feet away to the open ground next to the field tent and stacks of field equipment that included an eclectic assortment of steel jackhammers, pick axes, shovels, lightweight spades, geologic hammers, chisels, trowels, rock saws, brushes, strainers, bags of dry plaster, two-by-fours, and a 200-gallon freshwater tank.

"Why that'll do fine." Quantrill turned to his staff, standing at breathless attention awaiting his orders. "You heard the man—hop to it, folks," he commanded in a tone that was more cheerful and animated than bossy. As they scrambled off industriously, Quantrill turned back to Williston. "Now I'd be much obliged if I could take a gander at your diggings here, Doc, while they get everything ready."

"Why of course, Mr. Quantrill. Right this way."

As they stepped up to take a closer look, Quantrill's security team quietly took positions along the sandstone ledge around him. Despite the merciless noonday sun, they stood stony-faced behind their impenetrable sunglasses with their hands neatly crossed in front of them, the faint bulges beneath their armpits signifying concealed handguns. The only one that Higheagle knew by name was Quantrill's chief of security, Harry Boggs, a stodgy, walrus-mustached man in his early fifties with no nonsense in his face whatsoever. Three years ago, when Higheagle had first taken over as HydroGroup's senior project manager for the various Quantrill facilities, Boggs had performed a thorough background check on him and grilled him in person for two hours straight. Though their paths had rarely crossed since, Higheagle occasionally saw the security chief lurking about Quantrill's haz waste facility and refinery. Unlike Quantrill whom he liked and respected, Harry Boggs had always come across as shadowy and threatening. Higheagle prayed that he would never have the misfortune of crossing the man.

"Now as you can see, Mr. Quantrill, we have unearthed two different specimens: the carnivore *Allosaurus* and the herbivore *Stegosaurus*. It appears that the carnosaur has just delivered a savage bite to the neck of our stout-hearted Stego, who in return has driven his sharp tail spike into his attacker's abdomen."

"Looks like they were having quite a little fracas here when they were buried alive. Must have been a collapsed cutbank, I reckon."

Higheagle noticed the look of surprise on Williston's face. "Why that is a most astute observation, Mr. Quantrill. How did you know?"

"Just a lucky guess." The CEO winked mischievously. "I take it our theropod is *Allosaurus fragilis* and not *Allosaurus amplexus* based on its reduced size."

The surprised look persisted. "Why yes, that is correct."

"And I'm also guessing that our stegosaur is the species *stenops* and not *armatus* given the collar of bony ossicles covering its lower neck region?"

Now Williston's mouth fell open. "Mr. Quantrill, I must say I am—"

Suddenly a flock of birds blasted out from the piñon pines studding the slope, shrieking and cawing as if startled by something. Several of the bone diggers rose to their feet to see what had caused the commotion. Higheagle looked at his grandfather, who was studying the trees intently. A moment later the birds flew off to the west, wings flapping wildly, until they turned to little black dots against the bleached-blue sky above the mountains.

"I wonder what spooked them," said Quantrill.

"I don't know, but something's about to happen," said the old chief in a tone of premonition. "I can feel it coming."

Higheagle looked at him with puzzlement. "What is it, Grandfather?"

Before he could answer dozens of wild animals—coyotes, mule deer, rabbits, squirrels, mice, and assorted other small creatures—burst from the trees across the canyon. It was a crazy, Biblical-like scene and Higheagle could scarcely believe his eyes. He glanced back again at his grandfather, who's gaze was still fixed intently on the forest of piñon pines from which the birds and other animals had been flushed. *What the hell is going on?*

"Everyone, brace yourself!"

"Brace ourselves?" gulped Williston. "Brace ourselves for what?"

It was then Higheagle felt it.

A vague sense of motion, a weak but discernible ripple as some sort of energy passed through his body, giving him a little fluttery feeling in his stomach. He looked up at the top of the bluff, searching for some anomaly to match the strange sensation he felt in his gut, but there was nothing. Everything seemed normal. And yet there was an unmistakable change in the air, a frisson of danger that somehow his grandfather had sensed before everyone else.

"By thunder, I believe it's an earthquake!" cried Quantrill, and he made his body compact like a boxer preparing to defend a blow. "Hold on everyone, I expect we're in for the main shock now!"

"An earthquake? But there are no earthquakes in Colorado," insisted Williston. "This is a tectonically stable—"

There was another shockwave, a definite motion running up from the ground as they were hit savagely with another pulse of pent-up energy. This time the rolling sensation was much more powerful than before and punctuated by a series of abrupt jolts. Higheagle saw Dr. Williston go down, then his grandfather, Quantrill, Boggs, and two of the graduate students. And then he felt his own knees buckling as he was pitched to the ground like a bronc rider.

The entire bluff shook all around him. He felt a sharp implement dig into his back and saw a fist-sized cobble carom past in a blur, tumbling over the edge into the dry wash canyon below. Suddenly he saw rattlesnakes—he couldn't believe his eyes, the canyon floor was covered with them, like something out of *Indiana Jones*—wriggling through the grass, slithering between the rocks, struggling to escape the wave of energy. Then the ground motion turned even fiercer as big slabs and chunks of rock and loose sandy soil began to rain down from the rocky exposure above, pelting a dozen unfortunate victims like a hailstorm. The sandstone and mudstone walls heaved and groaned then the cycle was repeated as another wave hit, followed by an oscillation of the whole bluff.

Again, the earth shook violently and a thunderous roar echoed through the valley. There was power behind it—power and mystery to shame puny humankind—and Higheagle felt as if his whole body would explode from the catastrophic forces at work.

And then suddenly, thankfully, it was over.

The roaring sound was gone and the birds and animals had vanished and everything was eerily tranquil and there was only a lingering plume of yellow dust, rising up like a little tendril of cottonwood smoke. Higheagle looked towards the field tent and foldout dining table where Quantrill's staff had been setting up lunch. Both were flattened. The food and equipment were strewn about along with Quantrill's terrified staff and huge slabs and boulders of sandstone that had slid down from the exposure above. In less than a minute, the peaceful little base camp had been transformed into a wilderness of devastation.

Slowly, Higheagle rose to his feet. His legs felt heavy and his stomach was still fluttery. He looked at Quantrill and the others scattered about the dig site. They shook off the dust. They moaned and groaned. They bled from noses, mouths, and exposed craniums from the debris that had hailed down on them. The sky was aglitter with golden flecks of dust like falling confetti.

"Everyone all right? We lose anyone?"

"Your grandfather...I think I saw him go over the edge!" exclaimed Quantrill.

"What? Are you sure?"

Clamoring to the precipice, Higheagle couldn't believe his eyes. The old warhorse dangled precariously over the next ledge, his arm clinging to a scraggly juniper limb. Blood dripped from a nasty gash on his forehead and fell off into the space of the arroyo. Drip, drip, drip...

"Grandfather!"

"Hurry up—I can't hold much longer!"

"Stay there—I'm coming down!"

He started scrambling down feet first. The soil was loose and sandy and he found it difficult to find purchase. Finally, with considerable effort, he was able to make it to the narrow ledge sprouting the scrawny juniper tree. Now he could see the bottom of the arroyo. It was at least a thirty foot drop onto a patch of sharp, angular boulders.

"Here, take my hand!"

Gripping a branch of the bent juniper with one hand as he braced his feet against the main trunk, he held out his free hand to his grandfather. But the fledgling tree started to give way.

"Watch out, Joe!" warned Quantrill from above. "It's coming loose!"

"Quick, grandfather! Take my hand!"

Straining, the old chief reached up, but their fingers missed.

Higheagle reached down again as the juniper's roots began popping up.

This time their hands clasped together.

But suddenly Higheagle had nothing to support himself as the little tree jerked free from its roots. No time to think—the only option was for him to swing his grandfather up onto the ledge.

Mustering all his strength, he gripped him at the elbow and swung him like a pendulum over to a protruding knob of rock that jutted out from the narrow ledge.

From there, he was able to hoist the old man up all the way and then half-push, half-carry him up the unstable slope of sandy soil and regolith. When they were within reach of the group above, the burly Quantrill, Williston, and the head of security Harry Boggs leaned down, grabbed them by the scruffs of their shirts, and hauled them up onto the main ledge.

Higheagle blew out a sigh of relief mingled with equal parts exhilaration and exhaustion. His grandfather was damned lucky to be alive. In fact, given the powerful earth tremor, they all were.

"Damn that was close," wheezed his grandfather, wiping away the blood dripping from his gashed forehead with a dusty bandanna. "Thank you all for saving my ass. For a moment there, I thought I was done for."

"No, it was never in doubt, Chief—not with capable young Joe here," said Quantrill with a reverential gleam in his eye. "And now we best get you to the hospital."

CHAPTER 2

THE EARTHQUAKE ALARM on the fifth floor of the United States Geological Survey, National Earthquake Information Center in Golden, Colorado, blared at precisely 12:03:15 p.m. Mountain Standard Time. Dr. James Francis Nickerson jumped up from his seat, chucking aside the *Bulletin of the Seismological Society of America* reprint on late Cretaceous tectonic deformation in the Apennines he had been perusing.

The NEIC director and pioneering African-American seismologist known endearingly by the general public as the "Earthquake Man" hadn't even planned on coming in on a Sunday. But he had to put the finishing touches on his presentation for the upcoming Geological Society of America conference in Denver this week. However, after three hours of working on his PowerPoint slides, he had decided to take a little break and thumb through a technical paper he had been wanting to get to for some time now. Five minutes into the article, the EQ alarm outside his office shrieked like a klaxon, propelling him and his scientific team into instant action.

Rounding his desk, Nickerson dashed into the Seismic Drum Room as fast as his sixty-two-year-old legs would carry him. The styluses on a half dozen seismographs scratched and scrawled like tree branches clawing at a window. He felt his heart rate click up a notch at the excitement of Mother Earth yet again demonstrating her supreme, uncontestable, and utterly terrifying power. The alarm sounded at magnitude 4.5 and above for domestic tremors, and M 6.5 and above for shockwaves emanating from outside the country, so he knew it had to be a major disturbance.

From the Drum Room, he quickly made his way into the Situation Room where staff geophysicists Bill Schillerstrom and Brigid Donnelly were working feverishly at their computer workstations. Red lights flashed on the digital board above the six-foot projection screen hovering above the two scientists. The National Earthquake Information Center—the World Data Center for Seismology—maintained a minimum of two personnel round the clock to monitor earthquakes. The Center's overall mission: to rapidly determine the location and magnitude of all destructive earthquakes worldwide and to immediately disseminate this information to national and international emergency response agencies, scientists, and the general public.

"All hands on deck, boys and girls. Where's our epicenter?"

Brigid pointed to the large red star on the map of eastern Colorado shown on the 36-inch color monitor. "Luckily way out in the boonies in Elbert County, lat 39.3 degrees north, long 104 degrees west."

"Closest population centers?"

"Epicenter twenty miles east of Limon, fifty miles northeast of Colorado Springs, and seventy miles from us here in Golden."

Nickerson felt himself stiffen. "That puts our baby in the southern Denver-Julesburg Basin. But that can't be."

"That's what we thought too," said Bill. "Plains Seismotectonic Province—about as seismically quiescent as there is. But we've cross-checked it."

"I'm going to need confirmation. This shouldn't be happening."

"I'm on it." Swiping a bead of sweat away from his brow, Bill resumed punching away at his computer keyboard.

Nickerson turned to Brigid. "What's the moment magnitude?"

"Six-point-six."

Again the NEIC director was stunned. From the strong shaking, he had known the temblor was huge, but an M 6.6? This was Colorado not California, and this was the western Great Plains not the tectonically active Rocky Mountains, which had been in a continuous state of uplift since the Laramide Orogeny when dinosaurs still ruled the earth. At the same time, although destructive earthquakes were rare in this part of the country, he had to admit a 6.6 was certainly in the realm of possibility. The state had more than 13 recognized faults with assigned maximum credible earthquake magnitudes of 6.25 to 7.5, and the current earthquake was roughly the same size as the largest in recorded history, the 1882 quake north of Estes Park. Still, he couldn't remember the last time there had been a tremor in the state of sufficient intensity to pose a serious danger to civilian populations.

"Okay, I got it," announced Bill. "Confirmation from Caltech, CGS, UCB, and now UNR. Six-point-six across the board."

"What's the location uncertainty?"

The two young seismologists hammered away at their keyboards. "I'm pulling that up now," said Brigid. "Looks like a...plus-minus of six miles horizontal."

"Hypocenter?"

"The fault ruptured five kilometers below ground surface. A little over three miles."

Nickerson thought aloud. "Shallow focus quake."

"From our preliminary estimates the rupture occurred along a fault in the Precambrian gneiss."

"Basement of the Denver-Julesburg," observed Bill. "Those rocks are more than a billion years old and cut by a hell of a lot of old unmapped faults."

That may be, but there's still not supposed to be any seismic activity in that area. Especially with the fracking moratorium. What the hell's going on? "What about the uncertainty on the quake depth?"

"Plus or minus a quarter mile."

"Aftershocks?"

"Twelve so far," replied Brigid, her fingers flying across the keyboard. "All less than 3.0."

Nickerson pondered a moment, quickly synthesizing all the information. They would have to move quickly now. An M 6.6 would be a national news story and there were no doubt tens of thousands of terrified people out there in Elbert County and the surrounding areas trying to figure out what the hell was going on. Within the next five minutes, he and his staff of two would be inundated with phone calls from concerned citizens and swarmed by the news media. Everyone with a media ID badge from New York to LA would want to get an interview with the Earthquake Man. All the same, he still needed a few more questions answered before he could contact the North American Defense Communications System in Colorado Springs and get emergency response people moving into the impacted areas.

"All right, I've got to call NORAD and get some more staff in here pronto to deal with this. We've got maybe another minute or two until all hell breaks loose. Quickly show me the Shakemaps."

With a few quick clicks of her mouse, Brigid, on the left, pulled up a colored map showing the Modified Mercalli instrumental ground-shaking intensity, or MMI, around the epicenter. Meanwhile, Bill, on the right, pulled up a split screen showing the peak ground acceleration and velocity distribution. Nickerson closely analyzed the labeled, color-coded isocontours on both high resolution screens.

"The peak acceleration is around 65 percent g and the peak velocity is 60 centimeters per second within five miles of the quake," said Bill, pointing at the asymmetric contour pattern around the red star denoting the epicenter. "They both drop off rapidly within ten to fifteen miles. Looks like Colorado Springs, Castle Rock, and Southeast Denver have been spared. But we can expect heavy damage within five miles of the epicenter and moderate damage in Limon and the other nearby small towns."

"Lucky it was out in the sticks," said Brigid.

"Damned lucky," agreed Nickerson. "But there's still going to be some frightened and hurting people out there."

"I just hope nobody was killed," said Bill.

I hope so too, thought Nickerson, remembering back to the devastation wrought by the great Sumatran 9.1 earthquake of 2004 that killed nearly a quarter million people and left countless others homeless and destitute.

His two protégés looked up at him soberly. That was the dilemma about being an earthquake seismologist: on the one hand, there was the sheer exhilaration of studying awe-inspiring natural forces; but on the other, there was the death and destruction, the unspeakable tragedy.

Feeling a little sad, the Earthquake Man put a hand on each of their shoulders. "Well done, you two," he said softly.

"Thanks, Dr. Nickerson," said Brigid.

"Yeah, thank you sir," echoed Bill.

He let his smile of approval linger on them a moment longer. "I'm going to go call in the cavalry now. Let's see if we can't help some scared folks out."

CHAPTER 3

CHARLES PROMETHEUS QUANTRILL stepped into the emergency examination room at St. Thomas More Hospital in Cañon City, towering above Joseph Higheagle and his grandfather like a big old box elder. He had personally brought them down from the dig site in his Hummer and they were waiting for the doctor on call to come in and stitch up the nasty gash on John Higheagle's forehead.

"How you faring, Chief?"

Joseph Higheagle turned away from his grandfather and looked up with surprise. "Mr. Quantrill, you didn't have to come back—"

"Why I most surely did. I need to make sure old doc patches your grandfather up right. He sure as heck ought to since I just paid the hospital bill."

"You paid my grandfather's bill?"

"Left a check up at the front desk—told the gal with the blue hair to just fill in the amount when the doc was done. No need to thank me—it was the least I could do. The injury took place at my diggings and that makes me responsible. Plus now you and your grandfather won't sue me— or at least I hope you won't. I'm afraid that would make my head legal counsel, Jack Holland, very upset."

Quantrill watched with a suppressed smile as Higheagle and his grandfather the chief looked at one another, unsure of what to make of him or his unexpected financial disbursement. But the simple fact was that he had always taken a shine to young Joe—the consulting hydrogeologist had done a bang-up job for him the last few years—and he wanted to do a favor for him and his grandfather. Besides, he liked the cut of the old plait-haired chief, who reminded him of a Comanche horse trader he had known growing up in West Texas.

"We appreciate your offer," said John Higheagle, with a trace of irritation. "But it wouldn't be right for you to pay for me when I have my own health insurance."

"Sorry, Chief, but I ain't taking no for an answer. This one's on old Chuck Quantrill."

"But it's not your fault there was an earthquake," pointed out Joseph Higheagle.

"That may be. But at my diggings, I am still responsible for your safety and that of your grandfather."

Again, the two Cheyennes looked at one another, unsure of what to say. Quantrill gave a wry smile. He always got a kick out of shaking things up and doing the unexpected. As a businessman, he had learned that it tended to keep people on their toes and make them perform better under duress. After a moment, they both shrugged with reluctant acquiescence—as expected he had disarmed them.

"You are a very persuasive man, Mr. Quantrill," said John Higheagle. "You leave me no choice but to take you up on your generous offer."

"Thank you, Chief. I reckon I've just gotten awfully used to getting my way. Now where in the name of Captain Woodrow Call is that doctor?"

"The nurse told us he would be here in a few minutes," said Higheagle. "Have you heard anything more about the earthquake?"

"They're saying it was a 6.6."

"Where was the epicenter?"

"West of Limon. They're moving emergency response teams into the area now."

John Higheagle gave a puzzled look. "Limon? That far away? The way the ground shook, it felt a lot closer than that."

"I thought so too, Chief. And to be honest with you, I thought you were done for when I saw you roll over that edge. You must have Cheyenne Luck on your side."

"Cheyenne Luck? Is that what it was?"

"I reckon so." Quantrill gave a philosophical laugh. "So, gentlemen, not to change the subject but what did you think of the dig? I mean that is one hell of a find, isn't it?"

Higheagle nodded. "*Allosaurus* and *Stegosaurus* locked in mortal combat…it has to be one of the most incredible dinosaur discoveries of all time."

"I'm thinking bigger than the fighting *Velociraptor* and *Protoceratops* discovered by the Polish-Mongolian team in the Gobi Desert back in 1971. Hell, it may even be bigger than the four *Deinonychus* raptor pack hunters found attacking *Tenontosaurus* in 1964 by Yale's John Ostrom."

The two dusky Cheyennes looked at one another. "You certainly know your dinosaurs, Mr. Quantrill," complimented Higheagle.

"I'll say," seconded his grandfather. "I take it that your support of the museum is a little more than philanthropy."

"That would be true, Chief. You see, I grew up in a little fart of a town in West Texas and the most interesting thing that happened to me in my first eighteen years of my life—besides knocking helmets on the gridiron and rolling around in the hayloft with Jackie "Belle" Chorney and Lulu Gould—was hunting for fossils."

15

"What kind?"

"Permian mammal-like reptiles mostly. Especially, a big finbacked predator with sprawling limbs called *Dimetrodon* and a finbacked herbivore called *Edaphosaurus*. I have a good specimen of *Dimetrodon* back at my shop. There's also a fine specimen at the museum in Denver."

"Seen them both many times," said Higeagle. "So you were an amateur fossil-hunter growing up? That's how you got into dinosaurs?"

"Actually, the way it happened was I hooked up with a professor by the name of Al Romer."

"You worked with Al Romer? The legendary Harvard paleontologist? No way."

"It's the God's honest truth. I was his field helper for three summers. My father was a dirt-poor rancher and he couldn't afford to pay me to work our little spread. So when I was about eleven or twelve I set about looking for a paying job. One day I saw this fella poking around out at Williams Ranch and asked him what he was doing. He said he was looking for the bones of extinct reptiles. I told him I knew where all the best bones were and showed him three or four outcrops where they were literally spilling out of the hillsides. He hired me then and there as his assistant for five dollars a day. I worked for him for three summers—Old Alfred Sherwood Romer. He had this rickety old pickup truck that he drove all over West Texas collecting bones. He christened the bedeviled contraption Geraldine after the Geraldine Bone Bed, one of his favorite fossil localities. He was durned fond of those finbacks, especially *Dimetrodon*. He gave me a cartoon once that showed *Dimetrodon* digging up a human skull. Damndest thing I ever saw."

"That is one hell of a story," said Chief John Higeagle.

"I thought I would grow up to be a paleontologist, but instead I became an oil man. And now I've reinvented myself as a 'green' energy guru. Crazy the twists life takes."

"Did I miss something?"

The three men looked up with surprise to see the doctor.

"Well it's about time, Doc. We were beginning to worry about you."

"My apologies, Mr. Quantrill. I had to take care of a patient with a badly dislocated shoulder."

Suddenly the CEO felt his smart phone vibrating. He pulled it out and checked the caller ID, recognizing the number instantly. He punched the *Accept* button and put his ear to the cell.

"I need to talk to you—it's urgent," said the voice on the other end. It was his younger brother Jeb Quantrill—Chief Geologist, Executive Vice-President, and minority owner of Quantrill Ventures.

"Are you all right, Brother? Is it the earthquake?"

"Yes…I mean no. Look, I just need to talk to you all right? Are you alone?"

"No. Hold on a moment, I'll be right with you." He covered the cell then turned back to Higheagle and his grandfather. "I'm going to have to bid you farewell, gentlemen. I have to take this call."

"We'll see you later then, Mr. Quantrill," said Higheagle. "Thanks for everything."

"Don't mention it, Joe." He winked. "Adios fellas."

HE WALKED SWIFTLY down the hallway towards the waiting area. "What is it, Jeb? You sound worried."

The voice on the other end came across a little muffled and scratchy, a weak connection. "There's been a 6.6 earthquake and you're asking me *that*?"

"What do you mean?"

"We've got a serious problem on our hands."

Problem? Did he just say we've got a serious problem? He pushed through the double doors into the waiting area and started for the exit. His chief of security, Harry Boggs, looked up from the *American Hunter* magazine he was reading and signaled to the other two security men that it was time to go. The rest of Quantrill's staff had been left behind at the dig to clean up the mess caused by the earthquake.

"It's begun. The nightmare scenario we prayed would never happen has begun."

The CEO didn't like the panic in his brother's voice. "You don't know that for certain."

"No? Are you aware of the location of the epicenter?"

"They said it was near Limon." As Quantrill came to the automatic doors, Boggs swung in next to him with military precision. Covering his phone, he tipped his head towards the security chief. "Harry, I'll meet you at the car. This is going to take a minute."

"Yes, Mr. Quantrill."

"Sorry about that, Brother—I was momentarily distracted."

"I was talking about the goddamned epicenter. According to the National Warning Network alert, it's located twenty miles west of Limon. But that's not where the real epicenter is."

"I'm not sure I follow."

"You need to listen, damnit. Colorado has only four permanent seismographic stations that are part of the USGS Advanced National Seismic System national network. Because of the limited number of seismographs across the state, the NEIC's accuracy for triangulating an earthquake epicenter is only plus or minus five to ten miles."

"So?"

"So our seismic monitoring network has located the epicenter a hell of a lot more accurately than the NEIC. We've got twelve portable seismographs in our network and the data shows that the true epicenter is actually twenty-six miles west of Limon. That means the injection wellfield is closer to the epicenter than the USGS thinks. Six miles closer to be exact."

"So you believe our operation caused the earthquake. But that's impossible. Our wellfield is at least fifteen miles from either location. How can we be responsible?"

"I honestly don't know. But I still think we ought to shut down for awhile just to be certain."

"Shut down? You know that's not an option."

"Look, I've got a really bad feeling about this."

Quantrill squinted at Boggs. Standing by the Hummer, the doggedly loyal security chief stared back at him through his dark Ray Banz sunglasses, his hands crossed neatly in front of him. "I don't give much weight to gut feelings, especially when billions of dollars are at stake. I prefer scientific facts. And so far you haven't given me one iota of hard evidence about what caused the quake."

"Damnit, Chuck, don't you realize we could go to prison for this?"

"No one's going to prison. We haven't done anything wrong."

"We don't know that. Not yet anyway."

"If there is a problem then you and Wes are just going to have to fix it."

"We may not be able to. It may be beyond our control."

Quantrill kicked away a loose pebble from the edge of the planter. This conversation was going nowhere. He needed facts not speculation, firm resolve not panic. Jeb had always been a worrier, but this was ridiculous. He had to calm him down.

He spoke in a soothing voice. "There's no reason to get all in a lather. Here's what we're going to do. We're going to meet at seven o'clock tonight at my place and sort this all out. I need you and Wes to put together a full briefing. Once we've heard all the facts, we can decide how best to move forward. I know you're upset, but everything's going to be all right, I promise."

"You do realize that people may have been killed from this?"

"If that's true, it ain't from anything we did."

"We could be held responsible."

"No we won't. Now get a grip on yourself."

"Damnit, we could be on the hook for murder!"

"And I say we're not, Little Brother! And at seven o'clock tonight, you and Wes are going to prove it to me!"

CHAPTER 4

IN LESS THAN AN HOUR, the National Earthquake Information Center in Golden had transformed from a virtually empty government facility to a bustling emergency response command post. There were now not merely two but twenty geophysicists hammering away at computer keyboards, poring over seismograms, answering phones, and shuffling about in search of more bad coffee and electronic messages from seismographic stations scattered across the Western U.S. The styluses on a dozen seismographs busily scribbled their geophysical signatures as telephones rang in shrill unison and representatives from the national news media expounded on the ramifications of the 6.6 earthquake before boom microphones and cameras.

Standing with apparent calm amid the controlled pandemonium was Dr. James Nickerson, the Earthquake Man. He hovered above staff geophysicists Bill Schillerstom and Brigid Donnelly, who were seated around a large conference table in the Situation Room. They were busy assessing the probability of damaging aftershocks and fielding calls from police and fire departments, while the scientists at the computers lining the room were busy examining peak ground acceleration and velocity maps, studying P- and S-wave travel-time curves, and computing centroid moment tensor solutions.

Nickerson walked to the glass window and peered into the Drum Room. Here seismic waves from not only North America but from around the world were being monitored via satellite. Whenever a major earthquake rocked the continent, Nickerson knew that his next twenty four hours would be frantic and sleepless. Over the years he had learned to accept this exhausting fate because of the exhilaration he felt when he plunged into the task of unraveling a new earthquake's mystery. Each and every one was different and, despite the death and destruction that often accompanied them, their uniqueness brought something fascinating to his work.

Earthquakes had been a part of the planet since the Precambrian and even if they didn't kill, they never failed to scrawl their telltale signatures on the seismographs next door. Somewhere in the jagged lines representing the seismic P- and S-waves was the answer to the *when, where,* and *how* of each and every cataclysmic event. Nickerson knew he had only to assiduously study the wavy lines to find the answers to these questions.

For him, the *why* was more elusive. The seismic recordings themselves only provided part of the answer. The rest lay out of the subdiscipline of seismology and within the more tangible realm of stratigraphy and structural geology. To understand the causes of an earthquake, Nickerson needed to understand what the rocks below the earth's surface were like before they were twisted by gigantic folds and broken by wrenching faults. To accomplish this, he applied forces to the undeformed rocks and developed a model of how they got to their present state, constraining the problem with what was physically possible in the subsurface. He and his colleagues never merely examined seismic waves. They conducted simulations using elaborate computer models to illuminate the dark, mysterious world far below the earth's surface.

As Nickerson sat back down at the conference table, Bill Schillerstrom hung up the phone. "Here's the preliminary damage report. There's been no reported deaths, but telephone, communications, electricity, and gas lines have been disrupted in Limon, Matheson, Simla, and Ramah along Highway 24. Also severe damage has been reported in the town of Kiowa, in Deer Trail and Agate along I-70, and in—"

Nickerson held up a hand, stopping him right there. "Wait a second. This baby was a 6.6 and there's been no reported deaths? Not one?"

"Not a single person. Who knows maybe there is a God?"

"I wouldn't bet on it. How many injured?"

"Fifty-seven people so far, some severely. But still no dead."

"Let's keep our fingers crossed that holds up. What about damage?"

"Several water tanks near Limon sprung leaks. Two bridges collapsed along Highway 86 east of Kiowa. A fire broke out in Matheson from a ruptured fuel line. The buildings at several local ranches have been badly damaged and many have collapsed entirely. A tanker overturned on I-70, caught on fire, and blew up, but the driver was able to escape."

"Luckily the closest towns are fifteen to twenty miles from the epicenter," said Brigid. "Still, this one was felt far and wide. I just got off the phone with state geologist Mark Kelso. He says our quake was felt as far north as Sheridan, as far west as Salt Lake City, as far south as Taos, and as far east as Wichita."

"What's the extent of the surface rupture?"

Bill shuffled through his papers. "The preliminary reports from the emergency response people in the area of the epicenter are that there isn't any."

"You're telling me we just had a 6.6 and there's no evidence of surface displacement? Is that what you're telling me?"

The young seismologist nodded.

"That doesn't make any sense," said Brigid. "What do you think is going on, Doctor?"

"I don't know—so far this one has me stumped. What about aftershocks?"

"There's been twelve more," replied Bill. "All less than 2.0 in magnitude."

Nickerson nodded, but his mind was already moving in a different direction. Something about the epicentral location of the earthquake and the lack of surface rupture vexed the seismologist. He looked up at the large overhead flat screen showing the locations of the active and potentially active faults and earthquakes in Colorado between 1870 and the present day. The faults, epicentral locations for modern instrumentally-located earthquakes, and estimated epicenters for historic quakes were shown in red lines, circles, and polygons. The circles and polygons were sized according to the magnitude or estimated magnitude of the earthquakes, with larger symbols for larger magnitude quakes. A big red circle denoted the epicenter of the new M 6.6 quake. Nickerson could see from the map that there were now only three seismographically-located epicenters in all of Elbert County and no mapped active or potentially active faults. The county was conspicuously devoid of red markings compared to nearby counties to the west, lying within the Front Range. He found it puzzling that a major earthquake would take place in a geologically stable and seismically quiescent area, especially since a fracking ban was in place in this portion of the basin. It didn't make any sense.

"It's strange that it happened so far from the mountains," Brigid said, mimicking his thoughts.

"This is no simple coincidence—something isn't right. There hasn't been anything like this before in Elbert County that I can see. What's the biggest on record?"

Bill quickly clicked the mouse and brought up a colored text box on the big screen. "June 5, 1963. Magnitude 3.0. Hypocenter 33 kilometers below the surface."

"A whole lot deeper than our new fella."

"Twenty miles down versus three," Brigid said. "I think it's safe to say we've got a completely different focal mechanism at work here."

"We've got a lot more than that, boys and girls. We've got a bona fide conundrum on our hands."

"Maybe we've entered the Twilight Zone," said Brigid, and she began humming the creepy theme song to the legendary TV show hosted by Rod Serling.

They all laughed, but there was a nervous edge to it. Nickerson knew they were in strange, uncharted territory here—and it made him uneasy as he pointed again at the map. "I see the three epicenters here, Bill. What I want to know is how many total seismic events have been documented in Elbert County, including those not instrumentally-located?"

"Just the two you see there, plus our new bad boy."

"You're messing with me, right? Only three total, all seismographically-located? No estimated historicals of any kind?"

Shaking his head, Bill showed him his printout. "Nothing above a 3.0...*ever*. Even when fracking was allowed in the southern portion of the basin between 2000 and 2007."

Nickerson thought: *We really have entered the Twilight Zone. How else to describe the impossible?*

He turned his gaze once again to the map on the big screen, still perplexed. The largest historic earthquake in Colorado was the 1882 temblor that struck ten miles north of Estes Park. However, because the tremor shook the Centennial State before the invention of the modern seismograph, no one knew its precise Richter magnitude. The modern estimated magnitude for the earthquake was 6.6 based on indirect correlation to its modified Mercalli intensity. The estimated uncertainty was +/- 0.6, which meant the actual quake could have been anywhere from M 6.0 to M 7.2. Whatever its true magnitude, it was up until today the largest in the state's recorded history. And the fact still remained that there had been precious few above 5.0, none of which had occurred anywhere near the epicenter of today's quake.

That was what the Earthquake Man found most vexing.

What unique conditions had given rise to a major earthquake in an area where major earthquakes were totally unexpected?

CHAPTER 5

JOSEPH HIGHEAGLE'S HOUSE was a single-story Ranch in Littleton. It had a wood exterior in bad need of a fresh coat of paint, a pair of rusty old horseshoes nailed to the front door, and a trifecta of sugar maples and a knotty old apple tree out front. To the pleasant tinkling of wind chimes, Higheagle jiggled the front door open and waved his grandfather, who bore twelve fresh stitches on his forehead, inside. They had made good time on the way home from Cañon City; I-25 and the smaller thoroughfares had been surprisingly unclogged and damage free. When they stepped into the family room, his grandfather made a beeline for the couch, flopped down in it, and turned on the TV with a remote.

After a minute's worth of channel surfing, he settled on CNN. Veteran reporter Blair Gage appeared behind a desk with a split screen window on her left showing a distinguished-looking elderly man with a goatee, dark turtleneck, and sleek French beret tilted at a rakish angle. Along the bottom of the screen, the caption read:

JACK PATEY, "THE EARTHQUAKE PROPHET"

"Hey, it's that guy who predicts earthquakes," said the old chief.

"You mean that USGS guy, Dr. Nickerson?"

"No, you're thinking of the Earthquake Man. This is the other guy, the Earthquake Prophet."

Higheagle sat down in the recliner and studied the face on the screen as his grandfather turned up the volume. "Oh yeah, Jack Patey. He predicted that a major earthquake would take place in Southern California around the time of the Oscars last February. He said it would hit somewhere in the desert and one actually struck west of El Centro during the acceptance speech for best director."

"That's the dude. He ended up writing a book about it after he was fired from his job as the California state geologist. His boss told him to keep his mouth shut about his prediction and claimed that he had incited a panic. Hell, instead of firing the son of a bitch, they should have given him a fucking medal."

"Come on, Grandfather. He just got lucky—no one can really predict earthquakes."

"The Earthquake Prophet can. Quiet, let's listen to what he has to say."

REPORTER: *"According to your website, Dr. Patey, you predicted that an earthquake with a magnitude greater than 5.0 would strike along the Front Range between Colorado Springs and Denver this week. The Colorado Quake, as today's event is being called, is the tenth major earthquake that you have successfully predicted out of a total of thirteen since last February's Oscars. Can you tell our audience how you do it?"*

PATEY: *"Well, Blair, as you know, my theory is based on the fact that when the moon is new or full, there are stronger than normal gravitational stresses caused by the conjunction of the earth, moon, and sun. These time intervals of maximum gravitational pull are responsible for the unusually high tides, known as spring tides, that we see twice per month. When the earth, moon, and sun form a line, a condition known as syzygy, the solar reinforces the lunar and the tide's range is at its maximum. During these spring tides, there is added stress to the earth's tectonic plates and we typically see a larger number of destructive earthquakes. I call these time intervals seismic windows."*

REPORTER: *"These seismic windows, as you call them, are described in detail in your New York Times best-selling book* 'The Holy Grail of Seismology: Predicting Major Earthquakes and Saving Lives.' "

PATEY: *"That is correct, Blair."*

REPORTER: *"Please tell us how your theory relates to today's quake."*

PATEY: *"Yes, of course. Well at present a statistically above-average number of earthquakes are expected globally in the seismic window of October 23 through 31, which began today and runs through Halloween. This window is based on tonight's full moon, the very close lunar perigee—or the time when the moon is closest to the earth—early tomorrow morning, and the projected maximum Golden Gate tide of nine feet for this Tuesday, October 25. This will be the highest in two years. Now the reason I predicted a 5.0+ event specifically within the Front Range during this seismic window is because of the large number of lost pets reported in the area during the last two weeks. So I take two things into account, Blair. The gravitational cycle tells me when a destructive earthquake is expected. And the behavior of animals, especially household pets, tells me where a large event is most likely to occur."*

REPORTER: *"So animals like cats and dogs are picking up signals that an earthquake is imminent? That's why there's a correlation between lost pet ads and the timing of earthquakes?"*

PATEY: *"Exactly. We already know that dogs, cats, and other animals detect seismic P waves seconds before the S wave arrives. My theory is that animals also express seismic-escape behavior patterns days, or even weeks, in advance of a major event by picking up slight changes in the gravitational and electromagnetic field and connecting these perceptions with an impending earthquake. Basically, these animals can sense what's about to happen and they are trying to get out of the area, to safety."*

REPORTER: *"How were you able to get a tally of the number of lost pets in this case?"*

PATEY: *"As part of my SeismicWatch program, I have made arrangements with local and regional newspapers and earthquake trackers in every seismically active state in the country. The information is downloaded into my database on a daily basis. For the two-week period preceding today's earthquake, there were reports of two hundred and seventy-nine lost dogs and cats in the towns of Limon, which is the closest city to the quake, Denver, Castle Rock, Colorado Springs, and twenty small towns up and down the Front Range. The usual expected number for all of these areas is less than ten in a given two-week period. That's why I predicted a major earthquake in this area during my seismic window of October 23 through 31."*

REPORTER: *"Thank you, Dr. Patey. We're joined now by Dr. James Nickerson of the USGS National Earthquake Information Center in Golden, Colorado. Dr. Nickerson, can you tell us what the casualty figures are for this earthquake?"*

NICKERSON (appearing in a split-screen with Patey): *"There have been no reported deaths from the earthquake, Blair, but almost a hundred people have been injured."*

REPORTER: *"What about the financial loss from the earthquake?"*

NICKERSON: *"The economic loss from this event—which is the same magnitude as the biggest earthquake in the state's history in 1882—will exceed two hundred fifty million dollars."*

REPORTER: *"Is there anything that can be done to prevent these kind of losses in the future? That is, in terms of earthquake prediction?"*

NICKERSON: *"First of all, Blair, there is no such thing as earthquake prediction. There simply is no reliable or reproducible way to predict earthquakes. Neither the USGS or Caltech nor any other scientists in the United States or abroad has ever predicted a major earthquake."*

REPORTER: *"But Dr. Patey here posted on his SeismicWatch website that a magnitude 5.0 or greater earthquake would occur this week between Denver and Colorado Springs. Are you saying that he didn't predict the earthquake?"*

NICKERSON: *"I don't know what Dr. Patey posted on his website, but he does not know how to predict earthquakes. The only thing that can be done scientifically is to make long-range forecasts estimating the probability of potential future earthquakes. For example, USGS seismologists estimate that, over the next thirty years, the probability of a major earthquake occurring in Southern California is approximately sixty percent and in the Bay area is sixty-seven percent."*

REPORTER: *"Do you agree with that assessment Dr. Patey?"*

PATEY: *"Absolutely not, Blair. Look, I may not be able to pin down the exact location of the epicenter, the precise magnitude, or the exact hour of the day of an impending earthquake, but my technique has eighty percent accuracy within my seismic windows. The USGS just doesn't like to use the "P" word because* predictions *aren't one hundred percent reliable. And yet, as you just heard, they do long-term thirty year forecasting. The problem with their method is it doesn't heighten earthquake preparedness or take into account non-traditional ways of predicting earthquakes. It's human nature to become complacent if we are not made aware of the increased risks during periods of potential seismic activity. That's all I do—I inform people of potential spatial and temporal risks associated with earthquakes."*

"This Earthquake Prophet sure as hell sounds reasonable to me," said the old chief. "Why did the state fire his ass when they should have given him a promotion for warning everyone?"

"I still think he's more or less guessing," countered Higheagle. "There's no way to accurately predict whether an earthquake is going to happen or not."

REPORTER: *"So, Dr. Nickerson, can animals predict earthquakes?"*

NICKERSON: *"No one denies that animals can sense the primary P wave prior to the arrival of the more destructive secondary wave, or S wave, during a seismic event. But animal behavior still can't be used to predict earthquakes in any reliable, scientific manner. Even though there have been documented cases of unusual animal behavior prior to earthquakes, a reproducible connection between a specific behavior and an earthquake has never been established. Animals change their behavior for many reasons—defending their territory, hunger, mating, predators— and given that an earthquake can affect hundreds of thousands or even millions of people, it is likely that a few pets will, by chance, be acting strangely before an earthquake."*

PATEY: *"But this wasn't just a few pets. This was two hundred and seventy-nine when less than ten is the typical number."*

NICKERSON: *"So you say, Jack, but a high number of runaway pets still doesn't prove an earthquake is coming. The big question is still this: if we could accurately predict that a big earthquake was going to happen tomorrow, how can we use that prediction to save lives? The research shows that animals react just before a major event. That's not enough time to evacuate people."*

PATEY: *"But there is enough time. These cats and dogs along the Front Range sensed the earthquake more than a week in advance. And there were no foreshocks so what they must have been sensing are changes in the earth's gravitational, and perhaps electromagnetic, field."*

REPORTER: *"What would it take to prove to you, Dr. Nickerson, and the USGS that animals can be used to predict earthquakes?"*

NICKERSON: *"I don't think that anyone is trying to disprove it. All I'm saying is that animals typically don't react in time to allow people to be evacuated. Look, we had nearly a hundred people injured today and we were lucky, very lucky, no one died. If there were a foolproof way of monitoring animal behavior to get an advanced warning signal, then we would have implemented it by now. That's all I have to say."*

REPORTER: *"Thank you, Dr. Nickerson. Dr. Patey, do you have anything to add?"*

PATEY: *"Just one thing. These quakes aren't through yet. According to the data I've examined, we're due for another major temblor in the near future."*

REPORTER: *"Really? Can you tell us when and where?"*

NICKERSON: *"Stop this, Jack. This 'Earthquake Prophet' stuff is going to your head. All you're doing is scaring people. The citizens of this state have just been through a terrible tragedy. The last thing they need is a charlatan claiming he's the next Nostradamus."*

REPORTER: *"My question still stands, Dr. Patey."*

PATEY: *"Thank you, Blair. I'm afraid the Front Range is going to be hit again."*

REPORTER: *"Where?"*

PATEY: *"Near Castle Rock."*

REPORTER: *"How do you know?"*

PATEY: *"Because I have reports that there are countless animals— domesticated dogs and cats as well as wild antelope, coyotes, deer, prairie dogs, rabbits, and squirrels—still attempting to make it out of the area. These animals are still in an agitated state and that's why I'm convinced that there will be another event. Perhaps along a different fault or different segment of the fault where the seismic energy has built up."*

NICKERSON: *"This kind of talk is ridiculous, Jack—you're going to cause a panic. No wonder you were fired from—"*

REPORTER, urgently: *"Can you tell us when, Dr. Patey? All of America is waiting to hear what you have to say!"*

PATEY: *"All I can tell you is that an earthquake will strike again in the present seismic window."*

REPORTER: *"How big will it be?"*

PATEY: *"The magnitude of the quake will be 7.0 plus."*

REPORTER: *"Please, Dr. Patey, can you narrow down the date and time any more than that for our audience?"*

PATEY: *"I'm going to go out on a limb here, Blair. I believe the quake will strike east of Castle Rock next Monday—on Halloween night!"*

CHAPTER 6

"WELL THAT WAS ENTERTAINING," said Higheagle as the screen cut to commercial. He hit the *Mute* button on the remote so he and his grandfather could talk.

"You can say that again. But I'll bet you the Earthquake Prophet's prediction comes true."

"I'll take that bet. Ten bucks? Twenty? How about a hundred?"

"Let's make it dinner at the Buckhorn, you little pecker neck. It's been awhile since I've enjoyed some tasty broiled elk medallions and marinated rattlesnake."

"You've got a deal. But don't tell me you actually believe this guy can predict earthquakes based on lost pets?"

The old chief propped his feet on the pine coffee table. "Of course I do, but unlike you I know a thing or two about earthquakes."

"Please, grandfather, I'm a geologist. Or have you forgotten?"

"Okay Mr. Big Shot Geoscientist, so you remember that Sumatran earthquake and tsunami a few years back that killed almost a quarter million people?"

"How could anyone forget? That was devastating."

"Well, a herd of elephants knew it was coming. They began behaving strangely, stamping the ground and tugging at their chains long before the tsunami hit. Eventually they broke away and ran into the hills."

"That doesn't prove they knew an earthquake was coming. They may have sensed the change in atmospheric pressure from the approaching tsunami."

"True enough. But people all over the world have been reporting on strange animal behavior leading up to earthquakes for centuries. I've read up on it and it's nothing new. In ancient Greece, eyewitnesses reported that rats, snakes, and weasels deserted the city of Helice and headed for safety several days before a monster earthquake demolished the city. Then there was the Lisbon quake in 1755. The animals sensed danger and fled from low lying areas to higher ground long before the earthquake and tsunami hit."

"But as Nickerson said, we still don't know exactly what an animal senses days or weeks before a big event. You heard him. He said that a connection between a specific animal behavior and an impending earthquake has never been established."

"And I say Dr. Nickerson is wrong and the Earthquake Prophet is right. There's no reason to make it more complicated than it is. All Patey has done is come up with a scientific theory that explains what people have known for centuries. Plus I kind of like the son of a bitch for having the balls to go public before the Oscars."

"Yeah, I've got to admit that was cool."

"He didn't just call out the USGS and all of those California bureaucrats. He took on all those pompous academics at Cal Tech, UCLA, USC, Stanford, and the other universities. I don't know why they all dismissed him out of hand when his prediction was spot on. He was quoted in the newspaper a week before the telecast."

"I still think the guy's a little out there, Grandfather. I mean a French beret, come on? You want a beer?"

"Sure, but make it a Coors, not one of those fancy pants microbrews you keep in there."

"Roger that, Chief." Chuckling to himself, he headed towards the kitchen to grab the beers. When he reached the doorway, he glanced back appreciatively at the old man, who had taken the TV off *Mute* and was leaning back in his seat listening to more news on the quake. Even at seventy-four, John Higheagle looked strong as an ox from all the hiking he did in the foothills and all the weightlifting and biking he did at the gym. He had intelligent brown eyes, a wide nose that was hooked on the end, and long silver hair that would have tickled the middle of his back had it not been plaited along both ears in the traditional Cheyenne fashion. He was a retired tribal chief, lawyer, and former soldier who had served as a sergeant in the 7th Marine Regiment—the fabled "Magnificent Seventh"— in Korea. Since his retirement two months ago, he no longer lived or practiced law on the Northern Cheyenne Reservation in Lame Deer, Montana, but lived with his grandson in Denver. The old man had an air of mischief about him, which Higheagle knew was from his being a Contrary, a Cheyenne holy man who acted in opposite to serve an important tribal religious function and as a source of amusement. Since his grandfather had moved in, they were like the Odd Couple and sometimes fought like cats and dogs. But Higheagle loved him dearly and always made sure to listen attentively to his wise counsel.

His gaze lingered fondly on the old warhorse a moment longer before he walked to the fridge and grabbed a pair of ice-cold beers. Returning to the family room, he handed his grandfather a Coors and sat back down in the recliner with a Fat Tire in hand. His grandfather had switched from CNN to the Channel 4 News, where Dr. Nickerson was being interviewed again, this time by a local reporter.

"Shit, don't they ever give the guy a break?" said the old chief.

"Apparently not. I guess that's why they call him the 'Earthquake Man'."

"It's a hell of a fucking nickname—but not as good as the 'Earthquake Prophet'."

REPORTER: *"Dr. Nickerson, can you tell us anything new about the earthquake?"*

NICKERSON: *"The only new development is that we've refined our epicenter determination. The actual location is twenty miles due west of Limon on the Wilson Ranch. Thankfully, all of the people living there survived though the damage to the ranch was extensive..."*

As Nickerson went on, Higheagle suddenly thought of something and dashed into his office. He rifled through two of the drawers until he found a road map of Colorado and a ruler, then hurried back to the recliner. He set the map on the coffee table. He hadn't realized until now how close the epicenter was to Quantrill's waste treatment and hydrocarbon refining facility outside the town of Elbert. He located the approximate epicenter on the map. Using the ruler and map scale, he estimated that it was about thirty miles east of Quantrill's facility, twenty miles west of Limon, and fifty miles northeast of Colorado Springs.

"What the hell are you doing over there?" asked his grandfather.

"I was just wondering if there was any damage at Quantrill's facility."

"What are you hoping that there's a fresh new chemical leak that your company can clean up?"

"Not hoping—just wondering. I have to drill some wells and take some groundwater samples out there this week. I was trying to figure out if I might have to adjust some of the well locations based on this earthquake."

The old chief turned up the volume again as Dr. Nickerson disappeared from the screen and the station cut to pictures of cracked ceiling tiles, plaster walls, and windows in the town of Limon. These were followed by interviews of people in the towns and ranches east of the epicenter. Although a few individuals had been frightened out of their wits, most of the people actually seemed to be enjoying themselves.

Soon Nickerson came back on. For the next few minutes, his interview was interspersed with interviews of farmers, ranchers, small business owners, and others affected by the quake. Higheagle saw a noticeable difference in attitude between the seismologist and the general public. While Nickerson appeared tense and solemn, Joe Average Citizen seemed to be in an almost celebratory mood. He had survived Mother Nature's tectonic fury and would now be able to go back to his life virtually unscathed and tell his grandkids about it.

"Jesus, look at these people," said the old chief. "They sure as hell won't be joking around and high-fiving when the next one hits."

"Come on, Grandfather, there won't be a next one. The Earthquake Prophet's just trying to stir things up so he can sell more copies of his book."

The old Contrary gave a wily smile. "I don't think so."

"Oh you don't, do you?"

"Nope. And come Halloween night, I'll wager you and old Dr. Nickerson won't be doubting the Earthquake Prophet anymore either."

"Come on, you old fart, you really think the big one's going to hit?"

The old chief's eyes took on a puissant gleam. In that moment, he looked like he was from another time and place, as if he had harkened back to the days of their Cheyenne ancestors and transformed into a holy man conjuring up the spirits before a great buffalo hunt on the High Plains. "I don't think so, Grandson. I know so," he said.

Something about the look of resolve in his eyes made Higheagle's body go still. "You're serious, aren't you?"

"Deadly serious. You see, when I was hanging over that cliff staring death in the face, I had myself a vision."

"A vision?"

"A crazy fucking vision."

"What…what did you see, Grandfather?"

"The future, Grandson. I saw the future."

CHAPTER 7

CHARLES PROMETHEUS QUANTRILL'S private study at his mansion in the venerable Broadmoor neighborhood of Colorado Springs had a masculine, traditional Western flair. Everything was big, bold, and supremely costly, fully befitting of a man who had risen from unheralded origins in the Lone Star State to one of the richest men in the United States—indeed the entire world.

What made the room extraordinary was the priceless collection of prehistoric specimens and Western history artifacts exhibited in the glass display cases gracing the walls. One cabinet of curiosities bore a collection of uncommonly huge Cambrian trilobites and brachiopods, a fossilized fish from the Eocene Green River Formation, and a two-foot diameter Cretaceous coiled ammonite; while two others prominently displayed a set of stubby English Webley bulldog pistols, a collection of flint arrow points and bear claw necklaces representing various western Native American tribes, an exceedingly rare Cheyenne dentalium shell choker and set of ceremonial red cantlandite war pipes, and a pair of knee-high 1876 U.S. cavalry boots encased in golden spurs. Nicely rounding out the room were a handwoven Navaho rug once owned by Kit Carson, three priceless paintings by Charles Russell, and the stuffed head of a gargantuan bull elk Quantrill had bagged in the Medicine Bow Mountains last fall.

But what stole all the attention was the complete fossilized skeleton of *Dimetrodon grandis*, a cold-blooded protomammal that ruled the deltas of Texas as the most fearsome hunter of its day, forty million years before the dinosaurs. The skeleton stretched eight feet from the tip of its snout to the end of its tail, and its back was adorned with a large sail supported by bony rods, which in life had been covered by a webbing of scaly skin. The skull was large with broadly curved, almost smiling jaws lined with razor-sharp teeth. *Dimetrodon* was the first predator to literally dominate the terrestrial world, and this particular specimen had a special place in Quantrill's heart: Al Romer, the famous Harvard paleontologist, had given the magnificent specimen to the scrappy Texan when he was a boy.

Sensing some uneasiness in the room, Quantrill took a moment to study the three men he had summoned to his sprawling English-style country manor: Jeb Quantrill, Ph.D., age 62, Executive Vice-President, Chief Geologist, and minority owner of Quantrill Ventures, a leaner, more introspective, brainier version of his older brother; Wesley Johnston, age 59, also an Executive VP, Chief Engineer, pug-nosed, squatty, from the Hill Country not far from Austin, where he received his M.S. in civil engineering from the University of Texas; and Jack Holland, Esq., age 53, Chief In-House Counsel, bald, cadaverously thin, called *The Boil* (behind his back, of course) due to his complete lack of a sense of humor.

Quantrill cleared his throat and looked at his chief engineer. "All right Wes, go ahead and kick things off. And make sure you give enough background for our esteemed esquire here to render a sound legal opinion. Jack knows the big picture, just not all them technical details you and Jeb are so fond of."

"Yes, sir."

Still looking nervous, Wesley Johnston made his way to the satellite view map hanging from the display wall. He took a moment to collect his thoughts before launching into his presentation.

"As you all know, for the last ten years we've been pumping fluids along this pipeline here to our three-well injection network here." Using his laser pointer, he traced the pipeline from the facility to the well cluster approximately twenty miles to the east. "All of the wells are completed to different depths and have different screened intervals. This allows us to inject at different levels and not overpressure any one formation. We can also control the flow volume to each well or even shut one or more wells off at a given time. For the first three years of the injection program, we were pumping into deep well DW-105 screened in the metamorphic bedrock below a depth of ten thousand feet. During this time, our seismograph network at the injection well cluster recorded twenty-seven minor tremors, all of them below 1.0 in magnitude and none within a fifteen-mile radius of the wellfield. For point of reference, the USGS only records earthquakes above 1.0 and doesn't care about anything less than a 2.5.

"During the next three years, we injected into this intermediate well here, well IW-106. We experienced thirteen minor earthquakes, again none above a 1.0 and again no event within a fifteen-mile radius. After the second injection period, we pumped into the Hygiene Sandstone in well SW-107, which totals out at four thousand feet in this part of the Denver-Julesburg. This is our shallow well injection zone. We've recorded a total of nineteen seismic events since we've been injecting into this zone. All have been below 1.0 until today's 6.6 and the aftershocks in the 1.0 to 3.0 range that followed. Furthermore, all of the aftershocks have taken place more than fifteen miles from the injection well network."

"But now, for the first time, we've got big earthquakes on our hands," observed Jack Holland.

Johnston looked the attorney squarely in the eye. "I don't believe our deep well injection operation has anything to do with the earthquakes."

"Why not?"

"Because the epicenter of the main shock was fifteen miles away from the injection well network."

Quantrill glanced at his brother, whose opinion he valued most. "What do you think, Jeb? Is it possible the fluid could have traveled all the way from the well cluster to the epicenter?"

The chief geologist and second in command at Quantrill Ventures appeared to choose his words carefully. "I doubt the fluid injection could have pushed the waste fifteen miles horizontally in only ten years. But it may have increased the pore pressure enough to lower the shearing resistance of the rocks and trigger a bigger than usual earthquake along some fault that wasn't evident in our seismic survey."

"But how?" countered Johnston. "You didn't identify any active or even potentially active faults in the seismic profiling. And our surface injection and subsurface formation pressure gauges all show normal. You and I both checked them independently two hours ago."

"I suspect there are natural heterogeneities in the rocks that are somehow directing wastewater flow far away from the injection wells."

Quantrill looked at his two top scientists. "But you and Wes here sited this injection well network specifically because it was in a stable area in terms of earthquake potential. Are you telling me now that everything has changed and our operation has turned these tectonically quiet little Plains below our feet into California or Japan?"

"Just because a fault hasn't been mapped doesn't mean it's not there. You can only see so much in cores. It's not like an outcrop where you can see fractures over a large area."

"But you've told us before that the fracture orientation is to the north," countered Johnston.

"That's true," conceded Jeb.

Quantrill scrutinized his brother closely. "Let me get this straight. You're telling us the fractures from our original field tests in the Dakota and older Precambrian rocks aren't oriented to the east in the direction of the earthquakes?"

"That's correct. The fractures appear to be oriented for the most part towards the north. Actually, a little east of north, but not by much."

"I know I'm not the scientific expert, but it sounds to me, Brother, like our pumping fluids down those holes has nothing to do with today's quake."

"I agree," said Johnston.

Jeb drummed his fingers along the arm of his chair. "Okay, maybe I am being overly cautious. But we have to remember that peoples' lives are at stake. That's why I think we should either cut back on how much we're pumping or stop altogether for awhile until we've had time to properly assess the situation. There's got to be a relationship between the volume injected and the earthquake frequency for the low magnitude data that we haven't figured out yet. Maybe this new event and the aftershocks will shed light on it."

"I agree with Jeb," said the ever vigilant Holland. "Wouldn't it be prudent to either lower the injection rate or stop for awhile just to make certain?"

The table went silent. The men looked at one another for a moment before all eyes settled on the decision-maker: Quantrill. He realized that they were waiting for him to tell them what to do.

"I'm sorry, gentlemen, but I haven't seen enough evidence to justify stopping the program. Jeb, you and Wes keep studying the situation. But for the time being we're going to keep injecting at least a half million gallons per day. We're a business operation and we need to keep profitable."

Jeb leaned forward in his chair, his taut expression evidencing a hint of desperation. "Then let's at least pump into both the shallow and intermediate formations simultaneously, to be safe."

The powerful men gathered around the table looked at one another. "I think that's a good idea," Johnston agreed after a moment's reflection. "The depth where the fault ruptured is more than fifteen thousand feet below ground surface. It might help to redistribute the flow."

Quantrill saw how much it meant to Jeb that they proceed with some degree of caution going forward. He decided to throw him a bone. "All right, Brother, you've always been the smart one of the family. I've learned over the years to trust your judgment. Let's go ahead and split the flow between the Hygiene and the Dakota."

Relief spread instantly across Jeb's face, which pleased Quantrill. Although as CEO the buck ultimately stopped with him, he preferred to build a consensus with his inner circle—and especially his brilliant younger brother—on all major decisions, even if he disagreed with them.

"Wes and I will take care of it right away," said Jeb with renewed enthusiasm.

But Jack Holland still looked uneasy. "I still see a problem here. If the injection operation is not what's causing these earthquakes, then what the hell is?"

"We don't know the answer to that yet, Jack," said Quantrill. "But we will soon enough. That's priority number one."

"What about this environmental drilling project coming up?" Johnston

37

posed to the group. "Should we postpone it until we have a better handle on the situation?"

"What drilling project?" asked Holland.

"We're scheduled to drill some shallow groundwater monitoring wells this week at the waste treatment plant," said Jeb. "It's being done by our consultant HydroGroup."

"Who's in charge?" asked the attorney.

"Joseph Higheagle. The senior hydrogeologist."

"What's the investigation for?"

"To delineate chlorinated solvent contamination in groundwater from leaks associated with plant operations. The EPA's coming out later in the week to have a meeting. They just want some more sampling is all."

"Do any of you anticipate any problems with this investigation?" asked Holland, looking around the table. "You know, with the EPA or this Higheagle fellow?"

Quantrill and Johnston looked at Jeb.

"No, it's routine," said the chief geologist. "It should be no problem at all."

CHAPTER 8

DR. JAMES NICKERSON splashed some tapwater on his face. The icy cold water revived him instantly, but peering into the bathroom mirror, he still saw a tired old man staring back at him.

I'm getting too old for this crap, he thought irritably.

He snatched a paper towel to dry his hands and headed back to his office. As he sat back down in his stiff, high-backed office chair, he remembered back to his first earthquake.

Hebgen Lake, Montana, August 17, 1959.

He was thirteen years old at the time. His family was enjoying a summer vacation in Yellowstone and had rented a cabin on the lake. The 7.1 magnitude earthquake struck before midnight, tilting Hebgen Lake like a pinball machine, submerging cabins at one end, lifting docks dry at the other, and sending a landslide down the Madison River Canyon that dammed up the river and created another 175-foot-deep lake in the process. The avalanche of rock, mud, and debris that rumbled down through the valley killed nearly thirty people.

Luckily, no one in his family died that night. But he still remembered the violent ground shaking, the roar of the landslide, the devastating power of the earth's forces at work. The next morning he watched the National Guardsmen pull the battered corpses from the rubble. He remembered staring out at the devastation all around the lodge: the gaping fissures in the road, the collapsed cabins, the aprons of rocky debris, the soot-blackened ground and tendrils of smoke lifting into the sky from the smoldering remains of a wood cabin that had caught fire. But what had terrified him most was the sight of the broken, lifeless bodies being pulled from the debris. One of the unfortunate victims was a boy no older than he; at the time, it had seemed poignantly unfair to him that someone his own age should die.

It was on that day that Nickerson vowed that he would one day save people from tragedies like what he had witnessed. If only earthquakes could be reliably predicted, then people wouldn't have to—

"Dr. Nickerson, are you all right?" a voice broke through his reverie.

"What, I...? Oh, hello, Brigid."

The young geophysicist stepped into his office. "Is everything okay?"

"Yes, I'm fine...I was just thinking."

"I'm sorry to bother you, but this thing with Dr. Patey has everyone on edge."

"Dr. Patey? Don't you mean the Earthquake Prophet?"

"If his prediction comes true, we're all going to look like fools."

"Halloween night? Come on, the guy's nothing but a rock star."

"A lot of us aren't so sure."

"A lot of us?"

"Most of the staff."

He suppressed a gulp. "Really?"

"At first, we tried to laugh off the prediction as a bunch of pseudoscience. For years we've looked down our noses at him and his wild theories—but now everything's changed. We're scared to death that he's actually been right all this time and we've been acting like a bunch of academic snobs."

"Brigid, you know as well as I that there is no such thing as earthquake prediction."

"I used to think that…but…but I just read Dr. Kirschvink's paper."

"Earthquake Prediction by Animals: Evolution and Sensory Perception?"

"So you've read it. Then you know he makes a strong case that animals respond to seismic precursor signals such as changes in ground tilting and electrical and magnetic field variations."

"Yes, I'm quite familiar with Dr. Kirschvink's seismic escape-response system theory."

"Then you know what he recommends. Installing magnetic devices and electrical, tilt, and hygro-sensors in seismically active regions to give advanced warning for destructive earthquakes that can be correlated to animal behavior."

"As I've said, I'm quite familiar with Dr. Kirschvink's theory."

"I know Dr. Patey's a little out there, but he's basically only saying the same thing as Dr. Kirschvink."

"Dr. Kirschvink happens to be a respected evolutionary scientist and geobiology expert. There's no comparison between the two of them."

"That may be, but that doesn't change the fact that the staff is really worked up about this. Everyone's scared to death that another earthquake is going to hit on Halloween night and we did nothing to warn the public. I'm serious, there's a bad vibe going around. People are talking about not even coming in on Monday."

He couldn't believe that his staff was coming unraveled like this. My God, this was the United States Geological Survey—not the goddamned Cub Scouts! But at the same time, he knew that the human mind was enormously fragile. Even the most rational, objective scientist was not immune to invoking supernatural or mysterious explanations for certain phenomena.

Not wanting to hurt her feelings and unsure of how to respond, he turned his gaze away from her and peered at the pictures on the wall behind his desk, taking a moment to gather his thoughts. Gazing back at him were his three biggest heroes: Martin Luther King, Jr., the pioneering civil rights leader; John Milne, British mining geologist, father of modern seismology, and inventor of the seismograph; and John Wesley Powell, founder of the USGS and leader of the first expedition down the Grand Canyon.

Suddenly his telephone rang. He looked at the phone number on the digital readout. It was his boss, Nathaniel Watkins, the USGS director and science advisor to the president.

"Brigid, I've got to take this."

"Okay, but people are really worked up about this."

"Don't worry, I'll take care of it," he said, though he didn't have the faintest idea how he might accomplish the difficult task. "But right now I have to take this call."

"You promise you'll take care of it?"

"Yes I promise." He smiled reassuringly then waved her out the door and picked up the phone. "Director Watkins, how are you?"

"Not good, James, not good at all. My office is being bombarded with emails from angry citizens. They want to know why our agency can't predict earthquakes like the Earthquake Prophet. As if we're supposed to peer into some sort of crystal fucking ball."

"Mr. Director, you've got to trust me on this. This man is a loony tune."

"He also happens to have a Ph.D. from Cal Tech, was up until recently the California state geologist, and is a widely published author on earthquakes. People are listening to him, damnit!"

"I understand, sir. But what do you want me to do about it?"

"I want you to debate him."

Nickerson prayed that he didn't just hear what he thought he had heard. "Excuse me, sir, I don't think I—"

"You're going to debate him, James—we have no other choice. We've arranged a slot for you on *Newsline* for this Sunday night."

Nickerson swallowed hard. *Newsline, the prime time news show? Heaven help me.* He tried to find his voice, but it was nowhere to be found.

"If you handle this right, I promise an additional twenty-five million in your NEIC budget for next year. Just think what you could do with that kind of money, James. Think of all the computer hardware and software upgrades, the educational programs, the research papers, conferences, and training seminars. With that kind of money you could increase earthquake awareness to an unprecedented level."

"I understand, sir. But why the hard sell?"

"Because we need you to bury this bastard once and for all."

"We're talking about a debate on a news show not military combat, right?"

"He hit the 99th percentile, James. Which means that there's statistically only a one percent probability that his seismic window predictions could be matching the actual earthquake dates by chance alone. In other words, there's some kind of method to the madness, statistically speaking. Now how can that be if the guy's a crackpot who was fired from his job? We just want him to go away, James. The accuracy of his predictions is proving to be messy for the Survey."

Nickerson felt himself being set up like a bowling pin. "Mr. Director, I'm not sure I'm comfortable with this."

"You can cut the sanctimonious bullshit, James, because you're going to do this. And that comes from Secretary Jackson, not me, by the way."

The Secretary of the Interior? He's involved in this? Shit!

"When the Secretary wants something to go away, it needs to go away. The position of the United States Government—which, as you know, includes the USGS—is that there is no such thing as earthquake prediction. If the insurance industry or American Bar Association were to ever have any remotely credible basis for believing otherwise, then we've got a big problem on our hands. Do you understand now why this is so important?"

Nickerson said nothing. Biting his lip, he rose from his chair, went to the window, and gazed out at the gauzy sky and cottonwoods waving in the wind. A pair of turkey vultures perched on one of the limbs peered back at him. They were hideous creatures with their giant bat-like wings, hooked beaks, and dark soulless eyes. They reminded him of Director Watkins on the other end of the line, a scavenger picking at his carcass. *Damn him for putting me in this position!*

"So you'll do it, James? You'll take care of this for us?" It was a command, not a question.

The words hung there a moment, like a threatening storm cloud.

Nickerson hesitated. "I'll try my best, sir."

"No, you're going to do better than that, James. You're going to take care of this."

CHAPTER 9

THREE DAYS LATER—on Thursday October 27, 2008—four days before Halloween, Nina Curry was listening to the thrum of her supervisor's Prius engine as they drove along a paved county road seven miles west of the Quantrill Ventures facility. Her ash-blonde hair was perched along the rim of her slender shoulders and her well-sculpted face carried a hint of a smile. It was the same look of satisfaction that had been appearing often these past two weeks. Since she had moved to Denver and started her new job at the Environmental Protection Agency's Region 8 headquarters downtown.

There was just something about wiping the slate clean and making a fresh start in life. She had spent six wonderful years as an environmental engineer with the EPA Region 9 office in San Francisco, but it had definitely been time to move on. Relationships were a challenge—that would never change—but this last one had been an absolute disaster.

She glanced out of the corner of her eye at her new boss. If not for Richard Hamilton, she wouldn't have been able to transfer to Denver. Over the past two years, she had seen him on several occasions at environmental conferences and he always reminded her that he had an opening for her at the EPA office in the Mile High City if she so desired. She had never even considered taking him up on his offer until two months earlier when things had gotten out of control with her ex-boyfriend and he began to stalk her. She had called Richard on a Tuesday and by the following Friday the transfer was official. Which was no small feat given the EPA's cumbersome bureaucracy.

Studying him discretely as they drove, she had to admit that she had something of a crush on him, though he was happily married and she would never jeopardize her career by having a relationship with a married man. He was the Director of the Hazardous Waste Management Division and a powerful player in the EPA Region 8 hierarchy. She had seen him deliver at least a half dozen speeches at technical conferences and he was always head and shoulders above the other speakers.

As if reading her mind, he looked over at her and smiled. "So, Miz Curry, any last minute questions about today's agenda?"

"I did have one question."

"Good, fire away."

"After the primary meeting with Jeb Quantrill, we're going to meet briefly with Charles Quantrill on the wind farm project, correct?"

"That's right."

"And following that meeting, you're going over to the refinery to do your inspection while I oversee the drilling at the waste facility with this Joseph Higheagle fellow from HydroGroup?"

"You've got it. My inspection should take less than two hours. We'll be out of there by lunchtime."

"Really, that quick?"

"Yes, as a dutiful government employee, I always put food before work. You should know that about me by now."

"Silly me, how could I forget?" She grinned. "So tell me what's Joseph Higheagle like?"

"The guy knows his stuff. He's probably the only environmental consultant I agree with more than half the time. You're going to like him."

"He's Cheyenne, right?"

"Full-blooded. But I promise he won't take your scalp."

"Very funny. What about Charles Quantrill? What's he like?"

"Well let's see. If I had to describe him in a single sound bite, I would say that he was once a big brash Texas oil man who has evolved over time into an environmentally proactive alternative energy guru."

"It sounded like you were just reading from a resume."

"Did it now? Well how about this: did you know that Quantrill Ventures has the highest 'green' rating of any Fortune 100 energy company in the U.S.?"

"Actually, I did know that."

"So then you also know that he and his brother take environmental compliance very seriously. Like many of us at the EPA, they actually believe that incorporating sustainability and triple bottom line into their business model is nothing more than sound business practice."

"Okay, now you definitely sound like a PR guy. Come on, what's Charles Quantrill really like?"

"For starters, he doesn't seem like a billionaire. He's really down to earth in an old fashioned cowboy kind of way. He's also a gym rat. He's sixty-five years old but he looks a decade younger than that because he takes such good care of himself."

"I heard that his employees love working for him and his brother Jeb. Supposedly they pay their people well above their competitors. The word is that it's kind of an obsession for Charles in particular. I heard that it's because he grew up dirt poor in West Texas and doesn't want his employees to endure what he did growing up."

"You really have been busy Googling our CEO friend, haven't you?

You might want to do some real work once in a while, Miz Curry. After all, when I brought you here from San Francisco, I told everybody how great you were."

She chuckled. "I just wanted to come up to speed on the project—and that includes knowing something about the people we're regulating. What else do you know about him?"

"What is this a Bruce Wayne infatuation? Or are you going to up and quit on me—after I worked my tail off to bring you to Denver—and ask Quantrill for a job?"

"I just find him intriguing is all. It's not every day you get to sit across the table from a billionaire—on more or less equal terms. So what else do you know about him?"

"Besides that he owns a luxury box for every professional sport's team in town, gives tens of millions of dollars to charity every year, and hobnobs with U.S. senators? Well, let's see, he's also a huge paleontology buff."

"A paleontology buff? I didn't see anything on that."

"Wait until you see his downstairs lobby. It's like the Smithsonian."

"I can't wait."

They laughed and drove on in amiable silence. Nina stared out the window, grateful to have a boss with a genuine sense of humor that she could banter back and forth with like she was back in college. As they neared the facility, she noticed the long line of tankers along the shoulder of the road. There were more than a hundred of them, extending for nearly a mile. Hamilton slowed down as they started to pass the tankers in the rear.

"My God, look at this," she said. "I read in the reports that Quantrill treats a million gallons of hazardous waste per day, but I didn't imagine this."

"It's a big operation. Biggest in the U.S."

"I can see now why." She couldn't help but blink in awe at the sight of so many tanker trucks waiting to deliver their nasty chemical payloads.

Two minutes later, they came to a halt at the visitor's check-in and guard gate. Hamilton rolled down his window.

"Richard Hamilton and Nina Curry to meet with Jeb Quantrill."

The guard handed out two passes and a sign-in sheet. They scrawled out their names and affiliations before continuing to the main office.

It was a sprawling, four-story building done in a modernistic style, enveloped on all sides by lush ryegrass in intricate lawns, exquisitely sculpted hedges, and throngs of huge blue spruce and lodgepole pine. The office building housed the upper management of Quantrill Waste Services; Quantrill Energy Services, which included wind, solar, and geothermal power subsidiaries as well as conventional nuclear and petroleum-based entities; Quantrill Developments, the real estate arm of Charles and Jeb Quantrill's hugely profitable operation; and Sweetwater, the mineral water subsidiary owned by Charles Quantrill personally. To the north of the main building was a smaller, more spartan office for the plant personnel of Waste Services and the waste treatment plant itself. To the east was the same type of office building for Quantrill refining operations staff, and the refinery proper.

Hamilton pulled into one of the visitor's parking spaces. Stepping from the car, they made their way to the front entrance, shuffled through a revolving door, and entered the lobby.

CHAPTER 10

NINA saw instantly that her boss wasn't joking: the lobby did look more like a natural history museum than the ground floor of a Fortune 100 company. The sunlight radiating down from the central atrium illuminated row upon row of glass cases displaying a myriad of ancient fossils. There were marine fossils from Early Cambrian through Cretaceous times, including trilobites, brachiopods, cephalopods, armored jawless fish, corals, and crinoids. There was also a wide assortment of terrestrial vertebrates—early amphibians, mammal-like reptiles, dinosaurs, and large mammals—spanning the Permian Period through modern times.

But what caught her eye most of all were the life-size models of ancient lifeforms: a Permian finbacked *Dimetrodon* attacking a plump amphibious *Eryops*; a giant Jurassic meat-eating *Ceratosaurus* going up against an angry *Stegosaurus*; a lone *Utahraptor* in a crouching position with its vicious toe claw raised; a pair of saber-toothed cats attempting to bring down a woolly mammoth; and three barrel-chested Neanderthals armed with spears engaging a monstrous cave bear. All of the reproductions, she quickly realized, appeared to be to precise scale and correct to the last anatomical detail.

"This place is amazing," she exclaimed, her eyes big as plums.

"I told you he was an earth history buff," said Hamilton. "I love coming here for meetings."

She continued to stare in awe at the shaggy-bearded Neanderthals and beyond at the horn-snouted *Ceratosaurus* attacking the stegosaur. "I had no idea Quantrill was so into this."

"He's the Museum of Nature and Science's biggest donor. He supports digs in Colorado, Montana, Utah, and New Mexico, as well as one in Outer Mongolia and another in Argentina. Pretty wild, huh?"

"I'll say."

They stepped up to the battling Jurassic dinosaurs. "By the way, Joseph Higheagle's something of a paleontology buff too. It's part of his family history. You'll have to ask him about it."

"What do you mean it's part of his family history?"

"Well, his great-great grandfather, a Cheyenne warrior named High Eagle, once stole a giant dinosaur skull."

"He actually stole a dinosaur skull?"

"It happened right after the Civil War during the first-ever dinosaur hunting expedition into the American West. The Orser expedition. Joseph told Charles and Jeb Quantrill and I about it before our last meeting."

"Where did this all happen?"

"The expedition was into the Painted Hills in northern Colorado. That's where Joseph's great-great grandfather stole the *Triceratops* skull right from under the nose of the cavalry."

"Good heavens. How did he do that?"

"He and his brother snuck into the Orser camp late one night, took the skull, and hauled it off in a wagon. They covered the wheels with animal furs so they wouldn't make any sound."

"Jesus. It sounds like a Western movie."

"Yeah, that's what I said. But it wasn't just any old dinosaur fossil—it was the very first *Triceratops* ever found by a white man. The theft caused a great stir in the camp."

"I can imagine."

"The military commander in charge of the expedition was a legendary Indian fighter named General Kane. He came after them with over two hundred cavalrymen and Pawnee scouts. But the Cheyenne and their Sioux allies refused to give up the skull without a fierce fight. They didn't know at the time that it belonged to a dinosaur. They believed that the skull belonged to the Great White Buffalo Chief, the ancestor of all the buffalo. And that it would protect them from the white man. That's why they wouldn't give it up. It was big medicine."

Nina felt herself taut with excitement. "What happened next?"

"General Kane and the Indians fought several battles, but High Eagle and his brother managed to get away with the skull. Eventually General Kane caught up with them, took the skull back, and forced them onto the reservation. But after the Indian wars he gave it back to them."

"Gave it back to them? No way."

"I know, I couldn't believe it either, but this Kane was no ordinary guy. By then he had quit the Army altogether and gone on to become a big-time rancher. After High Eagle and his brother had lived on the reservation for a few years, the general recruited them to work on his ranch along the South Platte. Together, they raised cattle and later buffalo. After working for a few years, High Eagle and his brother were given a stake in the ranch."

"What happened to the *Triceratops* skull?"

"The general gave it back to the two brothers as a gift. They kept it on display in a barn. Over the years, people from the Northern Cheyenne reservation in Lame Deer and from the Southern Cheyenne rez in Oklahoma used to make pilgrimages to the ranch to pay tribute to the sacred skull. They passed it on to their descendants and the skull now belongs to Joseph Higheagle and his grandfather."

Nina nodded her head with delight. "That's an amazing story."

"I know. I liked it so much, I took Joe out to lunch after the meeting and had him tell it to me again." They stared thoughtfully at the horn-snouted ceratosaur before Hamilton glanced at his watch. "I'd like to stay here all day, but we'd better get going. Our meeting's about to start."

He led her to a bank of high-tech elevators that looked like something out of *Star Trek*. The doors opened. They stepped inside, rode the elevator to the third floor, and made their way to the receptionist's desk, built of solid teakwood. There was a waiting area with huge leather sofas, plush chairs, and a glass table in front of the desk. Nina quickly scanned the magazines on the table: *Colorado Business*, *Chemical Engineering*, *Natural History*, *Business Week*, *Forbes*, *The Armchair Paleontologist*, *Big Game Hunter*, and *The Insider*, Quantrill's intracompany newsletter. In the glass case next to the table was a massive skull of an *Albertosaurus*, the smaller but no less lethal cousin of T-Rex. It's dagger-teeth and exquisitely perforated cranium glinted in the sunlight shining down through the central atrium behind the receptionist's desk.

Richard Hamilton stepped forward to the desk.

"Morning Cynthia."

"Good morning, Mr. Hamilton. They told me to tell you that they'll be available in just a few minutes."

"They?"

She smiled. "Charles and Jeb both. Looks like it's your lucky day."

CHAPTER 11

CHARLES PROMETHEUS QUANTRILL sat behind his sprawling English oak desk with a conspicuous frown as he listened to his in-house counsel, Jack Holland, and his chief engineer, Wesley Johnston.

"Regardless of whether facility operations are causing the earthquakes or not," argued *The Boil*, his bald pate gleaming in the overhead lighting, "the current situation will become untenable if there is another one."

"But we have nothing to do with it, Jack," countered the CEO.

"Jeb and I aren't so sure," ventured Johnston meekly.

"What now Jeb's got you scared too? Didn't you just tell us all on Sunday night that you didn't believe the injection has anything to do with the earthquakes? Wasn't it you who said that the epicenter was fifteen miles away from the injection well network and twenty-five miles from the facility so we couldn't be responsible?"

"The situation's changed."

"How has the situation changed? Even before you split the flow between the shallow and intermediate zones, the injection pressure in all three zones was well within the acceptable range, correct?"

"Yes, both the injection fluid pressure and formation fluid pressure are holding fine at 600 to 1,000 psi. I guess I just have a bad feeling is all."

"It's that damned Earthquake Prophet and his prediction," confessed Jack Holland. "It's got us all on edge."

Quantrill couldn't believe his ears. Were these grown men he was talking to or superstitious children? "Dr. Patey is nothing but a charlatan. He just wants some publicity so he can sell more copies of his stupid book."

"That may be, but it still doesn't change the fact that we could all go to prison for this. As your corporate counsel, I'm advising you to shut down the program temporarily until we can get more definitive answers. If something were to happen on Hallow—"

"Good Lord, fellas, have you plum lost your minds?" he cut the attorney off. "You've let this Earthquake Prophet get inside your heads. You should know better—the both of you."

He raked them with a look of reproof before producing a monogrammed handkerchief from his suit pocket and dabbing irritably at his damp brow.

"We just feel there's too much risk when we don't know why these events are happening," explained Holland. "Why nothing above a 1.0 for a full decade and now a 6.6? It doesn't make any sense."

Johnston nodded. "If another earthquake were to strike, we could be in a hell of a lot of—"

"Trouble—you're damn right!" interrupted a new voice. "In fact, you can count on it."

The three men looked up to see Jeb Quantrill, who had slipped into the room quiet as a ghost and now turned and closed the door behind him.

Quantrill felt a twitch cross his face at the sudden intrusion. "Jeb, what a surprise. So now it's three against one."

"If that's what it's going to take to get you to listen, Brother, then so be it." He walked over to the sprawling business couch in the corner of the room and sat down, crossing one knee over the other, his expression cool and commanding.

Quantrill could tell his younger brother meant business. "Look Jeb, you've already said the injection is happening too far away from the epicenter for our operation to be responsible. You said there's no way the waste could have moved fifteen miles in only ten years."

"No, what I said was that there were likely heterogeneities in the subsurface that are preferentially directing wastewater flow far away from the injection wells. Somehow, the fluids are moving far beyond the well cluster before raising the fluid pressure in these reservoirs. According to the injection wellfield seismograph network, the epicenters of all the quakes—all the small ones below 1.0 and the recent 6.6—have been fifteen miles or further from the injection well cluster. The formation fluid pressure is exceeded not at the borehole itself, but at some critical distance away from the borehole. And that's the point at which rupture is occurring."

"And have you identified any of these...heterogeneities?"

"Not yet, but I'm still haven't gone through all the seismograph data. We need to scale back the flow rate to two hundred gpm until we have a better handle on this earthquake problem."

"Brother, there is no earthquake problem. We've been injecting for ten years, and in all that time, there's never been an event above a 1.0 until last Sunday. Furthermore, as you and Wes have pointed out, none of the earthquakes have been closer than fifteen miles from the injection wellfield. And there's never been a correlation between the timing and volume of the fluid injected and the small tremors that we've recorded. So I ask you, how can we be responsible?"

"I admit I'm at a loss to explain it. But until we know for sure, there's too much risk. Luckily no one was killed this past Sunday, but there was still two hundred and fifty million in damage. We need to shut down until we've figured this thing out."

Quantrill rose from his chair and stood by the window, a craggy expressionless figure against the backdrop of rugged mountains. "I ain't gonna cut back or shut down until I know for certain there's a correlation between the injection and the earthquakes. Even then, I'd rely on you and Wes to get more creative. We've got options. We've already split the flow between the shallow and the intermediate zones. Maybe we need to pump into all three at once so the flow is more equally distributed."

"That would certainly help," concurred Johnston.

"No, that's not enough," protested Jeb. "There's more to this now. Late last night I got a call from someone."

Quantrill jerked away from the window. "Who?"

"An old friend. You know him too: James Nickerson."

"That earthquake guy from the USGS?" gasped Holland in disbelief. "You two know him?"

At first, Quantrill was surprised by the news too, but after thinking about it for a moment, he realized that it was not that surprising given the current earthquake situation and his brother's and Nickerson's history together. All the same, the news gave him a feeling of dread. He stepped away from the window and looked at the attorney. "I've only met him a few times. Jeb's the one that was once close to the man."

Holland still appeared stunned. "How do you know him, Jeb?"

"We went to graduate school at Stanford and worked out in Midland together when we were just starting out. It's true we were close once, but I haven't seen him in years."

"And late last night he decides to just call you out of the blue?"

"He wants information."

"What kind of information?"

"He wants two things. First, he wants us to send him the seismic reflection profiles we shot across Elbert, Lincoln, and northeast El Paso counties in the mid-80s. He found out about it from Applied Geophysics, the company that performed the survey."

"And the second?"

"He wants our earthquake seismograph data."

Quantrill felt his gut clench. "From the injection wellfield?"

"No, luckily he doesn't know about that. He wants the data from our haz waste facility network. He wants to meet with me today to go over it along with Mark Kelso, the state geologist. Apparently, Kelso is furious that we haven't informed him or the USGS that we have an independent seismic monitoring network. He wants to know why we haven't already sent him our data from the recent quake."

Quantrill felt the vein in his neck tightening. *My God, the situation is even worse than I imagined. What other surprises do you have for me, Little Brother?* "How in the hell did Jim Nickerson find out we have a seismograph at the haz waste facility?"

"He didn't. Somehow Kelso found out. He must have made some calls."

Quantrill shook his head. "Damn, this is a nightmare. You said Nickerson and Kelso want to meet today?"

"At lunchtime."

"That soon?"

"Obviously, we can't give them the seismograph data," said Johnston.

"Why not?" asked Holland.

"Because it will help them pinpoint the rupture point of the earthquake," replied Jeb.

"Which could eventually point to us," said Quantrill. He looked at his brother. "There's no way you can meet with them—you'll have to call it off."

"If I call it off now, it will look suspicious."

Holland was still in a state of shock. "So what you're telling us is that the director of the USGS National Earthquake Information Center—who happens to be an old friend—and the Colorado state geologist have asked you to help them find out what's causing the earthquakes? This is a fucking disaster!"

"You can say that again. But they're not going to stop until they get what they want. That's why I agree with Wes that we need to reduce the flow to two hundred gpm, distributed amongst all three units, and run the rest through the wastewater treatment system for a couple of weeks until we figure this out."

Quantrill frowned. "I've already told you, I'm not going to cut back until you give me proof that the injection is causing the earthquakes. I'm not pulling up the tent stakes without a damned good reason."

"We're only talking about cutting back to two hundred gpm for Christ sake."

"You've heard my final word on the matter." He raised a finger. "You are not to give Nickerson or Kelso any data, do you hear me? Explain to them that we're a big corporation and we have to run everything through legal, which will take six to eight weeks. Meanwhile, you and Wes gather all the data you need to make your case and keep me informed."

"So that's it?" said Jeb, shaking his head in disgust. "You're not going to do anything?"

Quantrill felt a stab of anger, but forced himself to remain calm.

"Until you and Wes here prove to me that our injection program is causing those damned quakes, I don't want to hear no more about it. I can't shut down a billion dollar operation based on the crazy ramblings of a man who calls himself the Earthquake Prophet. That, gentlemen, would be bad for business."

At that moment, the phone on Quantrill's desk rang, surprising them all.

He quickly checked the caller ID. It was the front desk.

He pressed the intercom button. "Yes, what is it, Cynthia?"

"I'm sorry to bother you, Mr. Quantrill, but your brother Jeb instructed me to notify him when Richard Hamilton and Nina Curry arrived. Well, sir, they're here."

Jeb stepped towards the phone. "Thank you, Cynthia. Please have them wait for me in Conference Room B. I'll be over in a minute."

"Yes, sir. Oh, there's one more thing."

"Yes, Cynthia."

"Apparently there's also a Dr. Nickerson who is here to see you. He's at the front gate right now. They just notified me."

Quantrill gave an involuntary start and shot a look at his brother.

Jeb looked at his watch. "He's early."

Holland motioned urgently towards the phone. "Mute that damned thing!"

Quantrill spoke into the speakerphone. "Just a second, Cynthia." He hit the mute button and looked again at his brother and lead attorney. "Who the hell shows up nearly two hours early for a meeting?"

"He must want the information badly," explained Jeb. "Obviously, we can't turn him away. He'll be suspicious and that will only make the situation worse."

"Can't you just tell him you're tied up in meetings and can't be disturbed?" asked Johnston.

"He'll just come back. I know him. Look, he's only trying to find out what's causing the earthquakes. You can hardly blame the man for doing his job."

"Jeb's right. If there's one thing certain about old Jim Nickerson, it's he's as relentless as a bloodhound. No, I reckon that you and I ought to meet quickly with Richard Hamilton and his new engineer from the EPA. Then you take care of Nickerson and Kelso while I finish up with the EPA on the wind farm issues. You were good friends with the man once—I take it you can handle him. I'll poke my head in once I've wrapped up with Hamilton and the new gal."

"All right, I'll take care of it," said Jeb, his tone sounding more confident than Quantrill suspected he felt inside.

The brawny CEO hit the mute button again and spoke directly into the speakerphone. "Cynthia, when Dr. Nickerson arrives, please have him wait for Jeb in Conference Room C."

"Yes, Mr. Quantrill."

He punched off the intercom button and looked at Jeb. "All right, Little Brother, let's kick off this rodeo."

CHAPTER 12

JAMES NICKERSON, PH.D. sat across a gleaming cherrywood conference table from his old friend. The inevitable ravages of Father Time had taken more of a toll on Jeb Quantrill than he had expected. The dark circles around his eyes, streaks of silver in his sandy hair, hollow cheekbones—all of these bespoke of work-related strain along with the natural aging process and an inherent melancholy that seemed to come from deep within. But there was still the acute intelligence in his eyes that Nickerson remembered from their Stanford and Midland days together. Indeed, that was his old friend's most distinguishing characteristic.

"Thanks for meeting with us under such short notice, Jeb." The NEIC director motioned towards a humorless, tight-buttoned man seated to his right. "This is Mark Kelso, the state geologist."

Jeb reached his hand across the table. "Nice to meet you Mark." He smiled, but to Nickerson it seemed forced, as though he would have preferred not to meet with them at all. "So how can I help you two gentlemen?"

"Well, as I told you late last night, my staff and I are busy trying to piece together the tectonics out here. We've still got a lot of unanswered questions about the geological setting and focal mechanism that we're trying to work out. There are some records we'd like to get our hands on—namely the deep seismic reflection profiles you shot at your Stasney #1 and #2 oilfields and the seismographic data from your network here at the facility. But more importantly, we'd like to borrow some of your expertise."

"I think you might be putting too much faith in my abilities, James. I'm not a seismologist and we don't have any on staff."

"I still think you can help us. Word is no one knows this part of the Denver-Julesburg Basin as well as you."

The compliment didn't appear to register. "Who's working on this with you? Is it just the USGS and Colorado Geological Survey, or are there other entities?"

"We're also working with the Department of Oil and Gas," replied Kelso officiously.

"So you have the best and the brightest from three state agencies. I don't see why you need an old armchair geologist like me. It's been a lot of years since I even did any drilling, let alone basin analysis or balanced cross-section work."

"I realize that but let me tell you what we've got. The preliminary indication is that a blind thrust fault in the Precambrian basement may be the cause of the recent earthquake."

"Hold on a second—blind thrust, you say? As in a low angle reverse fault with no visible surface rupture?"

Nickerson nodded. "The problem is there hasn't been any evidence of historical seismicity in the area and no documented faults capable of the slip or energy release we saw from the recent quake."

"A blind thrust? I can't believe it. I haven't mapped any faults like that out here in this part of the basin."

"But you have drilled deep into the Precambrian basement. Is there anything you can tell me about the microfracture orientations?"

"Mostly about five degrees east of north. What was the orientation of the fault plane?"

"It's dipping to the west, towards the Front Range."

"That doesn't make sense. The principal stress should be coming from the other direction."

"It's not, and we've completed twenty different solutions. Somehow there's compression going on out here, which is strange. We've done balanced cross-section work and the forces required are unreasonably large to get the sections to balance out."

"You have to remember that balanced sections are theoretical models. You can't always take deformed layers of rock and restore them to their pre-faulted and pre-folded condition and remain within geometric and kinematic constraints. Besides, the solutions aren't even unique."

"The bottom line is there are adjustments going on in the deep crustal blocks that don't seem to be feasible without a significant change in...fluid pressure."

The room went suddenly quiet. Nickerson thought he saw a little twitch on Jeb's face, but it was gone in a flash. *What the hell just happened?*

"So have you found anything that might indicate whether there have been fluid pressure changes?" asked Jeb, recovering quickly.

"No, that's the problem. We were thinking that the adjustments might be the result of oil and gas withdrawal, fracking, or water-flooding of mature reservoirs to increase oil production. But the records of the Colorado Geological Survey and Department of Oil and Gas show that there hasn't been any permitted fracking in the basin since last year, nor has there been any water-flooding in more than twenty years by any of the majors or independents out here."

"We're thinking the earthquake may have resulted from subsidence or the past fracking and water-flooding," said Kelso. "Maybe it took awhile for those old basement rocks to feel the effects."

Nickerson eyed his old friend closely. "You don't know anyone out here who might be water-flooding or illegally fracking those old reservoirs, do you?"

"There could be someone. All I know is it sure as heck isn't us."

"Well, in any case, we'd appreciate it if we could get that Stasney reflection data and your seismograph data from here at the facility. That would be of great help to us."

Jeb glanced away and Nickerson realized that he was either about to get the corporate brush off or complete rejection. "I'm afraid, gentlemen, that's going to be…difficult."

"Difficult?"

"Of course, it's not up to me. It's in the hands of our legal department."

"Are you saying you won't give us the data?"

"No, I'm not saying that. Our legal department is in the process of evaluating your request. Apparently, it's going to take six to eight weeks."

"Six to eight weeks? Why so long?"

"I'm sorry but we have to follow our standard company protocols for requests of this nature. And I should warn you in advance that our legal department are sticklers when it comes to proprietary information or outside requests. They may very well decide that we can't release any information so I wouldn't get your hopes up."

If Nickerson wasn't mistaken, it sounded like the second in command at Quantrill Ventures was giving him the old corporate two-step. But why? The fact that Jeb was an old graduate school buddy and professional colleague made it all the more puzzling. He couldn't escape the suspicion that his old friend was withholding something.

Feeling embarrassed, he looked over at Kelso, who he could see was not taking the news well. Even on a good day, he was something of a sourpuss, hot head, or both—and right now he looked as though he had just swallowed a mouthful of bile. After a moment, Nickerson turned back to Jeb, hoping to persuade him to give him a break and find a way to hand over the data. But first he wanted clarification.

"So you're telling me that we can't have access to your deep seismic reflection profiles or your earthquake data from your seismograph network here at the facility?"

"That's not what I said."

"I'm sorry, then what did you say?"

"I said that it was out of my hands and it was up to our legal department to evaluate your request. I also informed you that it would take six to eight weeks."

"That's an awfully long time, Jeb."

"That's our legal department's standard review time for outside requests of company information. We are a private firm, not a public entity, and are under no obligation to provide our data to anyone."

"This is ridiculous," muttered Kelso. "We drove all the way out here for this crap?"

Nickerson raised a hand, restraining his less diplomatic colleague. "We understand, Jeb, that you have to adhere to company policy. But is there some way you can at least expedite our request?"

The geologist's face seemed to soften. "I can try."

"Good, that's all we ask."

"But as I've told you, it's unlikely you will hear back any sooner than several weeks and your request will probably be denied. I just don't want you to get your hopes up."

Kelso shook his head in disgust. "I don't understand why you have to get your legal department's permission at all. Need I remind you that we just had a magnitude 6.6 earthquake that injured more than a hundred people and caused over two hundred fifty million dollars in damage? What's it going to take for you to hand over this data? Does someone have to fucking die?"

"That's enough, Mark," snapped Nickerson, trying to maintain at least a modicum of cordiality. "We're not here to antagonize Mr. Quantrill."

"Well, you seem to be doing a heck of a job doing just that," boomed a deep authoritative voice, taking everyone by surprise.

The three men at the table looked up to see Charles Quantrill standing in the open doorway, his massive frame blotting out all but a sliver of sunlight slanting in from the indoor atrium behind him. Nickerson felt a tightening at his collar. Though Quantrill bore a non-combative grin, he still looked as fearsome as a Kodiak bear. But to the seismologist's surprise, the big man closed the door casually behind him, walked over to them, and with studied nonchalance, extended a hand first to the NEIC director then Mark Kelso before taking a seat at the head of the table.

"Don't mind me, gentlemen. Consider me nothing but a little ol' fly on the wall."

Nickerson couldn't help a little smile. In tromps the illustrious CEO with a cocksure grin on his face, like an emperor beholden to no one, then he casually sits down and instructs everyone to ignore him. But there was no way one could ignore *Charles Prometheus Quantrill*.

"Come on now, don't let me spoil your party. Please pick up where y'all left off."

"We were just explaining to Jeb here how useful the data from your oilfield reflection survey and on-site seismographic network would be to us. We were hoping that you would expedite the review by your legal department and submit the data to us as soon as possible."

Quantrill smiled pleasantly. "I'm sure quite a few of our competitors would like to get their hands on those reflection profiles too."

"Is that what you're concerned about, that your competitors could gain access to proprietary information? If that's what's causing the holdup, I promise we'll—"

"I'm sorry, James," interrupted Jeb, "but I don't believe you're in a position to promise anything. And even if you could provide some sort of guarantee, we have company rules that must be followed. As I've been explaining to you and Mark. What kind of businessmen would my brother and I be if we ignored our own legal department?"

"He's got a point, fellas. That's why I've always regarded him as the smart one."

Kelso fidgeted in his chair, a humorless scowl on his bureaucratic ferret face. "But the data from your seismograph array close to the epicenter is of critical value. It will help us pinpoint the earthquake with far better accuracy than we have with our three current USGS stations spread all over the state."

"We understand that," said Jeb. "But as I've explained to you, we still have an internal process that needs to be followed."

"We appreciate your position," said Nickerson, struggling to hold in his exasperation. "But if there are further disturbances in this portion of the Denver Basin, I can't emphasize enough how much your data could help us. The problem is we have to triangulate over such a large area, our current accuracy for locating an epicenter is only plus or minus five to ten miles. Without a close-in seismograph network to provide accurate location and depth control, we lose valuable time in emergency response. It is critical for first responders to get to likely areas of extensive damage and casualties as quickly as possible. Furthermore, your data will help us more accurately map the active fault or faults responsible for these earthquakes."

"Now I may be just an old country boy," said Quantrill with a mock self-deprecating air, "but it seems to me that it's the responsibility of the U.S. government to establish an appropriate seismograph network, not Quantrill Ventures or any other private company. Personally, I'd like to see Uncle Sam do a better job of protecting its people. I reckon the first step ought to be to install enough seismograph networks in the state that the epicenter of any earthquake can be ascertained in real-time."

Again Kelso started to protest, but Nickerson could tell that the battle was lost, that further discussion would prove futile. For the second time, he silenced the state geologist with a wave of his hand. It was a troublesome situation. He had the suspicion that his old friend Jeb and brother Charles were withholding something. That they were hiding behind company policy as a means to stall or deceive him. But why would they do that? What could they possibly stand to gain?

Then again, maybe he was just being paranoid. With its emphasis on secrecy and profitability, the corporate world was vastly different from the public sector, research, or academia. Maybe businessmen like Charles and Jeb Quantrill just saw and did things differently than the USGS. And yet his mind still wouldn't let go. What if he was right after all and they really were stonewalling? What could he do about it?

And then the answer hit him: Quantrill had solved his problem for him.

"After consideration, gentlemen, I think you're right. It would be advantageous to have our own seismograph network in the area as a precautionary measure. That's why we're going to install our own local network of portable digital seismographs near the epicenter. That way we'll have our own data and won't need to impose on Quantrill Ventures any further."

He had intended the proposition to be a game changer, but even he was taken aback at the shock that registered on the faces of the two famous brothers.

"I think this will be the best approach for all concerned. We should have the new seismograph network up by the end of next week. Of course, it would be best if we had your data so that we could position the network in the optimal location, but we understand you have your company protocols. So you gentlemen are off the hook so to speak. Even with the new network, we would, of course, appreciate any data you can spare us once you have cleared it through your legal department."

The room remained silent for several seconds as the two dumbstruck brothers considered how to respond. As the tense seconds ticked off, Kelso smiled smugly, putting an exclamation point on the triumph. Meanwhile, Nickerson could see that Jeb was so overcome with shock and mortification that all he wanted to do was end the meeting as quickly as possible.

Finally, Charles Quantrill recovered his composure and gave a cordial smile. "Well, I guess that wraps it up then. Thank you, gentlemen."

"I'll show you out," said Jeb.

Nickerson studied him: the man looked nervous as a cat. Something was definitely going on here. Did he dare push them a step further?

"Oh, there is one more thing," he said.

The two powerful brothers looked at him warily.

"If you wouldn't mind, Mark and I would appreciate a little tour of the facility. Call it a non-official damage inspection. You wouldn't mind showing us around, would you, Jeb?"

For the second time the room went uncomfortably silent.

But again Charles Quantrill—ever the clever businessman—regrouped quickly. "Why I think that's a fine idea. You don't mind, do you, Jeb?"

"No, I don't mind." The voice sounded robotic.

"Great," said Nickerson. "Let's get started then."

CHAPTER 13

JOSEPH HIGHEAGLE watched as the twenty-three foot boom of the CME-75 hollow-stem auger drill rig locked into position. He was about to install his second groundwater monitoring well of the day and fifth of the past two days, as part of his contaminant plume delineation investigation. The rig stood along the eastern property boundary of the hazardous waste treatment plant, a labyrinthine maze of aboveground storage tanks, steel conveyance piping, and biological, air stripping, and carbon adsorption waste treatment units. Plant personnel in blue work clothes and hard hats shuffled about the waste facility like fastidious ants. All morning long he had felt a periodic rumbling beneath his feet as the noisy tanker trucks chugged their way into the facility and were promptly pumped out. Quantrill Ventures was as busy as an international airport.

Once the rig was positioned, Higheagle hopped into his company truck and moved it closer to the drilling rig. As he turned off the ignition, he saw Quantrill's chief of security, Harry Boggs, and another member of Quantrill's security team watching him from a distance. They were standing outside the analytical laboratory at the north end of the parking lot. Something in the way the security chief and his stiff-looking cohort scrutinized him made him feel uncomfortable.

He looked away.

Stepping out of the truck, he pulled down the tailgate and arranged his logbook, Munsell soil color chart, grain size booklet, and other field supplies on the flat gate. Next he recalibrated his organic vapor meter, a metal instrument the size of a flashlight used to detect volatile chemicals in air. By the time he was finished, the lead auger flight began to drive into the ground. He listened to the powerful throttling of the big rig as the augers churned through the soil, letting out a little groan as they fought their way through the compact silty clay. Over the next few minutes, he felt the vibrations of the rig hammer rapping the earth, pounding out his soil samples below the ground in five foot intervals.

Once the drillers had reached the boring total depth of twenty-five feet, he looked up to see a woman walking up. She was carrying a clipboard and wore standard field clothing and OSHA Level D personal protective equipment: a hard hat, steel-toed work boots, and safety glasses. Richard Hamilton at the EPA had left a message that his new project manager, an engineer named Nina Curry, might stop by today to oversee part of the drilling. The woman came to a halt at the yellow caution tape. Higheagle studied her a moment before casting a glance in the direction where he had last seen Boggs and his crony.

The two vaguely menacing security goons had moved on.

"Joseph Higheagle, right? Hi, I'm Nina Curry."

He stepped over to greet her. "You just transferred here from San Francisco. Nice to meet you. Richard told me you might stop by while he was performing his inspection at the refinery. Come on in."

He raised the yellow caution tape and she ducked under. "Thanks," she said with a smile.

"So how did your meeting go?"

"Very well, thank you."

"So now you've met the famous Quantrill brothers."

"Actually we spent most of the time with Jeb. We met with Charles too, though only briefly. Richard and I quickly ran him through the new federal wildlife sighting regs for the wind farm."

"So Richard's over at the refinery now?"

"He said he'd stop by to say hello on his way out."

"Well welcome to Colorado. Richard's a good man. You're lucky to have him as a boss."

"I know, I'm really glad I moved here." They stepped over to his truck near the drilling rig. "So have you found any VOCs?" She was referring to the volatile organic compounds expected to be present in the soil and groundwater.

"Not yet surprisingly. In fact my organic vapor meter hasn't registered a reading over three parts per million. Haven't seen any chemical discoloration or smelled any odors either. The soil seems clean. But we'll have to wait for the groundwater sample results to be certain."

"What's the lith log look like on this hole?"

Higheagle pointed down to his soil boring log. "Silty clay down to eight feet followed by medium-grained sand to total depth. They're pulling up the twenty-five foot sample now."

A moment later, the driller's helper brought three brass tubes filled with soil, representing the final sample collected from the total depth of the boring. Higheagle took out his spatula, sliced out a portion of the loose soil from the uppermost tube, placed the soil in a plastic bag, and began examining it in detail with a 20x hand lens.

"So what do you think about all this earthquake stuff?" she asked him as he worked. "Pretty crazy, huh?"

"I'll say."

"The reason I mention it is that a few minutes ago I saw that USGS guy, Dr. Nickerson. You know the seismologist who's been on TV non-stop the past few days."

"The Earthquake Man? You saw him out here?"

"He was walking down the hallway with another guy when Richard and I stepped out of the office with Jeb Quantrill. Do you think he's here to inspect for earthquake damage?"

"I doubt it. I spoke with Jeb earlier this morning and apparently there was no damage whatsoever. They've already performed integrity tests. All the pipelines at both facilities tested tight. And there was no evidence of rupture in any of the tanks."

"How did they check everything so quickly?"

Higheagle placed the tip of his organic vapor meter into the baggie filled with soil and took a reading: 1.2 ppm—nothing but background. "They have their own trained staff and equipment for tank and pipeline integrity testing. Quantrill Ventures has all kinds of capabilities."

"Really? Like what?"

"They've got their own full service analytical laboratory and their own specially-trained emergency spill response team. They're also qualified to perform utility clearances for underground lines. And they've got fully automated seismic monitoring and leak detection networks. You name it, they've got it. They take environmental compliance and health and safety very seriously."

"I saw the sign when Richard and I came in. Sixteen hundred forty-two days without an accident at the refinery, waste processing facility, or wind farm. That's quite a health and safety record."

"Well above industry standards."

"All the same, I'm sure they'd prefer not to go through another event like what happened on Sunday."

"Actually, Quantrill Ventures probably isn't too worried about it. All of their facilities have been designed to the highest seismic building code specifications. Basically up to a 7.5."

"A 7.5, really? That is impressive."

Jake the lead driller walked over from the CME-75 rig. "How you want us to set this well?" he asked Higheagle.

"Screen from ten to twenty-five, blank to ground surface. Filter pack from total depth to seven feet below grade. One foot of bentonite pellets then grout to surface."

"Same as the others then?"

"Yep."

Jake turned and walked towards the supply truck where his helper was already pulling out the PVC well casing. Higheagle capped and labeled his soil samples and began filling out his chain-of-custody form for the samples while he and Nina made idle chat. He had to admit he liked her; she seemed pleasant and easygoing for an EPA engineer and he was glad she wasn't busting his balls, like some sadistically fussy regulators seemed to enjoy doing.

"My God, what is that?"

Her urgent voice took him by surprise. "What are you talking about?"

She pointed. "That…what the heck is that?"

Turning, he saw the prairie grass on the other side of the fence bulging upward from some kind of pressure. Suddenly, a fountain of liquid shot thirty feet in the air. There was force behind it, like an exploding volcano, and Higheagle found himself standing there with his mouth open, gawking in awe. A few seconds later, the spray subsided but the liquid continued to pour out of an open hole, uprooting grass and earth and flowing over the ground in a torrent. The flow of liquid quickly cut out a ragged channel along the edge of the pipeline.

"Holy shit!" yelled Jake as he took a step towards the gushing river of pipeline fluid.

The next thing Higheagle knew Jeb Quantrill materialized from the south side of the waste treatment plant, rushing towards him with Dr. Nickerson and the other guy that Nina Curry had mentioned.

"What the hell did you do?" snarled the chief geologist as he came dashing up.

"I didn't do anything! It just exploded out of the ground!"

"Well, you must have done something, goddamnit!"

Higheagle looked at the liquid bubbling out of the ground like an artesian spring. "What is it?"

"Damn petroleum line! I need to shut off the flow! Joe, you're in charge. Set up a support zone between the rig and the equipment shed there. Don't let anyone near that pipe. It's only a crude oil line but, from the smell, it appears there might have been some buildup of some sulfur gas. I'll be back in a minute!"

He sprinted off towards one of the buildings as Nickerson and Kelso came running up.

Higheagle quickly assembled the group. "We've got a hydrocarbon leak from some kind of gas buildup. Jake, I need you to take everyone to the support zone between the rig and the shed there, and wait for me. I'm going to take a quick picture of the release before the line gets shut off and all the fluid seeps into the ground. That way they'll know where to dig to clean up the spill. I'll be right behind you."

"All right, you've got it!" barked Jake. "Come on, everyone, let's go!"

Nina, Nickerson, and Kelso hesitated a moment, their gaze fixed on the fluid bubbling up from the ground, before following Jake and his helper to the far side of the drill rig. Higheagle reached into the truck, snatched his digital camera, sprinted to the fence, and clicked off a few pictures of the ruptured pipeline and surrounding release. The odor coming from the broken line was similar to a natural hot springs, yet it was somehow different. Was it his imagination or was there a trace of a chlorinated solvent odor? Or maybe the wind was blowing solvent vapors in from the processing area.

He studied the fluid cutting out a channel along the length of the pipeline. Surprisingly, the liquid was clear, not dark like the weathered crude he had seen in shallow soils around oil fields. He knew, however, that some lighter-chain crude oil wasn't all that dark when it came out of the ground, more of a light maple syrup or honey color. Still it was odd. He studied the fluid more closely. Unfortunately now he couldn't tell what color it was. Clumps of soil and grass had collapsed into the shallow flow channel and it was hard to make out the color. He noticed another strange thing. Whatever was flowing out of the pipe was definitely flowing to the east, away from the facility, and not towards it.

But how was that possible? He looked again to be sure, but there was no doubt about it. The pipeline flow was outbound, away from the facility, despite the level slope.

He was struck with a thought. He sprinted to the truck and rifled through his work chest, quickly locating his Brunton compass, a clean decontaminated hand trowel, and a brass tube with plastic end caps. He dashed back to the fence and took a bearing on the orientation of the pipeline. A ten- to twelve-foot-long section of the pipeline was exposed from the channeling of the liquid. He estimated the flow at around four hundred gallons per minute, a significant flow through an open four-inch pipe. He took the reading on the line: it ran north 81 degrees east. He took a confirmatory reading just to be certain and again the little needle adjusted itself on N81°E.

Setting down the compass, he snatched up his soil sampling equipment and stepped to the edge of the fence where some of the liquid had pooled up into a little swale. Leaning down, he took his brass sample tube and drove it into the wet soupy surface soil, filling the tube and packing in the excess saturated soil with his hand trowel and then capping it off with a spare plastic end cap. When he was finished, he picked up all of his materials and dashed back towards the truck.

It was then he noticed Dr. Nickerson staring at him from the edge of the drilling rig.

Higheagle gave a businesslike wave so the man wouldn't be suspicious and proceeded to the truck, where he quickly wrote down the pipeline orientation in his field logbook, stuffed the soil sample in his ice chest, and put away his field equipment. When he was finished, he looked back at Nickerson, but the seismologist had returned to the group behind the drilling rig. Higheagle cast a glance across the fence at the ruptured line. The fluid had stopped flowing out of the ground and the liquid levels in the various pools and channels were holding constant or subsiding.

He walked quickly to the other side of the drilling rig where the others were waiting for him. Nina was writing furiously in her field notebook, while Nickerson looked at him expectantly.

"The leak has stopped and it looks like the situation is under control."

Jake nodded vigorously. "I seen groundwater loaded with sulfur gas explode right out of a borehole like that sucker just done! Nasty shit, sulfur gas!"

Higheagle saw that the Earthquake Man looked skeptical. "A sulfur gas explosion? Is that what we just saw, Mr. Higheagle?"

"I have no idea, Dr. Nickerson. You may want to ask them."

He tipped his head towards the group of men walking briskly towards them: Jeb and Charles Quantrill, Harry Boggs, and Wesley Johnston, looking none too pleased.

CHAPTER 14

HIGHEAGLE felt the hair on the back of his neck standing on end as Charles Quantrill stepped up to him, towering over him like a grizzly.

"Goddamnit, son, why are you drilling so close to my crude oil line!"

He took a deep breath to steady his nerves. "The utility clearance people didn't mark it out as an oil line, Mr. Quantrill. Look at the paint color—it's blue for a water line." He pointed to the dashed blue line sprayed onto the hard-packed gravel.

Quantrill glared at his cherubic, pasty-faced engineer. "What color is a damned oil line?"

"Yellow, sir," Wesley Johnston replied sheepishly.

"I'm sorry, Mr. Quantrill, but I figured it would be safe to drill ten feet from a water line. It's well marked."

"I don't think the drilling had anything to do with the ruptured line," Nina Curry said, arms crossed defiantly. "The drilling rig wasn't even in use when it happened."

Higheagle realized he had been right about her: she could be feisty if the situation called for it. He looked at Harry Boggs and saw that he was scowling at her. Behind his dark sunglasses, the security man reminded him of the cruel prison guard with the impenetrable shades in *Cool Hand Luke*.

"And I suppose you're an expert in such matters?" Quantrill snapped at Nina dismissively before turning to address the entire group. "We're fixing to evacuate the area. Our emergency response team will be here any minute and we need everyone to proceed to the main office building."

"The line's been shut off and our team will clean up the spill in no time," added Jeb in an assuaging voice. "We have everything under control."

"It's just crude oil, right?" asked Kelso.

"Of course it's just crude," bristled Quantrill. "But we still have to follow our facility emergency response plan. Y'all are going to have to evacuate the area immediately."

Higheagle felt caught in the middle. On the one hand, he wanted to support his client and do as he was instructed; on the other, he had a sneaky suspicion that something was going on. Why were Quantrill and the others acting like the fucking *Gestapo*? He and the drillers had done nothing wrong. Why did the line trend to the east, away from the facility? Why were Quantrill and the others claiming the liquid was incoming crude oil when it clearly wasn't? And why was the flow rate in the four hundred gpm range? Were they flushing the line?

"All right, everyone, let's evacuate the area," commanded Harry Boggs, stepping forward and waving everyone towards the main office building.

Nina shook her head. "I'm the EPA staff engineer assigned to this facility. I'm not going anywhere."

"I'm afraid there are no exceptions," said Boggs sternly. "Everyone is to come with me for a debriefing with our health and safety coordinator and to fill out an incident report."

"I'm not leaving until I check out that broken line."

Boggs stepped forward aggressively. "Are you even certified to be here? Let me see your 40 Hour OSHA health and safety training card and your 8-hour refresher card."

Her face reddened and Higheagle saw at once that Boggs had her. "I don't have it with me."

"Well then, you must leave this area immediately."

She glowered at Quantrill. "You're not going to get away with this. My boss, Richard Hamilton, is over at the refinery and he's going to have some serious questions about this."

"Mr. Hamilton will be promptly informed of what happened here, Ms. Curry. He will understand perfectly well that I'm not trying to get away with anything. We take health and safety very seriously here at Quantrill Ventures and you are in violation of OSHA requirements."

"All right, let's go," said Boggs, and he took her firmly by the elbow.

She jerked her arm away. "Let go of me. I have to contact my supervisor and the EPA on-scene coordinator and tell them what's happened here. The OSC will then contact the National Spill Center."

Quantrill looked at his brother. "What's she talking about? I thought we're the ones who handle the cleanups in the event of a release?"

"Not at a RCRA facility. The EPA will be sending in its own emergency response team."

"How long will it take them to get here?"

"They'll be coming from Denver so maybe two hours."

Higheagle looked at his watch. He knew he was walking a dangerous line trying to remain neutral. But what else could he do? Quantrill Ventures was his client and he could not contradict his client in front of a regulator. But if it were that simple, what had possessed him to take a compass reading on the broken pipeline and to collect a sample? He glanced at Nickerson, who along with Kelso and the drillers seemed unsure of what to make of the standoff between the EPA regulator and Quantrill. The Earthquake Man gave him a look that seemed to say, "I saw you take that sample and compass reading, bud—and when this is over, you and I are going to have a little talk."

"All right, people," snorted Quantrill. "Let's get moving."

"Hey, look over there," cried Jake the driller. He pointed to a dozen or so workmen tromping out towards the spill site in front of a remuda of heavy equipment. There were two backhoes, a loader, two end dump trucks, and a truck-mounted crane with steel pipes and fittings.

"That's our emergency response and pipe repair team," said Quantrill. "They'll have that line repaired and the soil cleaned up in no time."

Nina shook her head in disbelief. "You certainly have it all figured out, don't you?"

"Why yes I do, Ms. Curry." He tipped his black Stetson and gave a winsome smile. "That's why I'm the head honcho of this little ol' Fortune 100 outfit."

CHAPTER 15

NINA CURRY felt like smashing a chair against the wall as she dialed the number to the EPA on-scene coordinator. Her boss still wasn't back from the refinery and she had left her damned cell phone in her car, compelling her to use one of Quantrill's company phones to notify the EPA on-scene coordinator about the release. Like the others, she had been forced to give an interview with the Quantrill Ventures health and safety coordinator and to complete an incident report prior to making any outside calls. A uniformed security guard with a too-tight shirt, bulging biceps, and implacable expression stood ten feet away from her in the conference room, quietly watching her. The sight of the bastard made her livid; it was as if Quantrill wasn't just keeping an eye on her but trying to intimidate her.

Wait until Richard hears about this!

What bothered her most of all was how easily the CEO and his lackeys had whisked her and the others away from the spill. Somehow they had managed to seize control of the situation from her—the on-site representative of the lead regulatory agency. But what truly stung her was that they had legitimate justification for removing her from the plant. It had been clever of Boggs to ask her to present her OSHA health and safety training cards.

The phone picked up after two rings. "Albert Rehder here."

"Are you the EPA on-scene coordinator?"

"Yes, and who am I talking to?"

"Nina Curry, Environmental Engineer, Region 8." She knew it was all being recorded.

"What's the problem?"

"There's been an unauthorized release out here at the Quantrill Ventures facility near Elbert. It's about twenty-five miles northeast of Colorado Springs."

"What's the hazardous material."

"The facility's calling it crude oil."

"Crude oil's nonhaz. What's the release volume?"

"I don't know exactly. A pipeline ruptured and it was spraying up in the air and flowing over the ground. I'd say maybe two or three thousand gallons."

"What was the cause of the rupture?"

"I'm not sure. All I know is the line failed."

"Are there any surface water bodies or drainage ditches that could be immediately impacted by the release?"

"None that I saw."

"Is an emergency response team en route to contain the spill?"

"The on-site team is already here. The facility has its own OSHA-certified emergency response people."

"So the team is already controlling the spill?"

"Yes, but—"

"Hold on, I've got another call."

"Wait!" Rehder's voice was gone. *Shit!*

The security guard continued to stare at her as the conference room turned quiet as a crypt. The guy was unnerving; she felt like flipping him off. Impatiently fidgeting with the phone cord, she scanned the pictures on the walls showing awards won by Quantrill Ventures: a Colorado Department of Public Health and Environment 1996 Award for Excellence; a Colorado Business Association 2001 Award for the Top Colorado Business; a 2006 award for being on *Corporate Responsibility Magazine's* annual list of 100 Best Corporate Citizens; and a 2008 Outstanding Green Business Award from the U.S. Environmental Protection Agency.

She shook her head in disgust. The way these bastards were treating her, this had to be some kind of cruel joke!

After a moment, Rehder's voice returned. "Miss, you still there?"

"Yes."

"I've got an emergency dichlorobenzene spill on the other line. What I'm going to do is call the National Spill Center. The release doesn't sound like a priority spill since it's only crude. I'll come by there tomorrow morning and perform my inspection."

She turned her back to the security guard and put her mouth closer to the phone. "But they're acting strangely out here. They don't want me near the leak."

"Is an emergency response team taking care of the spill or not?"

"Yes, but—"

"Well then let them handle it. I've got to go now. Keep me posted if anything changes. Here's my cell number." He dictated the number to her. "Anything else?"

She couldn't believe that the OSC wasn't coming out to inspect the area until tomorrow. But she had done all she could and it was in his hands now. "What time should I meet you?"

"Ten."

"Ten? Can't you be here any earlier?"

"Not with this dichlorobenzene spill. Now I've got to go. I'll meet you there at ten. Do they have a guard gate?"

"Yes."

"Make sure they'll let me in without any hassle," and he was gone.

Hanging up the phone, she still felt burning anger inside. She looked at the security guard, standing with his arms crossed, muscles bursting out of his short-sleeved polyester shirt.

Assholes! she muttered under her breath, and she started out the room to find her boss.

CHAPTER 16

JOSEPH HIGHEAGLE studied Nina Curry as she emerged from the conference room. Stepping into the hallway, she walked purposefully towards him, Jeb Quantrill, and Richard Hamilton, who had just returned from the refinery. From her body language, it was obvious that she was angry. The security guard that had been in the room with her turned off the light and swung in behind her, somewhat aggressively Higheagle thought. That was strange: was he trying to intimidate her?

She walked up and came to a halt as the beefy security guard continued down the hallway. Higheagle noticed that she looked gorgeous when she was agitated, with added color in her cheeks, a touch of poutiness to her full lips, and an appealing sensuality that he hadn't noticed before. An appreciative smile crept up on his face. But to his dismay, he noticed that Richard Hamilton and Jeb Quantrill were both looking at him. *Busted!* Embarrassed, he instantly wiped the dreamy smile from his face.

Jeb Quantrill stepped forward politely and gestured towards her supervisor. "I was just bringing Richard here up to speed on what happened."

Her boss looked at her sympathetically. "Were you able to get in touch with the on-scene coordinator?"

"Yes, he'll be out here at ten o'clock tomorrow morning." She crossed her arms and looked sternly at Jeb. "Where's Dr. Nickerson and Mark Kelso?"

To Higheagle's surprise, Jeb showed no visible reaction to her hostile manner. "They've left," the geologist responded calmly. "As I was just telling Richard and Joe, I've just returned from the spill. Apparently the release occurred along a weak joint in the oil transmission line that comes in from our Stasney #1 and #2 fields east of here. They've already repaired the line and are digging the impacted soil up now. Soon, we'll be taking soil samples from the sidewalls and the base of the excavation. Thankfully, we got to the spill quickly and have successfully contained it."

The way Jeb described it made it sound like the situation was resolved, but Higheagle knew better. In his mind, there were still unanswered questions. But of course, he could say nothing about his concerns to Richard Hamilton or Nina Curry. He worked for Quantrill Ventures, not the EPA.

"But why all the fuss if it was just crude oil?" said Nina, still looking skeptical and combative.

"There's no fuss," replied Jeb, maintaining his calm and in-charge expression. "Like I said, everything is under control."

Higheagle hoped to avoid another unproductive argument between the two sides, or for her to alarm her boss unnecessarily, and quickly interjected a question. "Are you going to want me to take the confirmatory soil samples from the excavation?" he asked Jeb.

"No, my team will handle it." He turned to Richard and Nina. "It looked to me that the impacted area was maybe thirty feet long by ten feet wide. That will be the area of the excavation. I was going to have my team take eight soil samples along the base of the excavation and four along each sidewall."

"That will be acceptable," said Richard Hamilton. "But you should also take at least four samples from each excavated soil stockpile."

"Will do."

"What analyses are you going to run on the samples?" asked Nina.

Higheagle looked at Jeb. "I think you should run them for full range total petroleum hydrocarbons by Modified EPA Method 8015; benzene, toluene, ethylbenzene, and xylenes by EPA Method 8020; and polynuclear aromatic hydrocarbons by EPA Method 8270."

"No, that's not going to work," protested Nina. "They need to be run for full volatile and semi-volatile organics."

Jeb politely shook his head. "But the material is crude oil. It doesn't make sense to run the samples for full-range 8260 and 8270 analyses. It's a waste of time and money."

"That may be, but for completeness sake, you're going to need to analyze for full-range vols and semi-vols."

"But the only constituents are petroleum hydrocarbons and PAHs. You smelled the sulfur."

"That remains to be proven."

As they continued to debate, Higheagle had the uneasy feeling Jeb was either prevaricating or withholding something, but wasn't about to question his client in front of the EPA. He thought back to the original geyser spewing out of the ground and the incised channels that had quickly formed. The liquid hadn't been all that dark or viscous and the odor didn't smell exactly like crude oil, though it did have a pungent sulfur odor as Jeb said. But everything had happened so fast, was it possible Jeb was telling the truth? For some reason that seemed unlikely. Was Quantrill Ventures flushing the line? Or did the company have some proprietary, or perhaps even illicit, activity going on that they didn't want anyone to know about? To answer that question, he knew that all he had to do was have the soil sample he had collected analyzed—not by Quantrill's laboratory, but by an independent lab.

After a minute more of back and forth, Hamilton interceded diplomatically. "I think we can go forward with your recommended approach," he said to Jeb. "We don't need you to run the full 8260/8270, but we are going to need you to analyze for TPH, BTEX, and PAHs by EPA Methods 8015, 8020, and 8270." He turned to his subordinate. "Nina, are you okay with that?"

She gave a stubborn look, as if she would dig her heels in, but then took Higheagle by surprise by relenting. "Yes, I guess that will work," she said grudgingly.

"Good, then we're in agreement. We're going to head back to our office now. Nina will be back tomorrow morning at ten with the OSC."

"We'll have the analytical results from the soil samples completed by then," said Jeb in a helpful tone.

"That quickly?" asked Nina.

"We have our own on-site lab. They'll be running the analyses all night and we'll have the results for you in the morning."

"We're going to need the gas chromatographs for the samples too," insisted Hamilton.

"We'll have everything ready tomorrow when Nina arrives."

"Thanks, Jeb," said Higheagle, highlighting his client's willingness to cooperate.

"It's the least we can do. We'll see you and Nina tomorrow then."

Higheagle was glad that they had worked out an agreement. But he still felt wary and uncertain about what was going on. "I'll have the drillers back out here to install the last two wells and develop all six. Is eight o'clock all right?"

"That's fine, Joe. Again, Nina, I apologize for any inconvenience we may have caused you."

Higheagle studied her expression. Her stubborn look had dissipated and her face had returned to its natural color. "I appreciate that," she said.

"And so do I," echoed Richard Hamilton.

"Good," said Jeb. "I'll show the three of you out then."

CHAPTER 17

LATER THAT DAY, Charles Quantrill stood with his hands in his pockets watching his brother and Wesley Johnston supervise the cleanup of the release area.

The twenty or so emergency response employees—clad in full-face respirators, white Tyvek splash-resistant suits, and nitrile gloves—had not only contained the spill, they had already made significant progress in the remedial effort. The ruptured pipeline—as well as the toxic industrial solvent and heavy metal-impacted soil—had been removed. The excavation had been completed to about six feet below ground surface, well below the depth that the waste liquid had penetrated. A small volume of crude oil had been brought over by vacuum truck from the refinery and smeared along one of the sidewalls and near the top of the excavation to make it appear as if some minor hydrocarbon contamination remained. This would make the cleanup operation seem more plausible for Nina Curry and the EPA on-scene coordinator during tomorrow's inspection. It would appear as though the emergency response crew had inadvertently missed a minor amount of harmless crude oil.

The excavated soil had been loaded into end dumps, driven out onto the prairie, and thin spread over a large area so that the volatile solvent vapors in the soil would disperse. Uncontaminated soil had been scraped from the prairie, saturated with crude oil brought over from the refinery vacuum truck, and thoroughly mixed. The soil had then been stockpiled upon huge plastic sheets fifty feet from the excavation. It would be used to represent the soil removed from the release area excavation. For the EPA's benefit, samples of the crude-oil-impacted soil had been collected in sample jars and orange-flagged stakes had been placed where the samples had supposedly been collected. The samples were being submitted to the on-site Quantrill Ventures Analytical Testing Laboratory.

A new offset trench had been dug about thirty feet from the old pipeline and a new pipeline had been placed in the trench. The new pipeline was connected to the old line both upstream and downstream from the rupture point. Once the new pipeline had been set in the new trench, a smooth-roll compactor had been used to consolidate the soil above it. Quantrill knew that by quickly redirecting the pipeline, he could resume injecting waste into his deep well network to the east by as early as tonight.

All in all, he had suffered only a minor shut-down to his highly profitable operation.

Soil samples had also been collected in sample jars from the clean soil removed from the trench where the new pipeline had been placed. A small quantity of crude oil was added to the soil sample that was supposed to have been collected from the one remaining contaminated area along the excavation. The soil samples were then submitted to the on-site lab as representative of the confirmatory soil samples taken from the spill area excavation. The sample results would show that all of the crude oil contaminated soil had been removed except in one area, where crude oil had been knowingly placed. On the chain-of-custody form for the soil samples, Jeb had assigned sample numbers and depths to the clean soil and orange-flagged stakes had been driven into the sidewalls and base to show where the samples were supposedly collected.

As Quantrill gazed out onto the open prairie to the east, he felt another surge of pride at how swiftly and competently his task force had addressed the problem. The contaminated soil had been removed and the only remaining contamination was a smattering of deliberately-placed crude oil from the refinery. The old piping run had been transformed into a new one. The deep well injection program would continue unaffected. And the EPA would have all the documentation it would need to verify that the release had been adequately cleaned up.

Quantrill knew that potential problems remained, but these could be addressed in the meeting he had planned with his senior staff an hour from now. The cleanup itself was being expertly handled. He would have to be careful with Nina Curry and the on-scene coordinator, but he was confident he could bring them both under control.

Charles Prometheus Quantrill knew that even a natural disaster of epic proportions could not stop him from doing what he did best—and that was making oodles and oodles of money. His ultimate goal since he was a little boy had been to strike out on his own, make a fortune, and thereby become *somebody*. Someone whose name people would remember. Someone people would gaze upon with awe. Someone people would whisper about in admiring tones from nearby dining tables. From an early age, he had been determined to make Ma and Pa proud by making a name for himself and putting an end, once and for all, to the horrible cycle of poverty that had swallowed up the Quantrill family. That he had succeeded beyond his wildest dreams was a testament to his charisma, fortitude, and perseverance.

For Charles Prometheus Quantrill, the road to greatness had begun a half century earlier along the wind-whipped prairies of West Texas. That day, a black funnel had swooped down from the sky...

YOUNG QUANTRILL stared up at the black funnel swooping down from the sky. It was far larger than the harmless little dust-devils he usually saw swirling across the plains. He had just finished cashing in a bag of soda bottles at the country store and was on his way home to get dressed for his shoeshine job at the Petroleum Club in Midland. He rode a single-speed bicycle, legs pumping furiously, eyes peeled to the horizon where the maelstrom of death and destruction was closing in on his family's tiny, wood-framed home. He had to get to Ma, Jeb, and baby Corinna before they got swallowed up.

The sky was smudged a hazy brown, but the big black funnel still stood out prominently in the foreground. The wind bent the trees like saplings. Tattered newspapers and cotton fluttered past like jetsam. Pa was miles away, busy helping put up a new barn over at the Williams spread, which meant that in this critical time of need, young Chuck, as he was then known, was the man of the family.

When he reached his white picket fence, he jumped from his bike, ran across the dirt yard, and called out for Ma. With dust swirling everywhere, he could scarcely see more than a few feet. Tree branches and grains of sand pelted his face while rags, clothing, tin cans, and other small objects banged into his shins.

He heard a voice cry out and ran towards it. The curtain of dust parted for a flicker of an instant and he spotted a figure crouching next to the shed by the storm cellar. It was his mother, struggling to pull up one side of the heavy wooden door with one arm while holding baby Corinna in the other.

"I'm here, Ma!"

"Chuck!" She clutched him desperately with her free hand. "Your brother—I've lost your baby brother!"

"I'll fetch Jeb, Ma! Let's git you and Cory down in the cellar!"

It took all of his strength to pull open the big cellar door. He carefully led her down the wood-planked stairs, baby Corinna in her arms. Once he had assured their safety, he climbed back out of the cellar, took his bearings as best he could, and tore off into the raging storm. He was unable to see more than a few feet in front of him. The roar of the wind was deafening, assaulting his ears like a stampede of wild mustangs. He made for the house, his legs coming close to buckling as he fought against the gale.

With his vision limited, it took him several minutes to locate the house. Bowled over by the wind a half dozen times, he miraculously managed to stumble upon the front porch stairs. He breathed out a sigh of relief as his calloused hands ran along the familiar splintery wood. As he grappled his way up the first step, the front door was blown from its hinges and he was again knocked to the hard packed ground, this time with so much force that he felt the air leave his lungs.

Struggling to regain his breath, he wanted to cry something fierce. But he knew that crying wouldn't help him find his kid brother. Steeling himself, he struggled to his feet and set out again. Once he got his bearings, he managed to win the battle against the wind and relocate the stairs. With strenuous effort, he fought his way to the top step before the force of the gale again knocked him flat, this time onto the porch.

"Brother!" he cried desperately, laying on his stomach like a crocodile.

There was no answer but the fierce howl of the wind and rattling of the windows.

"Brother, where are you?" he called out again.

This time he thought he heard a sound trickle up through the howling wind. *Is that a voice?* He called out again, louder this time. A reply seemed to come from not too far away. Crocodile-walking to his right, he shouted out again.

"Brother, answer me!"

He thought he heard sobbing.

The noise seemed to be coming from beneath his feet. He reached down and ran his fingers between the battered wooden planks of the stairs.

He felt a little hand reach out.

"Jeb, is that you?"

"Brother, I'm scared," a little voice sniffled.

He slid down beneath the stairs and grabbed the terrified boy, who had wedged himself between a pair of sturdy cinder blocks. "It's all right," he said reassuringly, clutching him tight.

"I lost Ma. I didn't know where to go."

"I'm here, Little Brother. You're safe now."

He pulled his brother—his best friend that he loved more than anyone else in the world—up into his arms. Then, fighting his way against the stiff wind, he managed to half-drag, half-carry the boy to the storm cellar and deliver him safely into the outstretched arms of their mother. As soon as he fastened the cellar door, the black funnel cloud swooped down upon them.

The tornado's fury was like no other that young Quantrill had ever faced. The wind howled and shrieked like an angry ghost. The door rattled and groaned, but by some miracle managed to hold. He held his breath, praying for the safe deliverance of his beloved family. To his surprise, his prayers were answered. After five minutes of violent shaking, the rattling stopped and the eerie whistling sound died away.

He waited a few minutes just to be safe before opening the cellar door and helping the others outside. The sky was an angry purplish-black welt to the west, a hazy bluish gray to all other points of the compass. But to his relief the dark-black funnel was nowhere in sight. The prairie seemed serene and desolate, as if some great battle had just passed.

He and Ma quickly surveyed the damage. The house was still standing, though all the windows were broken, the front and back doors were missing, and dishes, lamps, and countless other objects were broken or overturned. It dawned on the boy that he and his family had been fortunate: the farmhouse must have only been hit by the edge of the twister.

Feeling a sense of relief at his family's good fortune, he decided that there was no reason that he shouldn't go to work. He glanced at his pocket watch. If he hurried, he just might be able to make it to the Petroleum Club on time.

After locating his wooden shoeshine box inside the house, he searched for his bicycle. He eventually found it wedged against the picket fence. It was banged up—several spokes bent, handlebars out of alignment—but it was still useable. Though sweat-soaked and smudged with dirt, he didn't have time to wash up or change and would have to go as he was. He stuffed his shoeshine box in the metal basket on the front of his bike and hopped on.

His mother stepped out of the house with baby Corinna and Jeb. "Good Lord, son, where are you off to now?"

"Work, Ma—I reckon y'all are safe." He pointed towards the blue sky. "I'll be back at suppertime to clean up this mess, do the rest of my chores, and warsh up. I promise, Ma."

He left her there, openmouthed, and rode the sixteen miles to Midland. He had to dart around smashed homes, overturned cars, tractors, and horsetrailers, and knocked-down telephone poles for the first three miles, until he got to the main road. The sweat poured from his body, his lungs heaved, and his legs felt like lead, but he made it to the Petroleum Club in a little less than an hour. He had an important job to do and he would not miss it on account of one measly tornado.

He parked his bike on the curb and flung himself through the solid oak doors. He loved the Petroleum Club, the place where Midland's wealthy oil men idled away the lunch hour, and sometimes the entire afternoon, drinking martinis, chomping char-broiled Longhorn steaks, shooting pool, playing poker, and laughing at dirty jokes. He loved the rich smell of the cigar and pipe smoke, the ripples of bibulous laughter, the exciting talk of whipstocks, football, greenbacks, and sinful women.

Parking himself in front of the two wooden chairs outside the coat room, he looked up at the big grandfather clock. He was three minutes late for work. He pulled out his cloth rag, polishes, and brushes and arranged them neatly at his shine station. He was feeling good about himself until Sid Luckett, the armadillo-faced manager of the club, stomped up to him.

"Mr. Wilkins wasn't here but one minute ago wantin' his shoes shined, boy. You're late and I'd like to know just where you been."

"It was the twister, Mr. Luckett, sir. I got here quick as I could."

"Twister, my ass." He grabbed the boy by the ear and yanked him to his feet. "You mule-sloppin' country bumpkin, don't tell tall tales to me, you hear?"

"But I'm not lying, Mr. Luckett, sir. There really was a twister and I got here quick as I could."

"And I say you're a liar, boy. Maybe you've forgotten that we got a depression on in these parts. There's at least a half dozen colored who'd kill to have this here job."

"I won't be late again, Mr. Luckett, sir."

"You'd better not, boy. Or you'll be back home sloppin' mule shit faster'n a bloodhound can lick a dish." He snorted contemptuously and stomped off.

When the anger cleared from his throat, young Quantrill went into the bathroom and quickly washed up. When he was finished, he returned to his shoeshine station, raised his head prayerfully towards the ceiling, and vowed that one day he would be an oil man rich enough to buy that goddamned club.

CHAPTER 18

IT WAS AFTER FOUR when Higheagle poked his head into his backyard sweat lodge and saw his grandfather seated in his traditional seat, a bent willow and canvas backrest with a furry buffalo hide headpad. To his surprise, the old man threw him a scolding look.

"Either get the hell out of here or come inside, but don't just stand there like an idiot. You're taking my steam."

"Sorry, Grandfather. But I have something important to tell you."

"Well if you want me to listen, you'd better get me a fucking beer."

"That's your request? Okay one cold one coming up." He ducked back inside his house, put on his swim trunks, grabbed a towel and pair of Fat Tires from the fridge, dashed back outside, slipped back into the sweat lodge, handed his grandfather one of the beers, and took a seat in the open backrest next to him, placing his head on his own buffalo hide headpad.

It was a traditional Cheyenne sweat lodge. It opened to the east and consisted of a dome of arched willow branches covered with deer hides and canvas and a thick floor mat of fragrant sage. To generate the steam, they heated big blocks of basalt on their electric outdoor grill and carried them into the sweat lodge with a shovel, placing the heated rocks in the pit in the center of the lodge.

Leaning back in his chair, Higheagle took a sip of his Fat Tire and sighed with satisfaction. The old man took a big swig for himself then grabbed the hatchet pipe at his feet and packed the bowl with hemp with his thumb. Three eagle feathers hung from the pipe's steel blade and several parallel lines were painted on the wooden stem in brilliant red, blue, and yellow. The pipe had belonged to Joseph's great-great grandfather, the Cheyenne warrior High Eagle, and had been passed down through the generations.

When the old chief finished packing the bowl, he raised the pipe and paid tribute to *Heammawihio* and the Four Sacred Directions—North, South, East, and West. Then he lit the sweet-smelling hemp and puffed on the pipe. Higheagle always felt a sense of joy watching his grandfather smoke the pipe in the old way; for as long as he could remember the ritual had been performed in precisely this fashion.

They passed the pipe back and forth several times before finishing the bowl off and tapping out the ashes into the firepit. Higheagle leaned back in his traditional backrest, feeling the beginnings of a nice buzz coming on. As he often did, he felt a swell of pride at the history of his tribe—the Cheyenne, the Called Out People. He thought back to his youth growing up along the banks of the South Platte, or Buffalo Tallow River as his people had referred to it long before any white man had ever set eyes on the meandering water course. In that moment, fully immersed in a world of solitude and powerful memories, he was proud to be a *Tsistsistas*, proud to be a Cheyenne.

"Okay, Grandson, tell me what it is on your mind."

"Some crazy shit happened today."

"Talk to me, maybe this old Contrary can help."

"I need your word that you will keep this between us."

"Oh, it's that kind of secret? You know you can always count on my discretion."

"I still want to hear you promise me."

"Very well, you have my word."

Higheagle looked at him. Even though he trusted the old man, he felt torn between maintaining his loyalty to his client—the hand that literally fed him—and his desire to confess to his grandfather what he had witnessed today, to uncover the ultimate truth of it, and to uphold what was right. He picked up the hollowed buffalo-horn spoon from the sage mat, dipped it into the water bucket, and flicked some water over the heated stones, producing a misty cloud that sent a warm, stew pot-like breath of moist air over their faces.

"I could be mistaken, but I think Quantrill's trying to pull one over on me. He and his brother both."

"What have they done?"

"I'm not one hundred percent sure, but my guess is that they've got some kind of waste disposal scam going on at the haz waste plant."

"What do you mean?"

"I believe they may be pumping untreated liquid hazardous waste off-site without anyone knowing about it."

"What makes you think that?"

Higheagle hesitated a moment before responding, wondering why in the hell he hadn't seen it coming. But he also felt guilty for even talking about his client in this way, as if Charles Quantrill was some kind of mafia kingpin or corrupt public official.

"A pipeline ruptured today out at the waste plant. They said it was crude oil coming out of the line, but the liquid looked clear to me. I only got a quick look, but they made such a fuss about it I can't help but think they're up to something. We're talking about a huge volume here. What I saw spraying out of the broken pipe was like a fire hose—maybe four hundred gallons per minute, possibly more."

"Where was the pipeline?"

"Right off the edge of the property. The strange thing is the liquid was flowing out of the ground to the east, not to the west where it would have been moving if it really was an oil transmission line."

"What caused the rupture?"

"I'm not sure. At first, they tried to blame me for puncturing the pipeline, saying that I had drilled into it. Then they backed off. I think the line was just weak, maybe from the earthquake."

The old man nodded thoughtfully, his silver hair hanging loosely down his bull-shouldered back. He reached for the spoon and flicked some water on the stones, sending up a cloud of steam. "What are you going to do?"

"I don't know—I'm in a bind. Quantrill Ventures may be up to no good, but that doesn't change the fact that they've always treated me well and given me a ton of work. They're worth over two million dollars in consulting fees to HydroGroup every year. Quantrill Ventures is easily our biggest client. Without them, we're finished—and so am I."

"I can see your dilemma. But my question still stands: what do you propose to do?"

"The first thing is to have the soil sample I took analyzed. That will tell me what kind of waste we're dealing with here. Whatever it is, it sure as hell isn't crude oil."

"Wait a second. You took a soil sample?"

"The liquid was pouring out from the pipe and I was standing right there. What was I supposed to do, just sit there and watch? I wanted to know what it was."

"Does Quantrill or his brother know you took a sample?"

Why is he looking at me with that worried look on his face, like I don't know what the fuck I'm doing? "No, and that's the way I have to keep it. Look Grandfather, I know that I rushed into this without thinking, but I had to find out what was leaking from that line. The only problem is someone saw me."

"Who?"

"Dr. Nickerson. That seismologist from the USGS."

"The Earthquake Man?"

"He must have been out there inspecting for earthquake damage. He was with the state geologist, Mark Kelso, but Kelso didn't see us. Only Nickerson did."

"Did he say anything to you about it?"

"No."

"He hasn't contacted you since?"

"No, but I have the feeling he will."

"What did you do with the sample?"

"I delivered the sample to EnviroTest instead of Quantrill's lab so Quantrill and his brother Jeb won't know about it."

"So you've taken a sample on your client's property without him knowing? If you were a lawyer and did something like this to your client, you would be disbarred."

"Thanks, Grandfather, for making me feel even more guilty than I already do. What do you want me to say? I told you I wasn't thinking—it was like a reflex. And Nickerson saw me."

"How do you know this fluid you saw isn't just water or some sort of cleaning solution they use to flush out their oil lines?"

"I thought about that. But why was the flow away from the facility then? And if it was only water or cleaning fluids, why wouldn't they just say that? There's nothing illegal about flushing out transmission lines with simple reagents to eliminate plugging or reduce corrosion."

"When will you get the lab results back?"

"I should have them by late tomorrow. I know the lab director at EnviroTest and he's doing them on a rush basis for no extra charge. He owes me a favor."

The old man took a last pull from his beer and set the bottle down. "Do you want my advice?"

"That's the reason I'm talking to you."

"You need to ask yourself one thing."

"What's that?"

"If what you suspect is happening is what is really happening, are you prepared to cut off the hand that feeds you to figure it out? Or, more importantly, to make things right?"

"I don't know, Grandfather. Right now, I just don't know."

"Then that is the question you must answer." And with that, he leaned back in his traditional willow and canvas backrest with the buffalo hide headpad, closed his eyes, and fell fast asleep.

CHAPTER 19

"SO, GENTLEMEN, THE CRITICAL QUESTION IS THIS…"

Charles Prometheus Quantrill let the words hover in the air, drawing out the moment like a master thespian, as he calmly steepled his long, bony fingers and leaned back in his chair with a philosophical expression on his broad, hardy face. Seated around the conference table with him and his brother were Holland, Johnston, and Boggs. Like his home office, the CEO's *sanctum sanctorum* at Quantrill Ventures was done in an eclectic style and packed with a fabulous array of rare fossils and priceless Western artifacts. The walls were hung with a triumvirate of Albert Bierstadt oil paintings: *Oregon Trail* from 1869, *Indians in Council* from 1872, and *Storm in the Rocky Mountains* from 1886, each one celebrating the rugged pageantry of the American West. The solid oak, floor-to-ceiling bookcases lining the room gleamed with fresh polish and were packed with business books, journals, magazines, and family pictures. In addition to the handsome conference table he and his inner circle were seated at, a large sofa and upholstered chairs were arranged across an antique Navaho rug, which, like the one in his home office at the Broadmoor, had once been owned by frontier explorer and Indian fighter Kit Carson.

But it was the pair of rippled-glass cabinets that stole the show. One displayed an assortment of trilobites, winged brachiopods, and coiled ammonites; a *Utahraptor* claw; dozens of precious gems and minerals; and the fossilized skull of *Smilodon fatalis*, the lethal saber-toothed cat of the Pleistocene that had used its long canines to slash through the throats of its victims. The other case held a variety of Indian wares: a steel-tipped arrow that had once belonged to the Arapaho Peace Chief Niwot, or "Left Hand," killed by the butcher Chivington in 1864 at Sand Creek; a horned scalplock, yellow buckskin leggings, and trade-blanket breechclout that had belonged to an unknown scout that had fought in Frank and Luther North's heralded Pawnee scout battalion in 1869; and beaded moccasins, a bearclaw necklace, a buffalo scrotum rattle, and strings of rare beads pillaged from a Lakota family at Slim Buttes in 1876.

"Just what in the hell did Joe Higheagle and that EPA gal see out there?" Quantrill finished his introductory oration, expelling a little gasp of air at the end to underscore the importance of the question.

As expected, his brother Jeb fielded the query. "It's hard to tell. When the line failed, the fluid came shooting out of the ground like a broken water main. And it didn't look like crude."

"How long did it spray up in the air?" asked Holland, his cadaverous frame looking spindly as a spider in his oversized leather chair.

"Maybe ten seconds."

"That's a pretty short time. And how far away were Higheagle and Nina Curry?"

"Joe was working at the back of his truck, maybe forty feet away. Nina was closer, about thirty-five. Their view was partially blocked by the fence."

"After the liquid shot up like a fountain, it flowed over the ground, right? How long did that last?"

"It took less than five minutes from the time of the release for me to get to the emergency shut-off and kill the flow. Before I started off, I told everyone to stay behind the rig and not to go anywhere near the leak."

"Who was present again?"

"Higheagle, Nina Curry, and the two drillers. Nickerson and Kelso were with me, maybe two hundred feet away from where the rupture occurred when it happened. Richard Hamilton was still at the refinery at the time so he didn't see anything. We hurried over to the drilling rig. I had Nickerson and Kelso assemble with the others behind the rig."

"How do you know whether they followed your instructions?"

"We don't for sure," interjected Quantrill. "But by the time Wes, Harry, and I got there, all of them were behind the rig. As long as they stayed there, they didn't see anything except the original release and then some bubbling up out of the ground."

Harry Boggs, the security chief, leaned his fleshy body forward, bringing his reptilian eyes even with the edge of the table. "Yeah, but there's the odor too. Unfortunately, they weren't wearing respirators."

"What's the importance of that?" asked Holland.

"It means they probably got a good whiff," explained Johnston. "The wind was blowing in from the northeast."

Quantrill felt a little twitch of worry. *Is this situation going to turn into a huge problem for me?*

Holland appeared confused. "But I thought this stuff smells just like crude oil?"

Glances were exchanged around the table. "It's not quite that simple, Jack," said Quantrill, nettled by the sound of defeat in his voice.

"We've been adding mercaptans to the liquid to give it a sulfur smell," explained Johnston. "They're organic sulfur compounds added to natural gas to give it a smell because it's odorless. It's the same stuff in hot springs, the same spray that skunks have."

"We've been adding the mercaptans in case we ever had an accidental release like this," explained Quantrill. "Or if we had someone poking around the line unnecessarily."

"So they only had perhaps ten seconds to see the liquid coming out of the hole and they definitely smelled the sulfur odor," Holland said, looking at Jeb. "It doesn't sound like enough to make them suspicious. Besides, the spill has been completely removed, has it not?"

"The contamination has been excavated, but we're going to do another visual check tomorrow and go over the excavation a final time with the OVM before the EPA comes out again."

"But we still don't know exactly what Higheagle or the girl saw," complained Boggs, pulling at his walrus-mustache with a trace of annoyance. "During that five minutes or so you were gone, they could have walked over to the fence to see what was coming out of the ground."

"They didn't write anything like that up in their incident reports."

Boggs shook his head. "Forget the incident reports—those don't tell us anything about what they actually saw out there."

"Harry's got a point," said Johnston. "And the truth is the mercaptans don't completely eliminate the solvent odor."

"Then I'll say it again: we need to find out what they know. Especially Higheagle and the girl since they're the most familiar with these types of constituents."

Holland took off his wire-frame glasses and rubbed his eyes. "So is it reasonable to assume that they have some idea of the operation?"

Everyone looked at Jeb.

"I think everything happened so fast that they couldn't have had time to figure anything out. They might have thought we overreacted a bit. But I'd wager they never gave it a second thought after they left this afternoon."

"Was Curry still in a lather?" asked Johnston.

"No, she actually apologized. I think she bought our explanation, but she's still going to be looking closely at the spill site tomorrow."

"What about Higheagle?" asked Holland. "He's the one that worries me the most."

"Me too," echoed Boggs. "That boy's too clever for my liking. I didn't like him three years ago when I interviewed him—and I like him even less now."

Quantrill didn't have that feeling about Higheagle. In fact, he had always admired the young Cheyenne and was quite pleased with his performance over the years on the various environmental projects at the refinery, haz waste facility, and wind farm. All the same, he looked to his brother's opinion on the matter since he was the one who had worked most closely with Higheagle.

"What do you think, Jeb? Can we trust our Injun friend?"

"He's an advocate, a contractor to us, and I believe his loyalty is beyond question. We all saw how he kept his mouth shut when Nina Curry was getting all huffy."

"He certainly didn't say anything that would help her," agreed Johnston.

Boggs frowned. "I realize he's been a loyal consultant, Mr. Quantrill. But I think at this point he could pose a serious danger. He certainly has the technical background."

Leaning back in his leather chair, the CEO looked at his brother. "Do you think he's got a thing for that gal Nina? You told me he was giving her an eye-eating stare just before they left."

"I know what I told you, but the fact is he hardly knows her. Today was the first time they met."

"Harry noted that they seemed to be getting along well when they were out on the rig. He was watching them through his binoculars."

"I don't care what this Indian fellow's done for you in the past, Chuck," interjected Holland. "He's sounding worse to me every minute. As your attorney, I advise you to get rid of him—quietly of course."

"I hear you loud and clear, Jack. But now ain't the time to draw attention to the operation."

"In that case we'd better at least find out what he knows," warned Boggs. "That incident report he filled out doesn't tell us diddly."

"I'm already one step ahead of you, Harry. What I propose is to call Joe's boss tonight and have them both come in for a little talk at lunchtime tomorrow."

Jeb's mouth fell open. "You're going to call in Ravi Sundaresan? You can't be serious?"

"I am dead serious, Brother."

"What are you going to talk about?"

"Not me, you and I together. We're going to make sure our boy's got his mind right."

"And just what the hell does that mean?"

"It means that we're going to remind him who pays his bills and of the client confidentiality agreement he signed. He needs to know that he will be in serious trouble if he so much as opens his mouth to Nina Curry. We finance HydroGroup to the tune of two million dollars per year. That should buy one hundred percent loyalty in my way of reckoning."

Holland smoothed his tie and gave a thoughtful look. "That should make our boy think twice about talking to the girl or anyone else. But it's still no guarantee."

"Damn right it's not," snapped Jeb. "In fact, it could all just as easily backfire and all we end up doing is alert him that something is going on. Or worse yet, piss him off. Have you thought of that?"

"Your job is to make sure that doesn't happen."

"You're going about this the wrong way. Higheagle's no fool. He's going to realize that we just want to find out what he knows and that we're trying to shut him up."

"Ravi will bring him under control. The only thing Ravi cares about is holding on to his two million dollars per year in consulting fees. But the key to the whole thing is you, Jeb."

"What the hell are you talking about?"

"You're the one Joe trusts. If you could question him about the spill in Ravi's presence, we could find out what he knows and take down his responses right then and there in front of his boss. That way he can't later change his mind or disclose anything he saw to a third party."

"I don't see what purpose that would serve. Higheagle's already filled out an incident report."

"But we still need confirmation of what he knows," said Boggs. "If you go over the incident report with him, we can double check his answers and get him to sign off on what he said before. Only we'd give the form a new name. Call it an accidental release form and have a nondisclosure agreement along with it. You could do it all while Higheagle and Ravi are both sitting there. Strong-arming our boy into signing right on the spot could put an end to this once and for all."

"This is all too heavy-handed," protested Jeb. "Higheagle's already signed our standard non-disclosure agreement. Isn't that enough? He and Ravi are going to recognize what you're doing."

"Heavy-handed or not, this is the way we're going to handle it," commanded Quantrill, brooking no further opposition. "Jack, have the form on my desk first thing tomorrow morning. Now as far as your role during the meeting, Harry, I believe it would be best if you leave the room before Jeb interviews Higheagle and they fill out the form. I don't want it to seem like we're piling on."

"Yes, sir."

"So are we all on board, gentlemen?"

Boggs, Holland, and Johnston nodded their assent. Jeb looked away, refusing to submit but at the same time not pressing the argument further.

Quantrill decided to let it go at that. He had as much of a consensus as he was going to get for the time being. Jeb would come around after stewing awhile. "All right then. Looks to me like we've got our damage control moving in the right direction. Wes, you and Jeb make sure that pipeline release area is all nice and purty for Ms. Curry when she comes out here tomorrow. I want that gal to be as happy as a pine borer in a fresh log when she sees how clean that area is."

"Yes, sir," said Johnston.

"Thank you, gentlemen," the CEO declared to close the meeting. "And remember, if each and every one of us acts out his role as scripted, then everything will work out just fine. That means especially you, Little Brother, since our Cheyenne friend trusts you the most."

CHAPTER 20

THE FOLLOWING MORNING—three days before Halloween—Dr. James Nickerson waited anxiously for Joseph Higheagle to answer on the other end of his phone while he scanned the abstract of an article in the *Journal of Geophysical Research*. Yesterday's experience at Quantrill Ventures had been strange, to say the least. He had been debating contacting Higheagle since returning to the office yesterday afternoon. But until now, he hadn't been able to convince himself to pick up the phone and make the call.

Was he afraid of what he might find? That was part of it, he realized. What exactly had transpired was at this point still murky, although it definitely had a whiff of shadiness about it. Worse yet, it appeared to involve his old friend Jeb Quantrill. Some stones were best left unturned—and yet Nickerson couldn't let it go.

When the Cheyenne finally answered, Nickerson heard the sound of heavy machinery in the background.

"Joe Higheagle."

"Hi Joe, this is James Nickerson from the USGS."

The phone was silent for several seconds. "What can I do for you?"

"Are you out at the facility?"

"I'm overseeing the well development."

"How's it looking out there? Have they got the spill cleaned up?"

"For the most part. Nina Curry of the EPA is over there now inspecting the excavation with the on-scene coordinator."

"That's good."

"Look, I'm really busy here. What did you want to talk to me about?"

Nickerson felt uneasy; this was turning out to be more difficult than he had anticipated. *Just come straight out and say it.* "I'd like to know what you think happened yesterday?"

Another pause, longer this time. "I'm not sure what you're talking about."

"I'm talking about the sample you took. You know that I saw you."

Higheagle didn't respond.

"I'd like to know why you took it."

Again no response.

"Are you having the sample analyzed?"

"Look, Dr. Nickerson, I represent Quantrill Ventures as an environmental consultant. I can't discuss the project with any outside parties without the company's consent."

So this is the way you want to play it. "Spare me the corporate confidentiality crap, Joe. I'm not stupid. Something's going on out there. That wasn't crude oil that sprayed up out of that busted line and you and I both damn well know it. That's why you took the sample—to find out what kind of contaminants are in the soil."

Again a tense silence.

"Look, Joe, I think that line failed because of the earthquake. Which means that the refinery and waste facility are vulnerable and probably not up to the seismic design codes they're purported to be. Next time there could be a fire or explosion and people could get hurt or even killed. That's why it's critical to know what types of contaminants are being pumped through that line. If there's flammable or explosive liquids running through there, there could be major problems. And if somebody knew about it and did nothing—well, you can see where this is heading."

"Are you threatening me? Because if I'm not mistaken that's what it sounds like to me."

"I just want to know what's going on."

"Why don't you tell me what you were doing out at the facility yesterday? Were you conducting a damage inspection?"

"No, that wasn't the reason."

"What was it then?"

"Mark Kelso, the state geologist, and I had a meeting with Charles and Jeb Quantrill. We're trying to get to the bottom of this earthquake and the associated aftershocks. We requested a copy of a seismic reflection profile performed by Quantrill Ventures two decades ago to help us in our efforts. We also asked for the data from an on-site seismographic network."

"Are they going to give it to you?"

"I doubt it. My old friend Jeb—"

"What do you mean your old friend Jeb?"

"We went to grad school and worked together in Midland when we both first started out in the oil business years ago."

"Is that so? Then perhaps you should be questioning him instead of me."

"He won't tell me anything despite our past friendship. In fact, I think he and his brother are stonewalling me."

"Why would they do that?"

"Not to protect company information, I can tell you that. Quantrill Ventures is up to something and I'm going to find out what it is."

Silence on the other end.

"Joe, are you still there?"

"I've got to get off now—your old friend's coming."

Nickerson felt his heart rate click up a notch. "Jeb? Jeb's there?"

"With Nina Curry. Looks like she's done with her inspection. I've got to go now."

"I want to see those sample results, Joe. Once you get them, you call me. Do you hear me?"

"Goodbye, Dr. Nickerson."

"Joe, listen to—"

But he was gone. Nickerson cursed and immediately punched in Jeb Quantrill's cell number.

A voice came on after two rings. "Hello?"

"I need to talk to you, Jeb."

"James, this is not a good time. I'm busy with the EPA."

Nickerson wasn't quite sure how to play it, so he simply plunged ahead. "I wanted to check in and see if there's any way you can expedite my information request. I figured you might have given it some thought and perhaps changed your mind."

"No, James, I haven't changed my mind. Otherwise, I would have contacted you."

"But the situation's changed now."

"How so?"

"Well, yesterday you had a pipeline failure."

"I don't see what that has to do with anything. We've dealt with the problem. The EPA has already certified that the spill site is essentially clean."

"I'm not talking about that. I'm talking about the fact that the earthquake has weakened the line and that's why it failed."

"That's pure conjecture. You don't know that."

"You need to send me the data I requested. Otherwise, Mark Kelso and I are going to have to conduct a full inspection. And believe me, we'll find something. You follow?"

Now a note of anger. "Why are you doing this, James? After what I did for you?"

"I wondered how long it would take you to bring that up."

"They would have killed you, James. You know that."

"You're absolutely right, it was a goddamned lynch mob. A lynch mob of Texas good old boys just like you."

"You know I'm not like that."

"Oh yes, I almost forgot, massah, you saved this old nigger's bacon. I owe you my life. This *nigger* owes you his life."

96

"Don't say that word to me, goddamnit. You know I don't like it."

"What's wrong? It's just a word."

"No, it's not and you damn well know it."

"All right, you saved my life and I'll always owe you for that. Eight against one—and somehow you managed to pull it off. Your powers of persuasion are enormous, Jeb, almost as good as your brother's. Yes indeed, suh, this *nigger* owes you his life."

"Stop it, goddamnit. I don't like that word."

"I'll stop as soon as you come clean."

"What the hell is that supposed to mean?"

"You know damn well what it means. You're involved in something, you and your brother both."

"I'm punching off now."

"The only reason I'm not doing anything about it is because of our friendship."

"We don't have a friendship. Not anymore."

"You'll always be my friend, Jeb. You risked everything for me."

"I'm punching off now."

"All right, but when you're ready to talk you let me know."

"I have nothing to say to you."

"Yes you do, old friend. Just make sure you don't wait too long to tell me."

CHAPTER 21

HIGHEAGLE stood with Nina Curry behind the tailgate of his truck, watching the steel surge block cable as it swooshed up and down, forcing groundwater in and out of the perforated monitoring well. Jeb Quantrill had escorted her over from the excavation site a moment earlier before stepping away to take a call. By his body language, it didn't seem to be going too well.

Higheagle too couldn't help but feel agitated. How crazy was the call he had just received from Dr. Nickerson? Even though he had been expecting it, he was still reeling. The world-renowned seismologist was pressing him with questions and he wasn't sure how to deal with the man. More importantly, what in the hell had he gotten himself into?

He thought back to what his grandfather had said last night: *Are you prepared to cut off the hand that feeds you to make things right?*

He realized that he was no closer to answering that question now than he was then. Thankfully, he didn't have to make the decision right now. He could wait until the soil sample results came back and he knew for certain what type of contaminants were running through the line. But even then, would the analytical results be conclusive? Quantrill Ventures may have been pumping haz waste off-site, but that didn't mean that the operation was necessarily illegal. Maybe they were just flushing out the line with some type of surfactant. Maybe the line wrapped around the perimeter of the facility and selected waste was treated at another off-site location. From the utility clearances he had observed firsthand, the subsurface piping at the facility was complex. Who was he to question what contaminants went where and how they were treated? Or maybe the wastewater was used as process water for some other legitimate on-site or off-site operation.

Still, he couldn't deny the feeling in his gut that something wasn't right. But if his suspicions proved correct, did he dare turn in his own client, and thereby risk losing his job and two million dollars per year in consulting fees for his company? From a professional career standpoint, such a step would be suicidal.

Nina Curry interrupted his thoughts. "You'll be pleased to know that they've removed most of the impacted soil at the excavation."

She had caught him in a vulnerable moment of introspection, but he quickly regained his composure, presenting a mask of bland technical efficiency. "I know—the emergency response team did a thorough job," he said, feigning an enthusiasm he didn't feel inside. "I checked out the excavation earlier this morning."

"There's only one dirty spot with hydrocarbons remaining. I still can't believe how quickly they cleaned it all up. Now I understand why Quantrill Ventures 'green' rating is so high."

I wouldn't bank on that this year, sister, he thought with a sense of dread. It was surprising what a turnaround she had undergone since yesterday. Now that she and the EPA on-scene coordinator had visually certified that the excavation was "clean," she was no longer on the warpath against Quantrill Ventures. Nor was she suspicious of operations at the facility. He remembered that she had been busy talking to the drillers and Kelso when Nickerson had caught him collecting the soil sample. Now the roles were reversed—and he was the distrustful one. And yet, looking at her, he couldn't help but feel that, if his suspicions about Quantrill Ventures proved correct and he ultimately confided in her, he would find in her a kindred spirit and valuable ally.

But at this point it was moot since he still didn't know anything for certain. Even once he did, he would have to tread carefully. If Quantrill Ventures ever found out what he was up to, not only would he risk financial ruin from losing his job and his firm's most important client, but he would risk incurring the formidable wrath of Quantrill's lawyers for violating client confidentiality. Like every HydroGroup employee who worked on a Quantrill Ventures project, he had signed the seven-page corporate non-disclosure agreement. He remembered going through it line by line with both Quantrill's in-house counsel, Jack Holland, and his security chief, Harry Boggs.

When Jeb finished his call and started walking back towards them, Higheagle felt his cell phone vibrate. His supervisor Ravi Sunderesan's number flashed on the visual display. Why would his boss be calling? He had already briefed him yesterday and again this morning on the pipeline release and progress of the cleanup.

He stepped to the side so he could have some privacy as Jeb came walking up to him and Nina Curry. "I'll be with you in just a sec—I have to take this." He took several more steps away before speaking into his cell. "Hello Ravi?"

"Joe, how is it going out there?"

"Fine, we're developing the first of the new wells. What's up?"

"I am coming out to see you."

"What do you mean? You're driving out here?"

"I will be there in ten minutes. We have a meeting with Mr. Quantrill and Mr. Boggs."

Higheagle felt blindsided and again looked at Jeb, but he was busy talking to Nina. The two of them looked uncomfortable. He stepped a few more feet away for more privacy. Did Jeb know about the meeting? Is that why he appeared to be agitated talking on the phone a moment ago?

"Ravi, I don't understand. What's this meeting about?"

"I'm not sure exactly. Just meet me at the office in ten minutes."

"Wait a second. Am I in trouble?"

"Let's just say that there are some issues that we need to resolve."

Issues—what issues? Translation: he was in fucking trouble. *Shit!*

He felt a frisson of genuine trepidation. "What about the well development?"

"You'll need to shut down until you return from the meeting."

"But the EPA is here."

"Who from the EPA?"

"Nina Curry?"

"She's there with you right now?"

Why is that such a big deal? "So is Jeb."

"Jeb's there?"

"You sound surprised."

"He's going to be at the meeting too.'

Jesus, this is a goddamned setup! "Ravi, I don't know what this is about, but something isn't—"

"Just be there, okay." And he was gone.

Shit! He stepped towards Jeb and Nina, who were still engaged in conversation. He made eye contact with Jeb. "I've just been told that we have a meeting up at the office."

"Yeah, I just found out myself."

Higheagle tried to read him. *Is he telling the truth?* "What do you want to do about the well development? I don't think I should leave the rig."

"We'll have the drillers break for lunch. The meeting shouldn't take too long." He turned to Nina. "You're welcome to stay, but we're going to hold off on any well development activities until we're finished with the meeting."

She looked at Higheagle, her face showing concern. She had picked up on his and Jeb's tense body language. "I guess I'll head back to the office," she said.

"I'll tell the drillers," said Jeb, and he started over to the rig.

Once he was out of earshot, Nina said, "Is everything all right?"

"Yes, everything's fine," Higheagle replied, but he knew his face betrayed him.

"Well, call me if you need anything. Anything at all."

She smiled warmly and he realized that she wasn't just talking about work. He felt a little flutter in his chest. "I'll do that," he said, and he glanced in the direction of the rig and saw Jeb staring at them disapprovingly.

"I wonder why he's looking at us like that," said Nina. "Are you sure everything's all right?"

"Positive." Again he felt torn between his loyalty to his client, and his desire to be honest with her and uncover the truth. But, like Nickerson, could she be trusted?

She pulled a business card from her pocket and handed it to him. "My cell number's on there. When the soil and groundwater analytical results come in, please give me a call."

"I will."

Smiling sympathetically, she turned and headed to her car.

A moment later Jeb returned. He wasn't smiling at all.

"Let's go on up," he said curtly, and Higheagle knew he was in for it now.

CHAPTER 22

QUANTRILL peered into his cabinet displaying the fossilized skull of *Smilodon fatalis*, imagining what the massive hunter must have looked like as it stalked and dispatched its prey. The deadly saber-toothed cat of the Pleistocene was not as fast or agile as an African lion, but Quantrill knew it was far more stoutly built and deadly in close quarters. *Smilodon's* frontal fangs were longer, thicker, and more curved than those of the modern lion, and with its far greater upper-body strength, powerful forearms, and paws equipped with sharp talons, it's *modus operendi* was to move in with quiet stealth and quickly overpower its prey, using its scimitar-shaped canines to deliver a deep stabbing bite to the throat, slicing through the carotid artery with swift, violent efficiency.

Heaven forbid this was how he was going to have to deal with Higheagle.

He turned away from the skull and looked at his chief of security. "So what did you find out about our boy, Harry?"

Boggs tossed back the rest of his coffee, set his mug down on the conference table, and flipped to the first page of his notepad. "He was born and raised on the Northern Cheyenne Reservation up in Lame Deer, Montana. Date of birth 1977, which makes him thirty-one. Born to Russell and Melissa Higheagle. Both full-blooded Northern Cheyennes, or as full blooded as a marauding Plains Indian can be, I suppose. He was raised by his grandfather, mostly. His parents were killed along with his grandmother when he was six years old."

Moving nimbly for a big man, Quantrill stepped to the table and sat down. "How did they die?"

"They were murdered right in front of the boy's eyes. The police called it a simple armed robbery, but the case was never solved."

My God, it must have been hard on the boy, losing his parents and grandmother like that, thought Quantrill sympathetically. "What about the father? What's his story?"

"He was a Marine. Fought in 'Nam. He was on a three-week stateside leave from overseas duty when the murder happened. He was a winner of the Distinguished Service Cross."

"A war hero. Somehow that doesn't surprise me. And the grandfather?"

"Also a Marine as well as a war hero—in Korea. Won two different combat decorations as well as a Purple Heart at Pork Chop Hill in '53."

Quantrill picked up one of the seven flint arrowheads from the little handwoven straw basket at his desk and eyed it appraisingly. "Injuns—goddamn if they don't love a good fight. It's in their blood, by thunder. Tell me more about this grandfather."

"Like I said, sir, John Higheagle raised the boy. He was a tribal lawyer and acting tribal chief, but he's now retired. He serves as an informal senior advisor in councils and provides some litigation support on water and mineral rights issues up on the rez. He and his grandson own a small ranch along the South Platte."

"What about Joe? I remember from his resume that he went to Dartmouth, but I don't recall how he performed there. Did he graduate *sigma cum laude* or did he guzzle beer and chase women?"

"Actually, he almost didn't make it. He was on academic probation his freshman year. Damned near flunked out."

"And after his freshman year?"

"He was a B-student his sophomore year and got straight As his last three years."

Quantrill appraised his opponent in a different light. "Impressive. I recall from his resume that he was a double major in geology and vertebrate paleontology. That must be why he took five years to graduate."

"He also had a minor."

"In what?"

"American history."

"Must have been a lot different than the history he learned growing up on the rez. Play any sports in college?"

"Lacrosse."

"Dartmouth's Division 1. Again, impressive. Was he any good?"

"He was team captain and first team All-American his junior and senior years. He's also played professional lacrosse the past three seasons for the Denver Outlaws."

Jesus, he never told me he played lacrosse. I need to get to an Outlaws game and see the son of a bitch play, thought Quantrill, staring up at the late 19th century Albert Bierstadt oil painting on the wall showing a lone, buckskin-clad Indian warrior with storm clouds sweeping over the Rockies in the background. "What about his geological career?"

"He's been with HydroGroup since graduating from Dartmouth. He's a senior hydrogeologist making ninety-five grand a year with the firm. He makes another twenty playing for the Outlaws in the summer."

"Political affiliation."

"Independent."

"Hmmm. So what do you think, Harry? Is this lacrosse-playing noble savage going to cause me problems?"

"I already told you, I don't like him. He knows too much and I'm not sure where his loyalty lies. At the very least, you need to keep an eye on him."

"What are you suggesting?"

"Round the clock surveillance for the next week or so. I can have Heiser do it."

"What about wiretapping?"

"According to his phone records, he mostly uses his cell. Except when he's at work. I think keeping him under surveillance is going to tell us what we need to know. For the short term at least."

"You think he saw something out there with that pipeline?"

"He saw more than he should have, I know that."

Quantrill stroked his chin, thinking things through. "So regardless of how our little meeting in the next few minutes goes, we put him under surveillance. Is that it?"

"Yes, sir. And we should start tonight."

They were interrupted by a ringing phone. Quantrill looked at the number, saw that it was his executive secretary. He punched the intercom button. "Yes, Cynthia?"

"Mr. Sundaresan is here to see you."

"Please show him to Conference Room A. Tell him we'll be over in a minute. Is Jeb back?"

"He and Mr. Higheagle are on their way over now too."

"Thank you, Cynthia."

He punched off the button and looked at Boggs. "All right, get Heiser on Higheagle when he leaves here today. We need to know where our boy's loyalties lie."

"I'll take care of it."

Quantrill rose from his seat. "I'm going to have a quick little chat with Ravi before everyone else gets there."

"I'll be over in a minute."

"I've got to tell you though, Harry, I've always liked young Joe. He's always done a bang-up job for me."

"I know that, sir. But he now poses a threat to your interests."

"Meaning?"

"He's going to have to be dealt with—and I mean firmly."

CHAPTER 23

AS THEY approached the door of Conference Room A at precisely five minutes before noon, Higheagle felt his stomach twisted in knots. He looked discretely at Jeb, but found his face unreadable. Wordlessly, the chief geologist opened the door and motioned him inside. Stepping into the room, Higheagle quickly scanned the three men—Quantrill, Ravi Sunderesan, and Harry Boggs—sitting around a mahogany conference table.

His boss was the first to look up as he entered the room. The principal engineer was bedecked in a gray suit, conservative tie, and stiff loafers and his cool, ascetic expression matched his outfit. Higheagle wondered how long Ravi had been here talking to Quantrill and Boggs. His gaze shifted to Quantrill. To his surprise, the powerful CEO didn't look as intimidating or threatening as expected. The gunmetal-gray eyes did not appear to harbor any hostility or displeasure and his broad mouth actually creased into a kindly, paternal smile. That, at least, was a good sign. He wore his usual sartorial accoutrements: a custom-tailored English suit, cowboy hat, bolo tie, and pointy-toed boots. Compared to his brother, dressed in dusty field clothes, he looked impeccably groomed. The last one he made eye contact with was Harry Boggs. Bedecked in a tan suit and staid tie, the security chief stared back at Higheagle with cool calculation mingled with the usual dose of distrust.

As Jeb closed the door behind him, the Cheyenne gave a little start. There was a jarring note of finality to it: he realized with despair that it was too late to turn back. He took another gulp of air and allowed his eyes to trace the deep mahogany paneling and the dark green, flowing drapes pulled to the side of the window. Dark billowy clouds had settled over the Front Range, dampening the morning's lustrous sunlight with an unwelcome hint of doom and gloom.

Quantrill broke the excruciating silence: "Please take a seat, Joe."

Higheagle did as instructed. He knew he was in for it, but what exactly had he done? His gaze met Quantrill's and the CEO looked him squarely in the eye. He gave a little gulp, feeling suddenly dry and constricted in his throat.

"Now Joe, you've always done a fine job for us all out here at Quantrill Ventures. As a matter of fact, the first time I met you, I said to myself there's a man who's all taters and no vine. But lately it seems…well, I'm not going to sugarcoat it…we've got ourselves a situation."

Higheagle looked helplessly at Ravi, then Jeb. "I'm not sure what you mean. Are you talking about the incident yesterday?"

"No, we're concerned about something else. In short, you seem to have lost sight of the fact that you represent our interests at this here facility."

"I don't understand."

"The long and short of it, Joe, is you're getting too cozy with the new EPA regulator, Nina Curry."

"But we hardly know each other. I mean, we're not even friends. And even if we were, it in no way would affect my judgment, or my ability to represent you as a consultant, Mr. Quantrill."

"I don't think you'd ever compromise your obligations as a consultant, Joe. But women got a funny way of making a man do things he wouldn't normally do."

"You cannot have a relationship with the EPA project manager for this facility," suddenly blurted his boss, Ravi Sunderesan, unable to conceal his displeasure. "It puts everyone in a difficult position."

Higheagle felt himself cluttering with rage and disbelief. "But there isn't any relationship."

"Not yet maybe," chimed in Boggs. "But we've seen the way you look at her—and we believe it could lead to future problems."

Higheagle glanced coolly at Jeb, who he now knew was complicit in all this, then glared flints at Boggs. "Even if I was interested in her, I don't believe that would be any of your damned business."

"That's where you're wrong. It is absolutely *my* business—and the business of everyone else at this table."

"Getting close to this woman, Joe," said Jeb in a sympathetic tone like his brother, "poses a conflict of interest. All of us here have been through some rough relationships and we know how easily things can turn sour. In a case like that, Ms. Curry might be tempted to lash out at us to get even with you."

"And it's *my* job to prevent anything like that happening in the first place," added Boggs.

"Are you saying that I shouldn't see her period, or that I'm not to have a relationship with her?"

"We're saying it's best for everyone if you don't have anything but professional contact with the gal," answered Quantrill. "Now I know she's awfully purty and she's got a lot of spunk, but she's with the EPA and could, therefore, pose problems for us all."

Boggs quickly echoed his boss. "Mr. Quantrill here is paying you and your company a lot of money to solve his environmental problems. From the company's standpoint, anything that has the potential to raise conflict of interest issues is unacceptable."

Realizing he was embroiled in a battle he couldn't win, Higheagle retreated into the dark-green leather. "All right, if it's that important to you, I'll stay away from her."

"Business meetings or field oversight situations are fine, but that's it," said Ravi, lecturing him like a controlling parent. "And you should know that this situation is not unique. An employee at a firm I used to work for was forced to resign because he was having a relationship with a woman at the Colorado Department of Public Health and the Environment. And when I was in California, I heard about a similar conflict of interest involving an Envirotech employee and a woman with Cal-EPA."

"We think highly of you, Joe, that's why we're telling you this," said Jeb. "If you can make sure to keep your work and private life separate, you'll never hear about this again."

"I wouldn't tell her anything about our little talk here either," Quantrill added. "As far as we're concerned, this is a private matter between Quantrill Ventures and HydroGroup."

Higheagle rubbed his palms together in his lap. "I understand. Is there anything else?"

"No, that should cover it," said Quantrill with a friendly smile. He looked for confirmation from Jeb and Boggs. "Unless y'all have something to add?"

"Oh, there is one thing," said Jeb. "We need you to complete this Accidental Release to the Environment form we have here. You've already signed a non-disclosure agreement that covers all work completed on behalf of Quantrill Ventures. But we need this supplemental release form signed ASAP. The form is an addendum to the incident report you completed yesterday. It's just a formality."

"I'll be leaving now then," Boggs said, lifting his hefty frame from his seat.

"Thank you, Harry," Quantrill said. He waited until the security man had closed the door behind him before continuing. "Now why don't you tell him about the form, Jeb."

"It's just our standard company form for accidental releases. We want to make sure we have a detailed record of what happened yesterday. This will be the official record of the event that will be submitted to the EPA."

"We've just gone over it with Ravi here," said Quantrill. He pointed to the blank form on the table in front of the principal engineer then pushed a copy across the table towards Higheagle.

Over the next fifteen minutes, they asked him about the rupture, the characteristics and volume of the liquid he had seen, and how he, Nina Curry, James Nickerson, Mark Kelso, and the drillers had responded to the incident. Higheagle wasn't fooled at all. He knew instinctively that they were up to something. Though he answered each question on the form, he revealed no information about what he had actually observed during the release. The current meeting was obviously some sort of sham proceeding in which they were trying to find out what damaging information he knew about the leak. Even Ravi appeared surprised at how specific and detailed the questions were, though he didn't offer a single word of protest throughout the entire interrogation. The shameless bastard—all he wanted was to preserve HydroGroup's two million dollars in annual environmental consulting fees.

Jeb was the only one who seemed to feel guilty about the whole charade. Higheagle could tell that he was just following orders from his brother, and probably Boggs and Jack Holland. Deep down, Jeb appeared to be disgusted with the whole kangaroo court proceeding. He apologized before asking several of the questions and moved through some of them hastily, receiving sharp looks from his brother.

But the strong-arm tactics only served to reinforce in Higheagle's mind that Quantrill Ventures—a widely respected Fortune 100 company and proud recipient of numerous "green" business awards—was truly crooked after all. Now he knew that his eyes and nose had not lied. The pipeline was not for crude oil, nor was it simply being flushed out as part of some standard pipeline O&M procedure. The fluid gushing out of the ground contained haz waste from the facility and it was being pumped to the east. The sulfur odor was artificially batched in with the waste stream to make it smell like a petroleum product. And now Higheagle, because of what he knew, posed a very real threat to the Quantrill Ventures operation.

He didn't know exactly what they were doing with the waste, but whatever it was, it was most certainly illegal. Perhaps they were using it as process or cooling water for some type of on-site operation. Maybe they were pumping it off-site to be used for hydraulic fracturing. Maybe they were conducting a shady research operation. Or maybe they were merely disposing of it off-site to save a bundle of money. There were many possibilities, but none of them changed the fact that Higheagle was in the midst of a terrible dilemma: whether or not to risk destroying himself and his company in order to find out the truth about his client.

It was a no-win situation all the way.

CHAPTER 24

WHEN NICKERSON picked up the phone and heard the voice of Nathaniel Watkins, USGS director and science advisor to the president, he instantly felt that sinking feeling again. One way or another, tomorrow the axe was going to fall when he went *mano a mano* versus the Earthquake Prophet on national television. All week long he had felt a nagging sense of dread. Even if he performed spectacularly, how ridiculous would he look if an earthquake actually did strike within Patey's seismic time window? If that happened, he could kiss his career goodbye.

"So, James, how are your preparations coming along?" asked the stentorian voice hailing from Washington, D.C.

Horrible! he wanted to say. *And by the way I want out—you can get another goddamned lackey to do your stupid PR!* "Ah, just fine, sir. I'm going over my notes, practicing, of course."

"Good. You know Secretary of Interior Jackson and I are both counting on you. If we let crackpots like Patey sway public opinion and dictate public policy, we might as well just hand the country over to the crazies. We're about scientific reason, James, not pop psychology."

"I understand, sir."

"So tell me how do you plan to win the day?"

"I'm just going to stick with the standard talking points on our website."

"I don't think I need to remind you there's a lot at stake, James."

"I'm aware of that, Mr. Director. I'm confident that the USGS will come out in a favorable light."

"As I said, Secretary Jackson and I are counting on it."

"I won't let you down, sir."

"That's what the secretary and I want to hear, James. By the way, have you found out anything new on the source of the quake?"

"Well, we've identified the preliminary focal mechanism. We're dealing with a thrust fault. There's no visible surface rupture so it's blind."

"A blind thrust, you say?"

"Actually, we think there may be more than one of them in the Precambrian gneiss basement rock."

"Good heavens, a blind thrust fault swarm? Sounds like Whittier Narrows and Northridge all over again. Do you think there's a chance for recurrence?"

"There's no way of knowing. There hasn't been any evidence of historical seismicity above a 3.0 within fifty miles of the epicenter. And there are no mapped faults capable of the slip or energy release we saw from Sunday's quake."

"What's the orientation of the fault plane based on the focal mechanism calcs?"

"North eighty-seven degrees west."

"Westward dip, towards the mountains. That's strange. Shouldn't the principal stress be coming from the east?"

"Yes sir, another mystery." He rose from his chair, went to the window, and stared up at the one-hundred-foot tall M embedded into Golden's Mount Zion to the southwest. Constructed in 1908, the emblem pointed out to all travelers the home of one of the foremost schools of mineral engineering in the world, the Colorado School of Mines. "We've done the balanced cross-section work and the forces required are ridiculously large to get the sections to balance out. That's why we believe the adjustments going on in the deep crustal blocks could be attributable to increased fluid pressure."

"You're talking about hydro-fracking or water flooding for oil or gas recovery. Are there any activities like that taking place in the area?"

"None that we've been able to identify. In fact, there's been a moratorium on fracking in the southern portion of the basin since last year. Furthermore, there's no permitted fracking or water-flooding wells on record in the area. But we're been working hard to obtain additional information."

"Additional information?"

"From Quantrill Ventures. Unfortunately, we're running into roadblocks."

"You're talking about Charles Quantrill's company?"

"We need his deep seismic reflection profile data from his Stasney #1 and #2 oilfields and seismograph network data from his haz waste facility. The data will not only help us pinpoint the epicenter of any other earthquakes far more accurately, but help us figure out what's taking place tectonically out there. But Quantrill doesn't seem to want to give us the data."

"What makes you say that?"

"He told us he has to run it through his legal department and that it's going to take six to eight weeks."

"Sounds like standard corporate policy to me. Quantrill Ventures is a very big, successful company."

"I think the situation's more complicated than that, sir. We're at loggerheads"

"Please tell me you didn't antagonize Charles Quantrill?"

Nickerson felt a stab of irritation. Who's side was the director on anyway? "No, of course not. Mark Kelso and I simply asked him for access to his data."

"Mark Kelso?"

"The state geologist. He's working with us on this."

"I see." A formal clearing of the throat. "I wouldn't do anything to upset Mr. Quantrill. He's very well connected in Washington."

"Are you talking about Senator Tanner, the head of the Senate Appropriations Committee?"

"Among others. I would just be careful not to ruffle any feathers."

Nickerson wanted clarification. "Are you telling me to back off, Mr. Director?"

"Let's just say you have plenty to keep you busy right now."

"I've already taken steps to ensure we don't have to rely on Quantrill's data, though I know it would help. I'm recommending that we quickly deploy a network of portable seismographs in the area of the epicenter. I'm putting together an emergency budget request as we speak."

"Get it to me as quickly as possible. How soon can you have the network installed?"

"By the end of next week, sir."

"Good, I want it done. But remember, the priority right now is still your debate with Dr. Patey. You must put this guy away once and for all."

"Yes, sir, I understand."

"Secretary Jackson and I are both counting on you."

"You've made that abundantly clear."

"Good—see to it. And remember, James, if you take care of this, there will be an additional twenty-five million in your budget for next year."

"I understand, Mr. Director. I promise I won't let you down."

"You'd better not, James. I don't even want to talk about the consequences if you should fail."

CHAPTER 25

NINA CURRY sat at her desk thinking of Joseph. She had the feeling something wasn't right out at Quantrill Ventures and was worried about him. At the same time, she had enjoyed spending time with him yesterday and today, even if it had been under duress. A part of her was afraid to admit her interest in this Native American gentleman—and he *was* a gentleman—who seemed so authentic compared to the other men she had dated over the years.

She secretly wondered what it would be like if they were together. He seemed to like her, but she suspected that, between the two of them, she was the more smitten. She knew she shouldn't even be thinking about a new relationship when she had just managed to extricate herself from a horrible one back in San Francisco. And yet, she couldn't deny that little tingle inside her, that little tug at her heartstrings, when she was with him. She had resigned herself to six months of burying herself in her new job at the EPA in Denver before even contemplating going on a date with anyone. But then this tall, dark Cheyenne fellow had somehow entered into her life.

She thought of how she felt when she was with him. When he stood close by, their bodies within inches of touching, she got goose bumps. When he looked her way, she sometimes lost her concentration. When she was alone with him, she felt a connection. She knew she had feelings for him, feelings she could not deny. Of course it was not love, or even lust, but she was definitely interested.

Her thoughts were broken by a voice at her door. "Ground control to Major Tom, ground control to Major Tom."

She looked up to see her boss smiling at her playfully. "Richard."

"For a second there, I thought we'd lost you."

"Sorry I was just thinking."

"So you're back from Quantrill's already. How'd it go?"

"They've cleaned up most of the spill. There was just one spot of crude oil left and they have probably removed that by now."

"So you and Albert Rehder were able to do a thorough inspection of the impacted area?"

"Yeah. Like I said, there was only a little crude oil that hadn't been excavated from the north sidewall. They had removed all of the contaminated soil and stockpiled it next to the excavation."

He entered the room and sat down, crossing one knee over the other to expose a fifty dollar pair of patterned socks. "What were the concentrations?"

"Ten to fifty thousand parts per million."

"What did they do about the line?"

"They rerouted it early this morning."

"Was there much vapor associated with the release?"

"Not too bad. The only thing is it smelled kind of funny. It had a strong sulfur odor, but it was different somehow."

Hamilton stroked his chin, pondering a moment, as he stared off at the colorful Salvador Dali print on her wall showing a surrealistic apparition of a face and a fruit dish on a beach of soft sand. "Most unprocessed hydrocarbons have a pretty strong sulfur smell—I'll bet that's what it was. Especially if you saw it on the ground and it was dark."

"Oh, it was dark all right. It looked just like heavy waste oil from a clarifier."

"Good. So it wasn't a big deal then."

She nodded. "They collected several soil samples from the base and sidewalls and ran a rush laboratory turnaround on them. Only one turned up dirty and even it wasn't that bad. Albert and I told them to go ahead and take two confirmatory soil samples from the hot spot along the north sidewall once they had removed the contaminated soil. They already emailed me the results and the dirty zone came up clean."

"Sounds like you've wrapped things up nicely. Crude oil is an unregulated hydrocarbon so we don't want to make too big a deal out of it. We've got more than enough nasty haz waste and radioactive sites to keep us knee deep in paperwork well into the next century."

Despite how well the cleanup had gone, she wondered if she should tell him that something still didn't seem quite right out at the facility and that Jeb Quantrill and Joseph Higheagle had acted a little oddly. However, she realized that she didn't have any real proof, only suspicions. Besides, she didn't want to alarm him unnecessarily.

"You do have a way of cutting through the BS, Richard," she said.

"That's why they pay me the big bucks. Fifty K a year."

"Yeah, right. That's closer to my wimpy salary."

"I may be able to do something about that."

"I knew there was a reason I liked you."

"Just keep your nose to the grindstone, Miz Curry." He smiled like a big brother. "Seriously, it sounds like you handled things well out there. The release has been cleaned up and they're going to get you a letter report by the end of the week. As long as the contamination along that north sidewall has been addressed, I don't think any further action is necessary."

"I agree. That's why I told them to go ahead and backfill the excavation with the clean soil they had stockpiled nearby."

He smoothed a wrinkle on his pleated pants. "What do you anticipate Albert's involvement will be?"

"Not much. He saw enough to warrant closure." She wasn't going to tell her boss that Albert Rehder had actually seemed a little perturbed at her for dragging him out there since the excavation site was so clean.

Hamilton's cell phone chirped, taking them both by surprise. He looked at the incoming phone number on the digital display and his easygoing expression vanished. "I'd better take this call. Thanks for the update."

"You're welcome. I'll talk to you later."

AS HE STEPPED OUT THE DOOR, the phone on her desk rang. She picked up. "Hello?"

"Nina, this is Joseph Higheagle."

She felt a little flutter in her chest. Was he really calling her already?

"We need to talk."

He sounded worried. She realized that her initial suspicion about something not being right out at Quantrill Ventures must have been correct. "Have you already gotten the analytical results back?"

"Not from the plume delineation investigation. But I have other data."

"Other data?"

"I have some soil data."

"Soil data? What soil data?"

"I took a sample in the area of the pipeline release."

"You did? When?"

"Yesterday, when Jeb went to shut off the line."

"So that's why you—"

"Look, I don't want to talk about this over the phone. In fact, I'm going way out on a limb even talking to you."

Now she knew why he had appeared on edge out at the facility: it had to do with the pipeline release and soil sample he had collected. "You can trust me, Joseph, if that's what you're worried about."

He did not reply.

She waited a tense moment, realizing that she was now involved in something. Was it possible that Quantrill Ventures had actually duped her? "Are you going to email me the soil analytical results?"

"No, we need to meet in person."

"All right. When do you want to meet?"

"Tonight. And you can't tell anyone else about this, not even Richard, until I know what we've got here. Do you understand?"

She felt a little tingle of excitement, as if she were a spy. "Yes, I understand. Where do you want to meet?"

"The Buckhorn Exchange—seven o'clock. And just so you know, I'm bringing in another expert."

"Who?"

"You'll see when you get there."

CHAPTER 26

LEANING BACK IN HIS LEATHER CHAIR, Quantrill felt his senses tingle as he took in the lonesome melody of the western wind knocking against his office window. He thought back to his youth and felt a ripple of pride at just how far he had come. The lung-stinging prairies, salt flats, dust bowls, and thorny mesquite thickets of his West Texas childhood seemed like a century ago.

I hope Pa up in heaven is proud of me and Jeb. God rest his poor, broken soul.

He thought back to when he and his brother were constant companions: splashing about in the cool water of Comanchero Creek, wolfing down barbecued ribs and corn on the cob at the county fair, basking lazily in the sun on the Sabbath, breaking headstrong ponies in the corral, tossing around a battered pigskin together. He fondly recalled the pride in Ma and Pa's tired, defeated eyes the one time they both got all As on their report cards. He had grown up in poverty and his childhood had consisted mostly of backbreaking work, but peering back through the mists of time, he remembered his early years as some of his best. The memories, growing fuzzier and more embellished with each passing year, caressed his soul and reminded him of a more innocent world, one in which he and his brother were consumed with a singular aspiration: becoming *somebody*.

He looked across his desk into Jeb's haggard face, wondering where all the time had gone. Sitting next to his brother was his chief engineer Wesley Johnston.

"Gentlemen, I appreciate your concerns, honestly I do. But I think you're overreacting. Why the two of you look as nervous as a pair of long-tailed cats in a roomful of rocking chairs."

"We're not asking to shut down the operation for good," said Jeb, his voice quiet yet plaintive. "All we're proposing is that we stop the injection for awhile, until we have a better handle on this earthquake situation."

Quantrill frowned, but let him continue.

"That line didn't rupture by chance. Wes and I checked the control panel and the manual flow meters. There's over four hundred and sixty gpm running through that pipe now."

"It can handle well over five hundred gallons per minute."

"Not along some of those old joints, it can't. The earthquake had to have weakened the line in places—like at that elbow where it ruptured."

Quantrill looked at his chief engineer. "Is that so, Wes?"

"It's the only explanation I can come up with for why it failed."

"But it's fixed now. Is there any reason to believe that it will cause us any more problems?"

Johnston shrugged. "We just don't know."

Jeb leaned forward in his chair. "We need to cut back the injection rate to two hundred gpm or less until we have a better handle on this situation. With everything that's happened, Wes and I haven't had time for a thorough evaluation."

"You two still haven't proved your case to me. There was one sizable event and a few low-magnitude aftershocks, but there's been nothing since. You showed me the seismograph data earlier this morning. You said yourself there's no definite correlation between the earthquakes and injection in terms of the timing of injection, fluid volume, or location of the epicenter."

"I know what I said. But until we know for sure I still think there's too much risk. Suppose this time someone gets killed?"

Quantrill rose from his chair and stood by the window, his massive frame like a statue of Pikes Peak granite against the backdrop of craggy mountain peaks. "I think you both have gotten yourselves worked up about this Earthquake Prophet and it's affecting your judgment. If you can't match fluid injection volumes to earthquake occurrence then there is no correlation."

"Be reasonable, Brother. We're only talking about cutting the flow in half and continuing to split it between the shallow and intermediate zones."

"Why would we do that when the injection and formation fluid pressure are both in the proper range, below 1,000 psi? It seems to me that you boys have already solved the situation by splitting the flow. There hasn't been a single aftershock in the past several days."

"It's not just the injection. What about Nickerson and Kelso? You know they're not going to just go away."

"They're no bother as long as we don't give them any of our reflection profiles."

"How can you say that when they're now installing their own seismograph network? There's just too many people that can cause problems for us now: Higheagle, Nickerson, Nina Curry, and Kelso. All Wes and I are recommending is that we reduce the flow to two hundred gpm and run the rest through the treatment system for a couple of weeks until we get this thing figured out."

Quantrill was growing tired of arguing. "Look, we've already been through this. We can't cut back the flow rate until you give me hard proof that the injection is causing the earthquakes. We can't afford to pull up the tent stakes without a damned good reason. We've got a business to run."

"We're only talking about cutting back to two hundred gpm for Christ sake."

"I think you two are just worked up because of this durned Earthquake Prophet."

"Maybe you're right. Maybe this guy has made us a little edgy. But it's better to be cautious, right? People's lives are at stake."

Quantrill weighed the options. He knew it was important to give his brother's concerns serious consideration. After all, Jeb was the brains of the partnership and his business recommendations always had merit from both a financial and PR standpoint, keeping the company out of regulatory trouble while at the same time maximizing profits. Should he take his brother's advice and scale back or shut down the operation? If there was another earthquake, perhaps even more devastating, he might very well be responsible for the deaths of innocent people. How could he possibly let that happen? How could he forgive himself? What if his wife Bunnie found out? Or his four grown children and his fourteen grandchildren? What would they think of him? How could he face them? And what if he hurt his own family? How could he knowingly let such a horrendous thing happen to those he loved?

He could never allow that to happen.

"All right, Brother, suppose I agree to reduce the flow? Will you and Wes get off my back then?"

Jeb looked at the engineer, who gave a nod. "Yes we will."

"Then you've got yourselves a deal. Go ahead and reduce the flow to two hundred gpm." He raised a warning finger. "But I will again remind you both that I am going to need to see some *real* evidence before I authorize a full-scale shutdown."

"I understand."

"Good, then it's settled."

Jeb's eyes lit up with a mixture of joy and relief. Quantrill realized how much the concession meant to him. He felt a touch guilty for being so stubborn, but he was the chief executive officer of a company worth tens of billions of dollars. What did his brother expect?

"You won't regret this, Chuck, I promise you."

"I'd better not, Little Brother. Now git on out of here before I change my mind."

CHAPTER 27

AS HIGHEAGLE shuffled through the front door of the Buckhorn Exchange, his grandfather's warning from an hour earlier resonated in his ears.

You're in the game now, Grandson. Don't come crying to me when Quantrill decides to play hardball and comes gunning for you.

But the more pressing concern at the moment was could he trust Dr. Nickerson and Nina Curry?

Stepping inside the restaurant, he took a deep breath to compose himself. All his troubles seemed to disappear as he remembered back fondly to the first time his grandfather had brought him to the legendary frontier dining establishment just a stone's throw from downtown Denver. He had been seven at the time—the devastating murder that had claimed his father, mother, and grandmother had happened the year before—and his grandfather had decided to take him to Denver to show the boy the world beyond the rez. During the three day excursion, they walked in awe among the towering skyscrapers and visited the State Capitol, Elitch Gardens, Denver Zoo, and the museums of natural history, art, and western history. But the one place that always stuck out in Higheagle's mind was the historic Old West dinery at 1000 Osage Street where one could feast on buffalo, rattlesnake, and bull elk and wash it all down with a tall glass of fresh squeezed lemonade.

After being seated at a corner table, he glanced around the dining room. The Buckhorn Exchange was as historic an institution to the Queen City of the Plains as the Willard Hotel was to Washington, D.C., and it showed in the sheer variety of Old West memorabilia gracing its interior. The walls were packed with an eclectic assemblage of cowboy and Indian artifacts, splotchy black and white daguerreotypes, and trophies of wild bear, moose, bighorn sheep, bison, elk, deer, and antelope. Glass cases exhibited an enormous number of antique guns—Springfield carbines and Winchester repeaters, Colt .45s and tiny Derringers, flintlocks and smoothbore muskets—as well as an abundance of miner and trapper wares.

By the time he had set down his business satchel and perused the mouthwatering menu, James Nickerson and Nina Curry walked up to his table. Though deep down he was nervous and still had lingering doubts, he composed a cordial smile as he rose from his seat to greet them.

"Thanks for coming under such short notice," he said, shaking their hands. "I hope you're ready for a heaping helping of marinated rattlesnake."

Nina rolled her eyes. "I can't wait."

"Me either," quipped Nickerson.

As they took their seats, Higheagle could tell that despite their outward levity, they were as tense as he was. After a minute of small talk, he turned to the business at hand. He reached into his business satchel, withdrew three manila folders, and set them onto the table in front of them.

"I have a copy of the soil data for both of you. But before I give it to you, we need to agree upon a few ground rules."

Nickerson raised an eyebrow. "Ground rules?"

"Actually, there's just one. You both have to promise me you won't talk to anyone else about this or take any action without my authorization. Quantrill Ventures is my client and is to be regarded as innocent until I say otherwise."

Nickerson and Nina looked at one another. "I'm okay with that," said Nina.

"Me too," said Nickerson. "But since we don't know exactly what we're getting into here, I think it's only fair that each of us retain the right to walk away from this whole thing if we want to, no questions asked. Does that seem reasonable to you, Nina?"

"Yes, I'd prefer that too," she said.

Higheagle nodded. "Agreed. Now let's take a look at the data." He quickly showed them a CAD drawing showing the soil sample collection point along the ruptured pipeline then handed them each a manila folder containing the lab report, retaining a third folder for himself. Opening his folder, he waited a few seconds to allow them to look over the map and analytical report before launching into his data summary.

"As you can see, there's a nasty hodgepodge of stuff running through that pipeline: TCE, PCE, 1,2-DCE, 1,1,1-TCA, pthalates, mineral spirits, BTEX, PCBs, lead, arsenic, and hexavalent chromium. In fact, most of the detected compounds associated with the release are known or probable human carcinogens."

Nina looked up from the lab report. "So the supposed crude oil leak wasn't crude oil, or even mostly petroleum hydrocarbons, at all?"

"I believe the spill was liquid waste from the treatment plant. I think they're pumping it off-site without treating it and covering up the smell with some kind of sulfur compound."

"But I saw the crude oil around the excavation," said Nina. "It was dark and viscous just like crude."

"I saw it too early this morning, but I think they planted it there. I didn't realize they were up to something until they called me into their office."

"Yeah, what happened with that?"

"They told me to stay away from you."

"Stay away from me?"

"That's what made me suspicious. And now with this analytical data I have hard proof that Quantrill Ventures is up to something."

A waitress in a blue jean skirt and red and white checkered, pearl-buttoned Western shirt swung by their table, took their drink orders—a Fat Tire for Higheagle, a Scotch and soda for Nickerson, and a chardonnay for Nina—and promptly shuffled off. Higheagle looked around a moment. He had the oddest feeling they were being watched. He scanned to the left and right, towards the front door then in the direction of the kitchen and adjacent smaller dining room, but there was nothing except wall trophies of glass-eyed mule deer and buffalo. Slowly, he lowered his gaze to Nina.

"They really told you to stay away from me?" she asked him.

"They said that I was becoming too friendly with you and it posed a conflict of interest for the company. They told me that I was only allowed to speak with you in business meetings. They also asked me a ton of questions about what I saw out there. They had this dummy questionnaire and everything. They called in my boss and made me look bad in front of him."

"They're obviously trying to keep you quiet," said Nickerson. "At least they didn't take you off the project. So what questions did they ask you?"

Higheagle told them.

When he was finished, Nickerson said, "So Quantrill's pumping liquid waste off-site. Why? To make a bundle of money, or is it some kind of research experiment?"

"I don't know yet. But if I had to wager, I would say it's about money."

"How much are we talking about here?"

"It depends on what their treatment, O&M, and equipment replacement costs are. But if I had to guess, I would say it would be in the hundreds of millions of dollars range, maybe more. It's the largest haz waste treatment facility in the country."

"The main question I have," said Nina, "is how much they're treating versus how much they're pumping off-site? I mean, they're still running wastewater through the waste facility's treatment system. I saw them changing out the carbon and replacing the air stripper packing this morning. And I know they're pumping wastewater to the evaporation ponds because I saw the outflow."

Higheagle had been puzzled about this too. "I think they're only treating a small volume. That would give them the cover they would need. By treating only a small percentage of the wastewater, Quantrill still takes in a bundle while maintaining the impression that the operation is legit."

"It would explain why they went ballistic over the original spill. And why they told you to stay away from me and summoned you to the sham meeting. Why would they do all that if it was only crude oil?"

"The answer is they wouldn't," said Nickerson. "Which leads us to the most important thing about all this. What if whatever they're pumping off-site is causing the earthquakes?"

Nina gave a look of puzzlement. "You mean like they're pumping the wastewater into the subsurface and that's what's causing them? But wouldn't we have seen earthquakes before now?"

"Not necessarily. Not if they carefully controlled the injection rate and formation pressure."

Higheagle was taken aback; if what Nickerson was suggesting was true, it changed the situation dramatically. "Do you have any evidence to support this?"

"Unfortunately no. But it would explain why Quantrill has been so reluctant to give up any data from his seismograph network or his reflection profiles. The same sort of thing was done out at the Rocky Mountain Arsenal, Rangely Oil Field, Paradox Valley, and Trinidad. At Rangely, over a two year period in the late 1960s, they were able to turn the earthquake activity on and off, again and again, through the starting and stopping of deep well injection. They could basically control earthquakes. The only difference is that there were still low level earthquakes during the course of the study, whereas in this case there have been no detected foreshocks above a 1.0 and only a limited number of aftershocks."

"Is that rare?" asked Nina.

"Extremely."

"But can earthquakes really be controlled like that?"

"At the low end of the injection pressure and flow rate ranges, definitely. Anything, let's say, less than two or three times gravity flow and less than 500 to 750 psi injection pressure. At Rangely, they demonstrated how it could work. The bottom line is that given an area of very stable geology—meaning the absence of faulting and historical seismicity of any kind—earthquakes are unlikely unless very high injection pressures cause hydraulic fracturing. If I had to make an educated guess, I would say that's what's happening here. But if Quantrill does have an injection network, it has to be near the epicenter. I should call Mark Kelso."

"What can he do?"

"He and his staff are still performing their damage assessment. There are parts of Elbert County they still haven't covered. He could take a look around, see if he comes up with anything."

"Wouldn't you have to tell him what we're up to?"

"Not necessarily. I could just tell him to keep on the lookout for any large aboveground storage tanks, pumping stations, hydro-fracking or water flooding wells, things like that."

The waitress returned with their drinks and took their orders. Higheagle opted for an appetizer of marinated rattlesnake with chipotle cream sauce and an entree of quail with prickly pear cactus glaze, while Nickerson and Nina both went for the smoked buffalo sausage with the red chile polenta and spicy wild game mustard. The waitress smiled approvingly at the selections and walked off.

Again, Higheagle had the strangest feeling they were being watched. He scanned the room for signs of prying eyes, but the only person who seemed to be looking at them was the goateed frontier scout and showman on the painting on the wall—Buffalo Bill Cody.

He again remembered his grandfather's warning: *Don't come crying to me when Quantrill decides to play hardball and comes gunning for you.*

Nickerson broke through his thoughts. "Okay, now that we've heard the evidence, where do we go from here?"

"Before we can answer that, I want to remind you again about our deal. We don't talk to anyone except each other. Quantrill Ventures is my top client so I alone decide whether we're going to call in the cavalry as well as when to do it. Now if Quantrill's guilty and I decide to drop out in the name of professional self-preservation, I would still, of course, make sure you have everything you need to take the company down."

"I think we're both good with that," said Nickerson. "Nina?"

"That's fine with me. We understand that Quantrill is your firm's most important client and that you need to walk a tightrope on this."

"So now that we're all on the same page," said Nickerson. "What's the next step?"

"I have assignments for each of us."

"You really have thought this thing through. So what are our assignments?"

"Mine is to find out where that off-site line goes and what it's used for. Yours is to continue to focus on the earthquakes in an effort to identify the location of this possible injection network, with help from Mark Kelso. And Nina's is to find out who could have helped get the original haz waste facility permit and the renewals approved with a minimum of regulatory oversight or public comment. Quantrill couldn't have handled this operation all by himself. He would have had to have had help from someone high up."

"Are you suggesting that someone from the Colorado Department of Public Health and the Environment or EPA could be involved?" asked Nina.

"I was thinking more along the lines of Senator Tanner."

"The chairman of the Senate Appropriations Committee? That Senator Tanner?"

"He's up for reelection next Tuesday and Quantrill's given him a lot of money over the years. In return, could Tanner have helped him navigate his way through the regulatory process?"

"He could have fast-tracked the approvals, controlled public hearings, and minimized revisions. Basically, a heavy-hitter like Senator Tanner could quietly do all kinds of things to see the permit and renewals through the system quickly without arousing public interest."

"If he lobbied on behalf of the facility, wouldn't there be notes from meetings with the EPA and CDPHE?"

"They would have also been required to complete biannual hazardous waste manifest reports."

"All right. Get whatever files you can get your hands on as quickly as possible."

"I'll get on it first thing tomorrow."

"When will we talk next?" asked Nickerson.

"I'll call you tomorrow."

Nina leaned forward eagerly. "This is exciting—I feel like a spy."

Higheagle looked furtively around the room again, still feeling a watchful presence. Was he being paranoid or did Quantrill have someone keeping an eye on him? He looked back at Nina, who was still smiling like a gangly teenager. He wished she would wipe that silly expression off her face. Didn't she understand that this was not a goddamned game?

It was at that precise moment he realized the three of them were in way over their heads. Charles Quantrill was most certainly not a man to be trifled with—and neither were Harry Boggs and the other bastards who worked for him.

CHAPTER 28

WHEN QUANTRILL'S CELL PHONE vibrated and he saw that it was Boggs, he couldn't help but feel a swirl of anxiety. Outside his Broadmoor mansion, a curtain of wintry night had descended over the high plains. He and his wife Bunnie had just sat down to a cozy homemade dinner of sizzling sirloin steak, overstuffed potatoes, and gourmet green bean casserole crowned with onion rings.

"I'll call you right back, Harry." Punching off the phone, he turned to his wife. "Sorry, honey, but I've got to take this call in private."

"Do you want me to leave?"

"No, I'll just step into the study."

"Should I keep your dinner warm?"

"No, I won't be but a minute."

"All right, hon."

He smiled at her—his college sweetheart and bride of twenty-eight years, a buxom, auburn–haired former beauty queen who also hailed from the Lone Star state—and she smiled back at him with those pearly whites and childlike innocence that was so, so precious to him. *If only she knew what I was up to, would she still smile like that?* he wondered, dreading the answer to his own question. He rose up from his chair and headed down the hall towards his office where he would have more privacy. When he reached his *sanctum sanctorum*, he closed the door, sat down at his desk, and dialed up his security chief on his hard line.

"What have you got for me, Harry?"

"Looks like our boy didn't take your advice."

"What happened?"

"He's meeting with Nickerson and Nina Curry right now."

"Where?"

"The Buckhorn Exchange. They're having dinner."

"Could be just a bunch of pointy-headed scientists getting together for a meal."

"I don't think so. He's given them both a file. Maybe ten or fifteen pages of material. My man can't make out what it says, but it can't be good."

"Who do you have on him, Heiser?"

"Yeah."

"Does Higheagle suspect he's under surveillance?"

"Heiser says he hasn't been made, but he thinks Higheagle might be a little suspicious. He's been looking around the room every once in a while, like he's searching for someone."

Quantrill felt an odd tingle in his left hand, realized he was squeezing the phone. *Good Lord am I tense?* He forced himself to think. So Higheagle had broken his client confidentiality and was going rogue on him. The decision would no doubt prove to be a grave mistake for the Cheyenne. But how best to handle him?

"The situation is escalating, sir."

Quantrill did not reply. He needed a moment to think. He stared off at the pair of stubby English Webley bulldog pistols and neat rows of flint Cheyenne arrow points in his glass case.

"Sir, did you hear me?"

"Yes, Harry, I heard you. I'm thinking, goddamnit."

"You're going to have to do something, sir. I know a man."

Quantrill dreaded what would come next, but was curious. "Go on."

"He's what you might call a *persuader*."

"You're talking about a thug, a common criminal."

"He's a professional, sir."

"What's his name?"

"I don't know his real name, of course. But he calls himself *Mr. Sperry*."

"Mr. Sperry? No first name?"

"No, sir."

Quantrill couldn't believe what he was hearing; it was like something out of a movie. "And I suppose Mr. Sperry also gets rid of people."

"For the right price, he can do whatever you want. Like I said, sir, he's a very persuasive man. I think it's time for you to consider...outsourcing."

Quantrill felt a warning alarm ringing in his ears. This was all happening too fast, and he was having trouble catching up. He found himself trapped in a morass of indecision.

"Listen to me, sir," said Boggs, his voice carrying a note of urgency. "With all that's happening, you're about to be engulfed in a shitstorm. If you do nothing, everything you do from this point on is likely to be too little, too late. You have to take decisive action now, or you will soon find yourself backed into a corner."

Again Quantrill took a moment to think, staring at the intricate patterns of his handwoven Navaho rug once owned by his hero Kit Carson. He wondered what the intrepid frontier scout would think of the modern world. A world where entrepreneurs like him pumped toxic waste down deep injection wells to make billions of dollars in order to go "green" and men like Harry Boggs spoke of hired killers as if they were lawyers or accountants.

"Sir, what do you want to do?"

He didn't like Boggs' aggressive tone. "Just keep on doing what you're doing. Keep a man on Higheagle and round the clock security at the injection well cluster. Right now, those have to be the top priorities."

"What about Nickerson and Nina Curry?"

"Don't worry about them."

"This isn't going to just go away, sir. I think someone should at least talk to Higheagle."

"You mean threaten him."

"He's violated the non-disclosure agreement. There should be a severe penalty for such a breach of conduct."

"You know I don't like solving problems with violence. Just keep Heiser on him and keep me posted."

"If it's all right with you, I'd like to handle it myself."

Quantrill was taken aback; it appeared to be personal for Boggs. *Does he just not like the kid or is he worried that his men won't get the job done?* Quantrill supposed it didn't matter; Boggs was the best he had and would make sure the job was done right. "All right, Harry. I'm much obliged. But you can forget about this Mr. Sperry fellow. I want you to know that I would never resort to something like that."

"Never say never, sir. What about Nickerson and Curry?"

Is Harry questioning my judgment or is he making sure I know what's at stake? "I've already told you, don't worry about them. We'll have to see how things develop."

"Very well, sir."

"I've got to eat my dinner now. Call me when you have something new."

After hanging up, Quantrill sat back in his chair and took a moment to steel his nerves. Boggs was right, the situation was escalating, that was for certain. But there was no way he was going to hire some thug or assassin to do his dirty work. He would have to find a less drastic solution. After collecting himself, he rose from his seat and headed back down the hallway into the kitchen, where his wife sat quietly eating, looking, as always, cute as a button. When she saw him, she gave a little start.

"Why honey, you look like you've seen a ghost."

"Oh, it's nothing. I'm fine."

"Are you sure? You don't look right."

"It's just work."

"Well, I hate to see you all shook up, just like old Elvis. Remember when we saw him in San Antone and I wore those golden ribbons and my brand new saddle shoes."

"Yes, I remember."

"Weren't those the days?"

"Yes, they sure were, darlin'."

She smiled innocently. "Can I get you anything, honey? I hate to see you so blue."

He composed a smile for her benefit. "No, I'm fine. Like I said, it's just work."

CHAPTER 29

SATURDAY AFTERNOON—two days before Halloween—Joseph Higheagle sat in his home office wondering if he had made the right decision bringing in Nina Curry and Dr. Nickerson. After all, he still had no hard proof of illicit activities and had no idea whether his two new federal partners could be trusted. Worst of all, he still felt a wrenching guilt about digging into the business affairs of his most important client, who had treated him and his firm well these past few years. Even if Quantrill was up to something, what good could possibly come from biting the hand that fed him?

He turned away from the analytical report he had been perusing and stared off at the wood-framed prints hanging from his wall. One displayed a bleeding buffalo with a pair of arrows lodged in its muscular hump, surrounded by a pack of hungry wolves licking their snouts and baring fangs. The other consisted of a panel of four colored drawings from the late 1860s rendered by his great-great grandfather, High Eagle, a respected Cheyenne Kit Fox warrior and, in his later years, statesman. The panel, entitled "Fighting the Wolf Men," depicted a running battle between his ancestor High Eagle and several other resplendently painted Cheyenne warriors and their hated enemies the Pawnees, culminating in the daring rescue of the Dog Soldier Chief Red Wolf with arrows and bullets zipping overhead. He felt a deep pride in his venerable ancestors; now if only the brightly feathered, Winchester-wielding horsemen could help him with his current quandary.

What in the hell was going on? More importantly, what was he going to do about it? Was this really important enough to throw away his whole career over? Judging by the sheer variety and toxicity of the compounds in question, Charles and Jeb Quantrill looked like they could be generating another Love Canal. But where did the waste fluids ultimately go and what did it all mean? Why were they doing it in the first place? Was it just for money or was there some other reason? And what assurances did he have that Nickerson and Nina Curry wouldn't somehow blow the whole thing and ruin his career?

Hearing the sound of an engine, he looked out the window to see his grandfather pulling into the driveway in the War Wagon—Higheagle's rusty, 1982 four-wheel-drive Ford pickup. The old man cut the engine, parked, grabbed the bag of groceries from the front seat, stepped out, and walked to the front door, singing an old braveheart song about counting coups on the hated Pawnee.

Higheagle went to the front door and opened it for him, eyeing the bag of groceries. "Get everything?"

"Yep, we got some mean ass Mexicali fry bread coming up."

"Good, I'm starving."

Higheagle closed the door behind the old chief. They stepped into the kitchen and started pulling out the groceries.

"So I didn't get a chance to talk to you last night, Grandfather. How was your date?"

"Not very good. I didn't get laid."

"Okay, that's too much information."

"What you think I'm too old to be coupling?"

"Coupling? Has anyone actually used that word since Wounded Knee?"

"I sure as hell hope so. Coupling is the essence of who we are as human beings. And here I had a beautiful young maiden in the throes of passion and yet we were unable to consummate the act."

"You mean *you* were unable to consummate the act."

The old man pulled out a tin measuring cup and teaspoon from the drawer as Higheagle reached for a heavy cast-iron skillet for cooking the fry bread. "No, that wasn't the problem."

"Then what was?"

"She was worried that I was too old and might have a heart attack if we went through with it. Imagine that, me, fit as a buffalo bull, a regular Casanova, rejected because of my age. If that's not discrimination in its most insidious form, I don't know what the fuck is."

Higheagle laughed. "Well, how old is she?"

The old Contrary smiled salaciously as he measured out a cup of unbleached flour. "Fifty-six."

"And you're seventy-four."

"Unfair isn't it? Here we are a mere eighteen years apart and I get thrown out to pasture like an old warhorse."

"Well it's probably for the best. What would Grandmother think of you running around like a hot-blooded teenager?"

The old chief's expression turned thoughtful. "I would think she would want me to be happy."

Higheagle rolled his eyes. "I don't think that's the kind of *happy* she had in mind."

"I don't know, maybe I'm going through a mid-life crisis."

"At seventy-four? How old do you think you're going to live to be—

one hundred and forty?"

"It's possible. But only the Mystery knows."

"Yes, only the Mystery knows."

They began preparing the fry bread and toppings. While Higheagle cooked refried beans, grated jalapeño jack cheese, laid out strips of fire-roasted green chile, cut slices of avocado, lettuce, and tomato, and heated the vegetable oil, the old man sifted together a cup of flour, salt, powdered milk, and baking powder into a large bowl, poured water over the flour mixture all at once, and stirred the dough with a fork. Once he had gotten it to form one big clump, he rubbed flour on his hands and worked the dough, without kneading it, until all the flour was thoroughly mixed to form a ball that was sticky on the inside but powdery on the outside. The dough was then cut into four pieces, each piece being shaped, stretched, and patted until they had formed disks about six inches in diameter. Once the oil was heated to the proper temperature, the old man took each of the disks and submersed them into the hot oil, flipping them once to ensure that both sides were cooked golden brown. With the preparation of the fry bread completed, they cooked scrambled eggs, loaded up the fry bread with eggs, refried beans, green chile strips, lettuce, tomatoes, and *salsa verde*, and sat down at the kitchen table to eat.

"So how did your meeting with the Earthquake Man and the EPA woman go?"

"It went well. I think we're going to make a good team."

"Have you figured out yet why Quantrill would pump wastewater off-site? There must be a reason."

"The most obvious one would be to make a butt load of money."

"How much?"

"Hundreds of millions of dollars per year, maybe more."

"But how?"

"By eliminating—or at least significantly reducing—his overall treatment costs."

"So doing this would allow Quantrill and his brother Jeb to underprice their competition?"

"Exactly. They would have virtually no physical, chemical, or biological treatment costs. No waste disposal costs. No operation and maintenance costs. And no shutdown or downtime-related costs. The bottom line is they would be able to significantly lower their overall treatment costs while at the same time increasing their treatment volume. Quantrill Ventures is the largest hazardous waste company in the U.S., which means that they treat the most waste. But what if they're not even treating it? What if they're just sending most of it off to never-never land?"

To Higheagle's surprise, his grandfather seemed more skeptical than convinced. "How do you know that Quantrill's not just conducting some kind of scientific experiment?"

"I don't for sure. But my gut tells me this is about *mucho deniro*. Quantrill Ventures is the highest volume haz waste treatment facility in the entire nation. The tanker trucks line up for miles outside the facility, which runs twenty-four seven. The whole operation is enormous."

"That may be. But I still don't understand why you're bringing in a pair of federal regulators you barely know into an investigation of your client before you know what's going on."

Higheagle felt himself on the defensive. "I know what's going on."

"Bullshit. You have a few scraps of data, but you still don't know a damned thing. You haven't figured out where the waste is being pumped, why Quantrill is doing it, and who all is involved. You seem certain he's doing it purely for profit, but he could have other reasons. Hell, you don't even know if what he's doing is even illegal."

"Okay, so I have some work to do."

"Now there's an understatement. You didn't hear what I said last night, did you?"

"You told me to ask myself whether I was willing to bite off the hand that feeds me. Well, I've made my decision: I'm going to do what's right."

"Bold talk comes easy when the water's only up to your ankles. Just remember if Quantrill has done the things you say he has, you could be putting not only yourself at risk, but Dr. Nickerson and Nina Curry as well. After all, if you're right about all this, Quantrill has every reason to make sure none of you talk."

Higheagle took a bite of fry bread heaped with green chile and refried pintos. "I get it, Grandfather. So you can stop lecturing me."

"You are my grandson—I don't give a damn if my lecturing offends you or not. That's why I'm going to continue to remind you to keep your eyes and ears open at all times. Otherwise, you could end up looking like those gooks I saw in Korea who had their guts hanging out and were trying to stuff them back into their bellies. Believe me, that was not a pretty sight."

"Are you trying to scare me?"

"I just want you to keep in mind that the man you're after is a billionaire with endless resources and probably a dozen high-ranking politicians and law enforcement officials in his pocket. Other than that I think you're in great shape."

"So let me get this straight. You think I'm in over my head and rushing in without thinking things through?"

"That about sums it up."

"Okay then, so what do you recommend I do, oh great and wise chieftain?"

"The first thing is to dust off that scattergun I gave you for your sixteenth birthday." He was referring to Higheagle's Ithaca 12-gauge slide-action shotgun with the specially designed "duckbill" choke that was particularly lethal at close range.

"That's your sage, chiefly advice?"

"That's it. And while you're dusting off your Ithaca, I want you to know I'll be cleaning and oiling my Winchester. Do you want to know why?"

"Not particularly."

"Because as a wise and exalted chief, I know that your youthful urge to do the right thing has not only brought the Earthquake Man and this EPA woman under the crosshairs, but me as well."

"Sorry, Grandfather, but I'm immune to your scare tactics. Besides, that old antique gun of yours won't even fire."

"Oh, Yellow Boy will fire all right. I can still snap the head off a duck at a hundred yards with that old repeater."

Higheagle couldn't help but smile. "Is that so?"

"Yes, that is so."

They both laughed and took another bite of fry bread. "You are one crazy old fart, Grandfather. But I guess that's why I love you."

"I love you too, Grandson. That is why I worry about you so."

"You don't have to worry about me. I know what I'm doing."

"Like hell you do."

They laughed again, a deep throaty bellow that harkened back to the days of warriors sitting about campfires recounting stories of coup counting and horse thievery. When they finished their meal, they quickly scrubbed the dishes.

Higheagle said, "I'm heading out for a while. I should be back in a couple of hours."

"Where are you going?"

"To see Nina Curry."

The old chief grinned approvingly. "You sly dog you. You've been holding back on me—you're doing all this to win her over, aren't you?"

"It's not what you think, Grandfather."

"Oh yes it is. But just remember one thing."

"What's that?"

"Don't you dare get that little filly pregnant, you little pecker neck."

"Like I said you're fucking crazy, Grandfather."

"Yes, but that's why you love me."

CHAPTER 30

CHARLES QUANTRILL gazed up at Pikes Peak, mantled with a soft veneer of fall snow. The mountain looked spectacular in a dreamy way with cottony clouds tickling its massive granite face and a periwinkle sky as a backdrop. As he made his way along his flagstone deck, he felt the vibration of his cell phone. He withdrew it from his jacket pocket and glanced at the caller ID number: Senator Tanner.

"Hello, Senator. What can I do for you?"

Tanner spoke without preamble. "The Senate Ethics Committee is going to make a public announcement on Monday and open a preliminary inquiry into my case."

Though this was not unexpected news given their meeting last week, Quantrill was still surprised. "The day before the election. The bastards."

"The *New York Times* is running with a front page story. I wanted to let you know. You could catch a little heat from this too."

"Nothing my PR people can't handle. But I must confess, the timing couldn't be worse."

"This Earthquake Prophet?"

"Among other things. He's got people stirred up."

"You worried about tomorrow?"

"Not now that you're no longer giving a speech at my wind farm. I couldn't afford to take a chance of the ground opening and gobbling you up in the middle of your speech. How did the *Times* get the story anyway?"

"Citizens for Responsibility and Ethics."

"So it wasn't George Soros and his minions?"

"Nope."

"So what do you think? Can they make any of these allegations stick?"

"The bastards don't care about making them stick. They just want to win the election."

"How many points will this cost you?"

"My pollsters are saying less than three."

"That's not bad. You're up by five."

"Unfortunately, that's still within the margin of error. I'm keeping my fingers crossed." He cleared his throat. "Look, I've got to run now. But I did want to give you a heads up before the *Times* story breaks and the

Ethics Committee makes the official announcement tomorrow morning."

"I appreciate it, Bill. Good luck on Tuesday."

"Thanks, but I hope I don't need it. Bye, Chuck."

Quantrill punched off and stepped inside his office. But before he had settled back into his seat, his cell phone chirped again. Checking the caller ID, he saw it was Boggs.

"What do you have for me, Harry."

"Two things—and you're not going to like either of them."

Quantrill braced himself for the bad news.

"Higheagle's with Nina Curry. He's at her apartment as we speak."

That brazen son of a bitch! "What's the second piece of bad news?"

"That damned state geologist Kelso is poking around out at Sweetwater."

"Kelso is out at the bottling plant right now?"

"Fortunately I don't think he knows anything. He appears to be just driving around in his truck, inspecting for earthquake damage and talking to people."

"On a Saturday? Did he go onto the adjacent well cluster property?"

"No. But he did drive up to the locked gate, look over the no trespassing sign, and write something down in a notebook. He's gone now. But there's no question he's out snooping around. And that can't be good for us."

"Who's on guard out there?"

"Eric Smith."

"Did Kelso see him?"

"No, he's in the control room. The security cameras at the front entrance recorded everything. That's how I know it was Kelso."

"He must be looking over prospective sites for the seismograph network he and Nickerson were talking about."

"What do you want to do about him?"

"Nothing. It's Higheagle that we need to worry about."

"I still think you should be calling in some special help."

"You mean this Mr. Sperry?"

"He's a professional, sir, and, as I've said, the situation is escalating. It's no longer just Higheagle we have to worry about, but Curry, Nickerson, and Kelso."

Quantrill considered his options. He did not want to resort to physical threats or violence, but Boggs was right, the situation was growing increasingly troublesome. Perhaps it wouldn't hurt to at least have Mr. Sperry on call in case things took a turn for the worse and he was forced to respond quickly.

"All right, contact your man."

"Yes, sir."

"But you make it clear to him that, if we do come to some sort of arrangement, he's going to have to take orders directly from me. I will not communicate through middlemen."

"Given your reputation, sir, I don't think that will be a problem. I'll talk to him."

"Have his dossier emailed to me by this evening. And I want to meet with him personally tomorrow."

"I'm sure that can be arranged. What do you want to do about Higheagle?"

Quantrill leaned back in his chair, looking up at the priceless oil that took up the entire north wall of the study: *Custer's Last Fight* by W.R. Leigh. The warriors were sharply defined in the foreground compared to Custer and his embattled battalion, who blended in with the haze on the salient in the background. He studied the positions of the warriors, took in their rippling muscles, the implied motion, the confidence, the hint of violence yet to come. He sensed panic and desperation in the faces of the soldiers. If all hell broke loose with this earthquake thing, would he too end up looking like Custer and his terror-stricken soldiers at the Little Bighorn?

"I think it's time, Harry, you had a little talk with Higheagle."

"Me, sir?"

"Heiser has pictures of him with Nina Curry and Nickerson, right?"

"Yes, sir."

"Well then, you need to ask him why he has violated his non-disclosure agreement. Do it all by the book—as if it were a simple formality—but make sure you drive the point home so there ain't any misunderstanding."

"You want me to do it?"

"You, Heiser, and Stolz. Take care of it tomorrow night."

"Yes, sir. I'm looking forward to it."

CHAPTER 31

THE FOLLOWING EVENING, the day before Halloween, James Nickerson, Ph.D. felt almost too nervous to speak as he stared out at the boom microphones, mounted cameras, and bustling network staffers at the CBS affiliate in downtown Denver. He was about to go on national television—before forty million Sunday night viewers—and was absolutely petrified. He had the terrible feeling he was about to embarrass not only himself, his immediate family, and colleagues at the USGS—but the entire United States government and global seismological community.

At the insistence of his boss, he had performed several dry runs the past few days with his staff in preparation for the televised debate. He had received words of encouragement from not only his colleagues at the NEIC, but the many seismologists he had worked with over the years from the USGS Earthquake Hazards Program, the National Earthquake Prediction Evaluation Council, NASA, and Caltech. But privately he knew that he would become a pariah of his profession if he showed the slightest whiff of failure. How could he have allowed himself to be put in this position?

"Thirty seconds to air," he heard a clipped voice say to his right.

He looked at Giselle Valdez, the *Newsline* host and *de facto* moderator. Her bleach-blonde hair was perfectly coiffed and she wore a dark-blue business suit with a gray collar. A confident smile played at the corners of her mouth. She had probably done these little point-counterpoint shows so many times before that they had become second nature to her. Looking at her, Nickerson couldn't escape the feeling that he had been set up, that even if he was on top of his game there was no way he could come out of tonight's debate as the clear cut winner for the simple reason that he was expected to win.

He turned his attention to his adversary. Seated on the other side of a glass table and to the left of their *Newsline* host, Jack Patey, the fabled Earthquake Prophet, appeared every bit as calm and composed as Giselle Valdez. With his California surfer boy good looks, hardy tan, and hint of stubble, the man had a certain rugged academic appeal that would no doubt play well on television. He looked every bit the part of the adventurous, hands-on field scientist and documentarian he had become since his firing as the California state geologist. Whereas Nickerson knew he himself looked like a bland government administrator who rarely stepped out of the office. He had a sudden sympathy for what Nixon must have felt like going up against the tan, glowing JFK in that historic debate.

Was hate too strong a word for what he felt towards Jack Patey? Somehow he doubted it. But what made it worse was that his fate might very well be in the hands of this lunatic. Did the guy really believe that a handful of runaway kittens and squawking parrots meant that the next Big One was coming? How could such a thing even be quantified? More importantly what in the hell had he done to deserve this? He felt a little bead of perspiration growing on his forehead and wiped it away. Jesus Christ, was he going to end up like Tricky Dick?

The clipped voice returned to his right: "We're going live in five, four, three...."

Nickerson took a deep breath and crossed his fingers.

"Welcome to *Newsline*," announced Giselle Valdez, looking like an overgrown Barbie as she served up her trademark plastic smile for her television audience. "Last Sunday's major earthquake along Colorado's Front Range has sparked debate about earthquake prediction. Tonight I have with me two professional scientists to give us opposing views on what science is capable of on this subject. On my right is Dr. James Nickerson, Director of the United States Geological Survey, National Earthquake Information Center, in Golden, Colorado. And on my left is Dr. Jack Patey, former California state geologist and current *New York Times* best-selling author of *The Holy Grail of Seismology: Predicting Major Earthquakes and Saving Lives.* Good evening, gentlemen."

"Good evening, Giselle," the two scientists said in unison.

"Let's start with you, Dr. Nickerson. As Dr. Patey states in the introduction to his book, the so-called 'holy grail' of earthquake seismology is the ability to predict major seismic events. Based on your scientific judgment is earthquake prediction possible?"

"No, Giselle, I'm afraid that earthquake prediction is currently a scientific impossibility."

"Could you please elaborate?"

"Certainly. Research into predicting earthquakes has been conducted for over one hundred years without quantifiable success. There have been many claims of scientific breakthroughs with regard to prediction, but they have always failed to withstand scrutiny. There just aren't any precursors—such as foreshocks, gas buildup, or groundwater level increases—that are reliable in any statistically significant way. No one denies that these precursors exist—there is just no way to quantify them. Because faulting is a non-linear process, it is sensitive to the structural details of the earth as a whole. Not just those in the immediate vicinity of the earthquake's point of origin, or hypocenter. Therefore, any small seismic event has some probability of expanding into a larger event."

"So what you're saying is that there's currently no way to predict earthquakes on a consistent basis."

"Precisely. However, we—meaning the international seismological community—can estimate earthquake hazards over the longer term. For example, we can perform earthquake hazard assessments by using past earthquake history to estimate the probability that a quake of a particular magnitude will occur in an area within a given period. We typically examine earthquake trends over decades. We can do a fairly good job of saying which faults are likely to generate earthquakes and how large the magnitude of those earthquakes is likely to be. So we can forecast in the long term and use this information to improve building codes, perform responsible land use planning, and make sure that we don't build in high-risk areas."

"So what kind of signals do scientists rely on to tell them whether an earthquake might happen or not?"

"In the past, people have tried to associate an impending earthquake with such varied phenomena as electromagnetic fields, ground movement, weather conditions, gas content, water levels in wells, animal behavior, and the phases of the moon. NASA is currently studying thermal anomalies associated with radon gas releases in regions of major earthquakes from satellite and ground-based data."

"How does that work?"

"Well, uranium-bearing rocks in the earth's crust emit small amounts of radon, and as faults shift in the days leading up to an earthquake, they create new openings from which radon can escape. That excess radon, in turn, releases alpha particles that give the atmosphere an ionic charge and allow the formation of aerosol-sized particles as ions mix with water. It's this latent heat that's picked up by satellites as thermal anomalies preceding some major earthquakes."

"So is this a promising field as far as earthquake prediction goes?"

"Let's just say it has some potential. The important thing to remember about all of these precursory phenomena is that not one of them has been adequately studied, let alone proven to be reliable."

"Thank you, Dr. Nickerson." She turned towards Patey. "What do you think, Dr. Patey? Is the outlook for earthquake prediction as bleak as Dr. Nickerson would lead us to believe?"

"One thing I know for certain, Giselle, is earthquake prediction is too important to leave solely in the hands of the so-called 'earthquake experts' in government and academia. The bottom line is that my predictions are three to five times better than chance. To put it another way, I can predict earthquakes above 5.0 with an eighty percent accuracy based on my seismic windows. These are the time periods of maximum tidal force when there are significant stresses on the earth's tectonic plates and major earthquakes typically occur."

"Can you tell our audience how your earthquake predictions relate to these seismic windows?"

"Well, the current seismic window is from October 23 to October 31—last Sunday to midnight tomorrow. This window is based on last Sunday's full moon, the very close lunar perigee last Monday morning, and the maximum Golden Gate tide of 9.2 feet last Tuesday. Which turned out to be the highest in two years. But I don't just rely on the tides—I look at other evidence, specifically unusual animal behavior. That's how I was able to successfully predict last Sunday's earthquake. In the two weeks leading up to the event, there were an unusually high number of lost pets reported along the Front Range. So I rely on two things: the timing of maximum tides and unusual animal behavior. The tides tell me when a destructive earthquake is expected, and the behavior of animals, especially household pets, narrows down the specific time and place."

"So the tide tables allow you to do long range prediction and the animals help you pinpoint where and when the earthquake will be?"

"That's correct, Giselle."

Nickerson couldn't help but feel disdain as the camera zoomed in on Patey for a close-up. *Jesus Christ, the man's a celebrity and nothing more. Please tell me the audience isn't buying this garbage!*

"What do you think, Dr. Nickerson? Can Dr. Patey really predict earthquakes?"

"Absolutely not, Giselle. Dr. Patey never has and never will be able to predict an earthquake with any degree of certainty. In fact, the accuracy of his predictions is no better than chance alone."

"That's not true," protested Patey.

"It most certainly is." He looked back at Valdez. "The best that anyone, including Dr. Patey, can expect to do when it comes to earthquake prediction is to calculate the long-term probability of potential future earthquakes. Based on historical slip rates and recurrence intervals for well-studied, seismically active faults."

"What about so-called earthquake sensitives? Can't certain people sense that an earthquake is about to happen?"

"There is no scientific explanation for the symptoms some people claim to have preceding an earthquake. In fact, more often than not there is no earthquake following the symptoms."

"What about animals and earthquake prediction?"

"What about it?"

"There are reports coming in from various counties—so far Arapahoe, Elbert, Douglas, El Paso, and Lincoln Counties—of both wild and domesticated animals showing strange behavior and trying to get out of the area. Public officials are being bombarded with calls and emails from concerned citizens from all over these counties. In spite of all of this evidence, you still don't believe that Dr. Patey may be onto something?"

Nickerson knew he had to be careful here because this was a sensitive issue for the public, which tended to see things in terms of black and white. There were many variables that affected animal behavior. An unusually large number of lost pet ads, dogs howling into the night, and caged birds becoming restless did not necessarily mean that a tremor was coming. In many instances, such animal behavior might represent nothing more than the psychological focusing effect. People often remembered strange behaviors only after an earthquake or other catastrophe took place. Without a dramatic event, they might not even remember the strange behavior.

"I'm aware of the reports, Giselle. And here's what's going on as far as animals are concerned. First, there is anecdotal evidence that animals can sense P waves—the first waveforms to arrive during a seismic event— prior to the arrival of the more destructive, slower-moving S waves. It is well documented that various creatures—mammals, fish, birds, reptiles, amphibians, insects—exhibit unusual behavior in the moments just before a seismic event. It is believed that this is a vibration-triggered early warning response that acts in the short time interval between the arrival of P and S waves. This time interval is typically a matter of a few seconds, depending on the distance from the hypocenter.

"There is also anecdotal evidence of frightened or erratic behavior on the part of several species of animals in the hours, days, or weeks preceding a major earthquake. This may be what is occurring now along the Front Range. But whatever it is exactly that allows animals to sense an impending earthquake, tsunami, or the oncoming S wave following the arrival of the P wave still eludes us. In other words, we don't know what the animals are responding to or how they're doing it. Dr. Patey claims that there is a correlation between lost pet ads in a given newspaper and the timing of earthquakes. But a thorough statistical analysis of this theory, published in last year's *Science*, concludes that there is no such correlation."

"That article was a sham," cried Patey. "It was a deliberate attempt by the IASPEI to discredit me."

Valdez raised an eyebrow. "IASPEI?"

"The International Association of Seismology and Physics of the Earth's Interior," answered Nickerson, feeling more confident now that Patey appeared to be growing agitated. "It's a subcommission on earthquake prediction tasked with identifying and evaluating precursory earthquake phenomena. Things like foreshocks, magnetic field variations, radon gas increases, groundwater table rises, curious animal behav—"

"That's all fine and dandy," interrupted Patey. "But I already have a scientific methodology to predict earthquakes at an eighty percent success rate. And I say that there is a high probability of an earthquake tomorrow somewhere between Denver and Colorado Springs."

Giselle Valdez leaned forward in her chair with excitement, clearly relishing the jousting between the two competing scientists. "Well now, ladies and gentlemen, it appears the Earthquake Prophet has spoken. Is that a guarantee, Dr. Patey?"

"Nothing in nature is guaranteed, Giselle. I'll have to stick with an eighty percent probability."

"What about the magnitude?"

"Seven plus, Giselle. A major event."

Nickerson sat there in shock. *Are you insane! How can you possibly say such an irresponsible thing on television? But then again, what if he turns out to be right?* Nickerson dreaded the thought with every ounce of his being.

Valdez's appraising gaze shifted back to him once again. "What do you think, Dr. Nickerson? Is the Big One going to hit tomorrow?"

He started to respond, but then immediately thought better of it. *Damnit, how in the hell did I allow myself to be put in this position?* Especially when all of his colleagues at the Survey were counting on him to defend real science against pseudo-science and celebrity worship. If only his hero and founder of the USGS, John Wesley Powell, could see him now, he would be rolling over in his goddamned grave!

"Let me just say, Giselle, that no one can accurately predict precisely where or when an earthquake will strike. There is, however, reason for optimism. Seismologists have new technologies and powerful computer programs at our disposal. We're using these tools to explore new ways that earthquakes might be predicted—or at least better forecasted—in the future. We can certainly hope that someday we'll live in a world where earthquakes can be predicted before they occur."

Patey scoffed. "I'm sorry, James, but that's just not good enough." He looked directly into the camera as it zoomed in for a close-up. "You people out there, I'm sorry but the Big One's coming tomorrow on Halloween—and you damn well better be ready for it!"

CHAPTER 32

JOSEPH HIGHEAGLE flipped off the TV remote and looked at his grandfather. "I'm telling you, that is one wild and crazy dude."

The old Contrary nodded. "He's definitely out there, but I don't think he's bullshitting. There's a method to the madness."

"I still think it's all just a publicity stunt. The Earthquake Prophet just wants to sell more copies of his best-selling book."

"And I say he's on to something."

"Okay, I guess if the Big One hits tomorrow during the last day of his seismic window, then you can count me in too as a true believer."

"You shouldn't wait for disaster to strike before you appreciate the scientific merits of his argument."

"Sorry, Grandfather, but that's the best I can do." He reached for his beaded buckskin jacket hanging from the chair. "I'm going to pick up our take-out."

"Make sure to get extra *salsa verde* for the tamalitos."

"Will do, Chief." He darted out the front door, fired the War Wagon, and drove a half mile south then four blocks west until he came to Littleton, Colorado's best south of the border eatery: Tortilla Flats. He pulled into a parking spot, killed the engine, slid from his rusty-springed seat, closed and locked the door, and started for the entrance.

Suddenly a black Lexus screeched to a halt in front of him. The rear door jerked open.

Before he had a chance to react, two thick-necked hulks jumped out of the front seats and came at him aggressively. He recognized them instantly as two of Quantrill's security men.

"Get in the car now—Mr. Boggs wants to talk to you!" snapped the taller of the two, a fit white-haired man with bulging biceps and a Minnesota accent. White Hair gave him a hard shove in the back and he stumbled towards the open door.

Peering inside, he saw Harry Boggs sitting in the back seat, chewing with disinterest on a plastic straw. Another shove in the back propelled him into the vehicle. The door slammed. He was greeted by the smell of powerful cologne and looked expectantly at Boggs, who stared back at him through slatted crocodile eyes as the Lexus pulled out of the parking lot.

There was a lengthy silence, pregnant with anticipation.

"You know why you're here, Joe?"

Higheagle said nothing, waiting for Boggs to elaborate.

"You're causing Mr. Quantrill problems. You violated your confidentiality agreement by talking to people about things you shouldn't be talking about."

Higheagle decided to play dumb; if nothing else, it might buy him time to think. "I don't know what you're talking about."

"Don't treat me like a fool, Joe. I know about your visits with Dr. Nickerson and Nina Curry. Here let me show you something—I think you're going to appreciate this."

Higheagle watched with a mixture of fascination and dread as the beefy security chief opened a manila envelope, withdrew a set of color photographs, and handed them to him. He began flipping through the pictures one at a time while Boggs looked on with a hostile smirk. There were not just photographs of him talking to Nickerson and Curry at the Buckhorn Exchange and outside in the parking lot, but also showing him entering and leaving both the NEIC building and Nina Curry's house. Which meant that his initial suspicion had been correct: Quantrill's men had been following him since Friday night.

"What were you thinking, Joe? That you could just talk to whomever you please about Mr. Quantrill's private business matters? That's what confidentiality agreements are for—to prevent idiots like you from shooting off their mouths and spreading false rumors."

Higheagle said nothing. He felt like a small child exposed by an adult.

"What's the matter, Joe, cat got your tongue?"

With a look of resignation, he handed back the photographs. He hated being outmaneuvered like this. He should have known that Quantrill would keep him under surveillance.

"What do you want?" he asked, struggling, in his defiance, to maintain a modicum of dignity and control over the situation.

"Put an end to this little witch hunt of yours and develop a quick case of amnesia or you will be destroyed. Consider this your one and only warning."

The Lexus took a right onto Santa Fe drive, heading south. Higheagle felt every nerve and fiber in his body resisting, but he knew Boggs was making no idle threat. There was no question Quantrill would destroy him, both figuratively and literally. In this fight, he had always been and would always be severely overmatched. His grandfather had been right: how naïve he had been to think that he could delve into the business operations of his billionaire client without a fight. And if Boggs was threatening him, that meant that he would probably also pay a visit to—

"This is your one chance, Joe, so don't screw it up. You have violated your confidentiality agreement and Mr. Quantrill is very displeased. However, he appreciates the work you have done for him in the past and that is why he is extending you this one-time olive branch. He did this against my strong objection I might add. So one last time, here it is. You put an end to your inquiries right now—or your career and your life as you know it is over. Mark my words, the next guy to pay you a visit will not be as docile or forgiving as me and my associates."

From the front seat, White Hair looked back over his shoulder and gave a sinister smile. Looking at the man, Higheagle could only imagine how much more lethal Quantrill's next enforcer might be compared to Boggs and his goons.

The security chief raised a liver-spotted hand and tapped it against the driver's headrest. "Stop the car and let him out."

"Yes, sir."

The Lexus pulled off to the right into the breakdown lane. Boggs stared mutely out the window in the direction of the passing traffic, his face expressionless. The front door opened. White Hair stepped out of the passenger seat and flicked open the right rear door.

"Don't forget, we'll be watching you at all times, Joe," Boggs said as a final warning.

Higheagle said nothing and slipped from the car.

"Show our friend some parting love, Mr. Heiser."

White Hair grinned malevolently. "My pleasure, sir."

Reacting instantly, Higheagle assumed a fighting stance, feet apart and hands out to defend himself. But he was no match for White Hair, who grabbed him by the arm and pitched him over his shoulder in a surprisingly fluid judo-like move, sending Higheagle tumbling down the trash-strewn slope next to Santa Fe Drive. At the bottom of the hill, he felt a sharp pain in his ribcage and back as he tumbled into a pile of discarded cinderblocks.

The last thing he saw was Boggs glaring down at him through the open car window as the Lexus tore off into the night.

CHAPTER 33

FROM BEHIND his solid mahogany desk, Charles Prometheus Quantrill stared into the chiseled face of the man known as Mr. Sperry, feeling a chill along the nape of his neck. With his buzz cut, ramrod stiff posture, and no-nonsense demeanor, the man looked every inch the alpha male gun for hire he was reputed to be; yet, there was an air of worldliness and erudition about the man that seemed to intimate a privileged, educated upbringing as opposed to a traditional military, intelligence, or law enforcement background. His wide mouth was creased into a faintly supercilious smile, his nose was sharp and curved like the beak of a predatory bird, and his eyes were an icy crystalline blue, like a dimly backlit stained glass window. They peered back at Quantrill with the cool calculation and analytical detachment of a true professional. If the eyes were indeed the key to a man's soul, there was no doubt in Quantrill's mind that his mysterious guest had killed with swift, violent, remorseless efficiency on many prior occasions.

"So Mr. Sperry, I take it you had a pleasant flight?"

"As a matter of fact I did."

"And your hotel accommodations."

"Fine. I've always enjoyed the Broadmoor this time of year."

In the brief silence that followed, the man's faint crocodile smile remained impressed upon his features. Quantrill couldn't help but feel unnerved in the man's presence and secretly wondered if he had made a terrible mistake in setting up this meeting. What in the world had possessed him to invite a professional assassin into his fine Broadmoor home?

The man cleared his throat, folded his hands in his lap with meticulous precision, and leaned forward in his chair. "So I take it Mr. Boggs has made clear to you my special areas of expertise."

Quantrill had the sense that, despite his guest's deferential body language, beneath the polished exterior he was secretly enjoying the CEO's discomfort. "Yes, I believe I'm clear on that point."

"Then please tell me about the assignment."

"I would like to retain your services regarding a certain individual."

"Who?"

"A geologist."

"A geologist? What did he do steal from you?"

Quantrill didn't appreciate the younger man's impertinent tone or prying manner and gave him a sharp look.

"My apologies, Mr. Quantrill—none of my business. Please go on."

Now that's more like it. "The man's name is Joseph Higheagle. He has violated his confidentiality agreement with Quantrill Ventures and may try and go public with some...shall we say...sensitive information. I'd like to keep you on call in case the situation escalates and I am forced to...you know..."

"Terminate him?"

"Lord no!" Quantrill held his hands up to make sure he was making himself clear. "Not terminate. Just...talk to."

His guest appeared amused. "Talk to?"

"In a convincing fashion."

"As you are no doubt aware, my particular skill set involves a little more than...talk. However, I can perform such services in special cases, or for special clients."

"Obviously I can pay you handsomely."

"Yes, of course there is that."

"There might also be others to...talk to."

"Others?"

"I'll give you the information on the relevant parties at the appropriate time. In the meantime, I will place you on retainer until such time as your particular services will be required."

The man gave a little nod and glanced up at the painting of the Battle of San Jacinto entitled *Remember the Alamo.* Somehow the belligerent-themed maelstrom of charging soldiers, swirling dust, and blood-soaked earth suited the gun for hire. And yet, Quantrill couldn't escape the feeling that Mr. Sperry had some terrible secret or defect in his personality that made him particularly dangerous and nothing like the heroes who had vanquished Santa Anna and his Mexican legions at San Jacinto.

"That's fine, Mr. Quantrill. As no doubt Mr. Boggs has told you, I am very proficient at what I do and can work on very short notice." He tapped his long, bony fingers across the arm of his chair; somehow the action reminded Quantrill of a drumroll before an execution. "Are broken bones or torn ligaments within the boundaries of what you consider *convincing*?"

Quantrill did his best not to appear unsettled by his guest, but it was not easy to bottle up one's emotions in the presence of such a nakedly brutal man. Even if he was socially refined and a much sought-after professional. "We can work out the details when the time comes."

"Let's talk about my retainer then. What did you have in mind, sport?"

Sport? Was this pompous bastard for real? Quantrill pondered a moment; he didn't want to appear cheap, but he had no idea what the going rate for such services was. At the same time, he wanted to appear in control and not have to ask. "Two thousand dollars a day wired to an account of your choosing," he said, hoping he sounded direct and firm.

The man's eyes lit up ever so slightly—a brief but unmistakable glimmer of avarice—and then just as quickly the little ember was gone. "That would be acceptable, Mr. Quantrill."

"Good. That settles it then. Enjoy your stay at the Broadmoor. When the time comes, either I or Mr. Boggs will call you personally."

Mr. Sperry gave a lopsided smile. "I'm looking forward to it."

Something about his expression struck Quantrill as odd. He suddenly realized that he had been wrong about the man: financial compensation was not what drove him. Instead, the sadistic bastard actually enjoyed what he did!

"One last thing," said Quantrill, wanting to be rid of him.

"Yes, sir?"

"Have you ever failed an assignment?"

"Never. But of course I'm a Yalie."

"You graduated from Yale?"

"You find that surprising, sport? Well, you shouldn't. I was the most popular undergrad in my class. Our motto was *Lux et veritas*."

"*Lux et veritas?*"

"Light and truth." And with that Mr. Sperry winked impishly and again gave a lopsided smile.

CHAPTER 34

"WHAT THE HELL HAPPENED TO YOU?"

Without responding, Higheagle closed the front door and shambled towards the couch where his grandfather was sitting. His ribs and lower back still hurt like hell from tumbling down the slope and smashing into the pile of cinder blocks; and he still felt a stinging sensation on his cheekbone from a patch of sharp-edged brush that had clipped him on the way down.

"I don't want to talk about it." Setting the Mexican take-out on the table, he let out a little groan.

The old chief eyed him closely. "It was Quantrill's men, wasn't it? Please tell me you gave as good as you got."

"I never had a chance. All I know is I'm in fucking pain—and I don't want to talk about it."

"So I guess it would be inappropriate for me to say I told you so?"

Higheagle glared flints at him.

"All right, I got the message." He looked eagerly at the plastic bag filled with the Mex take-out. "Smells good, let's eat."

Higheagle slumped into the recliner. "Glad to see you're worried about me."

"I thought you didn't want me to talk about it."

He shot him another glare.

"Ah, it's not so bad. Just remember you're Cheyenne—you're not only tougher but you heal faster than most people."

"That makes me feel so much better."

The old chief had already set out plates and silverware so they could eat right in the family room in front of the TV. He pulled out the green corn tamalitos, chicken chalupas, rice and beans, and assorted green and red salsas and *pico de gallo* and served up a heaping plateful for each of them. They both plunged in, and after a few minutes, Higheagle had to admit that he was beginning to feel better.

"So now that you've vented and put some food in your belly, tell me what the fuck happened."

Higheagle told him the whole story, from the time he left the house to walking all the way back on foot to Tortilla Flats.

"So the game has begun. Quantrill is playing hardball as expected."

"I don't need another lecture, Grandfather. I need to know what I should do."

"It's going to escalate. You know that."

"Are you trying to scare me again?"

"No, but I do want you to ask yourself if uncovering the truth is really worth it?"

"I'm in too deep to pull out now."

"No you're not. That security guy Boggs offered you an out. And I think you should seriously consider taking it."

"No way. After what they did, I want to get even with those bastards."

"Your pride has been hurt and you are vexed by the injustice of it all. I can understand how you feel, but just listen to me for a minute."

"All right, you've got one minute."

"In less than ten years, you have worked your way up at HydroGroup to Senior Hydrogeologist making nearly a hundred grand a year and you are only thirty-one years old. You have built up a reputation as a rising star in your field and yet, at this very moment, you want to risk throwing it all away. You have also, unintentionally, put Dr. Nickerson and Nina Curry at risk. You have to ask yourself if it is all worth it? Quantrill knows you are on to him now. He's going to hound you with a full court press until you, Nickerson, and Nina give in. You heard this Boggs fellow. If you walk away now, you can still save your job and your life. And probably theirs as well."

"Is that what you think I should do, just remain neutral and do nothing? Like Switzerland?"

"It may be the smartest decision in the long run."

"Well I think it stinks and I won't do it. You'd better think of something else."

The old chief calmly took a bite of tamalito smothered in *salsa verde* and cilantro sour cream. "It doesn't matter what I think is best. It's your life and career, not mine."

"Yes, but unfortunately whatever decision I make could affect you. Like you said, I have put Nickerson and Nina in jeopardy. If that's true then I have put you in danger as well."

"Don't worry about me. I have Yellow Boy."

"A one-hundred-fifty-year-old rifle isn't going to stop Quantrill and you know it." He sighed wearily. "Look, when it's all said and done, the best thing for me to do is probably just quit my job. How can I continue to work for HydroGroup when my firm's biggest client is a fraud?"

"What would quitting solve? Quantrill gets off scot free and you lose your job? That's not even a Pyrrhic victory—that's just crap."

"I can find another job."

"Listen to me. Quitting doesn't solve anything. Either go after Quantrill, or save your job and let someone else put him away for you, but don't quit your job. If you do that, Quantrill wins and you lose. Also, if you quit now, how are we going to solve the case?"

"*We?* You're not getting involved."

"As you said yourself I'm already involved."

"In that case my decision is easy. I'm not going to put you, Nickerson, or Nina in jeopardy. I'm calling it quits. As you said, it's not worth throwing everything away and putting other peoples' lives at risk."

The old chief pondered a moment then nodded gently. "I can respect your decision, my grandson. But is it final?"

"Yes, Grandfather, it's final. I'm done with this case—and that means so are you."

CHAPTER 35

THE NEXT MORNING, October 31, dawned bright, clear, and unseasonably warm and Halloween night promised to be the mildest in years for trick-or-treaters. As the sun rose, a smattering of soft billowy clouds, propelled by southerly winds, drifted unhurriedly across the pastel-blue sky. By eight o'clock the temperature was in the mid-fifties and the sun's rays settled over the high plains like a warm blanket, lending a peaceful glow to the rumpled landscape.

And yet, despite the sunny skies, Charles Quantrill couldn't help but feel a sense of dread. Though he hated to admit it, he was secretly terrified by the prospect of another devastating earthquake. Since the Earthquake Prophet had first made his forecast on national TV, Quantrill had told himself it was nothing but a publicity stunt. But with the nonstop media coverage and back and forth bantering between the competing Patey and Nickerson camps, the prediction—or prophecy, as the crackpots were calling it, as if it were some kind of Biblical event—had taken over everything else. And now that the ill-fated day—October 31—had arrived, even Quantrill found himself frantic with anticipation.

Staring out his office window, he scanned the quilted landscape beyond the haz waste facility and refinery for any anomaly, however mundane, that might hint at a coming tremor. What if by some chance the disgraced geologist had been right all along and a devastating earthquake did strike? Would Quantrill's secret operation be discovered and he be utterly ruined? Would he be held responsible for the countless lives lost and hundreds of millions of dollars in damage?

He gazed out at the massive operation he and his brother had built up together. If there was another earthquake, they might very well lose everything. In the distance he could see a line of vacuum trucks, tankers, and drum-toting eighteen wheelers snorting impatiently along the road at the waste hauler's entrance. The enormous vehicles stretched for two miles down the road. He knew that today, like every day for about the past ten years, he would be receiving more than a million gallons of liquid waste and contaminated water containing chlorinated solvents, metals, petroleum hydrocarbons, PCBs, and other toxic chemicals. By maintaining treatment costs significantly below his competitors and with a Colorado ban on deep well injection and land disposal of chlorinated solvents, PCBs, and many heavy metals, he had cornered the lion's share of the U.S. haz waste treatment market. This, in turn, had allowed him to become a turnkey carbon-based and alternative energy company and expand his operations into wind, solar, and geothermal power—thereby not just paying lip service to sustainability like his competitors, but actually putting it into practice.

Now, if he wasn't careful, it could all come to an end in the blink of an eye.

Thirty-five years of hard work down the drain.

With that in mind, he stepped inside his office and dialed a number.

"HELLO, RAVI. This is Chuck Quantrill. How you doing this morning?"

"I'm fine, Mr. Quantrill. Busy trying to keep everyone in this office billable."

"Now I don't mean to shake up your morning like a Broadmoor martini, Ravi, but we've got a small problem that needs fixing."

A moment's hesitation. "How can I help you?"

"Well, it's like this. Joe Higheagle has done a great job for me over the years, but I'm afraid his association with Nina Curry has become a bigger problem than we anticipated. My folks in legal are all up in arms about his conduct. It's been brought to our attention that, despite our warning, he's continued to meet with Ms. Curry outside of normal working hours. Now strictly speaking, what he's doing may not be a violation of the non-disclosure agreement he signed, but I just can't afford to take that chance. Quantrill Ventures is a publically visible company and, as I've said, we gave both you and him fair warning. In fact, if we so chose, we could bring legal action against both Mr. Higheagle and HydroGroup for violating the client confidentiality agreement. However, given the outstanding service your firm has provided over the years, I don't think we have to go that far. Therefore, what I suggest is that Higheagle be taken off the project and you assign a new senior project manager."

"I am very much relieved to hear you say this, Mr. Quantrill."

"Relieved?"

"That we will remain on the job, I mean."

So that's what he was worried about? I should have known Ravi wouldn't think twice about throwing Higheagle under the bus. "Now, I don't want you or him to take this personally or anything. And nothing formal needs to be written up. Hopefully, you can find some new projects for him and quietly cut him loose. But I'm afraid Joe's gonna have to go."

"That will be no problem. I am pleased that you have confidence in us to do the job."

"So you'll go ahead and tell him today then?"

"I don't need to. He has already tendered his resignation."

Quantrill felt the breath catch in his throat. "What did you just say?"

"He resigned just a few minutes ago. He left my office before you called. I tried to talk him out of it, but he said that he had accepted a job with another firm."

I should have known that boy might pull a stunt like this. Damnit, what the hell is he up to?

"His last day is this Friday. Of course, I tried to get him to stay. He's one of our best people."

Quantrill forced himself to push aside his anger and focus on the motivation behind, and implications of, Higheagle's decision. "How much did you offer him to stay?"

"That's confidential."

"Cut the crap, Ravi. How much?"

"Twenty-five percent more than he's making now."

"And in this down market he didn't take it. I can't believe it. That boy couldn't have gotten another job for that kind of money in Denver."

Ravi spoke nervously. "I do not know what company he is going with because he wouldn't tell me. But many firms would pay a great deal to have him."

Feeling his custom-tailored English suit clinging to him uncomfortably, Quantrill took off his jacket, tossing it onto the chair in front of his desk. "You said his last day is this Friday?"

"Yes."

"And he didn't give any other reason for quitting except that he's gotten another job. Are you sure you don't know the name of the new firm?"

"He wouldn't tell me."

"So you don't know why he's leaving or where he's going, do you? Well you'd damn well better find out. And you'd better keep the fact that I was going to cut him loose between you and me, or there will be hell to pay. We've got, near as I can tell, ten million dollars of remediation work to be done at my refinery and waste facility over the next few years and I expect complete confidentiality and loyalty to me. You hear!"

He pounded his fist into his desk. Suddenly a sharp pain shot through his head. He could feel a migraine coming on. Years ago, he had had a serious problem with migraines, but now he only got them on rare, unusually stressful occasions. In the event of an emergency, he kept lidocaine nasal spray on hand in his car and at his home and office. He rummaged through his desk drawer until he found a plastic bottle of the precious fluid. Grappling for it with unsteady fingers, he unscrewed the top, threw his head back, and took a big snort.

"I'm sorry, Mr. Quantrill. I promise you, if it had been anybody else in the firm besides Joseph who had become mixed up with this woman, I would have terminated him myself. But he has always done such an outstanding job for you."

Quantrill took a deep breath to steady himself; his temples were literally throbbing. "I know he has, but he mishandled this situation and we've got to make it right."

"If it's any consolation, he didn't seem at all bitter. I have his resignation letter right here. He said, 'I cannot in good conscience continue in my current capacity at HydroGroup knowing that I have not performed to the satisfaction of Quantrill Ventures, Inc. I offer my apology not only to Mr. Charles Quantrill but to his excellent staff, including Mr. Jeb Quantrill, Mr. Wesley Johnston, and Mr. Harry Boggs for my poor conduct.'"

The faux patronizing words froze Quantrill in his seat. It suddenly dawned on him that he had underestimated the clever Cheyenne far worse than he had imagined. Higheagle had prepared the overdrawn apology so he could slip out of his current position without alerting or antagonizing anyone, the cunning bastard.

"Well, it does seem like old Joe's awfully sincere, now doesn't it?"

"He truly felt as though he had let you down, Mr. Quantrill."

"Oh, cut the bullshit, Ravi. You know he's mad at me for dragging him into that conference room and putting him through the ringer."

"He didn't sound like that to me."

Quantrill was beginning to feel the salubrious effects of the lidocaine nasal spray. Thank God the medication was so fast acting. With his head beginning to clear, he realized that it was time for him to make a tactical retreat. Without knowing precisely what Higheagle was up to or how much of a threat he would ultimately prove to be, he had to downplay the situation and hope that Ravi would be able to serve as something of an informant. Which he no doubt would do if he wanted ten million dollars in consulting fees over the next five years.

"All right, Ravi, I reckon we're done here. I didn't mean to get all in a lather—I was just surprised by how suddenly this all came about. Tell Joe there's no hard feelings and that he did a bang-up job for me."

"He'll be very pleased to hear that. I'll be taking over as the senior project manager myself if that's all right with you."

"That'll be fine," Quantrill said in his most reassuring manner, feeling much better now. "We'll be in touch soon."

"I look forward to hearing from you."

"And Ravi, make sure your human resources folks find out where our boy's headed. I've got enough problems without having some disgruntled ex-employee of yours making my life difficult."

CHAPTER 36

DR. JAMES FRANCIS NICKERSON felt a frisson of dread in the air. The Earthquake Prophet's prediction hung over the National Earthquake Information Center like an axe waiting to fall. Everyone knew the stakes. If Patey's prediction proved correct, the USGS would be a laughingstock and the former California state geologist, and more importantly his scientific methodology, would have to be taken seriously. If Halloween night came and went without a seismic disturbance, then the USGS, as well as the professional and academic institutions that worked hand and hand with the agency, would be acquitted and everything would return to normal.

It all hung in the balance.

He stepped into his office, closed the door, and looked up at the framed picture of his hero John Wesley Powell. The Civil War major who lost an arm to a minie ball at Shiloh, founded the USGS, and led the first expedition down the Grand Canyon stared back at him with an expression of stern 19th century paternalism, as if to say, "With your performance in last night's debate, James, you have not only let the Survey down, you have let *me* down!"

Nickerson went to his desk. As he sat back down in his chair, his phone rang. He checked the caller ID, hoping to ignore the call, but to his chagrin it was Director Watkins.

Damn!

For a fleeting moment, he debated whether to pick up. But his boss would just leave a message and he would have to return it eventually. He lifted the phone just before the call was about to be transferred into voice mail.

"Director Watkins, what can I do for you?"

"You can start by apologizing. You were terrible last night. Absolutely terrible."

Nickerson felt his whole body deflate like a balloon.

"You didn't shut Patey down like you were supposed to. You let him have the last word and now he's gone off and scared the bejesus out of everyone. My office has received hundreds of phone calls. Secretary Jackson is not pleased. And when the secretary of the interior takes an interest in our affairs and is not pleased, that is *not* a good thing."

"Sir, I tried to tell you that I wasn't—"

"Oh, nonsense, we had no choice in the matter. There was too much public pressure. And now unfortunately, what happened last night is only the tip of the iceberg."

"What are you talking about?"

"You've put us in an awkward position, James. You've upset a lot of people."

Nickerson felt his career slipping away, like a rug pulled out from under his feet. Thirty-two years of service to the USGS gone in the blink of an eye—how was such a thing possible? He should have refused to debate Patey; if he had held fast from the start, Watkins would have been forced to have someone else do his dirty work and he wouldn't be in the position he was in now.

"Who have I upset, Mr. Director?"

"Besides Secretary Jackson and myself? Well you've somehow managed to get on Senator Tanner's blacklist."

"Quantrill's lackey."

"That's the chairman of the Senate Appropriations Committee you're talking about."

"What did he say?"

"He says you've been harassing Charles Quantrill."

"You know very well that I haven't been harassing anybody. Quantrill refuses to give us his deep seismic reflection profiles, or the earthquake data from his seismograph network. We need that data, sir."

"Well, you're not going to get it. And you can forget about your portable seismograph network near the epicenter."

"You can't be serious? Since when does a single U.S. senator and corporate CEO tell the USGS what it can and cannot do?"

"I'm not going to get into this with you. You just do as you're told."

"I already did and look where that's gotten me. It was you who told me to get the portable network up and running as quickly as possible. I rushed the budget request to you last Friday per your instructions. And now you're telling me that the whole thing's been scrapped?"

"The situation has changed—drastically."

Nickerson was nonplussed. *What in the hell has happened?* The director had agreed that they needed the new network to accurately pinpoint the epicenter of future earthquakes in the area.

"I don't understand, Mr. Director. Why are we killing the local network? You just got the budget request."

"The seismograph locations you've identified are on Quantrill's property and we can't have access."

"Why not? Those are the best locations."

"Because that damned state geologist friend of yours—Mark Kelso—has gone too far."

"Kelso?"

"He's trespassed onto Quantrill's Sweetwater-bottling plant and had verbal exchanges with Quantrill's security staff. He's stirring up a hornet's nest."

Nickerson felt his anger picking up. He looked down at a damage assessment and aftershock report on the recent quake, shaking his head with quiet indignation. "How do you know that? Oh, don't tell me, Senator Tanner."

"James, you're not seeing this the right way. Is Senator Tanner an insolent prick? Absolutely. Can he cut our funding in half inside of a week? Yes he can. So you'd better just shut up right now and tell this Kelso to back off. Do you understand me? Call off your dog—and I mean as soon as I hang up."

"What's going on, Nate? This isn't like you to just roll over like this."

The line went silent; Nickerson knew instantly that he shouldn't have said that. He stared out his office into the Drum Room. The restless scratching and scrawling of the seismographs added to the unbearable tension of the moment as he waited for his boss to respond.

"Since we've been colleagues for the past twelve years, James, I'm going to pretend you didn't say that. But let me make one thing perfectly clear. You are in deep shit. You have angered the wrong people. And by not taking control of last night's debate with Dr. Patey the Earthquake Prophet, you have made the Survey look bad in the eyes of the public. Or at the very least made us look weak."

Nickerson felt defeated. What could he possibly say? "I'll call Mark Kelso right away. Will that be all then?"

"No, there's one more thing."

Nickerson cringed and waited.

"You'd better pray there's not an earthquake today. Because if there is, you're out of a goddamned job!"

CHAPTER 37

LATER THAT DAY, with low-slanting afternoon rays poking through his west-facing office window, Joseph Higheagle sat hunched over his desk with the focused concentration of a neurosurgeon. He had spent the last hour studying a series of oil and gas pipeline maps, checking and rechecking every minute detail, hoping for some telltale clue about the off-site waste disposal operation, if there actually was one. But to his dismay he hadn't found anything. He rolled up each one of the maps, put them away in his bin, sat back in his chair, and stared out the window at the snow-capped mountains.

Somehow they looked cold and menacing. Or maybe that wasn't it at all—maybe it was just the conflicted feelings he felt inside. After all, it was all or nothing now that he had given notice that he was quitting HydroGroup. Last night, in order to prevent potential harm from coming to his grandfather, Nina, or Dr. Nickerson, he had made a decision to stay with the company and to put an end to his clandestine investigation of Quantrill Ventures. But after tossing and turning all night he had changed his mind. There was no way he was going to look the other way when he knew his client was a fraud, even if that meant putting others in harm's way. He wasn't about to stay at HydroGroup and pretend his client was doing nothing wrong, nor would he let Quantrill's men bully and threaten him. But now that he had actually given notice, he realized that the situation wasn't so simple. The harsh reality was that there was now no turning back and no place to run or hide. He and his cohorts were totally on their own and their lives would most likely be in peril, if what Harry Boggs had said was a true indication of what to expect.

After a moment, his gaze turned to the maps rolled up in the bin next to his desk. He had a feeling he had overlooked something. He still didn't know where Quantrill's supposed crude oil pipeline went. He had already pored over the oil and gas transmission line maps for the area, but none of the lines tied into Quantrill's waste facility. There were two separate lines that entered the refinery along the northern property boundary, but they were well marked on the maps and far from the waste facility line that had ruptured. Somehow he wasn't looking at this the right way.

And then he was struck with an idea.

He quickly rifled through the maps in his bin showing the locations of the oil and gas wells in the area of the Quantrill Ventures facility. After pulling out several maps, he found the one he was looking for and spread it onto his light table. The map showed the location of the facility, surrounding parcel numbers and property lines, producing oil and natural gas wells, and dry holes. He took out his field notebook and read off the compass bearing he had recorded for the pipeline. The line trended north 81 degrees east before it was redirected by Quantrill's workers. He took out his protractor, plotted the orientation of the line on the map, and projected the line out all the way to the eastern edge of Elbert County. He studied the wells along the line near the facility and saw nothing irregular. Then he examined the map further east of the facility. He saw clusters of eight to ten oil or gas wells, each separated by hundreds of feet, and individual exploratory wells far from any production cluster. The clusters were invariably oil or gas producers, and the wildcat wells distant from the clusters were dry holes.

Suddenly, his eye caught something that deviated from the pattern.

Next to Quantrill's Sweetwater mineral water bottling plant, he saw a well cluster where three dry holes had been drilled right next to one another. He took out his ruler and measured the distance from the three dry holes to the pipeline plotted in pencil. His pencil mark missed the three non-producing drillholes by no more than a few hundred feet. At the scale of the map, the difference was negligible. The line leaving the facility had to tie in to the wells, especially since Quantrill owned all of the properties in the area, including the nearby Sweetwater plant.

Sliding his chair across the floor, he fumbled through the notebooks on the shelf. He quickly found the one containing the drilling logs of oil and gas wells drilled in Elbert County that had been compiled for the environmental impact study conducted by HydroGroup. The well logs were arranged neatly in the notebook first by county, then by well number. Inspecting the map, he read off the well names: DW-105, IW-106, and SW-107. Examining the map legend, he saw that SW, IW, and DW stood for shallow well, intermediate well, and deep well.

He flipped the pages in the notebook until he came to the page on well DW-105. He looked over the log and saw that the total depth was about ten thousand feet below ground surface, over five hundred feet into Precambrian schist and gneiss. An unusually deep well. Next he looked over the log for intermediate well IW-106 next. It was completed just below seven thousand feet into the Jurassic Dakota and Lakota Sandstones and the Morrison Formation. Finally, he flipped to the log for shallow well SW-107 and saw that it had been drilled to the bottom of the Hygiene Sandstone, about four thousand feet below grade.

For several minutes, he flipped between the pages and studied the information. He was puzzled. The deep well had been drilled first and all three wells had been drilled within a six-month time frame, one right after another; yet, surprisingly, not one of them had produced oil or gas. He wondered why any company would drill three wells in the same location if the first one had shown no signs of production capability. The drill stem test results showed that no petroleum hydrocarbon gases or liquids were detected in any of the producing zones encountered in any of the wells. It made no sense that three boreholes had been drilled right next to one another and perforated casing set when there was no evidence that oil or gas was present.

Unless, of course, the wells had been drilled for another purpose.

He reached for the phone to call Nina Curry.

"HELLO, THIS IS NINA."

"I think I've figured out how Quantrill's doing it," he said without preamble.

"Joseph?"

"He's injecting the waste down deep wells and that's what caused the earthquakes. That line that ruptured runs from the facility towards Limon and feeds into three injection wells next to his Sweetwater bottling plant. Each one is set at a different depth. That's how he's doing it."

"We should talk with Dr. Nickerson again."

"We can conference him in right now." A moment later he had the NEIC director on the line. "Dr. Nickerson, it's Joe Higheagle. I've got Nina Curry on the line with me and we have important news for you. I think I know what's causing the earthquakes."

"You've got my attention."

"I believe Quantrill's injecting waste fluids down three nested injection wells. I've been able to locate them on a map and also look over the well logs. What I've found is consistent with an illegal deep well injection program."

"Okay, but do you have definite proof?"

"No, we'd need to inspect the injection site to know for sure. Even then, it would be best if we could collect samples."

"This is big," said Nina. "We need to meet again—the three of us."

Higheagle groaned inwardly. "Uh, there might be a slight problem with that."

"Why is that?"

"I should have told you both this last night when we talked, but I didn't want to alarm you. Quantrill's security people have been keeping an eye on us. Or maybe just me."

"You mean they've been following us?" said Nickerson.

"I don't know about you and Nina, but Quantrill's men definitely followed me to the Buckhorn on Friday night. They have photographs of the three of us together."

"How do you know?"

"Last night Boggs and two of his lackey's threw me into a car and forced me to have a not-so-friendly chat."

Nina's voice evidenced alarm: "You mean they kidnapped you?"

"For ten minutes anyway. They told me to stop poking around and asking questions, and they especially warned me not to talk to either of you. Look, these guys *are* serious. I don't think they've tapped my phone or anything. But I think they're keeping an eye on me for sure, and maybe you guys as well. They said that if I didn't back off they would bring in someone a little more...persuasive. I'm sorry, I should have told you both last night right after it happened, but I didn't want to scare the hell out of you."

"You're right, you should have told us earlier," admonished Nickerson. "But now that you have, I know Quantrill and he definitely means business. He didn't become a billionaire by backing down to people who pose a threat to him. He's going to come after us hard with thugs *and* lawyers. We should stop and think and make sure this is what we want."

"I say we meet in person and go over what we've got," said Nina. "Then we can decide."

"Unfortunately, I can't leave my office right now so if we meet we're going to have to do it here in Golden. But we still have a problem. How can we pull it off without Quantrill knowing about it?"

"Joseph, did you see anyone tailing you into work this morning?"

"No, but that doesn't mean they weren't there. I'm sure Quantrill's security guys know how to avoid detection."

"Pick me up at my office in fifteen minutes. If there's a tail, we'll just have lose it on our way up to Golden."

"It's risky, but it might be your only shot," agreed Nickerson. "Be here in an hour. Eighteenth Street and Illinois, fifth floor."

"I'll bring the maps, well logs, cross-sections, and analytical results," Higheagle said to Nina. "Were you able to find out anything from the Health Department or EPA files?"

"I was able to get my hands on quite a few records. I've uploaded all the electronic files, but I haven't finished going through the hard copy documents. Our electronic filing system's still a bit of a mess."

"Were you able to get the waste manifest reports?"

"Yeah, but I haven't had a chance to go through them."

"Just bring everything you've got. We're going to have to sort this out as we go."

163

"Sounds like a plan," said Nickerson. "I'll see you two in an hour. Oh, and be careful."

"We will," said Higheagle. "We definitely will."

CHAPTER 38

QUANTRILL looked at Harry Boggs with astonishment. Outside his office, the building was quiet as a tomb except for the occasional footstep or click of a computer keyboard from the smattering of senior-level employees who remained. More than a third of his work force had called in sick today, and those that had showed up were worried and anxious about the predicted earthquake, so at 3 p.m. he had decided to send people home early. He and a handful of senior staff members were the only ones yet to vacate the premises.

"Come on Harry, you've got to be kidding me."

The security chief stood in front of Quantrill's solid English oak desk, stubby hands folded behind his back, bearing his usual look, which was that of a man perpetually breaking bad news. The desk was clear of paperwork, a testament to the CEO's lean and efficient management style.

"I wish I was, sir, but I'm not. Jack Holland's done it all right. He's downloaded more than fifty confidential files and copied them onto a flash drive. Ed Stewart reported it to me just fifteen minutes ago." Stewart was the company's head of IT, network administrator, and chief of cyber security.

"What kind of files?"

"Pipeline schematics, injection well construction details, process and instrumentation diagrams—all kinds of stuff. Looks like he's hedging his bets in case he needs to cut a deal."

Quantrill felt as though he had been punched in the gut. "My God, Jack? He's been my chief legal counsel for seventeen years."

"He's not done yet either. He's still copying files."

"He's still here?"

"Yes, sir."

"I can't believe this. After everything we've been through together."

"At this point, sir, I would trust no one—including your brother."

Quantrill gave a wounded look. "Jeb? He would never betray me."

"If you say so, sir. But I would keep a close eye on him all the same."

At that instant the security chief's cell phone chirped. Quantrill didn't agree with Boggs' assessment of his younger brother, but the man's job was to protect the company. Quantrill knew it was in his best interest to defer to him in security matters.

"I'd better take this, Mr. Quantrill. It's Eric Smith out at Sweetwater."

The CEO nodded his approval and began leafing through a stack of papers on his desk. Taking the call, Boggs walked to the corner of the room and stood next to the glass case with the saber-toothed cat skull. He listened for several minutes, interjecting an occasional question and nodding every so often, before returning to the front of Quantrill's desk.

"I'm afraid, sir, that I have some more bad news."

Quantrill braced himself.

"Mark Kelso is out poking around at the injection well area again."

Good Lord, not again?

"This time he trespassed onto the Sweetwater property and actually tried to get into the control room. He didn't succeed, of course, but he did look inside the window and see Smith."

"How in the hell did he get inside the security fence?"

"We don't know yet."

Quantrill couldn't believe it; he had just looked over the security video footage this morning showing Kelso poking around on Saturday. And now the bastard was back out there again, digging up clues like Sherlock Holmes!

"Where is Kelso now?"

"Smith just threw him off the property. Unfortunately, we can't do anything more than that. The last thing we want is for the police to get involved."

Quantrill began pacing in front of the window. He felt like he was sinking in quicksand. He stared out at the towering Rockies—a broad swath of silvery, jagged, snow-capped peaks—and felt their coldness. Nature could be a harsh thing. In that moment, with the threat of an earthquake hanging over his head like an oppressive cloud and events spiraling out of control, the world seemed a terribly gelid and random place. How naïve he had been to believe he could control the waste injection.

Suddenly Boggs' cell phone chirped again.

"Bible and sword, Harry, what is it now?"

The security chief glanced at the incoming number, licked his lips. "It's Heiser. Should I take it?"

"Yes, but make it quick." The CEO stepped out onto the balcony to get some fresh air, closing the Pella sliding glass door behind him. *Is there no end to these problems?* Off in the distance, a herd of fifty or sixty pronghorns nibbled contentedly at long-stemmed prairie grass. He watched them for a minute until several heads poked up in the air alertly, as if the animals had spotted or caught a whiff of something, a predator perhaps.

Boggs opened the door. Quantrill saw instantly that he had more bad news.

"Just get it over with, Harry."

"Higheagle and Nina Curry are on the move."

Quantrill shook his head in disbelief. Could his luck get any worse?

"Heiser and Stolz are following them west on Colfax."

"Looks like our boy didn't get your message, Harry."

"No, sir, he didn't."

"Which means we have a real problem on our hands."

Boggs nodded solemnly.

"What do you recommend we do about it?"

"We need to bring in Mr. Sperry, sir. It's time."

"I'll be the one to decide if and when it's time to bring in your hired gun, not you."

"Yes, sir. But I would advise against waiting too long."

"I hear you, Harry. I hear you loud and clear. But it's not time."

"Yes, sir."

Feeling anxious and unsettled, Quantrill stared off at the herd of antelope in the distance. The animals were no longer milling about and munching grass. They were all peering alertly to the west. They appeared ready to make a run for it, as if something had spooked them.

"What's up with them?" wondered Boggs aloud.

But as soon as the words left the security chief's mouth, Quantrill realized what was happening. As if to confirm his fears, hundreds of birds blasted out from the stand of cottonwoods along the creek west of the facility, shrieking and cawing as if frightened by something. At the same instant, the prairie dogs at the base of the bluff on the far side of the creek disappeared into their holes, one right after another, until there were no heads peeping out from the prairie. A moment later, the antelope broke into a dead run and were quickly joined by a small pack of coyotes and jackrabbits that seemingly came out of nowhere. Suddenly birds filled the sky, a strange-looking hodge-podge of hawks, magpies, ravens, blue jays, and ordinary robins, wings flapping wildly.

And then Quantrill felt it.

It started as a little jolt rising up from the floor and running through his body like a weak electrical current. Then the air itself seemed to change.

"We're in for it now, Harry! Quick, get inside!"

They dove inside the office. Feeling a strong vibration rippling up from the floor, Quantrill grabbed onto his solid English oak desk to stabilize himself. His priceless Albert Bierstadt oil paintings fell from the wall one at a time, and his original Frederic Remington bronze sculpture toppled from its pedestal. Now the building began to sway like a helicopter sawing out of control. He saw Boggs fall to the floor. The ficus tree collapsed and books began tumbling from the big bookcases. His desk was suddenly cleared of paperwork as if an industrious secretary had swept through the room.

He heard shouting coming from outside his door and from nearby offices. The building was rolling under the pressure of the shock wave.

Both of his rippled-glass cabinets crashed to the floor, disgorging trilobites, winged brachiopods, coiled ammonites, precious gems, Native American artifacts, and his prized *Utahraptor* claw and *Smilodon fatalis* skull. He dove to the floor and covered his head. His big bull elk trophy fell from the wall, puncturing one of the Bierstadt's, as bits of lathe and plaster rained down from above.

For a moment the vibrations stopped. He glanced at Boggs, lying prone and helpless with a look of terror on his face and blood dribbling from a nasty gash in his head.

Then the building was rocked again, worse this time, and Quantrill felt a fantastic rolling sensation. He remained pressed against the floor, feeling a churning in the pit of his stomach. The whole building groaned heavily as it was thrown further out of plumb. He heard screaming coming from outside the window. Looking up, he saw one of the walls crack open as if some great monster had cleaved its way into the room.

And then the shaking stopped altogether.

Rising to his feet, he dusted off the fine talc-like powder from his suit. The floor was covered with fragments of glass, plaster, and wood from his broken furniture. His black leather chair was trapped beneath his broken desk. The wall behind his desk was now empty and cracked.

As he helped Boggs to his feet, a terrific explosion outside shook the building. They scrambled to the broken window and looked down at the truckers' entrance to the haz waste facility. A black funnel of smoke billowed out from a pair of overturned tankers. Quantrill saw several people scurrying to get away as the rear of both vehicles exploded, sending up twin blasts of fire and hunks of metal into the air.

Shaking his head in dismay, he turned away from the window. "It's happened, Harry. By thunder, the prophecy came true!"

The security chief said nothing, just stared dazedly at the roiling flames.

Heart racing, Quantrill dashed to the door and tried to open it. But it was jammed shut. He yanked hard on the handle and managed to jerk it open.

He came face to face with his brother.

"You bastard," hissed Jeb. "You crazy murdering bastard!"

CHAPTER 39

WAITING FOR THE GREEN ARROW, Higheagle tapped his fingers on the steering wheel to the rhythm of Jackson Browne's "Doctor My Eyes." The Kiowa guitar virtuoso Jesse Ed Davis was playing his swirling Stratocaster solo and Higheagle was enjoying it immensely. The urban landscape around him was anonymous: low-slung apartment buildings, an obsolete car wash, the obligatory 7-Eleven, a run-down Chinese restaurant, and a liquor store covered with steel-barred windows. When the *Go* signal came, he made sure the coast was clear then eased into the left hand turn.

"I still can't see anyone following us," said Nina, anxiously peering into the side view mirror.

"Oh, they're back there all right."

"How do you know?"

"I can feel them?"

"Feel them?"

"I'm an Indian, remember?"

"You're bullshitting, right?"

"Nope, I've got a sixth sense—it's in my blood. Trust me, they're back there."

She gave a look of bemusement, but he could tell that she didn't discount his extrasensory ability entirely. At the next intersection, he peered into his rearview mirror, but saw nothing. No matter, the bastards were back there somewhere, he just knew it. He pushed his foot down on the accelerator and drove on.

"What about the earthquake? Do you think it's going to hit today or not?" she asked him.

"I don't think so."

"Why not?"

"Because all the built-up elastic strain energy was just released during Sunday's quake. And even if it wasn't, the Earthquake Prophet's theory just doesn't hold water."

"Well, it happens to make a lot of sense to me."

"Come on, think about it. We know what's causing the earthquakes and it has nothing to do with unusually strong gravitational forces."

"I don't know, I still think Patey's onto something. In any case, why don't we bet on it?"

"Bet on whether there's an earthquake today?"

"Yeah, we've still got eight hours left."

"Okay, you've got a deal. What are the stakes?"

"How about dinner?"

"Hmm, a date."

"I didn't say that."

"Yeah you did. You just asked me out on a date."

"Okay, so I'm busted," she said with a guilty smile. "What are you going to do about it?"

"Arrest and handcuff you."

"Oh really? Can we start right now?"

"Sorry, but I'm afraid we have to catch the bad guys first."

They both laughed. He hit the gas pedal and glanced again in his rearview mirror. This time he saw something. Three cars back lurked a black Lexus. But was it the same one from the other night? He looked into the mirror again and caught a glimpse of a pair of faces. The one in the passenger seat was partially obscured, but seemed familiar. Then he realized who it was: White Hair, the guy named Heiser. But he couldn't make out the driver. Was it Boggs? Was the security chief even in the vehicle? He supposed it didn't matter—he had to lose the bastards regardless. He thought hard for a moment, trying to gauge how best to pull it off.

Nina looked at him. "What's going on?"

"I spotted our tail."

She turned around. "Really, someone's back—"

But her words were clipped off as there was a sudden ground jolt beneath their tires. Caught off guard, Higheagle struggled to control the War Wagon as the pickup truck appeared to have a will of its own. Like a wild stallion, it gave a sudden convulsive shudder and banked hard to the right.

And then the S-wave hit.

The paved street beneath them began to vibrate. A Chevy Blazer materialized from out of nowhere, swerving into the westbound lane to avoid hitting four cars idling at the intersection. It bore down upon Higheagle and Nina with a vengeance. The last thing they saw before the impact was a terrified teenage boy and girl, mouths open in terror.

Higheagle turned left to deflect the blow, hoping the Blazer might sideswipe them instead of crashing head-on, but it wasn't enough. The vehicle drove into them like a freight train, pitching the War Wagon to the left. The two vehicles coupled for a breathless instant, then the big Blazer slid past, scraping paint and ripping out the side view mirror and front fender.

With the ground still shaking fiercely, Higheagle's foot slid off the brake and onto the accelerator. He hurtled helplessly toward a Dodge minivan waiting at the light. The teenage boy driving the Blazer overcorrected when the War Wagon and Blazer disengaged, and reeled to the right. Then the Blazer went airborne, tearing through a sign for the Bruce Ehleringer Apartment Homes.

Landing, it careened wildly and smashed into an RV parked in front of the apartments. A paunchy old man who was pulling something from the RV dove out of the way at the last second, but he was too late. He bounced off the windshield and the cigarette dangling from his mouth flew onto the asphalt parking lot.

Now a third pulse of seismic energy blasted up through Speer Boulevard, rippling the asphalt surface like a snapping garden hose. Still struggling to control the War Wagon, Higheagle sideswiped a huge oak tree and the truck careened right, rolled over once, miraculously righted itself, and came to rest in the shadow of the tree.

Suddenly everything was quiet. Higheagle realized that the ground shaking had stopped. He checked to see if he was hurt. No blood, but his left arm was numb from slamming against the car door. He glanced in his rearview mirror to see if Quantrill's men were still chasing them. The black Lexus was back there, but to his surprise, as the vehicle started to pull out into the adjacent lane to follow in pursuit, it was smashed from behind by a runaway UPS truck and driven hard into the guard rail.

"Holy shit did we just get lucky! Come on, we've got to get out of here!"

He turned to help Nina from the passenger seat. But to his surprise, he found her slumped over like a ragdoll.

Damn, is she badly hurt?

He touched her gently. "Nina, are you all right?"

There was no response; she didn't budge.

"Nina, wake up!"

Again no response.

This can't be happening! He clawed at his seat belt, managed to unbuckle it, and checked to see if she was breathing. In the shadow of the gigantic oak, he couldn't tell. He quickly checked her pulse.

She was unconscious, but alive.

CHAPTER 40

DAZED AND DISORIENTED, Nina looked up to see a pair of faces peering down at her.

She couldn't tell who the people were but they looked like twins. Then she realized that there weren't two people at all—she was seeing double.

Wordlessly, the blurry figure reached over to pull her out, the movements as adept as a gymnast: smooth, athletic, confident.

"Joseph, is that you?" she asked woozily.

"Yes, it's me. I'm getting you out of here." His voice sounded distant like a dream.

She giggled. "I'm falling for you, you know."

"You're what?"

"I'm falling for you and your Cheyenne charm."

"I think you just hit your head and your brain is scrambled."

"No, that's not it. I'm definitely feeling a little tingly."

"Tingly? Uh-oh, I know I'm in trouble now. Sorry, but we're going to have to pick up this conversation later when you don't sound like you're high on peyote."

She giggled again—boy was he funny!—then tried to blink away the stars, but everything was still fuzzy. There was a crisp sliding sound as the seatbelt was unfastened and then she felt herself grasped by arms that, while not thick, were powerful.

"You're going to have to help me here," she heard him say.

Together, they pushed and pulled. A moment later she felt herself disentangled and they broke up into the sunlight. She squinted against the brightness and slowly Higheagle's face came into focus. She blinked several times and reached out to touch his hand.

It was warm.

"You're going to be okay," he said reassuringly.

Wearing the dumb expression of a baby, she squinted at this throwback to the lance-wielding horsemen of the Plains she had always admired from books and movies, and thought, *I may be dreaming, Joseph Higheagle, but I am falling for you.*

AFTER HELPING NINA from the car, Higheagle took a moment to get his bearings. The numbness had disappeared from his arm, but he still felt disoriented. He wasn't sure what had just happened between the two of them. Was he mistaken or did she just say that she was falling for him? Did he dare tell her that he was falling just as hard for her? No, there was no time for romance. He had to make sure that they were safe from Quantrill's goons.

He scanned the street again for the black Lexus. It took him a minute to locate the vehicle. The rear end was totaled from the impact with the UPS truck and there was no movement inside the car whatsoever. He expelled a sigh of relief: he wouldn't have to worry about White Hair and the other guy for the time being.

He turned his attention to the two kids in the Chevy Blazer. *Jesus, what a disaster!* The Blazer had collided so violently with the RV, its front was crumpled like an accordion and the windshield was shattered. The boy and girl were trapped inside the vehicle and a corpulent old man lay groaning on the pavement next to the RV. He had been knocked down, but wasn't bleeding and appeared to be conscious. And then Higheagle saw the disaster waiting to happen: a stream of gasoline was spreading slowly across the asphalt, moving directly towards the old man's burning cigarette.

He couldn't believe his eyes. *What's next a suicide bomber?*

Like a guided missile, he ran to the vehicle and opened the passenger door to pull the girl out first. She wasn't moving, except for her breathing, which came in ragged gasps. Like the male driver, she wasn't wearing a seatbelt, and her face was smeared with blood.

He grabbed the girl around the chest as Nina came wobbling up like a punch drunk boxer. "Here, let me help you," she said, reaching in the truck.

"Hurry, there isn't much time," he said to her.

Together they pulled the girl from the crumpled Blazer, carried her to the lawn, and laid her down gently on the grass. Other people were coming on the scene now—three people from the 7-Eleven and two other groups from the apartments across the street—but, thankfully, he didn't spot White Hair or his companion.

They dashed back to the wreck. Blurry vapor trails hovered around the Blazer; the smell of gasoline was overwhelming. Surprisingly, the old man was up on his feet. They helped him to the grass, then scrambled for the boy behind the wheel.

He was in worse shape than the girl. There was a gaping contusion on his forehead and rivulets of blood poured down his face. His right arm was twisted at an awkward angle, caught in the steering wheel. Higheagle could smell the blood on him, a sweet sickening stench that mingled with the pungent smell of the gasoline, as he reached to pull his arm free.

That's when it happened.

Flames leapt up from the stream of gasoline in a burst of blue and orange. The fire quickly surged laterally towards the Blazer's ruptured fuel tank.

He shook his head in disbelief: *If there actually is a Great Spirit, the dude needs to know that he's fucking piling on right now!*

They jerked on the boy's arm, trying to pull it free from the steering wheel, but it was as if he was resisting their efforts to save him.

The flames drew closer. Higheagle felt the molten heat on his face through the open window.

They pulled harder.

Now the fire was upon them, flames pouring through the window, gray smoke billowing up.

Still fighting desperately to free him, they finally managed to disentangle the boy from the steering wheel.

But as they tried to pull him from the truck, his leg caught on something.

Shit! You've got to be kidding me!

To Higheagle's hortative cries, they tugged furiously and finally managed to yank him through the open door. As flames engulfed the Blazer, they dragged him across the lawn, diving to the ground when they reached the others.

There was a tremendous explosion, a fiery flash of orange, followed by an eruption of black smoke and a wave of searing airborne heat. A second explosion followed the first, as the mammoth RV disappeared behind an expanding ball of fire. The main frames of both vehicles remained earthbound, but hunks of metal, glass, and rubber blasted in all directions, whizzing past like flak. The biggest pieces fell like gunshot ducks from the sky. Higheagle and Nina covered their heads as glass and lighter debris poured down on them; luckily, they were far enough away to avoid the heavy hunks and were low enough to the ground to avoid the whizzing metal.

When the worst was over, they peered up at the wreckage. Flames poured from the jumble of charred metal and rubber on the ground, rumbling like a storm. Thick black smoke billowed up from the flames. By now a crowd had gathered along the perimeter, all eyes fixed on the blaze in awed silence.

"We've got to get to Dr. Nickerson," said Higheagle.

"What about those guys tailing us?" asked Nina.

Higheagle looked at the Lexus again; still no movement inside the vehicle nor any sign of the goons on the street. "Their car is totaled. We don't have to worry about them."

"But how are we going to get to Golden? Your truck's a wreck."

He looked over at the War Wagon, battered but stolid like a trusty Sherman tank. "That old warhorse—why he's just getting warmed up. Come on, let's roll!"

CHAPTER 41

"YOU BASTARD—YOU CRAZY MURDERING BASTARD!"

Quantrill stood stunned before his brother. He wanted to retort, to contradict, to deny—but in the heat of the moment, he could summon not a single word in his own defense. In fact, he felt utterly ashamed. Even if he were blameless, just hearing his brother spew the venomous words made him feel as though he truly was guilty.

The facts were undeniable: the dreaded earthquake had struck and, this time, the devastation was catastrophic. Based on the violent ground shaking at the facility, hundreds, perhaps thousands, must have died or at least been severely injured. When the final tally was complete, countless people would no doubt be homeless and the damage would be in the billions.

It was an absolute disaster in every way imaginable. His business operation—indeed his very existence as CEO of Quantrill Ventures—was in peril. At this point, he would have to literally fight for his own survival—and mercilessly destroy those who posed a threat to him.

He glared back at his brother defiantly. "None of us anticipated this would happen. How could we?"

"So that justifies what we've done?"

"No, of course not. But we can't be sure if we have anything to do with this or not. In any case, this is neither the time or place to argue about it." He looked back into his office. "On your feet, Harry. I need you to check all the offices. Make sure everyone in the building is accounted for."

Boggs rose up on his stubby legs with an audible groan. "Yes, sir," he croaked, in obvious pain.

"My God, what have we done?" lamented Jeb, shaking his head in disbelief.

"We didn't do anything—nature did." Quantrill started down the hallway towards the main reception area, stepping around fallen pictures, splintered wood, and chunks of dry wall, lathe, and plaster. He had to perform a quick and dirty damage assessment.

Jeb followed after him. "Like hell we didn't do anything. You bastard, I should have never let you talk me into this insane scheme."

Quantrill kept walking. "You have no definite proof that these quakes are the result of the operation. And remember, if there is a connection then you're the one to blame. After all, it was your computer model that said that as long as we injected less than six hundred gpm, we would be fine."

"Controlling what happens in the subsurface is—and always has been—impossible."

"It's a little late to be telling me that, don't you think?"

"I thought we could do it, but I was wrong. These are global-scale forces we're talking about here. Five…ten…fifteen…twenty thousand feet down is a world damn near as alien as Mars. I understand that now. There's absolutely nothing homogeneous or predictable about it."

Quantrill came to a halt in the main reception area. It was empty. He looked out at the facility and breathed a sigh of relief when he saw that the damage was minimal. He saw a few overturned drums, broken pipes, and a collapsed maintenance shed, but that was all. More importantly, he didn't see anyone hurt. He turned his attention to the two burning tankers beyond the gate. Black smoke filled the sky, bent back by the wind.

"Good Lord," he muttered under his breath.

Jeb angrily crowded him, waving a finger in his face. "This goddamned operation is finished—and so are we."

"What's that supposed to mean?"

"It means innocent people have died from this and we're going to fucking jail."

"No one's going to jail, Brother. That I promise you."

"Look at those burning tankers out there. We caused those fires—and probably a hundred more like them."

Quantrill stared at the flaming tankers then looked at Jeb. There were tears in his eyes. He felt ashamed knowing that his brother very well could be right and they were responsible for two devastating earthquakes. But how could they have known when all the scientific data showed the risks were manageable? And even if they were responsible, Quantrill wasn't about to just sit by and allow himself to be destroyed over this.

"Now is neither the time for panic or recriminations. We need to respond to this crisis in a calm, deliberate manner."

"This crisis was caused by your greed."

"No, you're the one who's ultimately responsible. You were the one who insisted that we go 'green' *and* remain highly profitable. But no one just hands out paychecks for sustainability. You have to make money doing it. That's what you said and that's what we did."

"We could have found another way."

"Not with a thousand percent return on investment, we couldn't. Now look, you're not helping here. We have a situation to deal with whether you like it or not."

"Situation? Now there's an understatement," said a sharp voice.

They both looked up to see Harry Boggs storming down the hallway with Wesley Johnston. He looked like a different man. He was still covered in dry wall dust and a rivulet of blood trickled down his cracked head like Y.A. Tittle in the famous photograph. But his crisp brown eyes were infused with an intensity that Quantrill had seldom seen before.

"Ed Stewart is dead," announced the security chief.

Quantrill was stunned. "My God."

"He was crushed by a beam."

"Is that…is there anybody else?"

"Not in the building. I don't know about the haz waste plant or refinery."

"What about Jack?"

Boggs pursed his lips. "I couldn't find him."

"You mean he's left the building?"

"No, I just couldn't find him. His car's still here so he hasn't vacated the premises."

Goddamnit, we need to find him! Before he does something he'll regret!

Johnston said, "I'm going down to the plant and make sure everything's shut down. We're going to have a ton of inspectors out here in the next few days so we're going to have to curtail the off-site program for at least a few weeks. I'll go over the situation with Jeff and make sure the system is off and all the tanks and lines have been checked." He was referring to Jeff Russell, the daytime facility operations manager. "I'll have a full damage report to you within an hour."

"Thank you, Wes. We'll meet back here when you're done. Good luck."

The chief engineer hurried off.

Jeb Quantrill had pulled out his BlackBerry and was punching away. "I can't believe you're going to try and cover this up," he said when Johnston was beyond earshot. "Ed Stewart's dead and this is your reaction?"

"What else would you have me do?"

"This is not the time for a debate," said Boggs impatiently. "We need to move quickly."

"Harry's right. This isn't doing any of us any good."

"You're both fucking crazy. Don't you realize what we've done?"

"You need to calm down, Brother." Then to Boggs. "Harry, I need you to find Jack and bring him to me."

Jeb gave a suspicious look. "What the hell's going on? What do you want with Jack Holland?"

"Nothing. Go on, Harry."

"Yes, sir." He dashed off on his stubby rhino legs.

Quantrill watched him for a moment before turning back to Jeb, who was frantically hammering away at his BlackBerry. He noted the dark circles around his brother's eyes, the look of physical exhaustion. He looked like a war victim, a skeleton of human wreckage. For the first time, Quantrill realized the full extent of the inner turmoil his brother had gone through the past week.

"You're just making this harder on all of us, Jeb. You need to stop."

"You're treating this like an emergency response when you should be on your knees praying for forgiveness. Don't you realize what we've done? We've murdered innocent people. The waste operation is finished and so are we. We're going to go to prison the rest of our lives for this."

"I've already told you we ain't going to prison. We didn't do anything wrong. Besides, you don't know if anyone's died besides Ed Stewart."

"Like hell I don't." He held up his BlackBerry. "The earthquake was a 7.8—it's already all over the Net."

"Where's the epicenter?"

"Twenty miles east of Castle Rock." He clicked a button. "The death toll is expected to reach a thousand or more." He looked up from the screen and shook his head with disgust. "You and I are officially about to become mass murderers, Brother. Doesn't that make you feel proud?"

Quantrill felt a sudden shortness of breath.

"I'm finished with this fucking company."

"But there's still no proof. How could there be no seismic activity for ten years and then suddenly a 6.6 and 7.8? There weren't even any foreshocks before either quake. If our injection operation was the cause, why is there no correlation between the injection volume and the earthquakes? First we split the flow then we reduced it and yet the earthquakes got worse? How is that possible?"

"I don't know and I don't care. There's only one choice now—we have to turn ourselves in."

"What? Have you lost our mind?"

"It's the only thing that makes sense anymore."

"Stop it, you know that's not an option. You're assuming we caused the quakes yet you still don't have any proof. How can you explain the fact that the epicenters are more than fifteen miles apart from one another and more than fifteen miles from the injection well network?"

"Maybe the rupture is occurring along different segments of the fault or in associated faults."

"The first quake was fifteen thousand feet down in the Precambrian bedrock. How can you explain this new one when we've been injecting in the Hygiene and Dakota five to ten thousand feet above the bedrock?"

"I don't know, but it's happening. Maybe the timing isn't so important. Maybe the earthquakes are resulting from the injection into the deep zone and it's just a delayed effect."

"You don't have the foggiest idea what's causing these tremors. Now I understand that we have to shut down for awhile just to be safe. But once we make repairs, we're going to resume operations at gravity flow. You and Wes are going to put your heads together and come up with an injection program that doesn't cause any earthquakes. Do you understand?"

"Are you out of your fucking mind?" He started walking away.

"Where are you going?"

His brother didn't respond. Then after taking a few steps, he turned back around, his face filled with shame. "Can you imagine what Ma and Pa would think of us? Can you imagine?"

HE STARTED OFF AGAIN and Quantrill felt a wave of panic. "Where are you going?" he asked again.

"You know damn well where I'm going. To turn myself in."

"Y-You can't do this."

"Like hell I can't."

Following after him, Quantrill grabbed his arm as he came to the edge of the atrium. Below on the first floor, the full-sized prehistoric replicas glinted in the fading sunlight filtering down from the greenhouse roof. The twenty-foot-long *Ceratosaurus* looked uncannily lifelike with its rows of gleaming teeth and its thick counterbalancing tail held high off the ground as it swooped in on its prey *Stegosaurus*. For an instant, Quantrill imagined himself as the attacking ceratosaur and his brother the plate-backed herbivore.

He jerked hard on his brother's arm, spinning him around. "You can't do this—we have to talk this through."

"Get your fucking hands off me."

He pushed Quantrill away; the CEO chased after him and grabbed him again. "You're not listening to me! You can't do this!"

His brother tried to jerk his arm away, but this time Quantrill held on tight, refusing to let go. They were standing right next to the railing, directly above the battling dinosaurs.

"I just want to talk to you!"

"We're done fucking talking! We're going to jail!"

"Stop, Brother—we can work this out!"

"Let me go!" With a firm tug, he yanked himself free and started off again.

"Just listen to me!"

But his brother was beyond listening. He made for the stairs. As he reached for the handrail, Quantrill caught up with him and tried to take him in a bear hug.

"Just listen!" he pleaded.

But this time, Jeb would have none of it. He wheeled and punched Quantrill in the jaw. Quantrill's head jerked back, but he maintained his balance.

For a moment, they looked at one another, stunned.

It was then that the first aftershock hit.

A sudden sharp jolt followed by a sea-like rolling beneath their feet. Then the second aftershock rocked the building as another pressure wave surged upward from deep within the earth. This time the ground motion was even fiercer and Quantrill was thrown down the stairs. Below in the atrium, he could hear the sound of glass shattering and objects falling to the floor as the display cases and life-sized replicas were further destroyed. The terrifying cycle was repeated yet again as a third aftershock hit. Then, as abruptly as it had started, the shaking stopped.

Slowly, Quantrill rose to his feet. He looked around for his brother, but didn't see him anywhere. He thought back to the tornado when they were kids when he had set out in the thick curtain of dust to find Jeb.

"Brother, where are you?"

No answer.

"Brother!"

He heard a little grunt, saw a hand on the railing. He went to the edge.

Jeb was holding on with one hand for dear life. Directly below him, a glass case packed with fossils had toppled into the Neanderthal-cave bear exhibit, knocking over the bruin and one of the Neanderthal hunters. A black-sooted spear point that had been dislodged from the fallen hunter projected upward from the glass case.

"Brother, help me," pleaded Jeb, his face reddening under the strain.

Quantrill hesitated.

"Brother! Goddamnit, help me!"

If he came to his brother's aid, wouldn't Jeb still just go to the police and ruin them both? Why save him if all he could look forward to was life in prison?

He reached out and grabbed his brother's free hand. "All right, I'll help you. But you have to promise me you won't go to the police."

"Fuck you! I'd rather die!"

Quantrill felt a swell of panic; he didn't want to let his brother fall to his death, but what choice did he have if Jeb stubbornly persisted? "Just hold on. We can work this out."

"It's too late, Brother. We're going to burn in hell!"

"You've got to listen to reason. We didn't mean for this to happen."

"But it did happen and we're to fucking blame!"

"No one has to know. I promise to shut down the operation permanently. Our margins will go way down, but our infrastructure is in place and we'll still be able to grow. We'll be even greener than before, I promise."

"You're fucking crazy!"

"I'm going to give you one last chance, Little Brother. Can you keep your mouth shut?"

"Fuck you!"

"Goddamn you, I'm not joking around. You must promise me. Don't do it for yourself, do it for Ma and Pa. They wanted more than anything else for us to be *somebody*. And now that we are, you just want to throw it all away?"

"You threw it away a long time ago. I looked up to you, you bastard!"

In the deep recesses of his mind, Quantrill knew what he was about to do was wrong, but he felt like a cornered animal. If Jeb had his way, there was no future for either of them beyond a prison cell. Goddamnit, Ma and Pa had raised him to do more than rot away behind bars!

"This is your last chance. If I agree to shut down the operation permanently, can you promise me you'll keep quiet?"

"Never!"

Quantrill steeled himself for what he now knew he had to do. "Then we have nothing more to say. Goodbye, Little Brother."

"I'll see you in hell!"

He released his grip, letting his brother fall.

In a frozen surreal moment, he saw it all: the look of surprise followed quickly by terror; the wind milling arms fighting against gravity; the spear jutting up from the broken glass case; the sharp flint tip piercing his brother's back and driving up through his chest; the helpless, impaled figure twitching and convulsing; the gargle of blood spewing from poor Jeb's mouth before his body went slack.

When it was over, Quantrill turned away from the ghastly sight. Thinking he was going to be sick, he steadied himself against the railing.

It was then he heard a sound.

The chuff of a shoe on the floor below.

He felt a wave of panic. "Who is it? Who's there?"

No response but the echo of his voice across the hollow atrium.

"Who's there?" he called out again.

This time he heard the soft crunch of broken glass underfoot. The sound seemed to come from near the front entrance.

He crept noiselessly down the stairs to have a better look. The late afternoon sunlight was fading rapidly, the front of the building in heavy shadow.

He heard a patter of running feet, caught a sudden flash of movement. He looked towards the revolving door and saw a figure scramble inside, spin through, and quickly exit the building.

"Stop!" he cried, but the figure dashed on towards the parking lot.

Suddenly Boggs came running up. "What is it? What's happening?"

The stodgy security chief spotted Jeb impaled on the floor below. A pair of shaggy-bearded Neanderthals stood above the cadaver clutching fire-hardened wooden spears. Boggs looked over the gory scene with cold analytical detachment for several seconds, taking in every detail without uttering a word or showing any trace of emotion, before dashing to the large window overlooking the parking lot to catch a glimpse of the fleeing person.

Quantrill stared down in funereal silence at his brother's blood-soaked corpse, punctured through the heart.

A moment later Boggs returned.

"I killed him, Harry," said Quantrill, shaking his head in disbelief. "I killed him just as Cain took the life of Abel. I had him one second and the next I just let go and he...he fell to his death."

"I'm sorry, sir—I know you loved him." There was a moment of tense silence then the security chief cleared his throat and spoke in a low, urgent voice. "That was Jack Holland I just saw from the window. He hopped in his car and drove off."

Quantrill did not respond. He continued to stare down in disbelief at his dead brother, feeling as though he was about to have one of his terrible migraines.

Boggs raised his voice. "I said that was Jack Holland, sir. He just fled the building and drove off in his car."

"So he must have seen what happened."

"That's affirmative." Boggs tipped his head down at the impaled corpse, growing paler by the minute. "He's an eyewitness. Not only that, but he has the engineering plans on a flash drive. He can cause a lot of problems, sir. A lot of problems."

Quantrill felt the hinges of his sanity about to loosen. He couldn't believe that the situation had deteriorated to the point where he had killed his own brother.

"We have to act fast, sir. There's no time to lose."

Act fast? Does he mean there has to be more killing?

"It's the only way. Your options are swiftly becoming limited."

The room began to spin and Quantrill felt dizzy, claustrophobic, as if he was caught up in a nightmare. How could he have let things get so out of hand? He could feel a migraine coming on and had to get back to his office where his lidocaine nasal spray was.

"Sir, I told you it's time to call in Mr. Sperry. He can make all of this go away."

"It will never go away," muttered Quantrill, staring down at the mangled body, taking in the expression of betrayal and agony on the ravaged face. In that eerily surreal moment, he couldn't help but feel overwhelming self-loathing for what he'd done.

"I know you already miss your brother, sir, but time will heal the wounds. You cannot afford to waste another second. My man can have all of this neatly wrapped up within two days."

Quantrill slowly turned away from the skewered cadaver, still not quite believing what had happened. In that instant, the all-powerful energy tycoon looked old and infirm, like a mere shadow of what he had once been.

"Sir, there isn't much time. We have to move *now*."

Another heavy, reluctant sigh. "All right, you win, Harry. Call your man and have him stand by."

"Yes, sir."

"In the meantime, I'm going to pay my final respects to my poor dead brother."

CHAPTER 42

HIGHEAGLE parked his battered Ford pickup on 18th Street since reporters had laid claim to the entire east side of the street in front of the National Earthquake Information Center. He and Nina hopped out and walked swiftly towards the entrance on Illinois. He carried a nylon satchel and rolled-up maps, Nina a leather courier pack overflowing with EPA files. Once they reached the entrance, they headed straight for the elevators.

The walls of the public display room facing the elevator were covered with enlarged photographs of the devastation wrought by several of the world's major earthquakes: Kuril Islands, Japan, 1958, 8.7; Prince William Sound, Alaska, 1964, 9.2; Loma Prieta, Northern California, 1989, 7.0; Qaen, Iran, 1997, 7.1; off the coast of Northern Sumatra, 2004, 9.1. And the most recent deadly quake, last May 2008, Eastern Sichuan, China, 7.9. Looking at the destruction, Higheagle felt terribly small and insignificant, which was precisely how he had felt during today's earthquake.

They rode the elevator to the fifth floor, got off, walked down a corridor, past small exterior offices and walls covered with seismograms and colorful geologic cross-sections, and stopped behind a gathering of people. Standing on his toes, Higheagle saw Nickerson addressing twenty or more reporters. The styluses on the seismographic canisters behind him were busy scratching away while red lights flickered on the digital earthquake watch board overhead.

They continued further down the hall to a smaller room with a glass window that looked into the Seismic Drum Room where Nickerson was speaking. At the table in the center of the room, two scientists studied large printouts with squiggly red lines. Several others were busily hammering away at computer keyboards along the walls of the room.

Higheagle tapped gently on the window. Nickerson looked up and saw them. In the artificial light of the Drum Room, Higheagle noticed how haggard he looked. The media had been camped out here practically all week and it showed in the dark circles around his eyes. After answering a reporter's question, he looked back at them, held up five fingers, and pointed down the hallway. Higheagle realized that he was signaling to them that he would meet them in five minutes in his office. A handful of reporters on the other side of the glass turned and gave him and Nina the once over, wondering why they warranted the special attention of the NEIC director.

The two scientists walked out of the room and down the hallway to Nickerson's office. Higheagle was surprised at how spartan his professional digs were. Nickerson was, after all, the chief of the USGS National Earthquake Information Center, state of the art the world over for earthquake recording and investigation. Apparently government cutbacks went all the way to the very top. They took seats in the two threadbare chairs in front of his cluttered metal desk and waited.

As promised, Nickerson stepped into the room five minutes later. "Thanks for rescuing me—it's like the Nuremberg trials in there," he said, closing the door behind him.

"That bad?" said Higheagle.

"Put it this way, they want me fired and replaced by the Earthquake Prophet. How's that for irony?" He stepped forward with his hand cordially extended, his medium-sized frame bedecked in a modest short sleeve button-up shirt, cotton pants, and scuffed-up brown leather shoes. "They've got to pin the blame on someone for this disaster. After last night's debate, I'm an easy target. By the way, were you guys tailed?"

"We lost 'em."

"You want to tell me about it?"

Higheagle looked at Nina and they smiled. "It's a long story," she said. "Maybe another time."

"Okay then where do you want to begin?"

Higheagle slipped off the rubber band on his blueprint. "Why don't we take a look at this map first. It shows the wellfield where I believe Quantrill is injecting the waste. Can we spread it out on your table here?"

"Yes, of course." The seismologist pushed his tall task stool to the side and cleared off the maps on the drafting table. Higheagle set his geological log book on the table and unfolded the colored map. The three of them quietly hunched over the map, studying it closely.

"Do you know how many people have been killed?" Nina asked the seismologist.

"Around four hundred so far, but it's still early. I would expect three or four times that number before the night is out. We've updated our preliminary moment magnitude estimate from 7.8 to 7.9. The three main aftershocks were 5.8, 6.1, and 5.4."

Shaking his head sadly, Higheagle pointed to the map. "Here's the waste facility and further to the east is the location of the pipeline that ruptured last Thursday. I've drawn the compass bearing of the line on the map. The projected pipeline comes within about two hundred feet of these three wells here: DW-105, IW-106, and SW-107. They're right next to

Quantrill's Sweetwater mineral water bottling plant. I think he may be using the plant as a front."

"What do the symbols stand for?"

"DW for deep well, IW for intermediate, and SW for shallow. I believe Quantrill's using an old oil line to pump wastewater from the facility to the wells. Once the fluids reach the wells, they inject it down into three different zones."

"What depth are the wells perforated from?"

Higheagle opened his geological log notebook. "DW-105 is screened around ten thousand feet below ground surface, in Precambrian schist and gneiss. Intermediate well IW-106 is screened at around seven thousand feet in the Jurassic Dakota and Lakota Sandstones and the Morrison Formation. And shallow well SW-107 is perforated across the Hygiene Sandstone, about four thousand feet below grade."

"I see. But this still doesn't prove that Quantrill is using them as injection wells."

"No, but this does." Higheagle pointed to the well log for DW-105. "You see, each well has been recorded as a dry hole. The drill stem tests showed no indications of petroleum hydrocarbons, either as gas or liquid, in DW-105, which was drilled first. And that goes for each of the major production zones, all of which were tested. Why would Quantrill set casing if the holes were dry?"

"The answer is he wouldn't," said Nickerson, finishing the thought. "So he completed three dry hole wells in an area that he knew had no production capability. Why? Because he knew they would be used as liquid waste injection wells, not as oil or gas wells. The only problem is, all this time, he hasn't just been pumping the waste fluids into never-never land, he's been injecting it into a series of blind thrust faults in the metamorphic basement. I should have seen this. Our focal mechanism and balanced cross-section work on the first quake suggested that significant fluid pressure was required to initiate rupture."

"Okay, hold on you two—Structural Geo was a few years back for me," said Nina. "What's a blind thrust?"

Nickerson instantly launched into a doctorate level discussion of the characteristics of the deeply buried or "blind" faults, which could not be seen at the earth's surface. He first described how blind thrusts were low-angle reverse faults in which one mass of rock slid up and over another, like a child's triangular wood block being pushed up the inclined surface of another block to make a rectangle. Next he demonstrated how the concealed thrust faults were closely associated with large folds, violently contorted rock layers like the rumples in a rug when pushed along a floor. Finally, he explained how the folds in deeply buried rocks were produced by repeated earthquakes along the faults that were linked with them.

Higheagle recognized immediately what a strikingly novel concept this truly was. If correct, it meant that geologists had, for the past two centuries, misconstrued countless folds in tectonically active areas as the product of slow and steady deformation of rock, as taffy is bent between a pair of fingers, instead of as the product of punctuated bursts of movement. It meant that foothills and mountain belts could grow by earthquakes, dangerous ones far below the surface that scientists didn't know about and politicians didn't care about. There was nothing gradualistic about the process. It was episodic, catastrophic, and far more terrifying than the slow bending of crust over millions of years.

"So there you have it," concluded Nickerson with a flourish. "We've got a major blind thrust problem on our hands. The increased pore pressure from the injected waste has lowered the shearing resistance of the rocks along the fault planes and is triggering massive earthquakes. It's Rocky Mountain Arsenal all over again—only magnified more than a thousand fold."

Nina looked puzzled. "Rocky Mountain Arsenal?"

"The Army was injecting hazardous waste down an injection well from 1962 to 1965 and causing small earthquakes. The largest was a 5.3. The strange thing is the earthquakes continued after the injection program was terminated."

Higheagle thought: *So the formation pressures were still high enough to generate earthquakes. Which means that these recent quakes could continue for awhile even if Quantrill stops injecting.*

"So more people could die even if we put a stop to all this?" gasped Nina.

The seismologist nodded solemnly. "I considered Quantrill's facility a possible source. But once I saw that it was nearly thirty miles away from the epicenter of the first quake, I tucked the thought away. I convinced myself that the earthquakes were the result of adjustments going on in the deep crustal blocks. Because the distance from the epicenter was so great, I never considered that Quantrill might be using Sweetwater as a cover."

"Has there been any historical seismicity in the area?" asked Higheagle.

"There was a 3.0 west of Limon in 1963. The problem is that it occurred more than twenty kilometers deeper than the last two quakes and the slippage wasn't along a blind thrust."

"Anything more recent at shallow depth?"

"There have been a few in the last few years. All below 1.0—background."

"How close in depth were they to the recent quakes?" asked Nina.

"The hypocenters have generally been about five kilometers down. That's about fifteen thousand feet, roughly the same depth as last week's quakes. In comparison, the hypocenter of today's main event and the three big aftershocks was seven kilometers down. I could kick myself now, but frankly we've never gotten too excited about anything less than a 4.5. That's what our earthquake alarms are set for. We simply don't have the manpower to evaluate the small events in any detail. There are too many larger ones going on around the world all the time that require our attention."

Higheagle noticed something on the map. "Hmm, that's surprising."

"What's that?" asked Nina.

"Quantrill must have planned the disposal operation since at least 1995."

"Why 1995?"

"That's the year the three injection wells were constructed." He pointed to the map. "Where would the epicenters be on here?" he asked Nickerson.

The seismologist ran his index finger across the blueprint. "The epicenter of the first earthquake and the ensuing minor aftershocks was here, twenty miles east of Limon. The epicenter of today's quake and the three big aftershocks was approximately twenty miles further west."

Higheagle marked the two epicenters on his map with a red ink pen, grabbed the engineer scale ruler on the map table, and measured the map distance from each epicenter to the well cluster. Then, using a calculator, he quickly computed the actual distances using the scale of the map. When he was finished, he set the ruler down and looked at the other two.

"The distance from the well cluster to the epicenter of the first earthquake is fifteen miles."

"And the distance to the second epicenter?"

"Twenty-four miles."

Nickerson scratched his chin. "So the quakes are moving west."

"Quantrill was smart enough to install his injection wells far enough from his facility so that, if any earthquakes occurred, they could never be directly linked to his operation."

"Probably figured that whatever earthquakes there were would be small. Anything less than 4.5 wouldn't even trigger our alarms and would be assumed to be the result of normal crustal adjustment, oil field subsidence, or secondary recovery. Especially since a 3.0 was recorded thirty miles away in 1963 and since Colorado has had at least a few around 5.0 in the last hundred and fifty years. This is where Jeb comes in."

"What do you mean?"

"Well, I'll bet he studied the Rocky Mountain Arsenal, Rangely Oil

Field, and Trinidad data and calculated that if he kept the flow under a few hundred gpm and switched periodically from one injection well to another, they could eliminate the earthquakes, or at least manage them down into the 1.0 to 2.0 range where they wouldn't draw any attention. At the same time, they had to be prepared. That's why they placed the injection wells so far away and why they set up their own seismograph network. They had to cover their bases. From the fluid testing program at the Arsenal, they would have known that the Precambrian metamorphics could take water at four hundred gallons per minute under more than six hundred pounds of pressure. So if they distribute the flow among two or three different formations, the focal mechanisms would be all over the place. Here at the NEIC, we wouldn't be able to pinpoint what was going on, or maybe not even care if the quakes were just microevents in the 1.0 to 2.0 range. It also explains why Quantrill has built all of his facilities to the most stringent seismic design code."

"Ingenious—yet incredibly fucked up," said Nina. "Which is precisely why we can't let the bastard get away with it."

"You're right," said Higheagle. "We have to find a way to stop this."

They all looked at one another. "But the question is how?" said Nickerson.

CHAPTER 43

"THE FIRST STEP IS TO FIND THOSE INJECTION WELLS," said Nina after a moment's reflection. "We have to be certain they're being used to dispose of chemical waste. We also have to find out how Sweetwater fits into all this. Like you said, it must be some kind of front."

"You're right—that's got to be the next step," concurred Higheagle. "The question is can we get in?"

She looked at him evenly. "No, the real question is, can we get in without getting caught?"

Nickerson was shaking his head. "Now just hold on you two. If you think Quantrill's going to just let you sashay on out to his property and poke around, you've got another thing coming. Besides, you'd be trespassing and committing probably a half dozen other crimes to get the information you want. And how do you know he hasn't booby trapped those wells? At the very least he's bound to have a high-tech security system in place or guards, or maybe both." The seismologist zeroed in on Higheagle sternly. "And what about those goons he sent to threaten you. Do you really want them to pay you another visit?"

Nina realized that Nickerson was right: they hadn't thought this thing through. Still, they had to do something.

"None of what you just said changes the fact that we have to stop these bastards," she said, with a trace of defiance.

"We will. But we've also got to proceed carefully."

"As Nina says, the first thing is to locate the injection wells. Once we've done that we can bring the case before the proper authorities."

Nickerson raised a skeptical brow. "And just who are the *proper* authorities?"

"Nina's boss for starters." Higheagle looked at her. "Right?"

She realized that she hadn't thought that far ahead yet. She wasn't even sure that, if there was a federal criminal investigation, her department would be the one to handle it since the Justice Department and the legal arm of the EPA, the Criminal Investigations Division, were the ones that typically handled environmental crimes. Though she worked for the U.S. government, she was reluctant to hand the investigation over to a bunch of lawyer-bureaucrats. But what choice did they have?

"I would definitely report whatever we find out to Richard, but the problem is the case will most likely fall outside the EPA's jurisdiction."

Nickerson frowned. "Whose jurisdiction would it fall under?"

"The Justice Department would likely take the lead role on the case, working with the EPA's Criminal Investigations Division. But regardless of who we turn to, we still need to find out about the wells and pipeline for ourselves, and also how Sweetwater fits in. I wouldn't feel comfortable taking this to my boss or anyone else without absolute proof."

"Me neither," agreed Higheagle. "When we're ready to go down that road, there's a guy in the FBI that I'm planning on calling."

"Who's that?"

"His name is Josh Kane. He's a Special Agent in the Denver office."

"How do you know him?"

"I grew up with him. He's a friend. But we're jumping ahead of ourselves here. There's no way we're calling in Special Agent Kane or anyone else until we have irrefutable evidence of wrongdoing. Right now we're just making an educated guess. If we're right about Quantrill then no one's going to care about a little trespassing. When the final tally is complete, this earthquake will have killed a lot of innocent people and caused billions in damage. The EPA and FBI are going to be far more interested in who's responsible for the deaths than how the information on those responsible was gathered."

Nickerson shook his head. "I don't know. This is sounding awfully risky—we just don't know what we're getting into here. There's also Mark Kelso to think about."

"What about Kelso?"

"He's been poking around to the east of Quantrill's waste facility and out at the Sweetwater plant. Just before the quake, he left me a message saying he may have found something."

"Where is Kelso now?"

"I don't know. Probably still out there."

"You haven't heard from him since the quake?"

"Unfortunately not. I suppose he could be hurt or dead."

We should try and get in touch with him, thought Nina. "If he's still alive," she said, "we need to talk to him and find out what he knows. He might be able to help us."

"I agree with you, but I still think you two are rushing into this."

"We don't have a choice at this point. We have to find that well cluster."

"I'm not going to be able to talk you two out of this, am I?"

Higheagle shook his head. "Nope. So you might as well make sure we get it right."

"Why don't you come with us?" proposed Nina.

"I couldn't leave even if I wanted to. Those media hounds in the other room would just follow me and I'd be out of a job before the night's through. I'm on thin ice as it is with the director. If I got caught snooping around one of Quantrill's properties, I'm afraid that would be the final straw."

"That's all right, we'll take care of it," said Higheagle. "Besides, if you stay here, you'll be able to follow through in case something happens to us."

"Wait a second," interjected Nina. "What do you think is going to happen to us?"

"Remember the opening car trunk scene from *Goodfellas*. That's a good place to start."

She felt her heart skip a beat. *I wish I hadn't asked.*

"Do you think the pipeline may have ruptured somewhere?" Higheagle asked Nickerson.

"The earthquake was a 7.9. It definitely ruptured somewhere."

"If we can collect soil samples along a rupture point like I did at the facility, we can document the types of contaminants present and tie them back to the facility. We might even be able to collect vapor samples from the well vaults if there are any leaks in the entry pipe."

"Sounds like the makings of a dangerous plan. I don't think I want to hear any more. Just promise me that you two will get in and out of there quickly. Take pictures, collect samples, use an organic vapor sniffer if you have to, but move fast and don't take any unnecessary risks. Okay?"

There was a rap at the door and a woman in her early thirties poked her head in. "Dr. Nickerson, the reporters are asking for you again."

"Tell them I'll be there in one minute, Brigid. Thank you."

The door closed.

Nickerson gave a groan as he stood up from his chair. "Recharge your cell phones and keep them on at all times. And remember, in and out fast, keep me informed, and don't try any hero stuff."

She looked at Higheagle. He winked at her.

"Don't worry, it will be a piece of cake," said the Cheyenne with a mock cocksure grin that made her chuckle inside.

"Piece of cake, my ass," snorted Nickerson, and he stepped out the door.

CHAPTER 44

WHEN QUANTRILL got off the phone with his brother's wife, Nancy, it dawned on him, for the first time in his life, that he might actually be evil. Five minutes earlier when he had dialed up her number, he had watched in silent disbelief as the ambulance drove off with the body of Jeb and three other employees. Now, after having spent the last few minutes lying to and consoling Nancy, whom he had known for more than thirty years, he was beginning to come to terms with the unsettling epiphany of what he had become.

So that's it then...I *am* evil.

He had loved his younger brother as much as he had ever loved anyone—and yet he had murdered him in cold blood. How was he capable of such a desperate and heartless act?

Now he had his answer: *he was evil.*

And yet, he didn't feel evil.

He knew he should have hated himself for what he had done. Should have hated that he had forever transformed his life into something repugnant and immoral. Should have hated himself for bringing shame and dishonor to the Quantrill family. In a moment of mindless fury, he had destroyed the most important person in his life, a man who had brought him unspeakable joy over the years. Ultimately, he had not just killed a brother, best friend, or a coveted business partner—he had killed a part of himself.

And yet, he didn't feel the overwhelming sense of self-loathing from the act itself that he had thought he would feel. True, he felt guilt and shame. But mostly he felt incomplete, lost and uncertain in an uncertain world, a world where he no longer had his loyal business partner of thirty-five years and brother of more than six decades at his side. It was as though he had lost his right arm.

So I'm evil then. So be it. I've still got to carry on.

He looked solemnly around his once grand office, now a wilderness of devastation. The famous paintings decorating his walls and priceless artifacts in the glass cases were severely damaged. The furniture was in disarray. The carpet was filled with shards of broken glass and chips of lathe and plaster. And a gaping crack tore through the wall like a lightning bolt, zigzagging from one corner to the next. He felt like an emperor whose empire had crumbled around him and whose citizenry had abandoned him.

The deep well injection program had been risky, true, but at the same time it had been absolutely necessary from a financial standpoint. Without it, he and Jeb would never have been able to expand their operations into sustainability, clean energy, and all things "green." At the same time, he realized that his brother had been right all along: they had deluded themselves by thinking they could control the mysterious, unpredictable world far beneath the earth's surface without at least some collateral damage.

And now it was too late to turn back. He had crossed some terrible line and there was no going back. If he were to survive, more people would have to be silenced—it was as simple as that. Yet, he couldn't bring himself to unleash Mr. Sperry—not yet. A part of him would rather die or go to prison for the rest of his life than take any more lives. But the other part of him, the practical side, told him to just get on with the dirty business of tying up the loose ends and eliminating any and all threats. After all, he was a businessman not a priest, a cold pragmatist not a warm and fuzzy idealist.

His cell phone vibrated. He glanced at the caller ID number, recognized it as Senator Tanner's. He punched the green button, accepting the call.

"Senator Tanner."

"Thank God, you're alive Chuck. I was worried about you."

"Thank you, Bill."

"But I'm also mad as hell. What in God's name have you done?"

Quantrill was taken aback. "What are you talking about?"

"I spoke to Interior Secretary Jackson on your behalf and the next thing I know I'm being summoned to the senate majority leader's house."

"You were summoned to Gregory Vickers' house?"

"I've been told to discontinue my association with you, Chuck."

"Why?"

"There have been whispers."

"Whispers?"

"That what you're doing at that plant of yours may be causing these terrible earthquakes. Tell me the truth. What the hell is going on?"

Quantrill felt a sudden jolt of panic. "Nothing's going on," he said in his defense, playing the shocked, innocent victim. "I want to know who's making these allegations because there's going to be hell to pay!"

"Calm down—no one's making any allegations. But if you're involved in something, you'd damn well better tell me. I need to know if I'm going to get any blowback."

"There's nothing to tell."

"Then what's causing these earthquakes? They're happening right in your backyard."

"They're as much a mystery to me as they are to you. Hell, the only one who seems to know anything about them is this Earthquake Prophet, Dr. Patey. Dr. Nickerson at the USGS doesn't have a clue as to what's causing them."

"Dr. Nickerson is probably going to be fired over all this. That's what my sources tell me anyway."

Fired? Now that would be a stroke of good luck, he thought as a knock sounded at the door.

"Come in," he snapped.

Boggs and Wesley Johnston stepped meekly into the room, closing the door behind them.

Quantrill signaled that he would be with them in a moment. Then to Tanner he said, "I've got to go, Bill. Now you best disregard these rumors you're hearing because there ain't a grain of truth to any of them."

"You promise you have nothing to do with these quakes?"

Quantrill turned away from Boggs and Johnston, covered the phone, and responded in an agitated whisper. "How dare you ask me that? My brother Jeb's dead because of what happened today."

"Oh dear. I'm sorry, Chuck, I had no idea."

"They just took his body away."

"I apologize. I'm so sorry."

"I've got to go, Bill. Goodbye." He punched off and looked at Boggs and Johnston. The security chief stood there as solid and loyal as a bulldog, hands crossed in his front, a quiet look of competence and determination on his walrus-mustached face. Johnston looked nervous as a cat.

"Talk to me, gentlemen."

They approached his battered English oak desk. Johnston cleared his throat, fidgeted with his hands before speaking with bland technical precision. "I shut off the injection well conveyance line and took flow meter readings from the control panel. Prior to shutdown, we lost about twenty-five percent total flow along the line. We have flow meters set up at the pumping stations every three miles, so I know we lost the majority of flow the last six miles."

"You're talking about the piping run furthest from the facility and closest to the injection well cluster?"

"Yes, sir." He inclined his head toward Boggs. "I haven't inspected the line yet to find out precisely where the leaks are. But I would recommend posting additional security along the last two sections and near the injection wells."

Quantrill leaned forward in his high-backed leather chair. "What about the damage report for the facility itself?"

"No visible surface rupture or cracking in the storage tanks or treatment units that I could see. There was some leakage associated with one joint leading to the carbon unit and some minor drum spillage, but that was it. The liquid in the tanks sloshed around quite a bit, but the fluid levels have stabilized. Overall, the damage was far less than I expected. I'd have to say that our rigorous seismic design has paid off."

Quantrill gave a nod of approval. Whatever else happened, at least the haz waste facility was intact. Thus far, that was the only silver lining.

"Does the EPA have any jurisdiction over the injection well pipeline?" Boggs asked Johnston. "What I mean is, will inspectors come out again to check the line?"

"The Colorado Geological Survey will come out again, and maybe the Oil and Gas Commission, but not the EPA," answered Johnston. "Their jurisdiction only covers the facility."

Quantrill frowned. "We need to get that line repaired quickly and control the inspections."

"We'll have to keep them away for a few days until the line can be replaced," said Johnston. "I'd wager that there's not more than a handful of rupture points, and it will be obvious where from either surface staining or OVM readings."

"You'll need to check that line first thing tomorrow," said Quantrill. "You should have one of the tankers spray some crude near the breaks too. As for tonight, have security patrol the last two sections of pipeline around the injection wells. What about our power?"

"The phone lines and electrical are okay. I don't know if we've lost the high-voltage line surrounding the injection wells."

"We can worry about that tomorrow. You've done a fine job, Wes. Go on home now and get some rest."

"Yes, sir. And I'm real sorry about Jeb."

"I am too—he will be dearly missed," said Quantrill, and he meant it.

When Johnston left, Boggs pulled up a chair and sat down. Quantrill felt the tension in the air, the sense of anticipation. He knew what Boggs was about to say.

"Time is running out, sir. You have to make a decision."

Without responding, Quantrill reached into his drawer and calmly pulled out a Sig Sauer P-229 nine-millimeter pistol.

Boggs eyes widened. "Sir?"

Ignoring him, the CEO calmly jerked back the gleaming nickel slide and pointed the pistol at his security chief.

Boggs licked his dry lips. "Sir, I don't know what you're…"

Quantrill said nothing. He continued to point the pistol at his forehead, drawing out the moment.

"You know the problem with a gun, Harry?" he asked rhetorically.

A bead of sweat appeared on Boggs' heavy brow. He shook his head.

"The weakest, most incompetent, stupidest, cruelest man on the face of the earth can kill the best and brightest among us in the blink of an eye."

"'God created man—Samuel Colt made them both equal.'"

"My point exactly. The gunman doesn't have to have any actual skill. He can take away everything a man has—and everything he's ever going to have—without any ability whatsoever."

Boggs nodded, but Quantrill could tell he wasn't sure what to make of him. Slowly, he lowered the pistol and laid it down on his desk.

"I've had this gun for twenty years and not once have I ever fired it. I don't even know why I own the damned thing."

"Mr. Quantrill, sir, I understand what a difficult time this is for you with what happened to your brother. But you have to make a decision. Jack Holland, Higheagle, and the others pose a serious threat. Left unchecked, that threat will lead to your downfall and that of Quantrill Ventures. If you are to retain your business empire, you are going to have to play the game."

"So that's what this is, a game?"

"I didn't mean it like that, sir. I just meant that time is running out and you have to make a decision. Discontinuing the operation, repairing the broken line, throwing out some crude oil is not going to save you or your company. You are going to have to take more...*extreme measures*."

Quantrill took a deep breath and closed his eyes. His mind reached back to tossing pebbles with Jeb along the Brazos, then to the summer they drove through the Hill Country with Ma after Pa had died, telling her about the energy company they were putting together. Ma was skeptical at first, but Quantrill remembered the eventual glimmer of pride in her eyes that her two boys could possess such lofty aspirations. Goddamn if that day hadn't been something! And then when he and Jeb had managed to transform their little startup into a Fortune 100 outfit and enjoy thirty-five years of professional triumph. Now if that wasn't the American Dream, what in the hell was?

The dream stayed with him a moment longer, like a pleasant breeze tickling his face, before drifting off. He thought of everything he stood to lose if the truth behind the waste operation and his brother's death were discovered. His good name, his life, his house, his family, his company, all his material possessions—everything would be in jeopardy. It suddenly dawned on him that he could not give it all up so easily. Survival mattered. And at this point was that not all he had to cling to? Was he not at war against those who would destroy him and everything he had built up? Was he not a soldier with his back against the wall and the enemy at the gates?

The answer that came to him was a resounding *Damn straight!* He was a soldier all right. He was at war, and during wartime, a soldier had to kill. Taking down those that posed a threat to him was absolutely necessary if he was to have any hope of surviving.

He looked at Boggs. They held each other's gaze for several seconds. When he spoke, his voice had a newfound conviction and bite of iron to it. "Call your man and have him take care of it. Pay him whatever he wants."

"Just Holland and Higheagle?"

"No, all of them."

"So we're clear: Kelso, Curry, and Nickerson too?"

"Yes, kill them all."

CHAPTER 45

HIGHEAGLE AND NINA stared raptly at the television screen, the steam spiraling upwards from their matching Denver Broncos coffee mugs. Nickerson was again speaking with the media; his frenetic pace apparently hadn't let up since they had left him an hour earlier. They had been switching between channels to obtain information on the damage and road closures from the 7.9 earthquake. Nickerson appeared every few minutes on both channels, as did his nemesis, the Earthquake Prophet, whose credibility had risen dramatically with his successful—or, according to the USGS, just plain lucky—prediction of the quake.

The temblor had devastated every town within a twenty-mile radius, rattled persons within a hundred-mile radius, and been felt by most people indoors within a three-hundred-mile radius. According to the newscast, the ground motion was generated by movement along a blind thrust fault seven kilometers below the earth's surface, a hypocenter slightly deeper than the previous 6.6 quake. The event was felt in all states bordering Colorado and in two places that did not—Hot Springs, South Dakota, and Little Rock, Arkansas. The death toll was over six hundred now—mostly from Castle Rock and the small towns to the east—but large numbers of people were reported to be trapped beneath fallen structures and the official tally would take another day or two to complete. Most overpasses and buildings within a ten-mile radius were severely damaged if not completely demolished.

As Nickerson disappeared from the screen, Patey reappeared. Higheagle went to the window. He was tired of the damned Earthquake Prophet and his triumphant *I-Told-You-So* declarations. True, the guy had called it like Nostradamus, but somehow it all seemed to come down to nothing more than plain coincidence, a random roll of the dice.

Peering out the window, Higheagle scanned the street for White Hair and his associate. He wondered if they had gotten a new set of wheels and were still on his tail. Or maybe Quantrill had reached his breaking point and was sending in his Jason Bourne guy—as Boggs had threatened he would do if Higheagle continued to have contact with Nina and Nickerson. The situation was getting out of control. Was it time to call in his friend Special Agent Kane of the FBI?

His thoughts were broken by the sound of a throttling engine. He gave a start. To his relief, he saw that it was just his grandfather driving up. The old chief parked and got out of the truck, pausing to stretch his knotty body before shambling towards the back door. A moment later the door opened, a light flicked on, and he appeared in the hallway just outside the kitchen, his silvery plaited hair twinkling in the light.

"It's crazy out there," he said without preamble as he hung his beaded elkskin jacket on the battered coat rack. "The supermarkets are flooded with people. Everyone's buying things up like it's the apocalypse." As he turned around and stepped into the kitchen, he noticed Nina. "Oh, I'm sorry, I didn't see you there." He stepped forward, hand extended. "You must be Nina Curry. My grandson's told me about you, but I have to admit you're even lovelier in person."

They shook hands. "Nice to meet you," she said, blushing.

"You look like a woman of fine breeding. I'll bet you're from back East and you went to prep school. Am I right?"

She smiled bashfully.

The old chief's eyes lit up. "I knew it. What prep school did you go to?"

"Miss Porter's."

"Hey, what a coincidence, that's where I went."

She laughed. "That's funny because Miss Porter's is an all-girl prep school."

The old chief gave a look of mock surprise. "It is? I always wondered why I didn't fucking fit in."

He delivered a fake punch to her arm and all three of them laughed. Higheagle could see that she wasn't quite sure what to make of the old scalawag, but somehow he seemed to have won her over.

"Sorry, I forgot to warn you about my grandfather. He's a Contrary."

"A Contrary?"

"A Cheyenne holy man who says and does things in opposites and likes to clown around. The best way to describe it is a holy warrior and merry prankster rolled into one."

"It's a ritual that goes back two centuries with our people, maybe longer," said the old man with an obvious note of pride.

"He's also a chief, tribal lawyer, and, most importantly, a consummate ladies man so I would watch your step around him."

"I'll be sure to," she said playfully.

John Higheagle surveyed the duffel bag on the floor. "Where are you two going? Don't you know we just had a big earthquake?"

"We're going out to investigate."

Nina appeared confused. "Wait, does he...?"

"Yes, he knows everything. He's like my Yoda."

"I have no choice—I'm much smarter than him. That's why I'm a chief."

Higheagle rolled his eyes. "He's modest too."

The old Contrary kicked at the duffel bag. "So where are you two heading?"

"We think we've located the injection wells. We're going to try and find them and collect samples."

"After our talk last night, I thought you had decided to let sleeping dogs lie."

"I changed my mind. I'm sorry, Grandfather, I should have told you."

"So you've decided to go to war with Quantrill." He looked at Nina. "Is this what you really want, or has my grandson talked you into this?"

She hesitated. "I think...well it's complicated...I mean...yes, it's what I want."

"That didn't sound very convincing."

"Okay how about this? We absolutely, one hundred percent cannot let Charles Quantrill and his cronies at Quantrill Ventures get away with this."

"That's much better. But remember, if you're going to collect samples on Quantrill's property, you're going to need to pack some serious firepower. You've taken that into consideration, right?"

Nina looked worriedly at Higheagle *"Firepower? Did he just say firepower?"*

"He's just kidding."

"No, I'm not. I'm telling you, you're going to need to bring it if you're going to venture out to Quantrill's. If he's causing these earthquakes like you say, he's going to do whatever he can to keep people from poking around on his property. He didn't get to be a billionaire by failing to cover his backside."

"Stop it, Grandfather. You're scaring her."

She crossed her arms. "I can handle myself, thank you very much."

The old chief grinned. "I like her—she's feisty."

"I'm so glad you approve." She rolled her eyes sarcastically then turned to Joseph. "If you think we need to arm ourselves then I'm not going to be the one to argue with you. But let's not lose sight of our objective: to find the wells and collect samples. I'll be damned if I'm going to go to my boss and ask him to get the Department of Justice or EPA Enforcement involved without hard proof."

The old chief nodded with vigorous approval. "Did you learn to talk like that at Miss Porter's?"

"No, that was Princeton."

"Impressive. You know my grandson went to Dartmouth. Full scholarship."

"I can tell you're quite proud of him."

"He's okay."

"Enough you two!" Higheagle pulled out his field supply and equipment list so they could do one final check. "We need to get going. But first we need to make sure we have everything."

"Good idea," said the chief and he started from the room.

"Wait, Grandfather, where are you going?"

But the old man didn't respond. Higheagle sighed with exasperation and looked back at his list. "All right, we've got a hand auger, GPS plugger unit, binoculars, ice chests filled with ice, chain-of-custody forms, soil sample tubes, vacuum pump, Tedlar bags for the vapor samples, organic vapor meter, Draeger tubes for VOCs, well location map, two flashlights, pipe locating magnetometer....I guess that's it."

She snatched the list from him and looked it over. "You forgot the full tank of gas, case of beer, and bag of weed. College road trip, here we come."

The old Contrary walked back in carrying a rifle, shotgun, and two boxes of ammo.

Higheagle waved him off like an umpire. "We're not going to need any of that crap so you might as well put it all away. We're going to sneak in and out without being seen."

"Bullshit. Hope for the best, plan for the worst—that's what I always say." He shoved one of the weapons into his grandson's hands along with a box of spare magazines.

"What is that?" exclaimed Nina.

"Ithaca 12-gauge slide-action shotgun—I got it for him when he was twelve years old. It's got a five-round magazine and a duckbill choke."

"Duckbill choke?"

"Yeah, to increase the kill ratio. Look here, the shells are loaded and ejected on the underside of the receiver. That way you don't have hot, smoking casings flying into your face when you're a left handed shooter like me and my grandson. Yes siree, you don't need to be a CIA sniper to take someone down with this scattergun. It'll drop anything weighing a quarter ton or less in its tracks as long as you point it in the right direction."

"Okay, that was too much information," said Nina.

"You think?" quipped Higheagle. "But you've got to admit it's a beauty."

"But not as good as Yellow Boy here." The old chief held up his Model 1866 Winchester lever-action repeating rifle adorned, in the Plains Indian way, with brass tacks, vermillion, and eagle feathers. "This gun belonged to our ancestor High Eagle, who fought Custer at the Little Big Horn." He yanked back on the lever action and peered down the sight of the trusty old repeater, ravaged by time and yet seemingly all the better for it. "They sure as hell don't make 'em like this baby anymore."

"I don't think they make them like *you* anymore either," said Nina, drawing a hearty laugh from the two big Cheyennes. "By the way, are you and Yellow Boy coming with us?"

He grinned, exposing his dingy yellow teeth. "No, while you two are out roaming the prairie, I think Yellow Boy and I will stay right here and let Old Man Trouble come to us."

"Oh, come on, Grandfather, there's not going to be any trouble."

"Like hell there isn't. We're about to have the fight of our lives."

"What makes you say that?" asked Nina.

"Last night I had a vision. I dreamt of soldiers falling into camp."

"Soldiers falling into camp?"

"Yeah, that was the vision Sitting Bull had just before the Little Bighorn. And if memory serves, that was one hell of a fucking fight."

CHAPTER 46

USING A SMALL BUT POWERFUL PEN LIGHT, Mr. Sperry ran a professional eye over the rear door of the church. He saw no evidence it was triggered with an alarm, though he wouldn't know for certain until he broke in. He turned his attention to the lock. It was a simple pin tumbler, old but solid. In his expert criminal opinion, it would take less than a minute to pick it. If everything went smoothly, he would be in and out, with the job completed, in under three minutes.

This is going to be almost too easy, sport.

If this attorney Jack Holland thought he was safe hiding out in the house of the Lord, he had another thing coming to him. Boggs had said he was probably on the run. So why then had he gone home and talked to his wife for twenty minutes? And after that, how could he have been so dumb as to let someone follow him to a church? In the age of Twitter, Facebook, Google, and a dozen other Internet tools specifically designed to track down people whether they wanted to be tracked down or not, even a total amateur could get all the information he needed to locate someone in less than ten minutes.

All the same, he liked being in the field. He took a deep breath of the cool Halloween night air. Years ago, when he was fresh out of Yale and doing absolutely nothing except living off his prodigious family inheritance, playing video games 24/7, and enduring endless lectures from his Philadelphia blue-blood father and mother about how he had to "get serious" and "pursue a career," his life had definitely lacked direction and he had yet to find his inner passion. But then—thanks to a cocaine-induced epiphany while getting blown by Cynthia R. Hathaway, the renowned senator's daughter—he had figured it all out.

He would become an assassin.

Now if that wasn't "getting serious" just what in the hell was? True, he had thought at the time, he would have to live a double life as well as endure long periods of planning and reconnaissance between short, punctuated bursts of hyper-violent activity. But at least no one could say he wasn't pursuing a career or that the work wasn't challenging. How could his parents fault him for discovering his true calling as they had urged him to do since his lackluster days at Phillips Exeter?

So he became a self-taught contract killer, reading every police report, blog, book, and technical article he could get his hands on covering firearms, infiltration tactics, disguises, and the black art of murder-for-hire. Three years and nine successful contracts later, he realized how ludicrous it had been for him to consider any other profession. He discovered that he was a natural born killer. To his pleasant surprise, his privileged upbringing and mannerisms made him virtually incognito to his generally upper-class victims before he drew them in close, dispatched them, and disappeared without a trace. No one ever expected an East Coast prepster, upper-class Brahmin to be a murderer—people like that only appeared in Patricia Hightower novels. Truth be told, it was almost too easy.

This was not to say that he was a cold, ruthless killing machine. He did not kill with robotic precision and icy sangfroid. In fact, for him each killing was intensely personal. Or *special*, as he liked to call it. He understood his victims, felt for them in his own unique way. He appreciated what was going through their minds in those final fateful moments. He could see it in on their faces. It was always the same. What he enjoyed most of all was that human beings that were so vastly different could go through precisely the same series of emotional responses just before they were killed. It always started with surprise and ended up with pure animal fear as they realized they had only moments before their lives came to a premature, unexpected end.

It was that final look that got him off. That was what made it all so—how else to say it?—exhilarating.

Hearing the distant yap of a dog, he froze in the shadows and scanned the bland residential neighborhood for the tenth time. A row of two-story upper-middle class homes, circa late-1950s, stared back at him impassively. The neighborhood was well lit, but there was not a soul on the street. That brought a little smile to the edges of his broad mouth.

Sticking the pen light between his teeth, he withdrew a foldover leather pouch containing lock picks. He carefully removed the two tools he needed to pick the lock, a tension tool and feeler pick. He inserted the tension tool first, which held the pins inside the lock down, then began to delicately probe with the feeler tool. Finally, after managing to align each of the pins along the shear line of the cylinder, he felt a little click. With what seemed like a will of its own, the cylinder turned and the door unlocked.

No alarm. I'm in!

He slipped inside quickly, closing the door behind him. Putting away his pen light and tools, he took a moment to adjust his high-density Kevlar vest, strapped across his midriff beneath his L.L. Bean duck-hunting jacket, as his eyes adjusted to the darkness. Though he doubted he would need a bullet-proof vest against tonight's lowly adversary, one could never be too careful. He took a moment to get his bearings. Weak moonlight filtered through a pair of narrow windows. He was in a foyer that branched into a series of hallways.

From the military-style shoulder holster beneath his jacket, he withdrew his Smith and Wesson M1911A1 .45 semi-automatic pistol with the seven-round magazine and Pachmayr grip. He then grabbed his custom-designed suppressor, twisting it in gently to the nose of his specially adapted handpiece. The Smith and Wesson's suppressor dampened the explosion in the chamber so that the pistol gave off only a *pfft-pfft* sound similar to a muffled staple gun.

Now he was ready to move.

He started down the hallway that appeared to lead to the main chapel. His movements were wary and deliberate, but also confident, the stalking alpha male in action. His eyes were as watchful as a night owl on the hunt, only more intense. Inside, the excitement was beginning to pick up now, as always.

When he reached an adjoining hallway, he peered cautiously around the corner.

That's when he saw him. An old man in a pair of flannel pajamas, lumbering down the hallway. Thirty feet away, unsuspecting but coming straight toward him.

He ducked back behind the wall. Luckily, the old man hadn't seen him, but what should he do? He listened to the slippered feet padding across the carpet. The guy was definitely not his mark, most likely the pastor who lived at the church.

As the anxious seconds ticked off, he knew there was but one option. He hated to kill an innocent, but neither could he afford to leave behind an eyewitness.

The man plodded towards him, the footsteps growing louder.

He fought the excitement and fear pulsing through his body. It wasn't easy to contain himself despite his countless hours of monk-like study and training. He felt powerful, manly, confident in a way that his blue-blood parents would have seriously appreciated though, had they known, they would have no doubt disapproved of his chosen profession.

A drop of sweat plunged down his nose as he picked up the rhythmic sound of the old man's breathing. He felt his muscles arch with eagerness, like a sprinter before the gun.

And then the old man was right there.

He popped him with two quick shots to the face. They were delivered with the surgical precision of a professional soldier, though in truth the silver-spoon Philadelphian had never received any formal military training. The soft hollow-point bullets drove the pastor backward, each individual projectile flattening on impact and doubling in circumference in the fraction of a second it took to obliterate the victim's brain and stop his heart. The sound of the discharging weapon, though muffled by the suppressor, was louder than expected, as was the thud when the old man fell to the floor.

Damn!

Jack Holland—his reason for being here—was still somewhere in the church, perhaps this very instant getting away. He pricked an alert ear toward the chapel, but he heard nothing.

Suddenly there was a crashing sound down the hallway, and with it came the frantic knowledge that the assignment was incomplete.

The mark is getting away!

Now he moved quickly, alpha male in overdrive.

Another crashing sound, metal furniture being pushed aside.

He tore into another gear, the gear of a jaguar. The sound of his lightweight Docksiders pattered like Mozart's Final Trilogy against the walls of the hallway. He rounded a small archway and there he was, face to face with the man he had come to kill.

"This is a House of God!" cried Jack Holland, backing against the wall.

The preppy assassin's square jaw tensed then relaxed. The air seemed to turn savagely hot and primitive, reminding him of the lion hunt his father had taken him on for his thirteenth birthday on the African savanna.

"Where's Pastor Danforth?"

"He's gone to a better place, I'm sure."

He moved forward, slowly, studying his victim's potential escape routes. A pernicious smile took root.

Options severely limited.

Jack Holland retreated, moving along the wall, fearfully. Mr. Sperry's look narrowed as hard and straight as a trunk of ponderosa pine. As he closed the distance between them to ten feet, he pointed the nose of the gun at his victim.

"He sent you, didn't he? He sent you to kill me."

"If you mean Mr. Charles Prometheus Quantrill—billionaire entrepreneur and leading citizen of the fine state of Colorado—then the answer is yes, sport."

"You'll burn in hell for this."

"Oh, I doubt that very much, Mr. Holland. Now please prepare yourself for your final opus."

The lawyer shook like a willow, sweat dripping from his forehead. The man's courage seemed to ebb away before Mr. Sperry's very eyes, as if a plug had been pulled.

The assassin closed in to point-blank range, his face slightly contorted.

"I'm staring at the face of the devil."

"No, sport, you're staring at a man made in God's own image. Ta-ta, Mr. Holland." Smiling punctiliously, he let loose with his silenced firearm.

Three shots. Jack Holland's face dissolved and he collapsed to the floor.

When it was over, Mr. Sperry calmly put away his pistol and again pulled out his pen light. He knelt down beside the body, frozen in a death pose like the ash-covered corpses he had seen at Pompeii during last summer's bicycle tour of Italy. The pen light illuminated the blood pouring out in a giant, inky pool from Jack Holland's head, but the assassin was unfazed. He had seen far worse mutilation at point-blank range a mere two months ago with a Wall Street financier who had bilked his clients out of hundreds of millions of dollars. Turning over the corpse, he removed a thin leather wallet from the victim's pants pocket. He kept the fifty, six twenties, and five dollar bill he found inside, along with all the credit cards, and chucked the wallet.

His assignment complete, he turned off his pen light and slipped out the front door, making sure to leave it unlocked.

Then, with the stealth of a wolf, Mr. Sperry disappeared into the night.

CHAPTER 47

QUANTRILL sat drumming his long, bony fingers at his desk, waiting by the phone. He was expecting a call from his wife Bunnie. She was at home, safe but still frightened. He wanted to go home and reassure her, but there was no way he could leave his office at this critical juncture. Mr. Sperry was in play now, and in this fluid environment, Quantrill knew he had tactical and strategic decisions to make as commander in chief. Decisions that were best made here at the office with Boggs rather than at home with his skittish wife nosing about.

Privately, he wondered if he had not made a terrible mistake in allowing Boggs to turn loose a professional killer. What would Ma and Pa think of him for hiring an assassin? But he already knew the answer: they would shudder with shame. They would think he must have signed some kind of pact with the devil.

Which in a sense he had.

Through his hard work and determination, he had built up his oil and gas startup into an impressive private energy and haz waste disposal company. But it took the illegal deep well injection operation to push him high up onto the Forbes Fortune 100 List, to position Quantrill Ventures as a juggernaut in the "green" energy market, and to transform him into a billionaire—all in less than a decade.

Boggs appeared in the doorway.

"Come in, Harry."

The stodgy, walrus-mustached security chief carefully navigated his way around the smashed *Smilodon* skull, a pile of broken glass, and the battered Bierstadt leaning against the fallen credenza. Though Quantrill had tidied up a bit, the office—indeed the whole building—was still a disaster, another pitiful reminder of just how minuscule he was compared to the massive earth forces at work. It pained the CEO to see his priceless art and paleontological possessions destroyed and strewn about. Tomorrow he would have the room thoroughly cleaned and everything put back together or replaced.

"Good news or bad news, Harry."

"Both. Which do you want first?"

"The good."

"Mr. Sperry was successful. The first target has been eliminated."

"Jack...Jack's really dead?"

"Yes, sir. It's done."

Ruefully shaking his head, he drew a mental picture of his chief legal counsel for the past seventeen years. This killing business was harder than he had expected.

Boggs remained stoic, rigidly precise. "Now for the bad news."

Quantrill looked at him.

"There was collateral damage."

Quantrill felt a twist in his gut. He should have known it would be like this, that other innocent people would get caught in the crossfire. "What happened?"

"Holland was hiding out in a church. The pastor was killed too."

The CEO stared at the jagged crack running down the wall. *Good Lord, has it really come to this?*

"I'm afraid there's more bad news, sir. Heiser and Stolz got in a car accident during the quake and lost Higheagle. Actually, they didn't lose him. They were hit from behind by a UPS truck and driven into the railing. The Lexus was totaled. Stolz broke his collarbone and fractured his skull in the crash and Heiser has a bad concussion. Though he was able to get Stolz to the hospital."

"Where are they now?"

"Still at the hospital. I sent Toby Fleming and Atwood to pick up Heiser."

"And Mr. Sperry?"

"On his way to Denver to visit Higheagle and the girl."

"Harry, I'm not sure about—"

"Sir, you have to trust me on this: you have to do whatever it takes or you are finished. With all the confusion over the earthquake, this is your one chance to make everything right."

At that moment, the security chief's cell phone chirped. He looked at his boss. "Do you mind?"

Quantrill motioned for him to take the call and went to the window. Staring down at the burnt-out tankers, he thought of Ma and Pa. Again he felt ashamed for the violent path he had chosen. But another part of him just wanted to get all the killing over with so he would have it all behind him.

A minute later Boggs was off.

Quantrill looked at him. "What is it now?"

"Kelso's out at Sweetwater again. This time both Eric Smith and Tim Connors saw him."

"He's snooping around again after the earthquake? This bastard just doesn't quit."

"It's worse than that. It looks like he set up some device a few miles northwest of the well cluster. They saw him driving around and followed him."

A light bulb lit up in Quantrill's brain. "Damnit, it's a seismograph—he's trying to pinpoint the epicenter."

"He talked some farmer into using his place. He's been driving around out there all day talking to people in the damaged areas. The man's on a mission and needs to be stopped. Since Mr. Sperry's on the way to Denver to visit Higheagle, I'd like to take care of Kelso personally for you."

"Where is he?"

"He just left the bottling plant and is headed this way."

"What did you have in mind, Harry?"

"You don't need to know. But I promise it will look like an accident."

CHAPTER 48

NICKERSON stared up at the digital flat screen in his office, wondering at the insanity of it all and whether Aldous Huxley's famous quote "Maybe this world is another planet's hell" was no joke after all.

Jack Patey was up on the screen—standing at an improvised lectern with his trademark French beret—giving a press conference in front of a salivating pack of Pavlovian media. Behind him, the backlit NEIC building and starlit Rocky Mountains served as a rugged, appropriately scientific backdrop. Nickerson shook his head in disgust. With the Earthquake Prophet down on the street right below his office blathering to a hundred million viewers, the publicity couldn't have been worse for the beleaguered USGS. In fact, Patey was making every earthquake seismologist in the country look like a buffoon.

And yet the NEIC director couldn't bring himself to turn off the TV.

PATEY: *"...problem is that the USGS won't accept unusual animal behavior data because it doesn't fit with their current scientific paradigm. That's what's holding back research into this area—it's not money or partisan bickering, but dogmatism and narrow-mindedness. Researchers who work in earthquake prediction are lumped in the same category as fortune tellers, scam artists, and scaremongers. We saw it with Galileo, Darwin, and Alfred Wegener. If your theory doesn't match the prevailing dogma of the day, the mainstream opinion right or wrong, there's something wrong with you. But there's absolutely nothing wrong with me. The problem lies with the USGS. They could be saving lives but they refuse to."*

REPORTER #1 (up front): *"Dr. Patey, specifically how is it that the USGS is narrow-minded?"*

PATEY: *"Because the agency refuses to look at the overwhelming anecdotal evidence on pre-quake animal behavior. As recent events have demonstrated, a wide variety of animals are picking up the warning signals not just minutes or seconds before a seismic event, but several hours, days, sometimes even weeks before a major earthquake. Correct, careful observation and monitoring of animals can provide advance warning of earthquakes and tsunamis."*

REPORTER #2 (jostling her way forward): *"Dr. Patey, Cathy Jenkins of the* New York Times. *Some people claim that everything you're doing is just part of a publicity stunt to sell more copies of your book. What do you say to those charges?"*

PATEY (with an ingratiating smile): *"Well, Cathy, I have to respectfully disagree. Why would I need more publicity? My book is already a bestseller as recognized by that wonderful little rag of a newspaper you work for. What's it called again? Oh that's right* The New York Times.*"*

The barb was delivered with good humor and received a loud round of laughter from the peanut gallery. Nickerson couldn't help but marvel at the Earthquake Prophet; if nothing else, the man had a way with the media.

REPORTER #3 (one of the few not smiling): *"But isn't it true, Dr. Patey, that the evidence for animal behavior preceding an earthquake has not actually been proven scientifically?"*

PATEY: *"I believe that the evidence from the past two weeks conclusively demonstrates how a genetic seismic-escape response mechanism works in a wide variety of animal species. That's why, in my view, the most important thing is for the USGS, Caltech, and the various other seismological research and public notification programs to implement some sort of protocol. We should be in the business of saving lives and limiting property damage, not performing research for research's sake."*

REPORTER #2 (again fighting her way forward): *"How then do you counter the claim that lost pets, erratic animal behavior, and the like represent nothing more than a psychological focusing effect. In other words, people remember strange animal behaviors only after an earthquake or other catastrophe has taken place."*

PATEY: *"Miss...what's your name again?"*

REPORTER #2: *"Jenkins. Cathy Jenkins."*

PATEY (tipping up his beret to have a better look): *"Miss Jenkins, let me remind you that unusual patterns of animal behavior prior to earthquakes have been reported independently by people all over the world going back to the ancient Greeks. These eyewitnesses didn't just make this stuff up. They didn't suffer from tricks of memory or partisanship. The bottom line is that animals try to leave their normal places of security before an earthquake and that is that. It is beyond dispute. As I've said repeatedly over the years, the only question that remains is what to do about it."*

REPORTER #4: *"What do you propose, Dr. Patey?"*

PATEY: *"It's all laid out in my book. I propose that we set up a special national hotline and website where people can call or email in if they observe strange animal behavior. A computer would then analyze the incoming messages to determine where they originated. A sudden surge of calls or emails from a particular region might indicate that an earthquake was imminent. The information would be checked to make sure the observations were not caused by other circumstances known to affect the behavior of animals such as explosions, fireworks, or drastic changes in weather. Such a project would capture the imagination of millions of people, encourage large-scale public participation, and would be fun. Unfortunately, the USGS and other government and academic institutions that are part of the establishment would fight such a proposal tooth and nail, so we the people have to band together and rise up—"*

The phone on Nickerson's desk rang, distracting him. He checked the caller ID: Watkins. *Damn!* The call he had been dreading.

He turned down the volume on his TV then lifted the phone before he could talk himself out of not answering.

"Director Watkins."

"Are you watching this?"

"Uh…I regret to say, yes."

"Do you know how much trouble this maniac is causing us? He's crucifying us—and it's all because of you! You were supposed to destroy him!"

Nickerson felt his face sag into a frown. *Why even bother to defend myself? What's the point?*

"You have put the Survey in a terrible position!"

How am I going to get him to calm down? "I'm sorry, sir. I didn't mean to—"

"I'm afraid I'm going to have to dismiss you!"

Nickerson felt the air leave him all at once. "You're firing me?"

"It wasn't my call. It was Secretary Jackson's."

That's a lie—the secretary of the interior doesn't fire goddamned USGS employees! Slumping in his chair, he stared up at the ceiling with a dazed expression. *After thirty-two years, this is the way I go out?*

And then a sudden, desperate thought flashed through his mind.

"I know what's causing the earthquakes," he blurted.

"What did you say?"

"I know what's causing the earthquakes." He looked up at the picture of Martin Luther King, Jr., his childhood hero, and next to him John Milne, the father of modern seismology and inventor of the seismograph. The sight of the legendary civil rights leader and stalwart British geologist and mining engineer gave him a feeling of strength and conviction. After all, it wasn't his fault that the Earthquake Prophet was embarrassing the Survey. He had opposed the *Newsline* debate from the start!

"You know what's causing these things and you haven't told me. Why the hell not?"

"We're still gathering data. But I can assure you that we're close, very close."

"Who's *we*? Is it that goddamned Kelso?"

"Among others. But that's not what's important, sir. What is important is that we are about to solve this case."

"Case? What are you Clarence Darrow? What the hell is going on?"

Nickerson had to handle this delicately. "Quantrill Ventures, we believe, has been conducting an illegal deep well injection program. We think they're pumping wastewater deep into the subsurface far off-site of the waste facility and that's what's causing the quakes. I'm waiting for confirmation from two independent sources as we speak. And yes, one of them is Mark Kelso."

A long excruciating silence followed, unexpectedly, by a vehement outburst: "Have you gone completely mad? I told you to leave Charles Quantrill alone!"

"So Senator Tanner's boy is untouchable, is that it?"

"Don't be insolent with me, James. You know very well that it's a matter of our funding. As head of the Senate Appropriations Committee, Senator Tanner has us by the balls. He runs the show and he has the votes to do whatever the hell he wants given the current antigovernment climate. Hell James, you know how powerful he is. He's the one who convinced Secretary Jackson to terminate you."

"Well, terminated or not, I'm going to get to the bottom of this. People are dying out there."

There was another silence and, this time, he could tell the dynamics had shifted. The director had to at least consider what he was saying to protect his own interests. Like any government bureaucrat, Watkins wanted to protect his fiefdom from its enemies—both internal and external—at all costs, thereby securing substantial funding and assuring his own personal advancement.

"I can solve this puzzle, Mr. Director, if you'll only let me. And in the process, the Survey will come out looking like knights in shining armor."

"And the Earthquake Prophet?"

"If nothing else, this will shut him up. The evidence will speak for itself."

There was another lengthy silence as Watkins processed this information, mulling over the pros and cons. As the seconds drew out, Nickerson looked out upon his desk. Normally, it would have been clean and devoid of all but a couple of small piles of paperwork. Now it was heaped with a half-dozen used coffee mugs, seismograms, geologic cross-sections, professional papers, and assorted computer printouts.

"How solid is your proof?" asked the director.

"Not solid enough yet. But we're close."

"Who are these people you're working with?"

"With the exception of Mark Kelso, whom you already know about, that's need-to-know. But I can assure you that they both have excellent credentials. One of them is with the EPA and the other worked for Quantrill Ventures as their consultant until quite recently."

"So they're legit."

"Very much so."

"All right, James. If I give you a chance to make things right, you're going to have to make things right. Do you understand?"

Nickerson tried to steady his nerves. The director was going to back down and let him keep his job—as long as he made the USGS, and Watkins in particular, look good. Nickerson realized that this was his one and only chance at redemption.

"I understand, sir. I won't let the Survey down."

"Believe it or not, I'm confident you won't. But there's one more thing."

Nickerson braced himself; he hadn't expected conditions. "What's that?"

"You have twenty-four hours."

"Twenty-four hours? But sir, you can hardly expect me to—"

"Just get it goddamned done, James." And he hung up.

CHAPTER 49

DRIVING THROUGH A NO-MAN'S LAND on County Road 108, Mark Kelso felt like a spy on the run. *They* were following him again, lurking in the shadows with their headlights off, further back than before but still a ghostly presence. Beyond the reach of the headlights, the rolling prairie and farmland west of Quantrill's Sweetwater mineral water-bottling plant gave way to a monochromatic void of misty darkness. The fog had drifted in only minutes ago, enveloping his Toyota Landcruiser in a gauzy curtain. The windshield wipers flapped gently back and forth as the headlights strobed across the gravel road and beyond, providing occasional glimpses of the devastation wrought by the earthquake.

He cast a nervous glance into his rearview mirror. If only he could see them. He continued westward on County Road 108, directing an occasional eye to his GPS unit.

How can I lose them? There must be a way.

The fog broke and a farmhouse appeared to his right, a skeletal presence in the gloom of his headlights. The property looked like a war zone. The main house had collapsed in on its itself. A pair of outbuildings were completely demolished with hay bales and farm equipment strewn haphazardly about. To the right, the barn still stood surprisingly intact, though all the horses were gone and the wooden stall doors banged back and forth in the wind. To the left, a horse trailer was pitched on its side into a ditch with the legs of a dead equine sticking up from one of the gaps in the metal siding.

He glanced in his rearview mirror. No sign of his pursuers in the fog.

He turned into the farm's driveway, pulled behind a pair of huge box elders, cut the headlights, quietly killed the engine. Total darkness enveloped him. His heart thumped in his chest in a steady, urgent rhythm. He forced himself to remain calm, but it wasn't easy to be composed when dangerous people were stalking you.

If only I could see them, he thought for the tenth time.

He paused a moment, listening. The farm seemed preternaturally dark and silent: no lights, no human presence, no animals, only a vast shroud of blackness.

He pulled his cell phone from the charger, fumbled it to the floor. *Jesus, get ahold of yourself Kelso!* His fingers felt like they were made of tin. He reached down and felt along the floor for his phone. *Shit, where did it go?* Unable to quickly find it, he felt a wave of panic and undid his seatbelt. Again, he told himself to remain calm.

But to no avail.

Finally, after frantically probing beneath the seat for a minute, he found it. He then plugged his headset into the cell phone and slipped it on his head so he could talk while keeping his hands free.

At that moment he saw his pursuers.

To his left, a pair of dim driving lights materialized like a phantom, sweeping across a little slash of gravel road and the featureless farmland beyond.

They were here.

Through an opening in the mist, he could make out the black Grand Cherokee. It was the same car with the two men in it that had followed him to the farm earlier today. The same vehicle he had seen parked outside the Sweetwater plant. He watched the Jeep as it slowly passed, like a cruising tiger shark, then disappeared over the next rise.

He expelled a momentary sigh of relief.

He then punched a button and set the cell phone in the cup holder between the seats. After two rings, he had Nickerson on the line.

"James, it's me. I've got to talk to you."

"Mark, where the hell have you been? I thought you were dead."

"No, I'm okay. I was in Limon when the earthquake hit."

"You were supposed to call me three hours ago."

"I know—I'm sorry. But I didn't want to risk getting you into more trouble with Director Watkins until I knew for sure. Look, James, I have to hurry, they're following me."

"Following you? Who's following you?"

"Quantrill's security—two guys in a Jeep Cherokee. They've been following me off and on all day. Please just listen to me. I think Quantrill's using his Sweetwater-bottling plant as a front. I just came from there. I don't know exactly what he's up to, but I think—"

"Save your breath—we already know about it."

"What? You do?"

"Quantrill's running an illegal deep well injection operation. He's using old oil transmission lines and oil wells that have supposedly been plugged and abandoned but haven't been. The whole operation is neatly tucked next to Sweetwater."

"But how did you—?"

"I didn't, Joseph Higheagle did. He's headed out there right now with Nina Curry to collect samples. We think the line may have ruptured somewhere around those injection wells like it did at the facility. If they can collect samples, they can prove what Quantrill's been doing. Here, let me patch them in."

Kelso looked anxiously up at the rise beyond which the black Jeep had disappeared. Would Quantrill's security goons figure out he had doubled back and turn around and come after him?

He heard Nickerson's voice crackle again.

"Joseph, Nina, are you there?"

"Yeah, we're here." Kelso recognized Higheagle's voice.

"I've got Mark Kelso on the line. He just came from the Sweetwater plant."

"We're on our way there now," said Higheagle. "We were hoping to meet up with you."

"I don't think that's going to be possible," said Nickerson. "I'm afraid Mark's being followed."

"By who?"

"Quantrill's security men," said Kelso. "Two guys in a black Grand Cherokee."

"We need to get onto the property next to the plant to take samples. Is there security out there too?"

"I don't know. It might be just these guys that are following me. If I could draw them further away from the plant, that might give you time to look around. What kind of samples are you going to take?"

"Soil and maybe vapor samples. Is there visible damage in the area from the quake?"

"Extensive damage. Not at the Sweetwater plant itself because it's been designed to be earthquake-resistant just like the waste facility. But it's a disaster zone all around it."

"We think there could be some damage to the old oil line Quantrill is using. Where are you now?"

"County Road 108, about seven miles west of the plant. I was heading...oh shit, they're coming back."

"Who—who's coming back?" asked Nina.

Kelso watched in mute horror as the black Jeep emerged out of the foggy darkness, the twin headlight beams growing in intensity. "Quantrill's security people. I'm blown."

"Just stay calm, Mark," said Nickerson. "Have they seen you?"

"I don't think so. But they will soon enough."

"Is there any way you can distract them?" asked Higheagle.

"What do you mean?"

"Like you said, if you could draw them away from the water plant, Nina and I may be able to get in there quickly and collect the samples."

Kelso watched as the Jeep slowed, sweeping its headlights across the prairie. "I can try. How close are you?"

"Less than ten miles away. We're on North Elbert Road heading south."

He kept his gaze fixed on the Jeep. The copse of box elders provided less concealment from a car approaching from the west than from the east, which meant that they would see him any second now. "There's no time left. I'm going to pull out and head west on 108."

"We'll try to get to the 108/Elbert Road junction before you. That way we can ID these guys without them seeing us."

"Okay. I'll draw them away and then I'll try to lose them again."

"Sounds like a plan," said Nickerson. "Good luck to you all."

I'm definitely going to need it, thought Kelso, and he punched off.

CHAPTER 50

TENSE ANTICIPATION gripped his vitals as he watched the Jeep stalk towards the entrance to the farm, the mist clinging to the vehicle like a cloak of black cotton. There was no alternative now but to make a mad dash for it.

Without turning on his headlights, he quietly engaged the engine and crept slowly for the open front gate. To his dismay, the men in the Jeep spotted him and instantly lurched into motion, speeding down the small hill to cut him off. But as the vehicle slipped into a blocking position, Kelso turned on his high beams, swung the wheel right, plunged his foot down on the accelerator, and bounded across the shallow ditch that ran along the road, leaving his pursuers in his wake.

The tires squealed as they found purchase on the asphalt. Peeling out, Kelso headed west and looked into his rearview mirror.

The Jeep was turning around to give chase.

He punched the pedal to the floor. The Toyota Landcruiser jumped forward like a racehorse, rattling and bouncing down the county road.

As he topped the hill, he checked his speedometer: seventy-seven miles per hour and climbing.

He looked back again. The fog had lifted and the Jeep's high beams hit him from behind.

He sped up to eighty-five.

His heart thundered in his chest. It was an all-out chase.

He gripped the steering wheel tightly, feeling his teeth grinding inside his mouth, which had suddenly gone dry. Pressing the gas pedal to the floor, he again glanced in his rear view mirror.

To his dismay, the Jeep was no more than a hundred feet back now and closing in on him fast. *Damn!* The roar of its 6.1-liter V-8 engine mingled with the sound of the Toyota's revving engine and the gravel ricocheting against the grill.

A moment later he felt it.

The Jeep rammed him from behind, knocking him forward. His head smashed against the steering wheel.

"Jesus Fucking Christ!"

Again, he looked at his speedometer. Ninety-eight miles per hour. He knew that he would be hard pressed to get the Toyota up much past one hundred, but that might be the only way he could evade these bastards. Or maybe he should go off-road? He flicked an eye towards the drainage ditch and barbed wire fence to his right. No way he could turn off the main road safely at this speed.

His head snapped forward as he was rammed again from behind. The steering wheel slipped from his hands and the Toyota swerved. He regained control as his pursuers came up on his left flank. The man in the passenger seat had rolled down his window and pointed a gun at him. Caught by surprise, Kelso swung the steering wheel to the left to ram the Jeep, but the driver pulled away.

A shot rang out, followed quickly by another.

He ducked down and corrected the Toyota, expecting to be struck by a bullet. But, to his surprise, none found him or his vehicle. He pressed his right foot on the gas pedal, bringing the Toyota up over a hundred miles per hour, wondering how the shooter could possibly be such a poor marksman to miss his car entirely.

He kept the pedal to the floor as he swung into a soft right hand bend in the road.

Behind him, the Jeep's tires squealed and another crackle of gunfire echoed into the night. Kelso ducked, cursing under his breath. The Jeep closed in on his left. This time he heard a bullet ricochet off metal. He slowed momentarily and swerved to his left in a feint, but his attackers pulled away to avoid impact.

His heart faltered in his chest.

With the adrenaline bubbling inside him, Kelso yelled out like a preacher possessed and swung the wheel left. He heard the screech of wrenching metal as the Toyota rammed into the side of the Jeep. Breaking away, he jammed his foot down again on the accelerator and quickly brought his speed back up to just under one hundred miles per hour. The man in the passenger seat fired his gun twice more. But again the bullets peppered the road around the Explorer without hitting him or the vehicle itself.

Kelso couldn't understand why the guy didn't seem to be firing at him. He had clearly been in range, yet his adversary seemed to have deliberately chosen not to kill him. Or was he trying to hit his tires and force him to crash to make his death appear like an accident?

There was another staccato of gunfire. Hearing the noisy clanking of metal, he looked into his side mirror and saw his hubcap flying through the air. The Jeep charged up again from behind, but this time did not ram him. Kelso felt the centrifugal force pulling him towards the driver's side door as he went into the next curve.

It was then he saw it.

A great mass of machinery—the biggest tanker he had ever seen—hurtling towards him like an enraged rhinoceros. The fog had thinned and the headlights were so bright he had to cover his eyes against the powerful glare. The monstrous vehicle churned and bellowed as it closed in on him, hogging the middle of the road with wheels in both lanes.

He looked into his rearview mirror and saw the Jeep closing in from behind, boxing him in. It accelerated and rammed him from behind. His neck snapped forward again and he swerved into the oncoming lane. As he did so, he saw the huge tanker to his front shift over and come into a direct line with his Toyota.

Behind him, the Jeep slowed down and pulled back.

Suddenly Kelso realized what was happening: Quantrill's men had sandwiched him in the middle and the tanker was going to pulverize him!

A side road appeared up ahead—an entrance to a ranch? Whatever it was, it was his only chance.

Slamming on the breaks, he swerved hard left towards the entrance.

But he was too late.

The massive tanker roared down upon him like a runaway locomotive. At the last second, he covered his eyes and braced himself for the impact. He saw a brilliant flash of white light as the steering column drove through his chest, collapsing his lungs and skewering him into the back seat.

Then he felt nothing at all except a gauzy bliss.

CHAPTER 51

NINA CURRY shook her head in disbelief as she stared down at the leaping flames and mushroom cloud of smoke billowing up from the demolished Toyota Landcruiser. Following the script, she and Higheagle had turned off their headlights and pulled over to the side of the road at the junction of Elbert Road and County Road 108 to wait for Mark Kelso. Horrified by what they had just witnessed, they sat there mesmerized and utterly speechless as they peered down from a small hill overlooking the wreck.

There was a secondary explosion and the Toyota fragmented into a thousand different pieces. Even from their safe perch two hundred yards away, the boom was deafening. Their car windows rattled from the pressure wave. The finer, fire-hot particles drifted slowly down from the sky like spent Fourth of July fireworks.

She felt tears coming to her eyes. *What have we gotten ourselves into?*

"Shouldn't we do something?" she said after several stunned, mournful seconds.

"I don't think there's anything we can do," responded Higheagle softly, patting her on the shoulder to console her. "Mark Kelso's gone and they'll be coming after us next if we go down there." He pointed at the two hard-looking men climbing from the Jeep then at the man stepping down from the tanker, a compact stodgy frame silhouetted against the leaping flames. "Look who's behind the wheel of the tanker there."

"Harry Boggs. The bastard. I can't believe Quantrill's security people are actual murderers."

"It was premeditated all the way. Those guys in the Jeep must have told Boggs that Kelso was headed this way and they set a trap for him."

They watched as the two goons joined Boggs at the edge of the burning Toyota. They appeared to be inspecting the crash to make sure that their victim was dead. Watching the killers casually surveying the wreckage and raging inferno made Nina feel physically ill.

Higheagle's chin extended forward stubbornly. "We have to find those damned injection wells."

"Do you think that's a good idea? I mean these guys are killers."

"All the more reason why they need to be stopped. Mark Kelso and the hundreds of people who died in that earthquake today deserve better than this."

Nina knew he was right, but she was still scared. She was torn by a strong desire to catch the bad guys and an equally pervasive instinct for self-preservation.

"Unless we find those wells and collect samples, we're never going to nail Quantrill. We don't want the goddamned footsoldiers, we want the general giving the orders."

"All right," she relented. "We'd better head out to Sweetwater before my better judgment prevails."

"Somehow I thought you'd say that." He turned the War Wagon around and struck north, using the faint moonlight to guide the vehicle. Once they were a mile up the road, he turned the headlights back on and picked up his speed to sixty miles an hour. They didn't encounter anyone else on the road until they neared the epicenter and came across ambulances, police cars, fire trucks, and other emergency vehicles. But several hours had passed since the earthquake and most of the people requiring medical attention had already been ambulanced or airlifted out of the area.

When they reached County Road 109, they headed east and came across several destroyed farms, overturned farm equipment, and a large number of livestock that had wandered out of their enclosures. Nina found something ghostly about the devastation and emptiness around them. Wrecked cars, tractors, backhoes, scrapers, and combines lay strewn about the sepulchral landscape. There were demolished truck stops and shops, equipment sheds and shacks, mobile homes and farm houses, water towers and wind mills. Cattle, horses, and pigs clopped aimlessly along the side roads, heading west away from the danger. There were no lights on in Elbert or any of the other small towns they passed through. Nina wondered how far away from the epicenter electricity had been shut down.

Fifteen minutes later they reached the Sweetwater plant. A sprawling aluminum building and neat arrangement of ancillary buildings stood silhouetted against the dark night sky. Beyond the buildings loomed a series of oil pumpjacks, some operating and others long since shut down. They sat there a moment studying the layout. They didn't see anyone around, nor did they spot any vehicles in the parking lot. But after what had happened to Mark Kelso, that did little to assuage Nina's fears.

Higheagle flicked on the dome light. "According to the GPS the well cluster should be about a half mile north and another mile west of the main building."

Resetting the odometer to zero, he pulled out the base map and checked their GPS coordinates using his hand-held Trimble global positioning system plugger unit. Once he had the bearings, they drove fifty yards south of the gate and stopped the truck. Grabbing two pairs of bolt cutters from the flat bed, they cut a sizable opening through the chain link fence. After peeling back the fence, they snuck through the opening, drove past the main building on their right, took a left, and drove along a side road until they reached a locked gate. Upon cutting the lock, they continued north along a hardpacked dirt road, taking GPS readings every so often to pinpoint their location relative to the presumed injection well cluster.

After ten minutes and several wrong turns, they were able to locate the nested wells, which were ingeniously concealed beneath pump jacks. Higheagle parked the truck and killed the headlights. They stepped into the cool night air beneath a pregnant, cloud-obscured moon and a canopy of dimly illuminated stars. Nina gazed up at the three motionless pump jacks. Silhouetted against the night sky like gigantic teeter-totters, the pump jacks and the injection wells cryptically hidden beneath them were encircled by a high-voltage fence with three strands of high tension razor wire at the top.

"I'm surprised we found them so easily. Maybe Lady Luck is watching over at least us tonight," said Higheagle wishfully.

Nina shined her flashlight on the sign hanging from the security fence. It read DANGER – HIGH VOLTAGE in bold black and red lettering.

"I wouldn't break out the champagne just yet," she said. "We still have to get inside."

CHAPTER 52

MR. SPERRY pulled deeper into the shadows, his riveted gaze directed at the small ranch-style house. This one was going to be special. He had never killed an Indian before and tonight he had the opportunity to bag two of them. Still, he would have to be careful. Higheagle and his grandfather would both probably have firearms of some kind close at hand. He had read somewhere—was it *Natural History* magazine or perhaps one of the *Smithsonian* publications?—that modern-day Plains Indians worshipped guns just as much as their buffalo-hunting ancestors. Which meant that this contract was definitely not going to be as easy as it had been with that blundering attorney, Jack Holland. But then again, this was precisely the kind of challenge he lived for.

He paused beneath the maple tree in the front yard and surveyed the house a final time. He had already worked out his approach, having studied the layout for fifteen minutes now from both the street and back alley. There were only two entrances to the house: a front door and a back, both with wooden steps leading to the entrance. A dim outdoor light illuminated the steps to the front door, but there was no light on in the back. There didn't appear to be any dogs. He had observed one truck parked in back, registered in Higheagle's name. He would use stealth to get inside the house and then he would bring surprise and overwhelming firepower to bear.

They had never failed him before.

It was time to move. Stepping surreptitiously from the shadows, he walked along the driveway to the back door, the rubber soles of his Docksiders squeaking ever so lightly, and peered through the window. Unfortunately, the shades to all the windows in the house were drawn, but he could just make out the silhouettes of two figures through the rear window shade. Was it Higheagle and his grandfather? If so, they were sitting ducks. Maybe this was going to be easier than he thought. They were sitting down in what appeared to be the family room watching television. He would take the younger and more dangerous target first, popping him with a quick double tap to the head. Then he would take his time with the chief.

A real Cheyenne Indian chief, that's what the dossier said. How fucking impressive was that?

A devilish smile took hold of his face. He couldn't wait to see the final look on old Sitting Bull's face. Maybe he would sing some kind of Indian death chant at the end like the savages did in the old days.

He felt a tingle of excitement play through his nervous system. This was what he liked to call *the hunt.*

He checked the door. Locked.

Quietly, he pulled out his foldover leather pouch and carefully removed his tension tool and feeler pick set. There was enough light bleeding through the shade that he didn't have to use his pen light. He positioned the tension pick first then delicately probed with the feeler tool. After a moment he felt a little click and the door unlocked. Putting away his tools, he pushed the door forward, but it came to a clinking halt from the safety chain. He withdrew a small set of bolt cutters and quietly cut the chain.

A sound came from inside the house.

He ducked back behind the wall, freezing still as a statue. But it was only a ripple of laughter. He peered through the shade. Higheagle and his grandfather were still watching television.

He waited a few more seconds just to make sure. Then he checked to make sure that his Kevlar bullet-proof vest was secure. Check. From the holster beneath his hunting jacket, he withdrew his Smith and Wesson .45 semi-auto, then pulled his noise suppressor from his pocket and threaded it into the nose of the weapon.

Ready to move.

Taking a deep breath, he pushed open the back door. It squeaked, but the sound of the television coming from the other room was loud enough to dampen the noise. He slipped noiselessly into the hallway, leaving the door partly open behind him to enable a quick getaway. His Cadillac Escalade luxury SUV was parked in the alley and it would take him less than a minute to reach it once his assignment was complete.

Tiptoeing across the wooden floor, he felt his heart rate click up a notch. Through the opening to the kitchen, he saw Higheagle and his grandfather. They were facing the TV, their heads of long unbraided Indian hair—one a youthful raven black, the other an elderly silvery gray—spilling down the backs of their chairs. His breathing increased. He realized he was every bit as excited as he had been at the church earlier this evening. Lord, the look on Jack Holland's face at the end: it had been so perfect.

This one is definitely going to be special, sport.

He gave a supercilious smile as he turned the corner from the hallway to the family room and came upon Higheagle and his grandfather from behind. His smile deepened and the corners of his mouth twitched once, twice with excitement. His breathing accelerated. He raised the pistol towards High—

But wait, something was wrong.

He took two quick steps and saw an unthinkable sight.

The figures sitting in the chairs weren't Higheagle and his grandfather at all, but improvised dummies with wigs! *What the fuck?* he screeched to himself, staring in stunned disbelief.

Behind him, he heard a metallic click.

He froze.

"It's a good day to die, isn't it, motherfucker?"

The old chief? But where the hell is Higheagle?

"Drop the gun on the floor, turn around slowly, and you just might live."

The assassin still didn't move a muscle as his mind worked frantically, going over the options.

"Don't fuck with me. I was a Marine in Korea and have killed many a gook in my day. That was a long time ago and I'm itching to rekindle that old time feeling."

He turned around slowly, Smith & Wesson .45 still in hand. He blinked with surprise as he gazed upon his adversary.

The old renegade had prepared himself for battle. His face was painted half black, half red with a bright yellow zigzag dividing the two colors down the middle of his nose. In his huge hands, he gripped an old Winchester lever-action rifle adorned with brass tacks, vermilion, and eagle feathers in the old Plains Indian way. His unbraided silver hair hung wildly to the middle of his back and he wore no shirt, only a bone-pipe breastplate, beaded buckskin pants, and a sacred Cheyenne Dog Soldier Rope—a lengthy sash of bison silk elaborately decorated with quill and feathers. Looking at him, Mr. Sperry couldn't help but feel as if he had been transported back a century and a half to the wild, wild West.

"I said put the fucking gun down—slowly."

Keeping his eyes on the gun, he started to slowly raise his hands above his shoulders. "All right, you win, sport," he said with false compliance—and he dove for the couch.

But the chief was faster than expected.

The first shot caught the assassin square in the chest just before he bounced off the couch. The second struck him in the upper left arm, barely missing bone, as he leapt for the window. And the third hit him just above the bellybutton as he crashed backwards through the glass.

The last thing he saw as he scrambled over the back yard fence was the old Cheyenne whooping like a banshee, cracking off rounds with his Winchester like a kid at a shooting gallery.

And Mr. Sperry thought two things: *That is one crazy Indian bastard!* and, *Thank heavens for fucking Kevlar!*

CHAPTER 53

"HOW THE HELL ARE WE GOING TO GET IN THERE?" asked Nina, shining her flashlight up at the DANGER – HIGH VOLTAGE sign suspended from the electrified fence.

"I'm not sure," said Higheagle. "But let's try this first."

He tossed the metal bolt cutters against the fence. The tool dropped to the ground with an innocuous thump.

He grinned. "Looks like we picked the right night for a break in. The earthquake's cut off the power."

Nina still felt anxious. "We'd better hurry though. It could come back on."

He picked up the bolt cutters, strode to the metal gate, and cut through the lock. Nina pushed the gate open and they stepped inside. Using their flashlights, they quickly located the concrete pad and well vault beneath the south pump jack. The vault box beneath the stationary pump jack was marked "DW-105" in black block letters on a white background.

Bingo!

"I think we should start here first," said Higheagle.

"This is the deep well, right?"

"Yeah. I figure this is the one they've been injecting into since the hypocenters of the recent quakes have been five to seven kilometers down."

"All righty then, big boy, let's get the equipment." Again Nina felt the excitement of a cat burglar as they returned to the truck and began unloading the organic vapor meter, Draeger vapor detector tubes, ice chests, chain-of-custody forms, and other supplies. In less than five minutes, they had everything laid out neatly on the concrete pad next to the deep well. Once they had unloaded the equipment and calibrated the OVM, they shined their flashlights at the large, rectangular well vault, which was locked.

Higheagle grabbed the bolt cutters and cut the lock. The vault had a spring release mechanism to open the door. Nina pushed down on the release button and the door slowly opened.

Step one accomplished—they were in.

They pointed their flashlights down into the open vault. A steel, four-inch pipe rose out of the ground and elbowed towards the west where three feet of pipe ran horizontal to ground surface. On the top part of the pipe, above where it came out of the ground, there were a series of valves, meters, and gauges.

Nina was surprised at the lack of chemical odors. "That's funny I don't smell anything."

"I was thinking the same thing." Higheagle grabbed the organic vapor meter from the case and turned it on. While Nina shined the flashlight down into the open vault, he climbed down and waved the OVM around in the enclosure, monitoring for organic vapors. The instrument made a chirping sound as the concentration of volatile organic compounds in the vault rose from zero to two parts per million.

"Only two ppm," he said. "That's background. I was expecting the concentrations to be a lot higher."

"Maybe they haven't been injecting waste into the deep zone recently."

"Then why the deep focus earthquakes? Let's check the other two wells to confirm."

They gathered their field equipment and headed for the next closest pump jack, labeled SW-107. This time when they opened the vault, a potent chemical odor wafted up at them.

Nina covered her nose and took a step back, remembering back to when she was ten years old and changed her baby brother's stinky diaper for the first time. "That's nasty, but it looks like we've hit the jackpot."

"It's that same solvent-tinged sulfur odor we smelled at the facility. They've definitely been pumping into the shallow zone recently. We'd better put on our respirators to be safe."

Two minutes later, they both donned full-face respirators equipped with protective VOC cartridges to minimize inhalation exposure. Nina shined her flashlight on the pooled liquid at the bottom of the vault. "Look, there's a leak in the line," she said, her voice muffled by her mask.

Laying on his stomach, Higheagle touched the horizontal section of pipeline. "There's nothing flowing through it—no vibration of any kind. Quantrill must have stopped pumping since the earthquake."

Nina shined the flashlight onto the tubing hanger and the master valve before turning it onto the bottom of the vault. "The master valve has fallen off."

"Looks like we've found our smoking gun. I'm going to take a measurement." He put down his flashlight, picked up the OVM, and pointed it down into the vault. The instrument quietly hummed for several seconds as the digital readout showed the total VOC concentration rising to 5,000 ppm before going off scale and sounding the alarm.

"Looks like we've found our first vapor sampling point," said Nina.

"Let's get the sampling equipment."

It took them several minutes. First, they prepared the Draeger vapor detector tubes and bellows pump, which was used to identify which volatile organic compounds were present in the air stream and their concentrations. Higheagle broke the tip of one of the fiber-filled glass tubes for analyzing trichloroethylene vapors, inserted the tube into the end of the hand-held bellows pump, and leaned down into the vault to collect the first vapor sample. He stroked the bellows pump to draw air into the tube while Nina shined her flashlight into the vault. After three strokes, he stopped and read off the value on the Draeger tube, which was based on the length of discoloration of the fiber in the tube. Nina checked the instruction booklet to see the equivalent TCE concentration; it was over 1,000 parts per million. She recorded the value in her logbook along with the date, time, and sample location. They repeated the process for the two other most common chemicals identified in the groundwater at Quantrill's facility: perchloroethene and 1,1,1-trichloroethane. Both contaminants were present at concentrations over 500 ppm.

When they were finished with the qualitative sampling and analysis with the Draeger tubes, Higheagle turned on the vacuum pump to collect the air samples that would be quantitatively analyzed by the USEPA certified laboratory. The instrument started to hum like an electric shaver. After making some adjustments, he attached Teflon tubing to the suction side of the pump. Once he lowered the long tubing into the vault, the vacuum pump began drawing air. He attached an empty plastic sample bag to a tap on the other side of the pump, which quickly filled with air from the vault. He twisted a knob on the bag to seal it and repeated the process, filling three additional plastic bags and sealing them. When he was finished, he placed the bags in the empty ice chest.

Throughout the sampling, Nina continued to document everything in her field logbook and labeled the bags so that the laboratory could identify them. She then took photographs of the wells, vaults, and oil well pump jacks, stuffing the camera back in her daypack when she was finished.

Next they turned their attention to the soil sampling. Their plan was to walk above the buried pipeline and look for surface leaks where they could collect soil samples to verify the types of contaminants present. Using his Brunton compass, Higheagle first took a pipeline bearing where it elbowed to the west. Once they had the bearing, they gathered up their sampling equipment and followed the surface trace of the buried pipeline using their flashlights and a hand-held magnetometer, trying to find visual evidence of surface leakage.

After walking fifty yards in the direction of the bottling plant, they smelled a pronounced sulfur odor. The odor was not as strong as what they had smelled at the vault, but it was potent nonetheless. They scanned the ground with their flashlights and saw what appeared to be saturated soil.

Using a small hand trowel, Higheagle dug down about six inches and collected a soil sample to measure qualitatively for VOC vapors. He scooped up some of the damp soil, placed it in a plastic bag, and labeled the bag with a magic marker. Then he placed the tip of the organic vapor meter in the bag. As at the vault for shallow well SW-107, the OVM reading went off scale, indicating that the concentration of total volatiles was above 5,000 ppm.

They had found a leak in the line.

Now all they needed were samples of the impacted soil to send off to the lab. They pulled out the steel hand auger and Higheagle began to dig. The implement worked like a corkscrew, twisting and packing soil into the column of the auger. Once he had reached the two-foot depth, he loaded the drive sampler with a brass tube and pounded it into the ground to collect a soil sample. The process was repeated at three other locations. Nina labeled the samples with a sample number and depth designation. Then she sealed, taped, and stuffed the samples into the ice chests and recorded the necessary analytical methods to be used on the chain-of-custody form that would accompany the sample to the EPA-certified laboratory. The soil samples would be analyzed for the constituents found at Quantrill's facility, as well as for mercaptans, the compound they believed was responsible for the sulfur smell.

After twenty minutes, they finished up. "Looks like we're all set," said Nina, feeling a sense of accomplishment as she stuffed the last sample in an ice chest.

But Higheagle wasn't listening. He had become distracted by something and was staring intently to the south.

She wondered what had spooked him. "What is it, Joseph?"

"They're coming."

"What? Who's coming?"

"Quantrill's security. We've run out of time—*they're* coming for us."

He held up a hand for her to stop and listen. She pricked her ear alertly to the south in the direction he had pointed. Nothing but a faint susurrus of wind.

And then she heard it.

A low rumbling sound. It sounded like a distant revving car engine. She scanned the prairie to the south and east, but still she saw nothing.

"We have to go," he said with quiet urgency.

"What about the well vaults? They're still open."

"They already know we're here so there's no point in closing them now."

They grabbed the OVM, hand auger, ice chest, and sampling equipment and quickly stuffed everything into the back of the War Wagon.

The sound of the distant engine grew louder.

"Hurry, get in."

Again Nina looked to the south and east, but there was still no sign of a vehicle.

And then suddenly it was there.

Like a British Man of War emerging from the fog, a pair of headlights sliced through the darkened night next to a pumpjack not more than five hundred yards away. She felt her heart falter in her chest. The car was moving fast, racing towards them on a dirt road that linked up with the injection well access road they were on.

They jumped into the truck.

Higheagle fired the engine. "You'd better fasten your seatbelt. This is going to be a bit bumpy."

CHAPTER 54

HIGHEAGLE recognized the black Jeep Grand Cherokee as it sped towards them on the road to their left. It was the same vehicle that had chased down Mark Kelso. The goon in the passenger seat clutched a cell phone in one hand and a pistol in the other.

Rounding a soft turn, the Jeep came in hard and fast.

There was a crackle of gunfire followed by the zing of a bullet and a ricochet off the side of the War Wagon. Higheagle pressed his foot to the accelerator and tore off down the dirt access road.

The Jeep swung in behind them.

The War Wagon surged forward like a racehorse. But the road was filled with potholes and loose gravel and it took all of Higheagle's dexterity to navigate through the maze of pumpjacks. As he and Nina roared over the rough ground, the War Wagon churned up a cloud of dust, which the Cheyenne knew was their best defense against their pursuers.

The front tire hit a bump and they bounded in the air. They came down hard just before a curve and he was forced to slow down to control the vehicle. An instant later, the Jeep rammed them from behind. The impact jerked their heads forward then snapped them back as the equipment in the back smashed violently against the rear gate of the flatbed.

"We can't lose those samples!" Nina yelled over the sound of the straining engines.

"You should be worried about our lives!"

"Oh, you'll get us out of this. You come from a long line of Cheyenne warriors, remember?"

"At a moment like this, how could I forget!"

He pounded his foot into the gas pedal, bringing the War Wagon up to sixty miles per hour. A bullet zipped through the rear window, made a small hole, then exited through the windshield without shattering the glass. They ducked down, keeping their heads just below the top of the headrest. Another shot, the bullet smashing into the rear of the cab. The Jeep was hot on their tail and showed no sign of letting up.

"Goddamnit, I can't shake them!"

"You've got to do something! They're coming in again!"

"I'm going nearly seventy miles an hour on a dirt road potholed like the surface of the fucking moon! What more do you want?"

"Maybe you can force them off the road!"

And just how am I supposed to do that?

Yet he knew he had to do something quickly or they would in all likelihood perish. It was then that his headlights caught the silhouette of an active pumpjack—its giant grasshopper frame like something out of *War of the Worlds*—bobbing up and down in a dull mechanical rhythm.

He had a sudden idea.

The pumpjack was on the left hand side of the dirt road and flanked by another one to the west. If he came to a sudden stop, his pursuers might be forced to divert around him on the left to avoid a collision and thereby have no choice but to head straight into the second pumpjack. It probably wouldn't work, but it was worth a shot.

"Hold on tight!" he cried.

He sped up, and then, as he passed the first pumpjack on his left, he took the right hand turn of the road and slammed on the breaks. The tires skidded across the road and sent up a dust cloud.

Taken off guard, the driver of the Jeep swerved left to avoid the War Wagon as expected, but then, instead of crashing into the second pumpjack, the driver overcorrected and fishtailed badly in the loose gravel. To Higheagle's surprise, the Jeep flew over a berm and directly into a third pumpjack that he hadn't even seen.

There was the sound of a heavy collision followed first by a low sputtering blast like a backfiring Model T and then by an explosive *Boom!* The entire prairie suddenly lit up as if by a signal flare. The flames rose fifty feet into the air, the swelling black fuel cloud spreading west from the giant steel pumpjack.

It was a monstrous, angry fire.

Higheagle pulled the War Wagon off to the side of the dirt road. There was no movement inside the vehicle that he could see as the Jeep and oily pumpjack were both engulfed in an inferno. They sat there watching the flames and smoke shooting upward like a giant head of cauliflower for a full minute without saying a word.

"Do you think they're dead?" asked Nina as the flames licked at the Jeep and there was still no movement inside the vehicle.

"I don't think anyone could survive that," he answered.

"What should we do?"

"Get the hell out of here before more bad guys come after us."

"I agree wholeheartedly," she said.

To his surprise, she leaned in close and gave him a hug followed by a warm kiss. "What was that for?" he asked.

"That was for saving my life."

He leaned over, pulled her in close, and kissed her passionately.

When they pulled away, she gave a look of pleasant surprise. "What was that for?" she asked him.

"Oh, believe me. I've been wanting to do that since the first day we met."

And with that he gave a devilish grin and they drove off into the silken night.

CHAPTER 55

QUANTRILL sat in his battered office, waiting for Boggs to call. It had been over half an hour now since the security chief had reported in and he was growing anxious.

I really have signed a pact with the devil, he thought as he stared at the phone. In order to go "green" he had pumped toxic waste down deep injection wells—a clandestine, highly profitable operation which, for more than a decade, had harmed no one but was now causing terrible earthquakes that were killing people. By taking the life of his own brother and hundreds of innocent people in the name of, first, the almighty dollar and a major expansion into sustainable energy, and now, self-preservation, would he not be banished to fiery hell and damnation in the afterlife? And yet, he knew no other way out. He had committed himself to survival—no matter what the cost.

His cell phone vibrated. He jerked reflexively in his high-backed leather chair and quickly scanned the caller ID. He was surprised to see that it was Senator Tanner.

He tried to keep his voice calm and composed. "Senator, what can I do for you?"

"I just got off the phone with Interior Secretary Jackson. Apparently, Director Watkins is not going to fire Dr. Nickerson after all."

"Why not?"

"Because Nickerson says he knows what's causing the earthquakes and all he needs is the chance to prove it."

"I'm not sure I follow."

"Goddamnit, don't you dare play dumb with me, Chuck. You need to come clean and tell me what the hell you've gotten yourself mixed up in out there. And don't even think of lying to me—I know you're the one causing the earthquakes."

Quantrill was stunned. He was desperate to say something in his own defense, but he was rendered speechless. Whatever prevarication he put forward would sound ridiculous. *My God, it's all coming apart!*

The senator's voice sliced through his troubled thoughts like a dagger. "What have you gotten me into, you bastard?"

"Gotten you into?"

"Dr. Nickerson says that you may be causing the earthquakes through some kind of fluid injection program."

Quantrill knew he had to rally to his own defense and plant a seed of doubt in Tanner's mind. "You have been badly misinformed, Senator. There isn't any such program."

"I told you not to lie to me, damn you. Jesus Christ, what have you gotten me into?"

"Dr. Nickerson is spreading lies. He's just angry because we won't hand over our seismic profile data without first running the request through our legal department."

"You'd better be on the level with me. Who do you think greased the wheels and pushed your hazardous waste permits through the system in record time, the goddamned Easter Bunny?"

"You've got to calm down, Bill."

"How can I calm down when I hear that I may be tied to some illicit waste operation? You'd better fix this, goddamnit! I am not going to go to jail for some crazy wet dream that I had nothing to do with!"

"Bill, you're overreact—"

"Shut up! I'm hanging up now and I don't want to have anything more to do with you!"

"Bill, please just listen—"

But he was gone. Quantrill could feel a migraine coming on again. He reached for his lidocaine nasal spray in his desk drawer and took a snort. How much longer could he keep a lid on things? Now even Senator Tanner suspected what was going on. And where the hell was Boggs? This standing by and waiting was excruciating! Everything he had worked so hard to achieve—all he had done to make Ma and Pa proud—was in jeopardy. Even if he could manage the situation, when would it all end? How many people would he have to kill to keep things quiet?

His cell phone vibrated again, startling him.

He reached for it with shaky fingers and checked the caller ID, breathing a sigh of relief when he realized that it was Boggs.

"Where the hell have you been, Harry? I've been worried half to death!"

"I apologize, sir, but my cell died on me and I misplaced my charger."

Quantrill let out a heavy groan. His head felt like it was being squeezed in a vise from his migraine. He took another quick jolt of lidocaine and tried to calm himself down. Though he was angry at his security chief, it was soothing to hear his reassuring voice. If nothing else, the man was reliable.

"I'm sorry, Harry, but I've got a terrible headache. Go ahead."

"Is it the migraines, sir?"

"Yes, I'm afraid they're back."

"I'm sorry to hear that. But I wanted to let you know that Mark Kelso has been taken care of. He won't be bothering you anymore."

"You used the tanker?"

"You don't want to know the details, sir. On two other fronts, I'm afraid we've met with some…resistance."

"Did Mr. Sperry go to Higheagle's house?"

"Yes, but Higheagle wasn't there. Unfortunately, his grandfather was."

"The old chief put up a fight, didn't he?"

"I'm afraid so, sir. He's a former Marine and Korean War veteran. It seems he was armed and dangerous…managed to shoot our asset in the arm."

"What happened to Higheagle and Nina Curry?"

"Unfortunately, that's the even worse bad news. They were just seen at the injection wellfield."

Quantrill felt his whole body tense. "What?"

"Eric Smith just called it in, sir. He and Tim Connors were in pursuit of a man and a woman. Smith got the tag number. The man was definitely Higheagle. They weren't able to ID the woman, but I'm fairly certain it was Nina Curry. They were trespassing on your property in the area of the injection wells. I'm on my way there now. I regret to inform you that Connors is dead."

"Good lord, what happened?"

"There was a high speed chase. Somehow Higheagle pulled some kind of braking maneuver and Smith and Connors ended up crashing into one of the pumpjacks. Smith jumped clear of the Jeep before the explosion but Connors was trapped. Smith is badly hurt, sir. He's going to require major surgery. Dagdigian's out there now too. He just extinguished the fire."

"Poor Tim Connors. I loved that stubborn son of a bitch like my own son. He will be missed."

"Yes, sir, he will."

They fell into silence. Quantrill shook his head. Higheagle and his damned grandfather—how could amateurs do such a thing? Then he realized the answer. Those damned Cheyennes were tough, wily, resourceful bastards, especially when it came to a scrap. It was in their goddamned blood!

He massaged his temples, hoping to mitigate some of the throbbing pain. "We are deep in the shit here, Harry, and I expect results. Do you hear me? What were Higheagle and the girl doing out there, snooping around like Kelso?"

"I'm in the process of figuring that out, sir. Smith says that the lock on the gate was cut and the well vaults were open. However, nothing appears to be missing and there's no evidence of digging or anything. It looks as though all they did was open up the lids and examine the pipes. Dagdigian says there's a pretty strong odor coming out of one of the open vaults."

"If Higheagle knew what the wells were being used for, he may have collected air samples."

"That has yet to be confirmed, sir, but yes, that is the likely scenario we're looking at here."

Quantrill shook his throbbing head in dismay. The situation was getting worse by the minute—and so was his damned migraine. "How in the hell did Higheagle and that gal have enough time to get in and out of that area? There was supposed to be a guard there."

"Your instructions were to keep an eye on the eastern six-mile segment of pipe and that's what Dagdigian was doing. Smith and Connors, I'm afraid, were busy with me attending to Mark Kelso."

"But how did they get in there when the fence around the wells is electrified?"

"I'm afraid the power's down from the earthquake."

"Goddamnit, I want tighter, round-the-clock security around those wells until we get that fence up and running again."

"Yes, sir."

"Whatever happens, none of this can be reported to the police."

"Connors's death and Smith's injuries can be explained by the earthquake. But we still have to deal with Higheagle and Curry."

"No shit, Harry. And how do you intend to do that with your man out of commission?"

"Despite his wound, Mr. Sperry wants to finish the assignment. He has already applied a field dressing and is prepared to go back into action. But he wants another hundred grand."

Quantrill felt a jolt of anger to go along with the pain in his head. *Who in tarnation does he think he is asking for more money after failing his assignment?*

"I realize that you might be inclined to reject the new terms, but you may want to make an exception in this case."

"Why's that?"

"He's a dangerous man, sir. He's not one to be trifled with."

"So I should pay him more so he doesn't threaten me and because he was stupid enough to get himself shot, is that it?"

"He will take care of this quickly and efficiently. He's unconventional, I know, but he is very good at what he does. And persistent."

"You said before that he's never failed an assignment. Well now he has."

"In the end, he will make it right, I promise you."

"All right, I'll call the man myself and authorize the new payment. But he damn well better take care of it this time. Where do you think Higheagle and the girl will go?"

"They'd be foolish to return to either of their homes after what happened. I would look for them to contact Dr. Nickerson, or perhaps another third party. Either before or after they submit the samples."

"What's the next step then?"

"Dagdigian needs to take Smith to the hospital. I'll have Heiser and Bob Rouse stake out Nina Curry's place. I'll take Higheagle's with Fleming and Atwood once I've wrapped things up out here. And I'll have Mr. Sperry stake out Nickerson. I believe they'll try and make contact with him again."

"What if they go to the police?"

"After trespassing onto private property and getting two men killed? I don't think so."

"Two men? I thought it was just Tim Connors."

"They don't know that."

"This is turning into an ugly business, Harry. I don't know how you expect it to end the way we want when our men are dropping like flies."

"Don't worry, sir, they'll make a mistake. And when they do we'll pounce."

244

CHAPTER 56

PULLING THE WAR WAGON next to the curb at Third and Ash Street, Higheagle pulled the key from the ignition and stared up at Richard Hamilton's two-story Tudor manor with the cream-painted stucco and dark-brown timber trim. He didn't want to be here. He wanted to go to his friend Josh Kane, Special Agent with the FBI. But Nina had talked him into speaking with her boss first, arguing that the crimes committed by Quantrill were of an environmental nature first and foremost and that Richard needed to be fully briefed before any law enforcement agencies were brought into the picture.

The Tudor was illuminated by a pair of lantern-style lights near the doorway and a floodlight above the three-car garage. The house and grounds were exquisite and well tended, and Higheagle couldn't help but wonder how a government bureaucrat could afford a home in the tony Cranmer Park area. Maybe Hamilton or his wife had family money.

The two slid from the pickup and ambled up the winding flagstone walkway to the front door. Hewn from thick oak, the door held two solid brass knockers and a grapevine twig wreath decorated with crimson chili peppers and dried Indian corn.

Nina rang the doorbell. A moment later a light turned on upstairs and they heard voices. Through the vertical window Higheagle saw Richard Hamilton walking downstairs in a navy-blue night robe and leather slippers. Peering through the window, he frowned before reluctantly opening the door.

He looked them up and down for a moment, noticing the soil splotches on the knees of their trousers. "I'm not sure I want to hear what you two have been up to," he said tartly.

Higheagle looked past Hamilton at the attractive woman at the top of the stairs dressed in a silk gown, her coiffed hair in slight disarray.

Hamilton turned. "Everything's all right, honey. These are two of the jokers I work with that take their work a little too seriously sometimes. I'll be up in a few minutes."

Her disapproving gaze lingered a moment longer before she sauntered off. Hamilton motioned them inside.

"I'm sorry, Richard, but we just had to see you," said Nina without preamble.

After shutting the door behind them, he raised a finger for them to be quiet. "Shush, I don't want to wake up the kids. Let's talk in the kitchen."

He motioned for them to follow. They passed through a sitting room with Queen Anne chairs, a peach and cream sofa, hand-painted porcelain lamps with silk Shantung shades, and porcelain snuff boxes positioned carefully on top of marble-topped side tables. Again Higheagle noted the lavish decor. From the sitting room, Hamilton led them into the kitchen, which was also upscale and filled with countless Brookstones gadgets. He opened one of the kitchen cabinets and pulled out a box of Milano cookies.

"I don't know about the two of you, but I always like a good cookie when I'm woken up in the middle of the night." He yanked on the handle to the refrigerator and pulled out a carton of milk. "You two want anything?"

"I'm okay," answered Nina.

"A glass of water," said Higheagle.

Hamilton grabbed a bottle of Perrier from the refrigerator and a glass from the cupboard, handed them to Higheagle, and motioned for them to sit in the caned chairs around the pine, country-style kitchen table. He set his glass of milk and plateful of cookies on the table. Higheagle sat next to Nina and across from Hamilton.

"I already know this is going to be a long story, so you might as well get on with it."

Nina proceeded to describe the afternoon's and evening's harrowing events: the two men tailing them when the earthquake struck; the meeting with Nickerson; the murder of Mark Kelso; collecting the samples at the well cluster; and the subsequent chase and explosion that had resulted in the death of the two security men. For five minutes, Hamilton listened intently without interrupting, quietly sipping milk and nibbling cookies.

Throughout Nina's recollection of the events, Higheagle studied Hamilton. He wanted to know what the man was thinking and whether he could be trusted to help them solve the case. But the EPA Haz Waste Management Division director's face was inscrutable. For a flickering instant, Higheagle wondered if he was even buying their story. From Hamilton's perspective, it must have seemed too fantastic to believe.

When Nina was finished, her boss spoke bluntly: "You two are in a lot of trouble."

Higheagle looked at Nina; this wasn't what either of them had expected. "We're not the ones in trouble," he protested. "It's Quantrill Ventures that's in trouble, not us."

Hamilton shook his head. "That's not how the law will see it, I'm afraid. What you two have done is flagrantly illegal. Which in turn affects how we're going to have to handle this."

"No one's going to care that we trespassed, if that's what you mean. The only thing that matters is that Quantrill's been injecting waste illegally and murdering people—and we can prove it."

"On the contrary, you can't prove that he has anything to do with this. In fact, for all you know he could be innocent. If you want to prove he's guilty—and based on what you have told me I have my doubts—you don't go about it like the Keystone Cops. You don't go poking around on private property without a warrant and take samples and kill security guards. Who are the criminals here?"

"We didn't kill anyone, Richard," protested Nina.

"When you trespass on private property and a pair of security guards end up dead because of your actions, you're looking at manslaughter at least. And now you've made me an accessory after the fact. I can't believe that I'm sitting here talking to a pair of fugitives for Christ sakes."

Higheagle didn't like his tone or what he was saying. *We're not fucking fugitives—you're twisting this all around!*

Hamilton rubbed his eyes. "Look, I'm on your side and you can count on me to help. But you've got to see this from a law enforcement perspective."

"It's not our fault the guards were killed," argued Nina. "It was an accident. They were chasing after us and shooting at us. After the earthquake, I'm sure they were under orders from Quantrill to shoot anyone on sight who went near those wells. That's why Mark Kelso was killed. He was poking around out there too. He suspected something was going on and they killed him for it."

"Can you actually prove that?"

"Maybe not," said Higheagle. "But we can prove that Quantrill's causing the earthquakes."

"Really. How can that be when the wells are more than fifteen miles away from the epicenter?"

"Over a long period of time and with an interconnected fracture system, the waste could have been driven far from the wells."

"Are you kidding me, that's the best you have? That's nothing but total speculation."

"Look, the facts are there. The well locations. The orientation of the pipeline. The volatile organic compounds detected by the Draeger tubes. The OVM readings. The close proximity of the earthquakes. Quantrill is definitely injecting fluids into those wells and causing the earthquakes—and the lab results will prove it."

"Maybe. But the results still don't take away from the fact that you two have committed serious crimes. Not only did you trespass and get into a high-speed chase with two security guards who are apparently now dead, but you collected evidence illegally. Your case would be dismissed in any court of law. But even worse, what you've done may throw discredit upon the EPA. We have legal channels, a system of rules that are meant to be followed—and you didn't follow them. What in the hell were you two thinking?"

"We didn't have time to sort everything out before we went out there," admitted Nina. "We had to act fast."

"No, you acted like complete idiots. I just hope like hell this doesn't come back to bite us. How did you think I was going to react? Did you think I was going to pat you on the back and uncork the champagne? This guy is one of the richest men in the country. He's going to crush and humiliate us unless we have all of our ducks lined up in a row."

"All right, we get the message," said Higheagle, crossing his arms. "But instead of telling us about how badly we messed up, why don't you tell us what we should do now. We've got to do something."

"He's right, Richard. We can't let Quantrill get away with this. You know how many people have died from this earthquake? The death toll is over eight hundred and still climbing. We're talking about a mass murderer, not just some corporate sleazeball."

Higheagle couldn't understand why Hamilton wasn't more sympathetic. Had he been a bureaucrat so long that he wasn't willing to take any risks at all? "Look, Richard, we have enough evidence to prove to ourselves that he's guilty and that's what matters most. We can leave it to the EPA and Justice Department lawyers to decide how best to prosecute the case."

Nina was quick to concur. "We just need enough evidence for our enforcement people and the Justice Department to follow up with their own investigation."

Hamilton shook his head. "If Quantrill is guilty of breaking environmental laws, then this is an EPA, not a Justice Department or FBI, matter. But the EPA didn't initiate the investigation and the data was collected illegally. Do either of you have any idea what you're up against on this thing?"

"We should talk to Jeb," proposed Nina. "I'll bet he'd be willing to cooperate."

Hamilton waved his hand dismissively. "You'd better just stop right there because you're not talking to anyone. My ass is on the line now and I'm not about to have my whole career flushed down the toilet. From now on, we're going to do things my way."

"Okay, so what's your plan then?" asked Higheagle.

"The first step is for me to talk with the Regional Administrator and someone I know high up in Enforcement. But if I do this, you both have to promise to keep a lid on this thing." He wagged an admonishing finger. "I won't have the EPA coming out looking badly on this. If there is justification for an investigation, then our office will speak with the Department of Justice and secure a writ of access from a federal judge. But neither myself or the Regional Administrator are going to get the DOJ or FBI involved until we're absolutely certain. You have to understand that this could take several weeks, maybe longer, to build up a legally defensible case against Quantrill."

Higheagle shook his head emphatically. "Time's the one thing we don't have on our side. He could shut down the whole operation, repair the leaks, plug and abandon the injection wells, and clean up the surface releases in less than a week. We've got to catch him while he's vulnerable."

"If you think I'm going to let you two go cowboy on this, you've got another thing coming. This is not the goddamned wild west. I will not allow you to ruin my career or destroy the credibility of the EPA. We are not a rogue agency who goes around beating up on corporations. We don't trespass on private land and get into high-speed chases that result in the death of security guards. We're not fucking Earth First."

"Well, I'm not with the EPA or any other group for that matter—I'm a private citizen," protested Higheagle defiantly. "So here's what we're going to do. We're going to go ahead and submit the soil and vapor samples to the lab for analysis. The results will prove that Quantrill has been pumping toxic waste into those wells. We can worry about the rest later. I suspect that the national media won't be too concerned with all these bureaucratic protocols you're talking about."

Hamilton frowned. "And when questions are raised about the death of two security guards, what are you going to say then?"

"The truth," Nina said. "They were trying to kill us."

Hamilton's expression narrowed. "You two are going to be in deep trouble if you move forward with this without the official backing of the EPA."

"I'll take my chances," countered Higheagle.

"No, *we'll* take our chances," corrected Nina.

Hamilton ran a hand through his inky black hair. "Jesus Christ, are you two stubborn?" His eyes narrowed on Higheagle. "All right, I suppose it won't hurt to run the samples over to Environmental Chemistry or one of the other labs. But just remember, an EPA staff member was out with you collecting those samples—and you were both trespassing. That's what makes it my problem. Look, the only way you're going to get a writ of access and a full investigation by the EPA and DOJ is if you let me handle this my way. If Quantrill gets wind of exactly what went on out there, he will throw everything he's got into it and lock this thing up in court well into the next decade."

Higheagle looked at Nina. Like him, she hadn't counted on this kind of opposition from her boss. But Hamilton was right: they had acted hastily and, even if the analytical results came back positive, their case wasn't as airtight as either of them had hoped.

"Okay, Richard," said Higheagle. "I'm willing to play it your way. But you better be right about this."

Hamilton looked at his subordinate. "Nina?"

"If you think this is the best way."

"It's not the best way, it's the *only* way." He smiled reassuringly. "So where are you going to have the samples analyzed?"

"We'll night drop them at Cornerstone Analytical in Aurora and have them analyzed on a rush basis," answered Nina. "The lab's EPA and Health Department approved. Plus they'll have them done by late tomorrow afternoon. We'll have a complete report done by Friday."

"Your report better have some sort of disclaimer because, officially, the agency can't have anything to do with this. I presume you two are paying for the analyses out of your own pockets."

Higheagle studied the EPA director closely; for the first time, he wasn't sure if he trusted the man. "I guess we'll have to."

"Have either of you told anyone besides Dr. Nickerson and myself about all this?"

"Nope—no one else," said Higheagle quickly before Nina could say anything to the contrary. "But one of the guys in the black Jeep called in on his cell when they were chasing us. So Quantrill knows we were out there. Plus the security goons came upon us so quickly that we had to leave the well vaults open so he's going to know that we inspected the vaults and probably took samples."

Hamilton thought for a moment. "We're going to have to keep this thing under wraps until I know exactly what we've got. Where are you heading after you take the samples to Cornerstone?"

"We'll be at my place," said Higheagle.

Hamilton's expression softened. "Okay, good. Go there, wait for my call, and don't get any more crazy ideas without letting me know. What you did was the right thing. It's the way you went about it that has put the EPA in an awkward position. But it will all work out in the end. Let me talk to a couple of people then we'll see what the analytical results tell us and put together a plan. Sound good?"

"That'll work," said Higheagle, and Hamilton showed them out.

CHAPTER 57

"WHAT THE HELL ARE YOU DOING?" cried Nina as Higheagle cranked the steering wheel of the War Wagon to the right, screeching through the intersection at Monaco and Alameda.

"My friend lives around here." He put his foot to the pedal and headed south on Monaco.

Nina was stunned. "What does this friend have to do with us? I thought we were going to Cornerstone to drop off the samples."

"There's been a change of plans."

"I didn't agree to that."

"You're going to have to trust me."

"Where the hell are we?"

"Scenic Glendale."

"This isn't near Five Points, is it? I've heard stories about that place."

"No, Miss Curry," he said, faking a snobby upper-class British accent. "I'm pleased to report that our current location does not abut the apocalyptic gang neighborhood known as Five Points. I dare say that we should have you safely back to Greenwich in time for your afternoon tea."

"I'm not a wimp. I can handle a ghetto."

"Of course you can, Miss Porter's. You saw one in a Spike Lee movie once."

She laughed. He had her there, she had to admit.

He brought the War Wagon to a stop in front of a drab-looking apartment complex. As he put the vehicle into park, his cell phone rang.

"I need to take this," he said. "I'll just be a minute."

Actually it took almost five.

"Who was it?" she asked him when he was finished.

"My grandfather. Unfortunately, some guy just tried to kill him."

"Oh my God, is he okay?"

"Not a scratch. He's a tough old warhorse."

"Should we go get him?"

"After we're done here."

"What are we doing here anyway?"

"My friend's a chemist at Quanterra Laboratories." He grabbed his daypack and hopped out of the truck. "He's going to run the samples for us."

Nina hopped out too, closing the door behind her. "What happened to Cornerstone?"

"I think Quanterra's better."

"That's not it. You don't trust Richard."

"Not one hundred percent." They walked to the back of the War Wagon. Higheagle opened the hatch and hoisted the ice chest filled with the soil samples from the bed of the truck. "I just want to protect our investment."

"What's your friend's name?"

"Frank Colucci, or is it Colacci?"

"Sounds like the two of you are close. You really don't trust Richard?"

"Let's just say that you and I have risked too much to be tripped up by a wildcard."

"What about your FBI friend, Agent Kane? Are you sure we can trust him?"

"One hundred percent.'

"Then when are you going to call him? You said you were going to."

"When the time is right."

"What does that mean?"

"It means soon."

"How soon?"

"Tonight. There's a few things we need to take care of first. Starting with these samples." He tipped his head towards the second ice chest sitting on the flat bed of the truck, the one filled with the air samples. "Can you grab that one?"

She reached in and picked it up. Higheagle closed the hatch and they carried the ice chests across the lawn and up an outdoor staircase. Reaching Apartment 207, they set them down and Higheagle rang the buzzer. A moment later the door opened. A man in his late twenties with tousled hair and scratchy stubble appeared in the doorway, squinting into the light. Nina found him boyishly attractive, his eyes friendly, as he stood there in a tattered Grateful Dead t-shirt and a pair of sweat pants, both of which looked as though they needed a thorough washing.

"Evening, Frank. Do you always answer the door without checking who it is?"

"I looked through the keyhole and saw her."

"I'm Nina."

"I'm in love."

Higheagle shook his head. "No, you're not, Frank. You're just horny."

Frank shrugged cheerfully at Nina. "My covers blown—bummer." He looked at the ice chests at their feet. "Why are you hand-delivering samples to my apartment at eleven o'clock at night?"

Higheagle picked up his ice chest and bulled his way past his friend. "We need your help, Frank—and without lots of questions. Do you think you can oblige?"

"I suppose I can give it the old college try-a-roo."

He stepped aside politely, allowing Nina to enter the apartment, then closed and locked the door behind her. As he did so, Nina took a moment to survey the living room. There were empty pizza boxes and a dozen empty Schlitz malt liquor and Red Bull cans sitting on a big, straw-colored coffee table that carried a hundred bumps and bruises. The rest of the furniture was scarcely distinguishable because of the mélange of clothes, bicycle parts, and mountain biking and climbing magazines cluttering the room and adjoining hallway that led presumably to a bedroom. A spider web of earthquake-related stress cracks covered one of the walls, which was missing a pair of framed pictures. She saw two piles of broken glass along the edge of the carpet beneath where the now-missing pictures had been hung.

"You might have better luck with women, Frank, if you cleaned up this dump," snorted Higheagle.

"I'm simultaneously pleading the fifth and blaming it on the earthquake. Though you should have seen it last week. It was a hell of a lot worse."

"I can imagine. Now enough chit-chat—we have some important samples for you here. Four air and four soil. We need them analyzed and the results emailed to us by three o'clock tomorrow."

"Three o'clock? You're fucking with me, right?"

"No, and we want regular—not rush turnaround—prices."

Frank looked at Nina. "Okay, what is this about? Why is he talking to me like Donald Trump?"

She shrugged. "I'd tell you but then I'd have to kill you."

"No tell-tell, no analysis."

"Ah, come on, Frank," said Higheagle.

"Talk to me, Kemosabe."

"I can only disclose one thing. The samples are going to prove what's causing the earthquakes."

"You're fucking with me, right?"

"No, Frank, I'm not fucking with you."

"No shit?" He turned to Nina. "Tell me he's not fucking with me."

"He's not fucking with you."

"We just don't want you to get caught up in all this, Frank. People may be after us."

"What kind of people?"

"Dangerous people. That's why you have to help us."

"What are you getting me into?"

"There's no reason to be alarmed," said Nina. "I'm with the U.S. government."

"Okay, now you're scaring the fucking crap out of me."

"She's with the EPA. That's why she talks like that."

"Joseph and I have found out about an illegal waste disposal operation that we think is causing the earthquakes. The samples that you're going to analyze for us are going to prove who's responsible. So what you're doing is very important, Frank."

"Why didn't you say so in the first place? Sure, I'd like to be a hero and nail a bad guy. Who is the motherfucker?"

"We can't tell you, not yet." Higheagle pulled the daypack from his shoulder, unzipped it, grabbed the filled-out chain of custody forms, and handed them to him. "Here, we need you to sign these."

"Just so you know, Joe, I like the way *she* talks to me better. And why do I feel as though if I sign those I will be visited in the night by some guy named Rocco?"

"Just sign them, Frank. You want to be a hero, right?"

"Okay, now you're both scaring the crap out of me." He pushed a heap of mountain biking magazines and laundry from the couch, snatched up a ballpoint pen, and sat down to sign the COC forms. Once he had signed both of them, one for the air samples and the other for the soil samples, Higheagle and Nina signed them too, tearing off pink copies for their own documentation.

"Thanks, Frank," said Higheagle when they were finished. "I want you to know that I'm going to pay you back for this. I'm going to get you a date."

The lab analyst looked at Nina. "Isn't he great? He leaves them in a state of hopeless sexual dependency and then I come along and fail in every way to fulfill their expectations. Over the phone, they're all excited and they say, 'Oh, you're Joseph's friend. I can't wait to meet you.' And then, of course, when they actually do meet me, let's just say the thrill is gone."

Nina smiled tartly. "Yes, Joseph's quite the Casanova, isn't he? He's certainly capable of servicing my needs—just like a trusty stallion."

"Is he now? Please tell me mo—"

"Okay, that's enough you two. We've got to get going. You're a good man, Frank, to do this."

"Yes, I know." He smiled. "Now about that special price. The best I can do is one and a half times the rate of standard two-week turnaround."

"You know I can't afford that."

"What else can you offer then?"

"Two dates—I'll get you two dates. And I promise one of them won't run away from you until at least halfway through dinner. That's the best I can do."

Frank mulled it over. "Two dates and standard turnaround price? Okay, that'll work."

"You don't get out much, do you Frank?" said Nina.

"I'm in the lab a lot. Having private conversations with radionuclides and polynuclear aromatic hydrocarbons, if that's what you mean."

Gee, it hardly shows.

"It's the new millennium," Frank explained, as he rose from his seat. "It will be remembered as a sad time in our nation's history, a time when outrageously witty, strikingly handsome, hard-working heterosexual home boys like me had to go to great lengths to debase themselves just for a simple date. We are weak creatures in the weakest of times, I'm afraid."

Higheagle stood up from his chair too. "We'd love to stay and listen to *Dark Side of the Moon* played backwards all night with you, but we've got to go before more people start shooting at us."

Frank licked his lips worriedly. "People are shooting at you?"

"Just a few bad guys. But hopefully they won't come here." He pointed at the ice chests. "By the way, the one on the left has the air samples and the one on the right has the soil samples. And remember, we need those results by three o'clock tomorrow."

"Yes, sir." He looked helplessly at Nina as he rounded the coffee table. "Please get General Patton out of here before he asks me for another favor." He came to a halt at the door, opened it.

"One last thing," said Higheagle. "Make sure the QA/QC is flawless and don't let anyone know you're working on this."

"Don't worry, I'll do the analyses myself. Now off you go, General." He gave a mock salute.

"You're going to be a hero after this, Frank. Trust me, every consulting firm in the state will be sending samples to your lab."

The analyst's eyes lit up. "I can see the *Denver Post* headline. *Quanterra—The Lab That Toppled Billionaire Charles Quantrill.*" He covered his mouth. "Oh, that's right, I'm not supposed to say anything."

"Damn, how did you know?"

He held up the COC. "How could I miss it? It says *Quantrill Injection Wellfield* right on the form."

"I'd watch it if I were you. Just saying the man's name out loud could bring you bad karma."

"Then I'll just have to keep this all to my lonesome little self."

"That's right. In fact, talk to no one but me. For anyone else, this project doesn't exist."

"Roger that, General Patton." He ushered them out the door. "I just hope you two know what you're doing."

"Are you kidding?" said Nina as they stepped outside into the crisp October night. "We're making it all up as we go along."

CHAPTER 58

RICHARD HAMILTON stared out at the cars passing along Colorado Boulevard through the dirty glass of the payphone. It was after eleven and there were only a few vehicles on the road. He touched his gloved hand to the film of dirt on the glass and doodled a stick figure. Growing impatient, he glanced at his watch. *How long has it been? Should I call again?* Feeling a little chill, he bundled his cashmere overcoat tightly around himself then glanced at his watch again. *Might as well.* He punched the redial. While the phone rang, he studied the green and red 7-Eleven sign hovering fifty feet away, mumbling impatiently under his breath. *Come on, come on.* The phone rang four times. Just as he was about to hang up, he heard the voice he wanted to hear on the other end of the line.

"Chuck Quantrill speakin'."

"I've been calling for the last fifteen minutes."

"Richard?" The voice was surprised. "Is this a secure line?"

"Yes, I'm at a payphone."

"You do know that you're only supposed to contact me in the event of an emergency."

"What the fuck do you think this is?"

"I take it you have important information for me."

"Yes, and it's going to cost you."

"You're already drawing a sizable salary from me, son. A quarter of a million per year as I recollect. I can't pay you more than that."

"Higheagle and Nina Curry were just here. They told me *everything*. I managed to contain the situation, but it's going to cost you."

"What does this have to do with me?"

"Don't play games with me. You know damn well what this has to do with you."

"Like I said, you're already being paid what most people would consider a handsome sum."

"I want a quarter of a million above and beyond my current compensation."

"Why, Richard, I swear you're the lowest kind of carpetbagger imaginable. You act as if blackmail is a goddamned profession."

"Cut the bullshit. I want cash like always, all twenties. Same drop as usual. And I want it by Friday."

The phone went silent. "You know I can't get that much together in so short a spell."

"You'd better, or else a certain—"

"You don't need to remind me about the report and video and all that other crap you've got on me. I liked it a damn sight better when you laid it out for me as a business proposition."

"I thought we were closing a deal here, but I guess not. I'm hanging up now."

"All right, all right, I'll get you the money."

"Then it's a deal. A quarter of a million."

"It's a deal. But you just remember, if I get bushwhacked by the feds, there's no more Daddy Warbucks for you and that purty little family of yours."

Though Hamilton was loathe to admit it, he knew Quantrill was right. The game of blackmail he was playing depended entirely on the financial security of the brawny Texan. Without Quantrill, he was just another two-bit government bureaucrat with a low six-figure salary and an above-average pension.

"All right, your boy and Nina Curry just left my house. They broke into your oil field and took soil and vapor samples around the injection wells. They said that two security guards chased them and were both killed in an explosion."

"Only one of the guards was killed. Tell me something I don't know. Or maybe you should first explain just why in the hell you let them leave?"

"That's not part of our deal."

"What are they going to do with the samples?"

"They're dropping them off at Cornerstone Laboratories in Aurora and leaving them in the night drop. The samples are in two ice chests and will have forms inside with information on the site and samples. The soil samples will be in brass tubes, about six inches long. The vapor samples will be in Tedlar bags, about the size of half-gallon sized Ziplocs."

"Got an address?"

"It's 10703 East Bethany Drive. I'd get Boggs and his men on those samples right away. The night drop chute should be right near the front. Should be a piece of cake. Have them pop the air bags and shred them to destroy the vapor samples. And have them peel the tape off the brass soil sample tubes and toss the soil. Have them do it as far away from the laboratory as possible."

"For Christ sakes, Harry and his security team ain't stupid, Richard."

"Higheagle and Curry know everything. You shouldn't have kept Higheagle on as long as you did."

"They talk to anybody else besides you?"

"Just that earthquake guy, Dr. Nickerson. Like them, he's going to have to be dealt with."

"My team is already on it. How do you know they haven't told anyone else?"

"I don't. But they came to me first so they obviously trust me. They said they came straight to my house after leaving the site."

"What did you tell them?"

"That we had to play it my way and take things slowly with EPA Enforcement and the DOJ or we could blow the whole thing."

"Anything else?"

"I told them not to talk to anyone."

"If you were so damn convincing, why in the hell didn't you talk them into giving up altogether?"

"I tried, but they wouldn't listen. And you know damn well I'll never do anything to implicate myself. That's the way the game is played. There has never been anything to link me to you. Shit, you're making hundreds of millions of dollars in annual profit while I only get a quarter of a—"

"A half million this year," Quantrill reminded him.

"Scraps compared to what you're hauling in."

"I'm going to pretend you didn't say that and ask you where they're headed?"

"They said that once they drop off the samples, they're going to go back to Higheagle's. By the way, what's your brother think of all this? He couldn't possibly be okay with—"

"Jeb's dead. He was killed in the earthquake."

"Killed in the earthquake? Are you sure about that?"

"What the hell are you implying?"

"You know perfectly well what I'm implying. And just so you know, you'd better not get any similar ideas about me. I know I don't need to remind you that I have copies of a certain video and a detailed report in the hands of more attorneys and tucked away in more safety deposit boxes than you probably knew existed in this state. So let's be clear: whatever you've got planned for Higheagle and the others, you'd better not be considering for me."

"You just get me a replacement at EPA better than that Nina gal. You had her brought in here, and I still can't think of a good reason why you did it. She was too damn headstrong from the get-go."

"No, she was the perfect front. Firm but fair, just like me. She just got mixed up with Higheagle is all."

"I've got to get my men moving. Now you listen up. You've built up quite a little blackmail business over the years, I'll give you that. But if I were you, I wouldn't want to push my luck."

"You're in no position to threaten me."

"I reckon I am, son. Just remember, if I sink like the Lusitania, you're going down with me."

CHAPTER 59

DR. JAMES NICKERSON stared in horror at the TV screen. There were now three suspicious deaths of people closely linked to Charles Quantrill—Jeb Quantrill, Mark Kelso, and the newest to be flashed up on the screen, Jack Holland, Quantrill Ventures' chief legal counsel. The likelihood of the three deaths not being related was very remote indeed, and Nickerson knew he could be next.

He turned up the volume with his remote. The police had cordoned off the crime scene at a church in Colorado Springs, where they were now pulling the bullet-ridden bodies of both Jack Holland and the unfortunate pastor of the church and loading them into an ambulance. All in all, it was a tragic and disturbing sight.

But it was Jeb's death that tore the seismologist up inside. He remembered back to their days together in grad school at Stanford and their early years as young geoscientists in Midland. He couldn't believe his old friend was gone. They had drifted apart over the years, and yet Nickerson had always thought of them both as kindred spirits. *We were so young and full of promise back then,* he thought; *ready to set the world on fire with our great minds.* The truth was they had both been very successful. But Jeb's success was nothing but a house of cards, an edifice built from a crazy get-rich-quick-scheme he had concocted with his older brother. It saddened Nickerson to think what a sham and waste Jeb's life had ultimately proven to be.

He wondered exactly how his old friend had died. The TV reports had been vague about the cause of death, except to say that he had fallen. Had he died in the earthquake? Or had his brother Charles killed him? It didn't matter, thought Nickerson; the CEO was still responsible for his brother's death. There was no doubt in his mind that Charles was the one who had come up with the injection scheme in the first place and had coerced Jeb and the other senior employees into implementing it.

He thought of the case against Charles Quantrill. Unfortunately, nothing was yet proven beyond a reasonable doubt. None of the three mysterious deaths could be attributed to Quantrill or his henchmen. Even Kelso's death might be considered an accident. So how in the hell were they going to catch the CEO, especially with the situation becoming more deadly by the minute?

Nickerson checked his watch. Eleven-twenty. He wondered why he hadn't heard from Higheagle and Nina. It had been more than an hour since they had last spoken and he was growing increasingly anxious. The whole situation had taken on a surreal quality. Prior to yesterday, they were nothing but a simple group of scientists trying to unravel the mystery of the earthquakes. Now, shockingly, they were being chased and hunted by Quantrill's security team and perhaps even professional killers.

When his cell phone rang, he flinched. *Jesus, get a grip on yourself, James!* He checked the caller ID: it was Higheagle.

Finally!

He punched the *Talk* button. "Joe, where the hell have you been?"

"We had to pay a little visit to Nina's boss and pick up my grandfather. One of Quantrill's men paid my grandfather an unfriendly visit. We just left the house a few minutes ago."

In the background, Nickerson heard the sound of a revving engine and screeching tires. Where the hell were they going in such a hurry? "Is he all right?"

"Yep. He clipped the bastard and drove him off. My grandfather thinks he was a pro."

"I wonder if it was the same guy who killed Jack Holland?"

"You're talking about Quantrill's lawyer?"

"They just pulled him and a dead priest from a church in Colorado Springs. They were both shot."

"Jesus."

"Is your house under surveillance?"

"We didn't see anyone. But we came in from the back alley and they may have been out front. I don't think we're being followed. My grandfather was able to sneak out through the back and we haven't seen anyone. I think we're safe for the time being."

"Don't you think it's time we call in the cavalry?"

"I just did—my friend Special Agent Kane with the FBI I told you about. He's the only person I trust."

"I hope he knows what he's doing. This situation is out of control—Quantrill's going berserk. He's killed, or tried to kill, five people already. We're all being hunted now and time is running out."

"Five people? I thought there were only four: Holland, the priest, Kelso, and my grandfather."

"There's also Jeb Quantrill."

"Jeb's dead too? Jesus."

Nickerson could barely hear Higheagle's voice over the sound of the revving engine. He spoke loudly into the mouthpiece. "It's all over the news with him being a corporate big shot and all. They're saying that he fell accidentally to his death, but I'm not so sure given everything that's happened."

"So we now have not only Quantrill's security people, but a professional killer after us. What's next Al-Qaeda?"

"What about the samples? Have you submitted them to a lab?"

"Signed, sealed, delivered."

That was good news: the samples were the key to the case. Without them, there was no way they could link the mostly legitimate on-site waste operation to the illicit off-site deep well injection operation. "How soon can we meet?"

"We're a little behind schedule. I'm thinking twelve-thirty."

"Will this Special Agent Kane be there?"

"That's the plan. But I still have to call him to confirm. I haven't told him any of the details yet, only that I think I know what's causing the earthquakes and I want to meet."

The tires squealed in the background and again Nickerson wondered where in the hell they were driving in such a hurry. "Where are you going?"

"We're on our way to Cornerstone Labs to conduct a little experiment."

"A little experiment?"

"Before we meet with Agent Kane, we need to know if we've got a fox in the henhouse."

CHAPTER 60

POISED BETWEEN TENSION AND IMPATIENCE, Joseph Higheagle sat with his grandfather and Nina Curry watching the front entrance of Cornerstone Laboratories. He had parked the War Wagon in the adjacent parking lot, concealing the vehicle beyond the reach of the lamplights on a small hill overlooking the analytical laboratory. They had arrived five minutes ago and Higheagle had the heat on low to take away the chill of the fall air. The lab and parking lot were deserted: not a whisper of movement was visible at the sample drop-off station beyond the glass doors.

But he suspected there soon would be.

"Do you think they'll take the bait?" asked Nina from the backseat.

Higheagle swept his Leupold 10X binoculars across the driveway, parking lot, and front entrance of the lab. "I put the odds at three to one." He set down the binoculars, put on a CD, and adjusted the volume. An acoustic guitar began strumming lightly. After several seconds, an otherworldly flute joined in, an exquisite mingling of sound that was at once ancient and modern, as well as captivating to the ear.

"Is that Cheyenne?" asked Nina.

"No, it's R. Carlos Nakai. He's Navaho and Ute."

"It's beautiful." She gave a little sigh. "What do you Cheyenne call yourselves? Is there a name?"

"*Tsistsistas*," replied John Higheagle. "The ones who are similarly bred. We are *The People*."

"*Tsistsistas—The People*," she said slowly. "If the Cheyenne are the people, what does that make everyone else?"

"Strangers, the enemy, the differently bred," said the old chief. "Like you."

"So what you're saying is if you're not a Cheyenne, you're basically subhuman."

"You catch on quickly—for a white Princeton girl."

"Very funny," she said, and they all laughed.

Higheagle studied his grandfather in the faint moonlight creeping through the window. Sitting in the passenger seat, he had changed into regular clothes, but he still cradled his Winchester Yellow Boy repeating rifle in his oversized hands and there were still faded smudges of red, white, and yellow war paint on his leathery face. He looked like a throwback to the Old West with his silver hair tumbling down his broad shoulders, his repeating rifle adorned with eagle feathers, brass tacks, and vermilion, and the faded war paint on his face.

Nina broke the silence. "So tell me about this FBI agent friend of yours whose going to help us, this Agent Kane. How do you two know each other again?"

"It's a long story."

"We've got some time. Besides, if we're going to move forward together on this, I need to know that I can trust this guy. I'm not about to let the FBI come in and take over this case. So what's this guy's story? How do you know him?"

"Our great-great grandfather's fought against one another in the Indian wars. At least that's how it all got started."

"Oh, so this guy is the descendant of General Kane. Richard told me the story about the general and your ancestor High Eagle."

"Richard? Don't you mean Evil Richard?"

"I guess we're about to find out. But tell me the story—I want to hear it again."

"All right. It happened in 1869 when Brigadier General Joshua Kane led a paleontological expedition into Northern Colorado. It was called the Orser Expedition after Harvard paleontologist Henry Orser. That's where my great-great grandfather, a Cheyenne warrior named High Eagle, and his brother Alights On A Cloud stole a *Triceratops* skull right from under the nose of the general. And I don't mean just any old *Triceratops* skull. It was the very first *Triceratops* ever discovered."

"No, it wasn't," countered John Higheagle testily. "Our people had been picking up dinosaur bones from that valley for decades before the Orser Expedition."

"Okay so it was the first *Triceratops* found and described scientifically by a white man."

"My God, a subhuman?" quipped Nina. "What happened next?"

"General Kane—or Two Stars as our ancestors called him—came after them and tried to get the skull back. He had over two hundred cavalrymen and Pawnee scouts. But the Cheyenne and their Lakota allies refused to give up the skull. They thought the skull belonged to the Great White Buffalo Chief, the ancestor of all the buffalo, and they didn't want to give it up. The Indians and the cavalry ended up fighting three great battles, which our people won. My great-great grandfather and their Cheyenne band ended up keeping the skull, but Two Stars hunted them down and took it back. The Cheyenne were eventually forced onto the Southern Cheyenne Reservation. Meanwhile, Two Stars quit the army and started a ranch along the South Platte in Colorado. After my grandfather and his brother had lived on the reservation for a few years, the General recruited them to work on his ranch. Together, they raised cattle and later buffalo and eventually my grandfather and his brother were given a stake in the ranch. Together, they named it White Buffalo Ranch after the great skull. The ranch is still there today and it's where Josh Kane, my grandfather, and I grew up. We have our own individual houses on the ranch, but still share all the land. That's how we know each other."

"What happened to the *Triceratops* skull?"

"Two Stars gave it back to High Eagle and Alights On A Cloud as a gift and now it belongs to the Northern Cheyenne people. My grandfather and I are the curators. The specimen is too valuable to keep on display so we keep it in storage for our people to see."

"That's enough talk—someone's coming," pronounced John Higheagle. His gaze was focused intently on the illuminated street below.

Higheagle turned. "Are you sure, Grandfather?" he whispered.

"Yes, they're here."

Feeling a tremolo of excitement, Higheagle focused his binoculars down onto the street. He spotted a pair of midnight-blue Crown Victoria's with tinted windows, moving slowly and methodically like a pair of cruising killer whales. The vehicles paused at the main entrance. Then they quietly made their way to the front of the lab building before coming to a halt at the overnight sample drop-off on the right side of the building. A moment later three front doors opened. A short, stocky man stepped out of the lead car and a pair of tall, brawny men slipped from the second vehicle, all three wearing suits and plainly visible in the well-lit parking lot.

Higheagle felt his heart rate click up a notch. Suddenly, he felt very alert. He turned off the CD player. R. Carlos Nakai's melodic, otherworldly flute playing disappeared.

"Do you recognize any of them?" asked John Higheagle.

"That's definitely Boggs, Quantrill's head of security, out front. The guy next to him with the white hair is named Heiser. He's the one that tossed me down the hill yesterday and was following us earlier this afternoon when the earthquake hit. I don't recognize the third dude. He must be new." He handed the binoculars to his grandfather. "That's not the same guy who broke in and attacked you, is it?"

The old chief took the binoculars and peered through them, adjusting the knobs as he studied the men below. After a moment, he pulled the binoculars away and shook his head.

"No, that's not him. I never forget a face."

"So our hit man is still out there. But at least we know Richard Hamilton's true colors."

"I can't believe I trusted him—the bastard," muttered Nina bitterly. "Can I take a look?"

"Yeah sure," said the old chief, and he handed her the binoculars.

"You know the worst thing," she said, focusing on Boggs and his crew as they studied the layout. "I moved out here because of Richard. He recruited me. And now I find out he's Quantrill's lackey. How could I have been so stupid?"

"He didn't just fool you—he fooled all of us," said Higheagle. "Hell, I always liked the son of a bitch. Up until tonight, I always regarded him as one of the best regulators I've ever worked with. That's what's so ironic about all this."

"Okay you two, you can stop feeling sorry for yourselves. They're going inside now."

They watched as the two men with Boggs went to the door marked *Sample Drop-Off*, pulled out a set of tools, jimmied open the door, and quietly slipped inside the building. Higheagle couldn't help but feel a little tingle of excitement watching Quantrill's security men in action. It was hard not to be impressed with how stealthily and skillfully they penetrated their objective.

He looked at Nina and his grandfather. They too were mesmerized.

Less than five minutes later, he saw a flicker of movement and the two men reappeared with a portable dolly carrying several plastic ice chests. They pushed the dolly to one of the Crown Victorias and stuffed the ice chests inside the trunk.

"How about that? They're not even going to check them," said Nina.

"Not here anyway," said Higheagle.

"Quantrill's not going to be happy when he discovers that he's been duped," said John Higheagle. "I sure would like to see the look on his face."

"Are we going to follow them?" asked Nina.

Higheagle shook his head. "Too risky. Besides, we achieved what we came here for. We know that Richard's up to his neck in this shit."

"Hold on—they're leaving," he heard his grandfather exclaim.

They watched as Boggs and the other two men hopped into their respective cars, fired them up, and started off. But as they pulled out of the turnabout, their headlights flicked up the hill and swept across the War Wagon.

"Quick get down!" cried Higheagle.

The three dove down in their seats.

He held his breath and didn't move a muscle as the headlights seemed to linger on them interminably. He wondered if Boggs and his henchmen had spotted them. He felt his heart pounding, breath quickening at the prospect of discovery.

"Did they see us?" asked Nina.

"I don't know. Just stay down and keep totally still."

After a moment, the headlights moved off them and, once again, a silky darkness descended upon the War Wagon. Pulling himself up with the steering wheel, Higheagle stole a peak over the edge of the dashboard. The two dark Crown Victorias cruised across the parking lot, again like gliding killer whales, made the turn onto the street, and drove off into the night.

Higheagle expelled a deep sigh of relief. "You can get up now—they're gone."

His grandfather popped up like a jack-in-the-box, grinning from ear to ear. "When they open those ice chests, they're in for one big fucking surprise."

"So is Evil Richard," said Nina. "When the FBI comes knocking on his door."

CHAPTER 61

WHEN THE TELEPHONE RANG, Quantrill had just kissed his wife, Bunnie, goodnight and was heading back to his desk in his home office cradling an Old Forester bourbon. The office was tucked away on the first floor, southwest wing, of his resplendent English country manor. Outside the window, a light drizzle had begun to fall and occasional bursts of lightning lit up the steep-pitched roofs, turrets, dormers, and gables of the twenty-room mansion like something out of Edgar Allan Poe.

He checked the caller ID, saw that it was Boggs, and picked up just before the fourth ring. "What have you got, Harry? Not more bad news, I hope."

"I'm afraid so, Mr. Quantrill. The ice chests weren't at the lab."

"What the hell happened?"

"I don't think Higheagle dropped them off at Cornerstone. We broke into the night drop room as instructed and found two ice chests containing vials and bottles with water in them. There were no brass tubes and no air bags. The forms inside the ice chests don't have the signatures of Higheagle or the girl. Nor do they reference the site, the wells, or your name, sir."

"Did you double check?"

"Yes, we went back just to make sure. There's nothing there. We rechecked the forms too. There are two spaces at the bottom of both forms we took from the ice chests. One of them says *sampler* and the other says *relinquished by*. In both places, it says *Richard Najarian*. The company name listed for him says *Eocon Engineering*. Where it says *project name*, it says *Petroco Refinery*."

Quantrill felt a sense of desperation. "So what are you telling me, that Higheagle and the girl are trying to disguise where the samples really came from?"

"I'm thinking that one of three things had to have happened. One, Higheagle and the girl haven't dropped the samples off yet. Two, Hamilton's lying and they've taken the samples somewhere else. Or three, they decided after leaving Hamilton to drop them off at another lab."

Quantrill felt his tension diffuse momentarily as Boggs' reasoning sunk in. After a moment, he said, "All right, we've got to concentrate on finding Higheagle and the girl. But again I have to ask you, are you sure those samples aren't there?"

"I'm positive, sir. We checked thoroughly."

"And there's no other way to drop them off at that lab?"

"We checked the whole building. There's no other drop off place. There's not even another entrance, only a fire exit."

"All right, get the hell out of there and get back to Higheagle's. He probably has the samples with him. Where is Mr. Sperry?"

"He's paying a visit to Dr. Nickerson."

"Now?"

"Yes, sir. We should be hearing from him any minute."

CHAPTER 62

MR. SPERRY parked his Cadillac Escalade luxury SUV one block east of the USGS National Earthquake Information Center and stepped out of the car, leaving it unlocked. He had already made three passes around the building to get a feel for points of entry and escape. He couldn't believe his good fortune: during his last drive by, he had actually spotted his target in one of the fifth floor offices; and, at half past midnight, there didn't appear to be anyone else in the building. By some stroke of luck, or perhaps just mental and physical exhaustion, all the seismologists except the fabled Earthquake Man had gone home for the evening.

He began to feel a little stirring inside, bringing to mind a triumphant fencing victory over a fierce rival at Andover when he was at Exeter. This one was going to be truly special. After the near fiasco earlier with the Grandpa from Hell, he couldn't believe how quickly his luck had turned around.

Though he had been shot three times, only one of the wounds had required medical treatment. Fortunately, the bullet had torn through his upper arm just above the elbow without striking a major artery. He had cleaned the wound, sewed it up tight, applied a bandage, and taken a double dose of antibiotics and a morphine derivative that brought back strange memories of having sex with Chelsea Fortescue, a saintly little virgin he had deflowered on a weekend trip to Vassar while at Yale. Already he was feeling much better. From his extensive research into all things paramilitary, he knew how to deal with battle wounds and there was no way he was going to let one measly grazing bullet take him off the active roster.

Lux et veritas, sport, he whispered his Yale motto to himself. *Light and truth* indeed.

As he started towards the NEIC building, keeping furtively to the shadows, he felt a growing pulse of excitement that made him momentarily forget the throbbing pain in his arm. He thought of the chief. Man was he one tough old goat. He was also crazy as a loon, dressing up like goddamned Crazy Horse himself with his war paint and Winchester repeating rifle. But the craziest thing of all was that the wily old renegade had known he was coming. Like an animal in the wild, the Indian had sensed his presence long before his arrival and took appropriate contingency action.

He knew he was lucky to have made it out alive. If not for his Kevlar bullet-proof vest and pure luck on that third and final shot, he would be done for. But he would have another crack at the old man and his grandson. Still, he was glad they were not on his hit list at the moment. He would deal with them later. All he had to worry about right now was some nerdy old scientist who probably hadn't done anything more strenuous in twenty years than change out a light bulb.

He made his way to the rear entrance of the NEIC building, ran a professional eye over the alarmed door, pulled out a small nylon case, extracted a series of state-of-the-art electronic devices, and swiftly disarmed the lock. With a gloating smile on his face, he put away his tools. Then he slipped into the building, located the fire stairs, and quietly made his way up to the fifth floor. From his earlier pass, he knew where Dr. Nickerson's office was and how best to take him. He would creep up close like a stalking lion, remaining completely still and silent, then make a mad dash with his silenced Smith and Wesson blazing.

Pfft. Pfft. Pfft. It would be over in a matter of seconds.

Picturing the fateful scene, he felt a tingle in his stomach. As always he was supremely confident, though the incident with the unexpectedly tough old chief had left him a bit rattled. But again he reminded himself that John Higheagle was a Korean war veteran who came from a long line of warriors. In sharp contrast, his new mark was an elderly nerd with no combat experience or history of gun ownership. He would be a lamb before the slaughter.

When he reached the fifth floor, he stood frozen a moment studying the layout through the vertical window. The coast was clear: the hallway and conference room directly ahead were empty and he couldn't hear a single sound. He withdrew his Smith and Wesson M1911A1 .45 caliber semi-auto from the military-style shoulder holster beneath his L.L. Bean duck-hunting jacket and screwed the perforated silencer into the nose of the firearm until it was tight and secure.

Quietly opening the door, he stepped out into the hallway. After scanning in both directions, he then started to his left towards Nickerson's office, moving stealthy as a cat across the tiled floor.

He navigated his way past a pair of computer rooms then past a room with a bunch of scratching seismographs before reaching the corridor that led to the seismologist's office. The lights in the interior of the building were on, but Nickerson's office appeared to be the only one visibly illuminated from the street. He kept moving, his silenced pistol raised in a two-handed grip in his gloved hands. Another ten feet and he was at Nickerson's office.

The world famous seismologist sat behind his desk looking over some computer printouts. Quiet as a mouse, Mr. Sperry ducked into the office one door over and across the hall from Nickerson's, retreated into the shadows, and took a moment to study his victim.

The Earthquake Man was intently focused. Mr. Sperry could tell that he had no idea that his scientific lair had been penetrated and he was about to die a swift and violent death. The surprise would be total. This one was going to be special, he could tell, as he rechecked his semi-auto.

This was it—the moment of truth.

It was then the interruption came.

Headlights swept past Nickerson's office window and tires unexpectedly squealed to a halt down on the street below. The seismologist stood up abruptly from his seat and went to the window to have a look. With no view onto the street, the assassin quickly darted into the office across the hall to see for himself what the commotion was about.

A pair of unfamiliar cars pulled to the curb in front of the NEIC building. From one of the vehicles stepped Higheagle, his grandfather, and Nina Curry, a foxy little thing in the flesh the assassin saw at once. They were carrying several bags filled presumably with documents. From the other car emerged a man whom he instantly recognized as a law enforcement officer of some kind, most likely FBI. He quickly put together what they were doing here: Higheagle and his clever little companions were here to meet with Nickerson.

If he could somehow catch them by surprise, there might be an opportunity to roll up the whole group in one fell swoop.

Lux et veritas indeed!

He moved closer to the window. Higheagle clutched a cell phone to his ear and was walking with the others to the front entrance.

Suddenly the phone in Nickerson's office next door rang.

He crept back into the office across the hall. Once there, he watched and listened as the seismologist punched the *Speaker* button and spoke into the phone.

"Joe, you're here already—that was fast."

"We're coming up. Can you buzz us in?"

"I'll be right down. I have to let you in myself." Nickerson punched off and stood up from his chair.

Unsure of which direction he would take down the hallway to reach the elevators, the assassin pulled back deeper into the office, concealing himself behind the wooden desk. He heard a brisk padding of footsteps, saw a shadow pass, and then the footsteps faded away and he heard Nickerson push the button to the elevator. A moment later there was a dinging sound and he heard the heavy metal doors open and then close.

He quickly checked the large conference room next to the room with the scratching seismographs and another smaller conference room on the north side of the building. They would most likely use the larger conference room for their meeting. The room was closer to Nickerson's office, more centrally located, and would be able to comfortably seat the entire party of five and still allow them considerable space to examine the documents in their possession. When he was finished with his reconnaissance, he pulled out his cell phone and quickly punched in a number.

"Chuck Quantrill speakin'."

"It's me, sport. I only have a minute so listen up. I'm at the USGS in Golden. Dr. Nickerson has just gone downstairs to let in Higheagle and Curry. Higheagle's brought his grandfather with him and, by the looks of it, a federal agent. They'll be here in the next two minutes."

"How many total?"

"Five including Nickerson."

"Can you take them all?"

"That's what I want to talk to you about. This has turned into a much bigger assignment than I had anticipated."

"I'll pay you five hundred thousand dollars."

"No, you'll pay me two million. And I want it wired into my offshore account by noon tomorrow."

Quantrill made no immediate response; as expected, the CEO needed a moment to consider the new terms. In the meantime, the assassin stepped into the large conference room and again studied the layout. Central table, ten chairs, two doors in and out, glass windows on three sides. It was the perfect room for an ambush. Once they were all seated around the table, he would be able to take them down like ducks lined up in a row.

"We have a deal, sir," said Quantrill. "Call me when it's done."

"Until then—cheerio, sport," said Mr. Sperry, and he punched off.

He ducked into the office across the hall from the conference room. There he made one last survey of the kill zone, taking in the various lines of sight and avenues of escape. He had a good angled view into the room and had the advantage of heavy shadow and two different hallway escape options. He would eavesdrop on them for a few minutes before killing them. That way he could report to Quantrill precisely what they knew and to whom, beyond those in the room, they had transmitted the information.

He heard the ding of the elevator.

Feeling a throbbing pulse of excitement, he slipped deeper into the shadows of the office, waiting for the special moment to come.

CHAPTER 63

ONCE THE GROUP settled into their seats, Higheagle looked across the table at Special Agent Joshua Kane and wondered if he was making a big mistake bringing the FBI into the case. No doubt his friend could be trusted; it was Josh's superiors that worried Higheagle. The situation was already complicated enough. Were they simply making things worse by bringing the FBI into the fold? Would Josh or his supervisors even believe the wild story he was about to tell?

"So, Agent Kane," said Nina, her voice resonant as she sat forward in her seat, peering across the glossy conference table. "I heard the story about the *Triceratops* skull. Did Joseph's great-great grandfather really steal it from your great-great grandfather or is he pulling my leg?"

The FBI agent looked at Joseph and smiled. "It's all true."

"I'm glad to hear that. I have another question."

"Fire away."

"Can we trust you?"

He gave a look of surprise. "Trust me?"

"Trust that you won't take the information we're about to give you and either screw up the investigation or cut us out of the loop."

He appeared amused. "Why would you think I would cut you out of the loop?"

"Because you work for the FBI. J. Edgar Hoover may be long dead and gone, but old habits die hard."

"I think you've been watching too many movies."

"So you don't care about seeing your face on the six o'clock news?"

He grinned. "Look, I'm neither a seismologist nor an environmental scientist so I can tell you, from what I've heard so far, we're all going to have to work together on this one."

"As equal partners?"

"Until I've heard all the evidence, I can't make any promises."

She gave a stubborn look. "Then there's no deal." She gave Higheagle *the look* and he knew it was time for him to make his appeal. Nina and Nickerson had both insisted upon it. "Go on, tell him."

Kane looked at him.

"It's only fair, Josh," said the Cheyenne. "We've put our lives on the line. If we're going to go through with this then it has to be a team effort.

We're going to have to have unanimous buy-in from all the players on all decisions until we agree to hand over the case."

Kane's eyes narrowed slightly.

"This is the only way, Josh."

There was a lengthy silence as the special agent considered the proposal. "All right, you've got a deal," he finally agreed. "Now let's hear what you've got. Start from the beginning."

It took ten full minutes. Together, they described how Quantrill's illegal deep well injection operation was causing the earthquakes, how his hired guns were out chasing and killing people, and how Richard Hamilton was implicated in the whole, dirty mess. By the end of it, Special Agent Joshua Kane had taken a full five pages of notes and actually looked bewildered.

"This is a lot bigger than I thought," was all he could manage to say.

Higheagle noticed his grandfather staring intently at the open doorway. "What is it, Grandfather?"

"I'm not sure. I thought I heard something."

"I didn't hear anything," said Nickerson.

"I did," said Agent Kane.

CHAPTER 64

COVERTLY watching his targets talking in the conference room, Mr. Sperry thought of all the fun he could have with two million dollars. But then he realized that two million dollars was not all that much, all things considered. Especially since he had never been very good at saving money. With his extravagant tastes in fine cuisine, high-end prostitutes, and glitzy resorts around the globe, two million bucks wouldn't go as far as it should have. And then he got to thinking that not only was two million dollars not enough, but he wanted the whole money thing taken care of right now. Why the hell did he have to wait until the job was finished? I mean, it wasn't like it wasn't in the bag. As he had suspected, his victims weren't expecting anything was going to happen to them here at the USGS and their guard was down. It was going to be almost too easy. He would take the Feeb first, then the wily old Indian chief and his grandson, then Nickerson and Nina Curry, whom he would save for last.

He couldn't wait to see the final look on her face just before he unleashed his maelstrom of lead. It would be over in a matter of seconds.

Again he thought of the money. He wanted it right now.

The goddamned money—he definitely deserved more than two million measly dollars. Come on, were there not five people who could do serious harm to Quantrill in there? And wasn't the CEO of Quantrill Ventures a billionaire high up on the Forbes list?

His mind fast-forwarded to when it was all over. He would lounge around on a beach for a month or two before he would get bored and want to get back to wet work. He took an imaginary whiff of the sea air, felt the soft fine beach sand beneath his feet, gave a contented sigh. A little surf and sand and deep sea fishing off Cabo—not to mention a half-dozen high-grade Mexican whores whom he would spank and mount repeatedly—would be just what he needed after the current assignment.

But to make it all happen—at least the way he wanted it to happen—he had to play a little game.

Keeping his gaze fixed on his victims, he quietly pulled out his cell and punched in the number.

"Quantrill here."

He paused, letting the symphony of the moment wash over him. "It's me. It's done."

A note of surprise on the other end. "You killed them all?"

"Yes, sir." *Does my voice sound somehow different? Is it my imagination or do I sense hesitation?*

"You're positive?"

"What?"

"You're sure they're all dead."

"I'm a professional, sir. When I tell you they're dead, believe me they're dead. There's one more thing."

The line remained quiet. Again he wondered if Quantrill was actually onto his little charade or he was letting his imagination get the better of him.

"What's that?"

"I want double the amount and I want all the money wired to my account straight away."

"Four million dollars? That's not what we agreed to."

"The assignment was a challenging one and I feel I deserve more. You want this to go away forever, don't you?"

"Are you threatening me?"

"I never threaten my clients. I just happen to think this job is worth more than the previously agreed-upon price. I took significant risk and nearly lost my life tonight—on two occasions."

Another long pause. But this time when the voice returned it had softened considerably. "Very well, I suppose this warrants a sizable bonus. Congratulations on a job well done."

"Please make sure the money's transferred straight away. Four million dollars."

"I can guarantee it, Mr. Sperry. Now I believe this concludes our business arrangement. I bid you adios."

"Goodbye, Mr. Quantrill. It's been a genuine pleasure working for you, sport."

CHAPTER 65

SMILING, Mr. Sperry punched off and stepped towards the window of the office. As he did so, he emerged from the shadow and the artificial light of the hallway captured his reflection momentarily. One half of his face basked in the glow of the fluted light, while the other remained masked in shadowy darkness.

One half good, the other half evil, he mused. *No, no, no, sport, you're all evil—pure unadulterated evil!*

He stepped back out of the partial light, throwing his reflected face into complete blackness. He gave a crooked smile: it was like a sign from above.

He had his money and it was all going to be over in the next minute, he told himself again. *But you will treasure this moment for the rest of your life.*

It was then he heard an unexpected footfall.

WHEN HE HEARD THE SOUND, Higheagle felt his senses go into high alert. He scanned the hallway outside the conference room and the dark offices beyond, but didn't see anyone or anything unusual.

"Is there anyone else in the building?" Agent Kane asked Nickerson.

"No, just me."

"Are you one hundred percent certain?"

The seismologist shook his head.

There was another noise—this time it sounded like a light footfall.

Higheagle looked around the table: a twinge of fear registered on the faces. Kane brought his index finger to his mouth, shushing everyone quiet. Then he quietly withdrew his standard FBI issue Glock 17 nine-millimeter semi-automatic. The chief followed up by pulling out a Colt .45 pistol that looked like it belonged in a museum. Higheagle subsequently followed suit by reaching for his own Colt wedged into the crook of his back.

Nina's mouth opened with surprise. "What is this an NRA convention?"

Special Agent Kane hushed her with an emphatic finger in front of his mouth. He started towards the open door, clutching his semi-auto in a two handed grip with the nose pointed towards the ceiling. Higheagle and his grandfather quietly stepped towards the other door with their Colts.

A tense silence gripped the room.

Suddenly, out in the hallway, there was a distinct footstep and an unfamiliar voice broke through the silence.

Then all hell broke loose.

CHAPTER 66

Where the fuck did she come from? gasped Mr. Sperry in shock as he stood face to face with a young woman who appeared seemingly out of nowhere. The moment before she materialized, he had heard a light footfall on the linoleum floor and only then did he realize—too late!—that something was terribly wrong. If only the unfortunate little wench had walked past the office without glancing inside, he would have had just one more unarmed, defenseless civilian to put down. But now he had lost the thing he needed most of all: the element of surprise.

"What are you doing?" demanded the woman, but in the fraction of a second after the last syllable flew out of her mouth, his right arm swung up, his finger squeezed the trigger, and the hollow-point bullet drilled through her forehead, flattening on impact and destroying vital brain matter as it augered its way deep into her occipital lobe and came to rest at the rear of her cranium.

The woman was dead before she hit the floor.

He bolted from the room, tightly clutching the custom-installed Pachmayr grip of his silenced Smith and Wesson .45 semi-auto in a two-handed hold.

But already he could tell that it was too late.

The federal agent cleared the doorway of the conference room and opened fire from twenty feet away. There was no time to come at him at an oblique or to conceal himself behind an object so he somersaulted into the hallway, popped up like a jack-in-the-box, and returned precision fire with his silenced weapon.

Pfft. Pfft. Pfft.

The glass of the conference room and the office behind him exploded as he, Higheagle, and the FBI agent squeezed off several rounds that failed to find their mark. He dove behind a row of metal file cabinets, while the FBI agent took cover behind a bulky photocopier and Higheagle shepherded Dr. Nickerson and Nina Curry out of harm's way beneath the conference room table.

After popping in a fresh magazine, he unleashed two shots into the conference room to keep Higheagle and the others at bay. Then he let loose with three carefully placed shots at the FBI agent, who peered out from behind the photocopier. The Smith and Wesson shuddered in the assassin's gloved hand, and this time he heard a grunt.

Had he hit his mark?

Unsure, he cracked off two more shots to finish off the seven-round magazine. He quickly discarded it, slammed another mag home. Fully loaded, he carefully worked his way forward and wedged himself between a pair of heavy metal cabinets, slowly closing in on his adversary for the kill.

Then he thought of the damned chief. *Where in the hell is that clever son of a bitch?*

Again the corridor crackled with gunfire. He returned fire—the same strangely high-pitched staple-gun-like *pfft, pfft, pfft*—then ducked back behind the cabinet. More glass exploded, and this time shards of metal, splinters of wood, and pieces of insulation and wallboard whirled through the air as the bullets ricocheted down the hallway of the USGS building. Both sides squirted out a few more rounds until there was another lull in the shooting.

As he changed out the magazine a third time, he stole a careful glance into the corridor. Drips and spatters of blood covered the floor next to the photocopying machine. So he had clipped the Feeb after all. But was it just a flesh wound or had he put his adversary out of action?

Hearing a noise to his left, he peered again into the conference room and saw Higheagle herding Dr. Nickerson and Nina Curry towards the rear door. Not wanting them to escape, he sprayed them with lead. The conference room exploded in a maelstrom of splintered wood, slivers of metal, and chunks of dry wall and insulation. On the last shot, he saw Nickerson take one in the upper thigh as he reached for the door handle. The Earthquake Man let out a groan of pain and recoiled like a wounded animal, ducking back under the table with Higheagle and the girl.

Mr. Sperry slipped his hand into his pocket for another mag. Again he wondered: *Where in the hell is that diabolically clever chief?*

As he popped in the fresh magazine, the FBI agent stepped out from behind the copier and moved cautiously towards him, his Glock above his head in surrender. *What the fuck?* thought Mr. Sperry, withholding his fire. The agent was wounded all right—the assassin saw an inkblot of blood blossoming at his midriff—yet the man was surprisingly calm.

It was only then that Mr. Sperry realized that something was terribly wrong. Slowly, he looked back over his shoulder.

There stood the silver-haired chief smiling like a Cheshire cat, the pistol in his hand trained directly on his chest. Somehow the wily old fart had snuck up behind him in total silence while managing to communicate his intentions to, and work in unison with, the FBI agent and his grandson. But how had the clever old renegade done it! It was like goddamned magic!

"Put down your piece, asshole, or you're going to be sucking bitter grass from the root end."

The assassin felt his jaw twitch ever so slightly. "You know me, Chief. I don't think I can do that."

"That's fucking too bad for you then."

"Come on, sport, you're not going to—"

But the words were chopped off by a staccato of gunfire as the old chief unleashed five shots in a rapid burst. The preppy assassin had never before felt such a force as the bullets burrowed into his Kevlar body armor in a star-shaped cluster, knocking the wind out of him and driving him into the shattered conference room window, his free hand clawing at the broken glass in desperation just before he dropped his gun and his body crashed to the floor.

The back of his head hit hard. The last thing he saw before he blacked out was the old chief standing above him, muttering some sort of Indian chant and poking at him with a long metal pointer as if it were some kind of coup stick.

And this time all he could think was: *What the hell is this the Little Fucking Bighorn?*

CHAPTER 67

HIGHEAGLE took measure of the damage.

Dr. Nickerson was a wreck. Wounded in the leg but oblivious to his own suffering, he quietly sobbed over the prostrate body of his dead colleague, a woman named Brigid Donnelly, who had stumbled onto the scene and in the process saved everyone's life. Further down the hallway, Special Agent Joshua Kane had collapsed onto the floor. Blood bubbled slowly from the bullet hole in his gut. His eyes blazed with a combination of anger and excruciating pain. Nina Curry stood in the open doorway to the conference room looking dazed and confused, apparently unaware that her right forearm bore a grazing wound inflicted during the shootout. A few feet away lay the gunman, looking deceptively unthreatening and peaceful in his unconscious state. The thick, protective body armor beneath his shredded jacket was riddled with bullets.

John Higheagle picked up the killer's gun, kicked at the body gently with his foot, and motioned towards his grandson. " No wonder I couldn't kill the son of a bitch in two tries—he's got a bullet-proof vest. What should we do with him?"

"Cuff him," croaked Agent Kane. He slowly rose to his feet and produced a pair of handcuffs. "I'm calling in the cavalry."

"You sure you're all right?" asked Higheagle, taking the handcuffs from him.

"No, I'm not all right. But I happen to be too fucking young to die." He pulled out his cell phone and started to punch in a number.

Higheagle leaned down, rolled the killer over onto his stomach, and clamped the cuffs on him. At that moment, the killer's eyes fluttered open and he let out a little groan.

Shit, he's coming to!

"Watch out, he's dangerous," warned Nina.

"Don't worry, I've got my gun on him," said the old chief. "He's not going anywhere."

"Except a prison cell in Canyon City," said Higheagle.

"Hell, the son of a bitch should look at the bright side. He's going to be making some new friends at the facility shower stalls."

The Contrary touched him gently with the nose of his pistol, counting second coups on him. After a moment, the killer came around and stared up at the old chief. He blinked several times.

"You did it again—you wily old bastard."

John Higheagle pointed the pistol at his face, offering no reply.

The killer grinned with admiration. "I don't know how you did it, Chief. But you are extraordinarily clever."

"I'll take that as a compliment."

The smile lingered. "You're welcome, sport. But may I give you a piece of advice?"

"Advice?"

"Yes. I think it would be best for you and your friends here if you just let me go."

"Now why would we want to do that, sport?" said Higheagle.

The killer smiled dangerously. "Because if you don't, I'm going to kill each and every one of you. And I promise it will be extremely slow and painful."

The chilling words drew pronounced expressions of worry from Nina and Nickerson. Higheagle and his grandfather just looked at one another with amusement. The killer's supercilious, threatening grin widened.

The old chief shook his head. "Sorry, sport, but you're in no position to make threats. In fact, it's you who should be worried."

"Yeah, why is that?"

"Because you talk too much."

"You've got a problem with animated discourse, old sport?"

"Only when it involves dumbass *vehoes* like you." And with that, the Contrary took the butt of his pistol, knocked the killer unconscious, and counted coup on him one more time for good measure.

CHAPTER 68

CHARLES PROMETHEUS QUANTRILL felt the relief wash all over him. The reprehensible but absolutely necessary deed was done and they were all dead.

And yet he still felt dirty, a touch of evil. He wanted to take a shower and scrub himself clean. But first he had to contact Boggs and tell him to call off his team.

He dialed the number and made the call, informing the security chief that the job was complete and everyone could go on home and get some much needed rest. When finished, he took a hot soothing shower, dried himself off, and put on a comfortable bathrobe.

That's when he began to feel the emptiness inside. He went to the window and stared up at the twinkling stars. He couldn't help but feel regret for having Higheagle and his grandfather killed. He had always liked the young Cheyenne and, after surviving last Sunday's earthquake with the two men, he had taking something of a shine to the old chief too. But he convinced himself that there was no use worrying over it now.

Survival was what mattered most.

The only remaining concern was the soil and vapor samples, but with Higheagle and Nina Curry dead, this posed far less of a problem. Of course, he would still need Boggs to track down the samples. If they were analyzed and the analytical results somehow found their way into the hands of some scientific expert, they could prove troublesome. But he considered that prospect unlikely.

He opened the sliding glass door and took in the soft lullaby of the wind rubbing up against Cheyenne Mountain. Overall, he was confident that the situation had been brought under control. All of the parties that had posed a serious risk to him were now dead. The three members of his security team that had been injured in dangerous car wrecks had survived and their injuries appeared to be manageable. Though the critical samples had yet to be recovered, by tomorrow evening Wesley Johnston and his engineering team would be far along in repairing the pipeline running to the injection wells and in removing the contaminated soil at the various release points along the line. Richard Hamilton's blackmail salary appeared to be worth the price as his information had allowed Higheagle and the others to be tracked down and killed. All in all, the situation was under control and things were looking up.

After a few more minutes spent gazing up at the stars, Quantrill stepped back inside, poured himself an Old Forester, and sat down at his desk. Taking a satisfying jolt of the bourbon, his gaze drifted to the wall-sized painting of *Custer's Last Fight*. The general stood tall and proud in his creamy-white buckskin suit, big white hat, and scarlet cravat tied loosely around his neck. His loyal troopers clung desperately to Last Stand Hill all around him, the hallowed salient above the Little Bighorn River where he and the two hundred nine cavalrymen with him had perished, forever sealing his and their immortality. Quantrill examined the long sharp nose, deep-set blue eyes, and reddish-golden hair that was long and wavy like prairie grass. He saw something of himself in the cut of the general. The warriors hurled themselves at the Boy General and his men from every direction, and Quantrill saw a magnificence to the futility, to the boldness of the soldiers that were holding their ground in the face of overwhelming opposition.

Standing there looking at Custer in his last dying moments, Quantrill was reminded of his own mortality. He thought of how far he had come and where he was headed. A part of him couldn't help but feel shame for everything he'd done, but at the same time, he knew he had had no other choice if he were to survive. The sheer will to survive—with some semblance of his life and work intact—was what ultimately drove him now.

But that was not the way it had been in the beginning.

He remembered back to his boyhood days on the wind-whipped prairies of West Texas. He used to stare out of the cracked window of his one-room schoolhouse and dream of how he was going to set the world on fire with his great ideas. He recalled that pie-in-the-sky look, that boundless hope and energy captured in the photographs from those halcyon days. He remembered how his teachers had told him that he would go on to do great things and was destined to live the American Dream. But every night when he came home from school, he saw his father collapse into the family couch after a fourteen-hour workday. Night after night, he watched helplessly as the old man sunk into that battered couch, without complaint but dying inside.

After a few years, the boy's honey-warm vision of the American Dream faded like the sun over a salt flat. The way American Dreams were born, he began to learn, was a myth. They were certainly not made by men like Pa, though the man he worshipped above all others fully deserved a piece of the great American pie. He began to understand that the only way to truly live the American Dream was to be either lucky as hell, fiercely driven, or unapologetically unethical—and preferably all three. American

Dreams, he began to realize, were made mostly by men who cut down those in their path, who were propped up by family connections and those in positions of power, and who bent, and often broke, the rules. Somehow the human world worked on a grand scale of Social Darwinism, where the duplicitous, malicious, cunning, and ruthless prospered at the expense of people like his father. It became clear to him that it was virtually impossible to embody the American Dream without destroying other people or violating certain moral standards.

The culminating event of his childhood had been when he saw his father collapse from a heart attack in a crippled, pathetic heap on his seventeenth birthday. That tragic event, forever blazed into the mind of young Quantrill, was the final tone-setting event for the rest of his life. He knew, above all else, that when he died he didn't want to be a broken man like Pa. That man, the one young Quantrill had desperately loved more than any other, had busted his back for twenty-five years and had been no better off on the day he died than he was on the day his first son and namesake was born. That harsh lesson of young Quantrill's youth had gone on to grip him in its claws throughout his adult life.

When he had moved to Colorado decades earlier, he had known, even then, that nothing was going to stop him from reaching his goal of becoming one of the richest men in the state, indeed the whole country. He had spent his early years scrapping and sweating like a plough horse just to get by and he would never allow anyone or anything to cast an ugly shadow over his dreams or those of his family again. Pa had been unfairly denied an existence befitting a human being, and had ultimately ended his forty-five-year life as a failure. Charles Quantrill, Sr. had worked hard and played by the rules and his only reward had been a busted back, a broken heart, and a tumbleweed shack on a dust-choked prairie.

Quantrill took a pull of stiff bourbon and stared up at the embattled Custer. He realized that, unlike the Boy General and his poor father, he had fulfilled the true American Dream. Not the one of myth, not the embroidered touchy-feely one you learned about in school or read about in a magazine, but the real unvarnished one that most people didn't want to talk about or acknowledge. And in fulfilling the true American dream, he had thus paid tribute to Pa. He had carried the torch that the miserable wretch had not been granted the opportunity to carry. And having carried that torch, as horrible as bearing it had ultimately proven to be in terms of collateral damage, he had somehow managed to also vindicate his father.

And in the process, he had expunged the nightmare of his own impoverished childhood.

CHAPTER 69

THE FBI'S DENVER FIELD OFFICE was located in the Federal Building at 1961 Stout Street. The eighteen-story edifice wasn't particularly imposing, especially compared to the majestic State Capitol and other Corinthian-style government buildings a few blocks away. It looked somber, elephantine, and antiquated—a throwback to the bygone Hoover era. But what the office lacked in aesthetic grandeur, it more than made up for in the ability of its personnel. The playground of the Rockies appealed to many an FBI careerist, and the Denver office tended to attract a disproportionate share of the best and brightest from other field divisions and residencies around the country.

The Bureau occupied the top three floors of the building. Just under half of the three-hundred-odd employees were special agents and desk supervisors; the rest were support staff, including intelligence research specialists, management analysts, evidence technicians, computer operators, attorneys, radio dispatchers, and clerical support personnel.

On the eighteenth floor, Higheagle looked around the cherrywood conference room table, surveying his audience. Seated to his left was Dr. Nickerson and his grandfather, and on his right Nina Curry. Across the table loomed Henry Sharp, assistant special agent in charge of the Denver field office, and a smattering of subordinate FBI agents. Seated at the far end was Ben Carrington, Director of the EPA Office of Enforcement, Criminal Investigations Division, whom he knew from the Petroco Refinery enforcement project they had worked on together two years earlier.

The conference table was littered with legal pads, laptops, and information packets. The packets prepared by Higheagle and his two scientific cohorts contained the recent analytical results, seismic printouts, EPA file sheets, and a brief summary report of the overall findings of their investigation. With the death toll over a thousand now, and with Special Agent Kane still at the hospital and unable to be present as a liaison between the scientific team and the law enforcement contingent, the atmosphere was tense. Most of those present had been briefed on the case late last night following the attack at the NEIC, but there were several new faces in the room. Higheagle wished his friend Josh Kane could be here. Based on Henry Sharp's pompous introductory remarks and the stiff, law-

and-order way the man carried himself, Higheagle already had a bad feeling about the guy. He was still trying to figure out how best to handle him when Sharp took him by surprise by clearing his throat and turning the floor over to the Cheyenne.

"Thank you Special Agent Sharp. As we discussed last night, there are three separate injection wells screened at different depths that are being used to dispose of the liquid waste. From the soil and vapor samples we collected at the disposal site, we have a good handle on the constituents of concern in the injected fluid stream."

"So the results are in. What did you find?" asked Carrington.

"Nasty stuff: TCE, PCE, 1,1,1-TCA, 1,2-DCE, BTEX, heavy metals, PCBs, and every kind of PAH under the sun."

Sharp held up a hand. "In English please!"

"Very well, let's just call it a veritable toxic soup of hazardous, cancer-causing chemicals banned for deep well injection in the State of Colorado. The organics concentrations were more than ten thousand milligrams per kilogram for several of the compounds in soil and thousands of ppm in air. Oh, and did I mention that the samples were loaded with mercaptans?"

Sharp gave a look of puzzlement. "Mercaptans?"

"It's a sulfur compound Quantrill used to disguise the chemical odor of the other compounds," explained Nina. "It's the same as the rotten egg smell you get around hot springs."

The ASAC nodded. "All right, please continue Mr. Higheagle and Ms. Curry."

He and Nina spent the next few minutes describing the operation from the time the waste was delivered to Quantrill's waste facility through its injection deep into the subsurface. When they were finished, they turned the floor over to Dr. Nickerson. The NEIC director launched into a PowerPoint slideshow presentation that described in detail how the injection activities had led to the earthquakes.

"The thing that at first confounded me," explained the seismologist, "was why the epicenters were so far from the injection well cluster." Using a laser pointer, he pointed to the injection well cluster and the epicenters of the two large earthquakes and three main aftershocks on the flat-paneled screen. "But now I believe I have the answer. After much study, I have concluded that the liquids are moving through improperly plugged and abandoned oil wells."

Sharp gave a contentious look. "Let me get this straight. The earthquakes happened because of fluids moving through old oil wells?"

Nickerson nodded. "Last night I looked over all the oil and gas well completion and abandonment records. There are dozens of wells within a five- to twenty-mile radius of the injection wells that haven't been properly plugged and abandoned."

"Which explains why the shallow well contained the highest vapor concentrations," said Higheagle. "Because it's the one they've been injecting into recently. The contaminants are moving laterally through the upper injection zone, the Hygiene Sandstone, until they reach an improperly abandoned oil well. Then the contaminants are leaking in along the cracked, permeable concrete grout and along joints in the steel casing and going down thousands of feet."

"So the earthquakes aren't occurring because of the waste fluids injected into the deep Precambrian basement rock," said the man to the right of Sharp, who appeared to be the ASAC's assistant. "They're happening because of vertical fluid migration into the deep zone."

"Exactly," replied Higheagle. "The horizontal flow is high in the shallow zone, but once a leaky well is reached, the contaminants move deep down through the open casing as if it were an open vertical conduit. At the bottom of the well, the fluid pressure then forces the waste fluids out into the formation. The fluids then move along another set of fractures until they reach a major fault plane. Once there, the fluids lower the shearing resistance of the rocks and initiate rupture along a blind thrust, which in turn results in a major earthquake. That's what Jeb Quantrill didn't account for: the influence of improperly abandoned oil wells on the vertical transport of the liquid waste."

The table turned silent for a moment as the team digested this technical information. Higheagle looked at the EPA enforcement official Carrington, the only person in the room besides his two scientific cohorts that he actually trusted.

"One thing I'd like to know," said Carrington, "is how Quantrill's waste facility received a permit in the first place." He pointed down at the three EPA RCRA permit approval letters on the table in front of him provided by Nina. "The facility was first permitted in 1991. But the permit was granted without approval by the Colorado Department of Public Health and Environment."

"I can explain that," said Nina. "Back in 1991, EPA Region 8 section chiefs could grant initial TSD permits themselves because the regulations weren't fully in place yet."

Sharp leaned back in his cushioned chair. "So who granted the permit then?"

"It wasn't my boss Richard Hamilton. It was a guy named Mark Wolford. He was the Director of the Hazardous Waste Management Division before Hamilton."

"Is he still there?"

"He died of AIDS in 1996."

"I'm not sure I follow," said Carrington. "Are you saying that Hamilton and Wolford were both complicit in some sort of illegal activity to get the permit through?"

"No, I'm not saying that. All I know for sure is that the original permit and the first renewal were granted in 1991 and 1996 by Wolford, and the last two renewals were granted in 2001 and 2006 by Hamilton."

"What was Hamilton's position when the first two permits were issued?"

"He was the RCRA Implementation Branch Chief, working directly under Mark Wolford."

There was another silence around the table as several of those present mulled over this information, while others scanned the paperwork in their information packets. Higheagle and his grandfather took a moment to more closely examine the four RCRA permit approval letters. The original permit and first permit renewal were signed by Wolford, whereas the two most recent renewals were signed by Hamilton. Higheagle studied the signature on the original permit and the first renewal. Something about the signatures puzzled him, so he lined the cover page of all four permits side by side. The subtle distinctions between the signatures suddenly became more apparent. Though the original permit and the first renewal both bore the signature of Mark Wolford, the two signatures were not by the same man. The signature for the first renewal had characteristics in common with both the signature on the original permit and the two renewals signed by Richard Hamilton.

Higheagle jumped up from his seat. "I think I've figured it out!"

The others looked at him with astonishment.

"Richard forged Mark Wolford's signature during the first RCRA permit renewal. That's how he got in with Quantrill."

Sharp looked skeptical. "And your proof is?"

"It's right here." Higheagle pointed to the four RCRA permit signature pages laid out side by side in front of him. "This one's the original permit signed by Mark Wolford back when he had the authority to grant the initial permit himself. The next one is the first renewal, supposedly signed by Mark Wolford. And these last two were signed off by Richard Hamilton. Look at the signatures. The signature on the first renewal isn't the same as the one on the original permit. It's a cross between the original and the later permits Richard signed. He got ahold of Wolford's signature and copied it. Only he's not a very good forger. Look at the *a* in *Mark* and *Richard*. It's a hybrid. And look at the date of the signature. It was less than a month before Mark Wolford died."

Sharp, Carrington, and several others leaned over the table and studied the writing more closely. "So what are you saying, Mr. Higheagle?" demanded Sharp.

"I believe Richard Hamilton took advantage of the fact that Mark was dying of AIDS and forged his name on the permit. And by doing so, he got Quantrill out of any public comment. In short, he ensured that there would be no outside comment on the part of any party regarding the permit."

"Wouldn't there have been someone else involved for quality control?" asked Carrington.

Nina fielded the question. "Normally another senior-level person or a couple of junior staff members would review the permit and find deficiencies, but in this case there weren't any additional reviewers. Usually there will be requests for additional studies, soil stability testing, a more comprehensive endangered species protection program, but there's no record of these things either. Richard got the permit renewal without any internal or external comment, and made it appear as if Mark Wolford was the one who approved it."

"So are you saying he did it to cover his tracks?" asked Carrington.

"That would be the most logical explanation."

"Could Hamilton be blackmailing Quantrill?"

"We don't know," answered Higheagle. "But whatever the arrangement is, he must have figured out what Quantrill was up to around the time Mark Wolford was sick. He saw his golden opportunity and he took advantage of it. I'll bet he received a big payment from Quantrill for shepherding the renewal through the system without any comments whatsoever."

Nina nodded. "If we're right about this, then Richard has been protecting Quantrill's illegal waste operation since the beginning. He's been able to control the timing of inspections and audits as well as the entire permit review process. He's been able to select the staff on the project—including Miss Gullible here—and to control what they document and keep them from taking enforcement actions. And he's been able to quietly keep the Colorado Department of Public Health and the Environment at bay."

"All right, I've heard enough on this Hamilton," snorted Sharp. "What else have you got?"

"I have some meeting minutes from 1996 and earlier," said Nina. "Senator Tanner lobbied hard with the CDPHE and the EPA to get the permits through each time. He was at several meetings where Mark Wolford was present. He pulled a few strings for Quantrill. It looks like Richard purged the file, except for the old stuff before he was involved."

"Are you now telling me that a United States senator is complicit in this mess?" said Sharp. "No offense, Ms. Curry, but you're a scientist not a law enforcement expert. You'd better be careful what accusations you make."

"I'm not making accusations, Agent Sharp, except to say that Senator Tanner clearly exerted his influence here. He was at five meetings with the CDPHE and EPA between 1991 and 1996, and probably some afterwards. So there is a connection between Quantrill Ventures and the senator."

Sharp looked skeptical. "So Tanner lobbied hard for Quantrill. So what? That doesn't mean he knows about the waste operation."

"It's true the senator may not know what's going on," said Higheagle. "But a whole slew of others besides Quantrill are, or were, definitely involved. That list includes his brother Jeb, Harry Boggs, Wesley Johnston, and probably at least a half dozen others. Quantrill would have needed a number of key senior and mid-level facility employees to successfully run the operation."

The room went silent as the group digested the information. After a moment, Nina broke the silence, "So where do we go from here?"

"At this point, there's only one option," pronounced Nickerson.

Everyone looked at him.

"We have to give a press conference."

Sharp scoffed at the idea. "That's not going to happen."

"But the world needs to know about this. More than a thousand people have died and another five thousand have been injured. We have an obligation to get the facts out to the general public ASAP."

Now Sharp was shaking his head emphatically. "No way. This is an FBI investigation and we're not going to—"

"Under normal circumstances that would be the case, Henry—but not today."

All heads looked up to see Special Agent Joshua Kane at the door, his arm in a sling, looking a touch pale and heavily medicated, but otherwise serviceable.

"What the hell are you doing here, Special Agent?" growled Sharp. "You're supposed to be in the hospital."

"I've been discharged."

"More likely you snuck out."

"I'm fine, sir, really I am. And I'm here to tell you that I gave my word to these people."

"I don't care if you gave your left nut, they're not running this investigation. Nor do they have any say in how it is run. Is that clear?"

Higheagle shook his head in dismay. He had suspected this would happen.

Carrington cleared his throat. "Agent Sharp, might it not be in our mutual best interest to let the facts of the case come out by those that discovered them?"

Sharp squinted like a gunfighter. "What are you saying?"

"Let them give their press conference. In the meantime, you and I can communicate to our higher ups and with DOJ, as well as secure a writ of access from a federal judge. Richard Hamilton and Senator Tanner are high-ranking federal employees and it won't hurt to tread carefully on this one. There are going to be a lot of people above our pay grades getting their fingers into this. It will be advantageous for us both to adopt a wait-and-see approach. We can have our teams in place to arrest the appropriate parties within the next two hours."

The eyes now turned to Sharp. Higheagle had a bad feeling that he wasn't going to go for it, but to his surprise the ASAC relented.

"All right, Director Carrington. But I want it documented for the record that this is your crazy wet dream, not mine. And that you're the one vouching for these people. Also, my team will accompany the three subjects at all times until the proper arrests are made."

"Very well," agreed Carrington.

Sharp looked at Higheagle. "All right then. You and your merry band of scientists have two hours to do your press conference. Then we take over."

"Thank you, Special Agent—you won't regret it," said Nickerson. He turned to his cohorts. "Where should we hold the press conference?"

The old chief smiled. "There's only one place in this dusty old cowtown where people will listen."

"Is that so? Where's that?" snorted Sharp.

"The southeast corner of Lincoln and Colfax."

Nina's mouth fell open. "The State Capitol?"

Higheagle smiled inwardly. *It's fucking perfect!*

"Before you all get too excited," said Kane, "there's one thing I forgot to tell you."

Sharp gave a querulous expression. "What's that, Special Agent?"

"Morgan Seagrave escaped while being transferred to County. Don't ask me how."

Sharp and the other FBI agents froze in their seats along with everyone else except Carrington, who looked up with puzzlement. "Who the hell is Morgan Seagrave?" he asked.

"He's the professional assassin who tried to kill us last night," replied Higheagle, feeling a sudden wave of dread.

Like the others, Carrington now looked genuinely fearful. "Oh, that fellow. That is bad news—very bad news indeed."

CHAPTER 70

"GOOD TO SEE YOU, VERNON," said Quantrill, delivering a firm pat on a shoulder wrapped snugly in a purple monogrammed golf sweater.

"Howdy Chuck," replied the man, slipping a hand into Quantrill's oversized mitt. "Everything okay out at the shop?"

"Luckily, we escaped serious damage, but we still have some minor repairs. We'll be back up and running by tomorrow. I gave all my employees the day off except for a few key personnel. Folks are still scared and I think it's only fair they spend some time with their families."

"That's the right thing to do. No wonder your employees love you so much."

Quantrill felt a twinge of guilt. *If you knew that I am responsible for the deaths of over a thousand people and murdered my own brother in cold blood, would you still think I was such a good person?*

"Glad to see you're all in one piece, Chuck. The back nine beckons."

"See ya, Vern." He stepped up to the bar, looking around for his lunch and golf partners, Jay Cerny and Rich Richter, but he didn't see them. He looked at his watch and realized he was twenty minutes early.

"What can I get you, Mr. Quantrill?" asked the club's veteran bartender, Tabb Bubier, as the CEO placed his elbows on the elaborately carved oak bar.

"Hello there, Tabb. Why I'll have an Old Forester on the rocks."

"Yes, sir, Mr. Quantrill, coming right up." The bartender moved down to the other end of the bar to prepare the drinks.

Quantrill snatched a handful of roasted peanuts and began munching on them. He turned and gazed out the window at the 18th hole, a four-hundred-yard par 4 that was tightly bunkered on all sides of the green. Beyond the green in the far distance loomed the massive granite face of Pikes Peak, recently topped off with snow. After the regrettable losses of the past forty-eight hours, it was a peaceful, welcoming, spectacularly beautiful sight—representing a metaphorical rebirth of sorts.

His thoughts were broken by a voice to his right. "Hello, Mr. Quantrill."

The CEO turned. To his surprise, suddenly seated next to him was a man in a gray suit and silver bolo tie with a severely hooked nose, perfectly combed blond hair, and wire-framed glasses. That was odd—he could have sworn that he was alone at the bar. Where had this guy come from? More importantly, who was he? He obviously wasn't a member of the club because Quantrill couldn't recall seeing him here before.

The man smiled at him knowingly. He studied the face more closely. It was then he saw something familiar in the jut of the man's chin and the greenish hue of his eyes. He almost choked on his peanuts. Could it really be...?

"Yes, sir, it's me."

Quantrill shook his head in disbelief; this Mr. Sperry truly was a master of disguise. But what the hell was he doing here? "You had me fooled. If you hadn't said anything, I would never have known."

"Thank you, Mr. Quantrill. Now about why I'm here."

He felt a jolt of anxiety. The man before him may have been the consummate pro, but in person he was still terrifying. "Is it the money? I completed the transfer early this morning as you requested."

"No, the money's fine. In fact, it's more than generous."

"Then what's the problem?"

"I'm afraid circumstances have changed."

Quantrill brushed away the peanut skins clinging to the sleeve of his golf sweater. "Changed? Changed how?"

"I think you'll see when you look at the TV screen behind you."

"What? What are you talking about?" He looked down the oak bar and saw the bartender staring up at the television screen. *Why isn't Tabb fixing me my drink? What is it, more on the earthquake?* He turned back to his unexpected guest.

"I think you'd better take a closer look, Mr. Quantrill."

What in the hell is going on? He looked up at the screen again, this time more closely, as the bartender turned up the volume. There was an Indian man with a long pony tail speaking from a podium in front of the state capitol.

Quantrill's jaw dropped.

"But it can't be!" he whispered to the disguised assassin frantically. "You killed him last night! You killed them all last night!"

"Actually I didn't, sport. That's what I came here to talk to you about. But I'm afraid our time is running out."

Quantrill felt a sinking, desperate feeling in his stomach and noticed that Tabb the friendly, veteran bartender was staring oddly at him. "So they're still alive?"

"I'm afraid so."

Quantrill climbed off his barstool and stepped closer to the screen. Higheagle was talking about the samples collected near the injection wells and how they contained high levels of industrial pollutants. After a few seconds, a camera zoomed in on some of the people behind him and he saw Dr. Nickerson and Nina Curry. He watched in stunned silence as Higheagle described the various individuals involved in the operation, the probable murder of Jeb Quantrill, Jack Holland, and Mark Kelso, the attempt on Higheagle's grandfather's life, and the subsequent attempt on the lives of Higheagle and the others at the NEIC. So engrossed was Quantrill that he didn't notice as the bartender slipped out quietly from behind the bar and snuck into the adjoining hallway to speak with the club manager—an older, white-haired man clad in a bright green blazer.

Quantrill turned away from the TV and wagged a finger at his unexpected guest. "What in the hell have you done? Did you cut some kind of deal?"

"I did nothing of the sort. I regret to say that I failed in my mission."

"But...but how?"

"It's a long story. And I'm on the run now so I'm afraid I'm going to have to keep the money."

"On the run?"

"Last night they caught me. It was that damned Indian chief—he's a wily old fox. And then early this morning they attempted to transfer me to the county jail and I escaped. I'm a professional, Mr. Quantrill, and that's why I'm here. I wanted to apologize to you in person. I also wanted to know if you still want me to fulfill the contract...once the dust settles, that is."

"Kill them? Now? After this? Are you insane?"

Mr. Sperry's jaw tightened. "You shouldn't talk to me that way, sport."

Quantrill looked back at the TV; he felt it all slipping away. "My God, what has happened?"

"I understand you're upset. So I take it that you don't want me to kill them?"

But Quantrill wasn't listening. "What am I going to do?"

The assassin looked warily to his left. "Regrettably, sport, our time has run out. We have to go now."

Twisting in his seat, Quantrill saw the club manager and two security men rushing towards him. He felt a surge of fear and lightheadedness as the room began to spin around him. He turned back towards the disguised Mr. Sperry, but already the man had vanished.

Good Lord, where in the hell did he go so fast? He's like a ghost.

Quantrill realized that he was all alone now. His only option was to make a run for it. Trying not to bring attention to himself, he slipped discretely from his seat and headed for the side door that led to the parking lot. Once outside, he dashed down the steps and hurried for his Cadillac parked in the front row.

Halfway to the vehicle, he chanced a look over his shoulder. His three pursuers had cleared the door and were coming quickly after him, the club manager in the lead. He turned abruptly on his pursuers.

"I was just leaving. Was there something you wanted to say to me, John?" He directed his fierce gaze at the club manager.

Now that he had caught up with the powerful CEO, the club manager looked unsure of what to do next. "You'd better just be on your way, Mr. Quantrill," he equivocated. "We don't want any trouble here at the club."

Though tense as brick, Quantrill managed to retain his composure. "Neither do I. So if you'd be kind enough to back off, gentlemen, I will be out of your hair."

"Then go now, sir. And please don't come back. You're not welcome here."

Quantrill started to protest, but then thought better of it. Instead, he bit his tongue, tipped his head courteously, slipped into his silver Cadillac, and drove off. Though it seemed unimaginable, the billionaire energy entrepreneur was now a lowly, desperate criminal on the run.

CHAPTER 71

SEVENTEEN MINUTES LATER, as he approached his sparkling English country manor near First Street and Beech Avenue of the Broadmoor, he spotted a fleet of government vehicles parked inside the electric gate. If he went inside, his life as he knew it would be over in a matter of seconds. Without slowing down, he continued past his turreted mansion, breathing a sigh of relief as he looked in his rearview mirror and saw that, miraculously, he hadn't been spotted. He stepped on the gas pedal, took a right, and headed towards Cheyenne Road.

He was not going to let them catch him.

Three minutes and two disregarded red lights later, he felt a migraine coming on. *Damn not again,* he thought. Feeling a severe throbbing in his temples, he pulled over to the side of the road and opened his glove box. He rummaged around for a moment, cursing to himself, until he spotted the familiar plastic lidocaine nasal spray bottle. Grappling for it with unsteady fingers, he unscrewed the top, threw his head back, and took a big snort of the soothing, precious fluid.

While he waited for the medication to take effect, he stared up at massive Pike's Peak to the west. If only he hadn't hired Higheagle's firm to begin with, he would never have had the Cheyenne sniffing around his facility and holding press conferences on the steps of the capitol. But how could he possibly have known back then what a problem the hydrogeologist would become? The kid had been as loyal as a puppy and the quality of his work was outstanding. How could he have known that his multibillion dollar operation would come crashing down because of this young man?

When his head cleared, he pulled back onto the road and headed north, unsure of where he wanted to go. On a whim, he turned left onto Highway 24 and struck west. Maybe he could hide out somewhere in the mountains. Passing Manitou Springs and Cave of the Winds, he soon came upon the turnoff for Pikes Peak. He was about to drive past when he felt a tug inside and yanked the steering wheel hard to the left, barely missing, in a touch of irony, a massive tanker loaded with chemical waste.

Onward and upward he drove, past the quaking aspen and Rocky Mountain juniper and into lush forests of Douglas fir and ponderosa pine, from the montane into the alpine, towards the granite crags inhabited by bighorn sheep and golden eagles. The pain in his head had disappeared completely. Soon he was above the tree line, some two thousand feet from the summit, zigzagging his way up the imposing granite batholith.

When he reached the summit, he took another snort of nasal spray just to be safe before stepping out of the car into the cold mountain air. It was dry and brisk and didn't carry a drop of moisture. Strangely, it didn't feel cold to him, even though he was dressed only in golf clothes. He felt invigorated and alive, as if he were a young boy again in West Texas.

He walked to the large viewing platform.

He looked west towards the Continental Divide. Then southwest towards the mighty Sangre de Cristos. Then east towards Kansas, the direction from which Zebulon Montgomery Pike had ventured in the early 1800s, though the famous military explorer had, ironically, failed to actually reach the top of the mountain that now bore his name.

After watching a young mother scold her two sons who were throwing pebbles at one another, Quantrill drifted over to a monument made of smoothly polished Pikes Peak granite and read the inscription on one of the bronze plaques. It commemorated the 100th anniversary of the writing of "America the Beautiful" by Katherine Lee Bates. With tears in his eyes, he looked at the images inscribed into the plaque: the pilgrims making the daring crossing of the Atlantic; the founding fathers signing the Declaration of Independence; and beautiful little montages of the cracked Liberty Bell, the Statue of Liberty, Mount Rushmore, and Pikes Peak itself. Studying the images, he felt proud to be a part of the restless spirit that was America.

These were his images. This was his America. He was absolutely American.

"Ten minutes till closing, sir."

The voice rattled Quantrill from his reverie. He squinted at the man in the drab-green ranger's outfit, standing twenty feet away. "But I don't want to leave."

"I'd like to stay up here forever too, sir. But the fruited plains below beckon us both." He smiled pleasantly, stepped off the platform, and headed around the edge of the Summit House to begin clearing the area. The mother and her two sons walked towards the parking lot.

Quantrill didn't want to return to his life below. He wanted to stay right here and feel the way he did now forever. Suddenly the pain in his head returned with a vengeance. He took another hit of lidocaine nasal spray, but it had no effect. He dragged himself away from the monument to the east side of the viewing platform. He felt as though his head had been kicked by a horse. Again, he pulled out his nasal spray and took a jolt.

But the relief did not come.

He inhaled again, harder this time. After a few moments, he still felt nothing. The light around him flashed like a strobe; the colors of objects seemed to change. Clutching his head between his hands, he looked in the direction of the ranger. He saw two men where there should have been only one.

He tried to take another breath from the inhaler, but fumbled it to the ground. He picked it up and drew frantically on it again. Still the numbing spray had no effect. He stumbled towards the stone wall, threw his arms over its top, and propped himself up.

"Sir, are you all right?" asked the ranger.

Quantrill couldn't hear him, nor could he see that the ranger was walking briskly towards him. He wanted only for the pain to end. He wanted only to somehow remain in the blissful world he had been in ten minutes earlier. He pulled himself up onto the wall, using the high-powered binocular along the edge of the wall for support.

"Sir, what are you doing? Get down from there!"

Quantrill ignored him. He stared down at the granitic world spread beneath him: monolithic spires, walls of talus, huge curved columns that—to his migraine-ravaged brain—registered only as a fuzzy mass of grayish brown.

"Stay where you are, sir! Don't move!"

Quantrill heard urgent boots running towards him, but still he did not turn towards the sound. He wanted more than anything else to crawl into a fetal position and hide away in the warm womb of a world beyond the reach of the law. He had no desire to live in a world where his life, as he knew it, was no more.

The ranger lunged for his feet.

Quantrill spread his arms out, like the wings of the huge black ravens gliding above the great mountain, and jumped.

Two hundred sixty brawny pounds knifed through the cold mountain air.

For those precious microseconds before the impact, his head was clear once again. He felt the life force just as he had as a boy, skipping flat stones across the Brazos with his beloved brother and digging up the bones of ancient protomammals with his childhood hero, Harvard paleontologist Al Romer.

In that instant where he flew like a great mountain bird, he saw the face of his brother, the best friend he had ever known, and Ma and Pa. They all smiled at him encouragingly.

There was a sickening snapping sound as Quantrill's head crashed onto the concrete loading platform twenty-five feet below and his spine broke into two separate strands. From there, the massive broken body slid down the slope of the dock onto the old cog rail line, built more than a century earlier, and came to rest on the saw-toothed cog pulley.

By the time the ranger reached him, the big man was staring up dully, his oversized glassy eyes like those of the mighty bull elk hanging from his office wall. There was no blood on his face or head. He carried a slight smile, not a grin or smirk, but a peaceful and fulfilled expression.

The ranger knelt down to check his pulse. He felt nothing.

Kee-Raw! Kee-Raw!

The ranger's eyes flicked towards the sky. A pair of huge, dark ravens glided gracefully along the edge of the great mountain.

Charles Prometheus Quantrill was dead.

EPILOGUE

ONE YEAR LATER

GRINNING MISCHIEVOUSLY, Joseph Higheagle and his grandfather the Contrary yanked off the canvas cover with dramatic flourish.

The crowd stepped forward to have a closer look. The skull was as big as a Volkswagen Beetle, with a giant horn over each eye and a third smaller protuberance directly over the mouth. A sharp, almost birdlike beak projected from the tip of its snout and a large shield of bone, or frill, extended from the back of its skull. The margin of the frill was ornamented with a bony structure that formed a sort of scalloping like a seashell. All in all, it was a spectacular sight, and though Higheagle had seen it many times before, he still felt a shiver of excitement as he gazed upon the breathtaking paleontological wonder passed down from his venerable warrior ancestors.

"That's one hell of a *Triceratops*," exclaimed Dr. Nickerson.

"It had better be—it's the type specimen," said Higheagle proudly.

"To think it was stolen right from under my great-great grandfather's nose," said Special Agent Kane with a smile.

Higheagle chuckled. "Yes, but he stole it back from *my* great-great grandfather and then later gave it back to him. So it all evened out in the end."

"Just like the Quantrill case," said Kane.

Several pairs of eyes narrowed on him skeptically.

The FBI agent shrugged. "Okay, so there's a few loose ends. But we've gotten most of the bad guys."

"Let's tally the score," said Nina. "Quantrill and his brother are dead. Wesley Johnston, Harry Boggs, and nine others are serving ten to twenty. And you've managed to seize two hundred seventy million in assets to pay for the earthquake damage."

"Impressive isn't it?"

"I'm afraid not. The wives of six of these crooks have claimed abject poverty yet they still have tens of millions of dollars in their bank accounts, and that maniac the...what's his name?—"

"Morgan Seagrave III," said Higheagle. "He goes by the code name Mr. Sperry."

"Yes, that maniac Mr. Sperry still hasn't been found yet and could still be after us."

"We're doing our best to track him down," said Kane.

"Yet you still have no idea where the hell he is."

"Actually, we've just received word that he may be in South America contracting his services out to a major drug cartel. But that has yet to be confirmed."

"That's really reassuring, Special Agent," said John Higheagle. "Let's face it, you have no goddamned idea where this psycho killer is. For all you know, he could be watching us right now."

"Come on, folks," said Nickerson. "We didn't come here to talk about all this. We came here to marvel at this incredible specimen."

"He does have a point," said Higheagle.

There were vigorous nods all around. As the group stepped forward for a closer look, the Cheyenne gave a little sigh of satisfaction. Before them was no cast replica, it was the original find—cleaned up, stabilized with steel support rods, and released from its tomb of sandstone matrix. He took a moment to study the monstrous horns, the giant curved snout, the massive crenulated shield looming behind the fossilized head. Beyond the skull, as one peered through the open barn door, the fading western sky was a bedazzling purplish pink, making the sharp horns appear like warriors' lance points against the fiery clouds. It was a spectacular scene, made all the more spectacular by the assortment of gifts from Cheyenne worshippers laid out before the massive horned beast. Arranged in a half-circle around the *Triceratops* skull were painted buffalo skulls, strings of beads and trinkets, twists of sage and tobacco, strips of buffalo hide, silk and calico, bundles of medicine sticks, pouches filled with herbs and tobacco, and a quiver filled with painted arrows.

"This is incredible," gushed Nina. "But shouldn't it be in a museum?"

"No, it belongs to our people," said John Higheagle emphatically. "A *Triceratops* it may be in the eyes of science—but to we Cheyennes it is, and always will be, the Great White Buffalo Chief. That skull was dug up from the sacred Painted Hills where our people long lived. It will always belong to us and serve as our deity."

"Speaking of digging things up," said Kane. "During our investigation, I managed to come across both Charles and Jeb Quantrill's personal diaries."

"I hope you burned them," said Nina.

"Actually, I found them intriguing. When I first started reading, I thought it would be like reading Himmler or Göebbels. But it was nothing like that at all. These were just two regular, hard-working boys from West Texas who wanted to build up something special. But somewhere along the way, they got their priorities mixed up. I'm telling you, these diaries were definitely not what I expected. They both hated what they were doing, but they firmly believed it was the only way they could achieve triple bottom line."

"Triple bottom line? What the hell's that?" asked the old chief.

"The three pillars of corporate responsibility and sustainability: social, economic, and environmental. You know the three P's: people, planet, and profit—in that order."

"This is revisionist BS," said Nina. "Are you trying to make us all teary-eyed over these two brothers when they killed over a thousand people?"

"No, I just thought you might want to know *why*."

"I already know why they did it. They were greedy bastards."

"If I know my friend, Jeb, it wasn't that simple," said Nickerson. "What else did they say in their diaries?"

"Well first off, the whole operation was Charles Quantrill's brainchild. By the early nineties he wanted to transform the company from a small but respectable oil, waste handling, and real-estate outfit into a sustainable energy juggernaut. Jeb was never comfortable with his brother's vision, not from day one. But he too couldn't resist the temptation to become a leading green energy company. Plus his older brother held so much sway over him that he would do anything for him. That's the thing, they truly loved each other. It comes through in everything they wrote. Ultimately, Jeb and Wesley Johnston designed the whole operation, but it was Charles who was the true visionary. Surprisingly, the whole operation would never have been discovered if there had never been any earthquakes. For ten years, there weren't any."

"Why Special Agent," observed Nina sarcastically, "you sound like you almost admire them."

"I don't admire them. I'm just trying to understand them."

"Well, you're going to have to try and understand them some other time," said John Higheagle. "It's time to perform the ceremony."

"Ceremony?" inquired Nina. "What kind of ceremony?"

"We're going to purify ourselves from the evil spirits these two energy tycoons have brought into this world."

"And how do you propose to do that?" asked Nickerson.

"In a minute I will show you. But first I must get ready."

From a side table, he grabbed a double-trailed headdress containing alternating red and white eagle feathers and placed it on his head. Next he grabbed a bundled medicine pipe, a large pestle and mortar for mixing paint, a buffalo bladder bag, and an elaborately beaded pouch holding tobacco, powders, and paints. Once he had gathered everything, he commanded the group to sit down in a semi-circle facing the giant dinosaur skull.

"First, I will paint you all then we will give thanks in a prayer to the Great White Buffalo Chief. It is because of him that we live in harmony again and are at peace with our Mother, the Earth. The Quantrill brothers have made her angry, but the natural balance has been restored. She is at peace once again and there are no more earthquakes. Also, I am going to ask the Great White Buffalo Chief to protect us in the future."

"Protect us?" said Nickerson. "Protect us from what?"

"Why Mr. Sperry, of course. You know he will be back."

They all looked at him, horrified.

"I'm just kidding!"

"You had me, you old scalawag!" cried Nickerson.

"Me too!" echoed Nina.

They all laughed, filling the barn with a ripple of good cheer. Higheagle felt a wave of euphoria mingled with pride. How could he feel anything less in the company of such fine people and in the presence of the Great White Buffalo Chief of his ancestors? Just being near the colossal, primordial mass of bone sent a shiver of pride through his body. The sacred object made him feel a profound sense of inner peace and a connection to the historic past of his Cheyenne ancestors, the Called Out People.

As the laughter died away, his grandfather handed him the cantlandite medicine pipe to commence the ceremony.

It was then that a funny thing happened.

They looked up at the great skull. And from that day forward, they would both swear that the Great White Buffalo Chief was smiling.

AUTHOR'S NOTE

BLIND THRUST was conceived and written by the author as a work of fiction. The novel is based on his experiences in California and Texas as a Registered Professional Geologist in assessing earthquake hazards and fault classifications on behalf of real-estate developers in environmental site assessments. However, the novel is ultimately a work of the imagination and entertainment and should be read as nothing more. The names, characters, places, government entities, corporations, and incidents are products of the author's imagination or are used fictitiously and are not to be construed as real. Any resemblance to actual events, locales, businesses, companies, organizations, or persons, living or dead, is entirely coincidental.

Despite the massive earthquake hazards depicted in *Blind Thrust*, the citizens of Elbert County will be pleased to know that there has never been a major, catastrophic earthquake in Castle Rock, Limon, or any immediately surrounding area in modern times. The southern portion of the Denver-Julesburg Basin within the Plains Seismotectonic Province is, in fact, as seismically quiescent and safe as any geographic province in the State of Colorado. Fortunately, this means that if you are an inhabitant of Elbert County, it is highly unlikely that you will ever require a real-life Dwayne "The Rock" Johnson to swoop in and save you in his rescue chopper.

There is no historic dig site known as "Felch Quarry 3" located in Garden Park, Colorado, six miles north of Cañon City. However, Felch Quarries 1 and 2 in the Garden Park Paleontological Resource Area are quite real. These quarries bear impressive Jurassic dinosaur remains, which the author has had the pleasure to examine first hand with his family in the stifling heat of midsummer. First discovered in 1877, the Felch Quarry sites produced numerous holotypes of both Jurassic herbivores and theropods named by O. C. Marsh, the longtime adversary to the greatest Saurian bone hunter of all time, the erudite, dapper, and fanatically opinionated Edwin Drinker Cope. Most of the specimens recovered from the Felch Quarries are exhibited at the National Museum of Natural History in Washington, D.C.

In the Mile High City, there is indeed a Museum of Nature and Science, an FBI Field Office, a USEPA Region 8 Office, and a Buckhorn

Exchange Restaurant; and in Golden and Colorado Springs, respectively, there is indeed a USGS National Earthquake Information Center as well as a Broadmoor Hotel and residential neighborhood. However, to the best of the author's knowledge no one bearing any resemblance to the fictional characters portrayed in *Blind Thrust* has ever undertaken activities similar to the events dramatized in the novel at these inspiring locations. The author holds the utmost respect for the USEPA, USGS, and FBI and has not made any attempt to portray any federal agency in a bad light. In fact, all three governmental agencies were instrumental and generous in answering questions and providing assistance to the author. Thanks are given to USEPA, USGS, and FBI personnel in the *Acknowledgements* in the subsequent pages.

There is no Quantrill Ventures, Inc. engaged in the fossil fuels and clean energy markets in Colorado that the author is aware of. Therefore, in the novel the company's illicit, shadowy, and ultimately murderous activities have been entirely fictionalized and, in reality, would be unlikely to occur in the real world of a Fortune 100 energy company. The brothers Charles and Jeb Quantrill, of course, have no real-life counterpart and are wholly the creation of the author's imagination. Similarly, all of the Quantrill Ventures, Inc. employees portrayed in the novel as primary or secondary characters (including geologists, engineers, plant managers, lawyers, IT managers, security personnel, receptionists, and secretaries) are the products of my unconventional brainwaves and have no real-life counterpart, at least that the author is aware of.

ACKNOWLEDGEMENTS

TO DEVELOP THE STORY line, characters, and scenes for *Blind Thrust*, I consulted hundreds of non-fiction books, magazine and newspaper articles, blogs, Web sites, and numerous individuals and visited each and every real-world Colorado setting fictionalized in the novel in person. All in all, there are too many resources to name here. However, I would be remiss if I didn't give credit to the critical individuals who dramatically improved the quality of the manuscript from its initial to its final stage. Any technical mistakes, typographical errors, or examples of overreach due to artistic license, however, are the fault of me and me alone.

I would personally like to thank the following for their support and assistance. First and foremost, I would like to thank Waverly Person, the former director of the U.S. Geological Survey's National Earthquake Information Center in Golden; Dr. Lucile M. Jones, USGS seismologist, Visiting Research Associate at the Seismological Laboratory of Caltech, and Science Advisor for Risk Reduction for the USGS Natural Hazards Mission Area in Los Angeles; Tim Rehder, Senior Environmental Scientist at the USEPA Region 8 Office in Denver; and the many professionals from the FBI Denver Field Office for patiently answering my questions and providing the critical technical and/or scientific research and federal government perspective for the development of the novel. *Blind Thrust* greatly benefitted from the expert advice given by these people and agencies. Any technical mistakes or inaccuracies due to artistic liberties, of course, belong to me and not these helpful professionals and governmental agencies.

Second, I would like to thank my wife Christine, an exceptional and highly professional book editor, who painstakingly reviewed and copy-edited the novel.

Third, I would like to thank my former literary agent, Cherry Weiner of the Cherry Weiner Literary Agency, for thoroughly reviewing, vetting, and copy-editing the manuscript, and for making countless improvements to the finished novel before I chose to publish the novel independently.

Fourth, I would like to thank Stephen King's former editor, Patrick LoBrutto, and Quinn Fitzpatrick, former book critic for the *Rocky Mountain News*, for thoroughly copy-editing the various drafts of the novel and providing detailed reviews.

Fifth, I would like to show my appreciation for author James Patterson and author-literary agent Donald Maass for their positive reviews and constructive criticism of my first completed novel, *The Coalition*. They took the time to give me genuine feedback and without their encouragement I might not be as determined and resilient an author as I am today.

I would also like to thank Austin and Anne Marquis, Betsy and Steve Hall, Fred Taylor, Mo Shafroth, Tim and Carey Romer, Governor Roy Romer, Peter and Lorrie Frautschi, Brigid Donnelly, John Welch, Link Nicoll, Rik Hall, George Foster, Margot Patterson, Cathy and Jon Jenkins, Danny and Elena Bilello, Charlie Fial, Vincent Bilello, Elizabeth Gardner, and the other book reviewers and professional contributors large and small who have given generously of their time over the years, as well as to those who have given me loyal support as I have ventured on this incredible odyssey of suspense novel writing.

Lastly, I want to thank anyone and everyone who bought this book and my loyal fans and supporters who helped promote this work. You know who you are and I salute you.

ABOUT BESTSELLING, AWARD-WINNING AUTHOR SAMUEL MARQUIS AND FORTHCOMING TITLES

"Marquis is brilliant and bold…It's hard not to think, "What's he going to come up with next?"
—SP Review - 4.5-Star Review (for *The Slush Pile Brigade*)

"A promising thriller writer with a fine hero, great research, and a high level of authenticity."
—Donald Maass, Author of Writing 21st Century Fiction

"*The Coalition* has a lot of good action and suspense, an unusual female assassin, and the potential to be another *The Day After Tomorrow*."
—James Patterson, #1 *New York Times* Bestselling Author

"With *Blind Thrust* and his other works, Samuel Marquis has written true breakout novels that compare favorably with—and even exceed—recent thrillers on the *New York Times* Bestseller List."
—Pat LoBrutto, Former Editor for Stephen King and Eric Van Lustbader (Bourne Series)

Samuel Marquis is a bestselling, award-winning suspense author. He works by day as a Vice-President–Hydrogeologist with an environmental firm in Boulder, Colorado, and by night as an iconoclastic spinner of historical and modern suspense yarns. He holds a Master of Science degree in Geology, is a Registered Professional Geologist in eleven states, and is a recognized expert in groundwater contaminant hydrogeology, having served as a hydrogeologic expert witness in several class action litigation cases. He also has a deep and abiding interest in military history and intelligence, specifically related to the Golden Age of Piracy, Plains Indian Wars, World War II, and the current War on Terror.

His technical scientific background and passion for military history and intelligence have served Marquis well as a suspense writer. His first two thrillers, *The Slush Pile Brigade* and *Blind Thrust*, were both #1 *Denver Post* bestsellers for fiction, and his first three novels received national book award recognition. *The Slush Pile Brigade* was an award-winning finalist in the mystery category of the Beverly Hills Book Awards. *Blind Thrust* was the winner of the Next Generation Indie Book Awards in the suspense category, an award-winning suspense finalist of both the USA Best Book Awards and Beverly Hills Book Awards, and a *Foreword Reviews'* Book of the Year award finalist (thriller & suspense). His third novel, *The Coalition*, was the winner of the Beverly Hills Book Awards for a political thriller.

Former Colorado Governor Roy Romer said, "*Blind Thrust* kept me up until 1 a.m. two nights in a row. I could not put it down. An intriguing mystery that intertwined geology, fracking, and places in Colorado that I know well. Great fun." Kirkus Reviews proclaimed *The Coalition* an "entertaining thriller" and declared that "Marquis has written a tight plot with genuine suspense." James Patterson compared *The Coalition* to *The Day After Tomorrow*, the classic thriller by Allan Folsom. Other book reviewers have compared Book #1 of Marquis's World War Two Trilogy, *Bodyguard of Deception,* to the spy novels of John le Carré, Daniel Silva, Ken Follett, and Alan Furst.

Below is the list of suspense novels that Samuel Marquis has published or will be publishing in 2015-2017 along with the release dates of both previously published and forthcoming titles.

The Nick Lassiter Series
The Slush Pile Brigade – September 2015 – The #1 *Denver* Post Bestseller and Award-Winning Finalist Beverly Hills Book Awards
The Fourth Pularchek – 2017

The Joe Higheagle Series
Blind Thrust – October 2015 – The #1 *Denver Post* Bestseller; Winner Next Generation Indie Book Awards; Award-Winning Finalist USA Best Book Awards, Beverly Hills Book Awards, Foreword Reviews' Book of the Year, and Next Generation Indie Book Awards
Cluster of Lies – September 2016

The World War Two Trilogy
Bodyguard of Deception – March 2016
Roman Moon – January 2017

Standalone Espionage Thriller Novels
The Coalition – January 2016 – Winner Beverly Hills Book Awards

Thank You for Your Support!

To Order Samuel Marquis Books and Contact Samuel:

Visit Samuel Marquis's website, join his mailing list, learn about his forthcoming suspense novels and book events, and order his books at www.samuelmarquisbooks.com. Please send all fan mail (including criticism) to samuelmarquisbooks@gmail.com.

Made in the USA
Middletown, DE
01 November 2022

13900229R00196